Praise for
Vicki Hinze

"Hinze has written a masterful, complicated tale of...
tum with each turn of a page. Her writing flows surely, moving from one character to the next, one setting to another, with readers keeping the swift pace."
—*Publisher's Weekly*

"[Hinze] keeps the pace brisk and the tension high. Don't start reading too late at night—you may see 2:00 a.m."
—Crosswalk.com

"As expected, *Deadly Ties* filled my need for encouragement, and though it explored some rather disturbing issues, its consistent reminder of God's omnipotence was a welcomed comfort."
—TheChristianManifesto.com

"Fans of Christian suspense will enjoy Hinze's latest thriller."
—*Library Journal*

"Excellent characterization and a compelling plot draw the reader in and never let go. Perhaps most importantly, the novel addresses the universal question of the purpose of pain and the importance of faith when all hope seems lost. Evil is unapologetically painted black and bold, making the redemptive power of Christ seem all that much more powerful. *Deadly Ties* is absolutely magnificent."
—FictionAddict.com

"I literally couldn't put down *Forget Me Not* by Vicki Hinze. The suspense kept me flipping pages until long after midnight, and I loved the plot twists. Highly recommended!"
—COLLEEN COBLE, author of *The Lightkeeper's Bride* and the Rock Harbor series

"*Forget Me Not* took off like a bullet from a shotgun and gripped me all the way to the exciting end. With tight plotting, twists and turns, a sweet romance, and lots of action, I'll be making room on my romantic suspense shelf for more books from Vicki Hinze!"

—SUSAN MAY WARREN, award-winning author of *Nothing but Trouble*

Praise for
Not This Time

"Vicki Hinze's new thriller, *Not This Time,* hones suspense to a razored edge. Riveting, relentless, and fraught with betrayals, here is a novel that cuts both to the bone and to the heart. *Not This Time* should be retitled *Not to be Missed.*"

—JAMES ROLLINS, *New York Times* best-selling author of *The Devil Colony*

"In *Not This Time,* Vicki Hinze has created a tense, suspenseful story, peopled with vivid characters and set against a backdrop of deadly danger. I can always count on Vicki for an absorbing story I'll remember long after I've closed the book, and *Not This Time* was no exception. Do yourself a favor and pick this book as your next read."

—KAY HOOPER, *New York Times* best-selling author

"Vicki Hinze has created a 'keeper'! *Not This Time* is engrossing, entertaining, filled with excellently drawn and very real people, and a story that keeps you turning the pages!"

—HEATHER GRAHAM, *New York Times* best-selling author

"Hinze paints her tale on a broad canvas, her writing expertly controlled, rich in imagination, deep in characterization. It's a race against time and shadowy instincts, the narrative loud with surprises, the premise all-too-believable."

—STEVE BERRY, *New York Times* best-selling author of *The Jefferson Key*

CROSSROADS CRISIS CENTER, BOOK THREE

NOT THIS TIME

A Novel

VICKI HINZE

MULTNOMAH
BOOKS

Not This Time
Published by Multnomah Books
12265 Oracle Boulevard, Suite 200
Colorado Springs, Colorado 80921

Scripture quotations are taken from the Holy Bible, New International Version®. NIV®. Copyright © 1973, 1978, 1984 by Biblica Inc.™ Used by permission of Zondervan. All rights reserved worldwide. www.zondervan.com.

The characters and events in this book are fictional, and any resemblance to actual persons or events is coincidental.

ISBN 978-1-60142-207-1
ISBN 978-1-60142-275-0 (electronic)

Cover design by Kelly Howard

Published in the United States by WaterBrook Multnomah, an imprint of the Crown Publishing Group, a division of Random House Inc., New York.

Multnomah and its mountain colophon are registered trademarks of Random House Inc.

Library of Congress Cataloging-in-Publication Data
Hinze, Vicki.
    Not this time : a novel / Vicki Hinze.—1st ed.
        p. cm.—(Crossroads crisis center ; bk. 3)
    ISBN 978-1-60142-207-1—ISBN 978-1-60142-275-0 (electronic)
    I. Title.
    PS3558.I574N68 2012
    813'.54—dc23
                                    2011029988

Printed in the United States of America
2012—First Edition

10 9 8 7 6 5 4 3 2 1

To Julee Schwarzburg.
Thank you for helping me find my way and taking this journey with me.

ಲ〜ಲ

To my children. Thank you for the privilege of being your mother.
And to my Heart, my Sunshine, my Rainbow, and the Angel Boy who to me
hung the Moon and Stars.
I'll love you all forever and forever, no matter what.

1

❦

He was late.

The country club's parking lot was nearly full, but Detective Jeff Meyers spotted an empty slot in the last of five rows. He parked and cut the engine, grabbed the invitation to Harvey and Roxy Talbot's remarriage off the center console, and then rushed through the humid heat back to the main entrance.

Cold air blasted him in the face. He breathed deeply, relishing it. No doubt all the Crossroads Crisis Center staff were already out in the courtyard. He hated to show up for a classy event late *and* sweaty, but thanks to clashing factions at Ruby's Diner over the coming mayoral election, there hadn't been time to shower and change clothes.

Bypassing a grouping of sofa and chairs, Jeff headed toward the back of the building. With all its polish and gold-framed original art, the club was too elegant for his tastes, but the people were friendly enough to make it semi-comfortable. There was no need to ask anyone where to go, which was a good thing, since not a soul was in sight—*kind of funny, that*—but Annie and Nora, the self-appointed Seagrove Village wedding planners, had made sure if a body found the front door, there'd be no confusion.

Rose petals on the cool marble floor created a path between white stretch columns to a set of french doors that led outside to the courtyard. A sign would have worked, but the club didn't allow them. There were limits to its tolerance for things that pricked at its perception of class.

Since Roxy had her heart set on the inner courtyard, they had scheduled the ceremony later in the day to avoid the relentless heat, but it still radiated. With reluctance, Jeff left the cool lobby and closed the french doors behind him. Doing his job or not, he would get his ears blistered by Nora for being late. His only hope was that the village matriarch was so focused on the ceremony she wouldn't notice. She was getting up in age and bat-blind, seeing walls only when she bumped into them, but Jeff had never known Ben Brandt's housekeeper to miss a thing that mattered to her, which meant Jeff was going to get reamed. He resigned himself to it.

Nora had put everyone on notice. This ceremony had to be perfect for Harvey and Roxy. Dr. Harvey Talbot worked at Ben's crisis center and Nora worked for Ben. That put Harvey under Nora's protective wing as one of her "boys." She was beloved in the village, and anyone who messed with her would answer to everyone—Jeff included.

Truly, Harvey and Roxy getting back together was a miracle, and all the villagers were glad to see it. They never should have gotten divorced. Harvey hadn't wanted it, but Roxy was with the FBI and she'd pulled a case that involved NINA—Nihilists in Anarchy—a group of terrorists with a criminal wing so ruthless, it gave Homeland Security, law enforcement, and crooks cold chills. Roxy had divorced Harvey to get him out of the line of fire so NINA wouldn't hurt him or use him to get to her. Not that she'd explained that to Harvey, which is why he'd been as miserable as a man on death row. Apparently, so had she.

Jeff followed the rose-petal trail onto a stone walkway that wound between fat shrubs and fountains that cooled the air with a welcome mist. He'd like to pause to cool down but didn't dare; if he was lucky, he'd get to hear the "I do agains."

Intended to seat fifty, the intimate courtyard was surrounded on all sides by brick buildings that held in the heat. He rushed his steps, rounded a cluster of petite palms and spiny palmettos—and came to a dead halt.

Bodies lay everywhere.

All the white-slatted chairs stood empty, and every guest who should have been in one was sprawled on the ground. Under the arch draped in leafy greenery and pink roses lay Harvey and Roxy and Reverend Brown.

Jeff didn't dare move. Hyperalert, he scanned the scene. The Crossroads group was clustered together. Nora lay facedown, her arm outstretched as if reaching for her companion, Clyde Parker, who was flat on his back with a toppled chair parked half on his stomach. It wasn't moving. With breaths, that chair should be moving.

Jeff whipped out his phone and hit speed dial, phoning the station. *Busy.* No surprise; most who'd answer were here, supine on the grass. The silence in the courtyard was deafening. They all lay motionless. *What had happened here?*

His heart thudding, he pulled his gun, continued searching. *Nothing.* Fearing a trap, he checked the rooftops but saw only clear blue sky. The lingering scent of something pungent burned his nose. It sure wasn't the flowers, but he couldn't tag its source. The building's walls had trapped the scent, but now a breeze stirred. Whatever the smell, it was faint and fading fast; another minute or two and it'd be gone.

Chemical. Get out of here. You're getting exposed.

He ignored the warning. He was already exposed, and these people mattered to him; he couldn't just leave them. Keeping his eyes peeled, he thumbed off the safety and readied for rapid firing, then moved toward the people closest to him: Beth Dawson and her SaBe Inc. co-owner, Sara Jones-Tayton. Sara's husband, Robert, wasn't with her. *Strange.* He seldom missed a social event, and Sara rarely attended one without him. Beth and Sara volunteered at Crossroads, kept the center's computers safe from hackers, and helped out Quantico when it got in a pinch. Crumpled on the grass behind the chairs, they too must have arrived late and not made the last half-dozen steps to their seats.

His mouth went stone dry. These were all his friends—many of them since birth. Were they all dead?

Nothing. Not one unexpected sight or sound or movement. He tried the station again. *Still busy.*

A table draped in crisp white linen stood between the others and him. Flowers and crystal filled one end; a two-tier wedding cake, the other. The breeze bent all the leaves to the north, and that faint, pungent smell had disappeared. Whatever it was, it'd dissipated.

Get out, Jeff. Wait for Hazmat.

The internal battle escalated to a war. He should wait for a hazardous-material team, but his heart wouldn't let him. Covering his mouth and nose with his handkerchief, he stepped behind the table and bumped his back against the brick building, then slid down the rough wall to Beth. *Don't let her be dead. Please.*

In a cold sweat, he squatted and pressed his fingers to her throat. A steady thump pulsed against his fingertips. She was alive. *Thank God.*

"Beth?"

No answer.

"Beth?" They had dated a couple times. He had been crazy about her, but she just hadn't been into him, so they settled for being friends. "Can you hear me?"

No response.

What about the others?

No. Backup first. You need backup.

Reverting to his life as a beat cop, he reached for the radio clipped to his collar before remembering he no longer had one and his phone was already in his hand. Darting, wary, he tried the station yet again. Finally, it rang.

"Seagrove Village Police."

The rookie, Kyle Perry. "It's Jeff Meyer. Who's there with clout?"

"The chief's in, but he's in conference."

"Get him."

"I can't, Detective. He said not to disturb him."

It was quicker to switch than to fight a rookie under orders. "Who else is there?"

"Coroner Green."

Hank would do. "Get him on the phone."

A moment later, Hank came on the line. "Hey, why aren't you at the ceremony?"

"I just got here. Everyone's out cold, Hank." Jeff briefed him, requested backup, and then added, "I need a Hazmat team—medical too, but put them in a holding pattern away from the building until Hazmat gives an all clear."

"What do you think happened?"

Sara Jones-Tayton was breathing. Shallow and slow, pulse thready but there. "I don't know." Jeff stood, his knees crackling. Still no one conscious in sight. He moved on to the next closest group. "No signs of a struggle. They're just all on the ground, out cold."

"White powder? Oily residue? Funny smell? Anything like that?"

"No residue or powder. I caught a whiff of something when I arrived, but it's gone now. There's nothing else to see—wait a second." Beth lay on her side, her hand buried beneath her. He looked closely, then checked the others, homing in on their hands. Beth, Sara, Kelly Walker, and Lisa Harper all had strings tied to their fingers—and Roxy did too. "Five women have strings tied to their fingers. Looks like monofilament."

"Fishing line?"

"Appears so." He followed the lines to where they converged. "All five lead to one place—the wedding cake." Jeff double-checked, then added, "To the bride. She's half buried in the bottom layer of the cake—not Roxy, the plastic bride that usually sits on top of the cake." He moved closer. The plastic was cracked, its edges jagged. "The plastic groom was ripped off." Jeff checked beneath the table. "He's missing."

"T-T-The plastic groom is missing." Hank stuttered. "H-Harvey—"

"Is here."

"Then what does it mean?"

"I don't know, but this was no accident." Not with those strings. Jeff didn't like where his mind was going, yet he'd have to be a brick short to ignore the obvious. "Professionals knocked out everyone and singled out specific targets."

"Oh man. Not NINA again." Hank sounded as nervous as Jeff felt.

The international terrorist organization that, to fund its ideological objectives, black-marketed anything of value—weapons, intelligence, drugs, people. "It's crossed my mind already." They'd had two run-ins with NINA; of course it'd crossed his mind.

"I could see NINA coming after Kelly or Lisa—and Roxy busted up their human-trafficking operation—but why Beth and Sara? They can't identify anyone in NINA."

"They helped us take NINA down in the human-trafficking case." When it came to computers, Beth and Sara were two of the best on the planet. Their SaBe was a megasuccessful software company, and everyone in the village knew they helped out the government all the time. Quantico tried repeatedly to hire Beth full time but couldn't afford her, and before Sara married Robert Tayton, she'd spent nearly as much time at Quantico as she had at home. NINA could want them both out of the way for that. "Revenge, maybe?"

Jeff turned to examine the next of the fallen. Darla Green, the widow of the deceased mayor, lay alone. Jeff wiggled his fingers into position on her throat. *Breathing.* He moved on.

Hank grunted. "NINA can't afford idle revenge. If they're behind this—"

"Who else has the ability or guts to pull off something like this?"

"No one who'd actually do it. But that means there's more to it than revenge."

"We don't even know what *it* is yet." Jeff kept moving through the crowd, person to person, finding throat pulses and growing more and more relieved. "Whatever it is, we never saw it coming. They came in and did what they wanted—they could have killed them all." That truth sent shards of fear slicing through Jeff's veins. His friends—all his friends—could have been murdered on his watch.

"But they didn't kill them."

"Not this time." Jeff gazed down, then glanced over, seemingly seeing double senior women. His heart sank, then slammed against his chest wall. "Maybe something is still in the air, Hank. I'm seeing two Noras."

"Probably Nathara, Nora's identical twin. She's here from New Orleans to take Nora to some eye specialist."

"Oh." Jeff had never seen her before. He blew out a relieved breath and checked them both. *Strong. Steady.* He moved on, past Nora and her sister, and placed his fingertips on the next throat. *Nothing.*

He tried again.

Still nothing.

Tried a third time but it just wasn't there. No pulse.

A lump rose in Jeff's throat. "Oh, man."

"What?"

Jeff's eyes burned. *Bury it. You're a professional. Remember it.* His throat went thick and strain flooded his voice. "You'll need to come out too, Hank. I—I, um, can't lock down the crime scene by myself, and the rookie won't be much help."

"Got it. Backup's already on the way."

Not the kind of help he required. "I need backup *and* high-powered help."

"How high?" Uncertainty elevated Hank's voice.

A tear leaked from Jeff's eye. "All the way." Hank was sharp on the uptake. The chief was too. They'd know to contact Homeland Security and to get the FBI on-scene immediately.

"Al won't like it. Not without some preliminary work being done first."

Hank Green was wrong on that. "The chief will dial the phone." Jeff looked into sightless eyes that once had twinkled kindness and his own vision blurred. He gently swept the eyelids closed with his fingertips and searched for his voice. "This has to be some kind of chemical attack. We don't have the resources—"

"Let's don't jump to conclusions, Jeff."

He started snapping photos with his cell phone. Hank, not the chief, was reluctant to call in outsiders. Why? Protecting the village tourism? He was running for mayor... "You either jump or get dragged into this one, Hank. Chemical is all that makes sense."

"We don't have to rush to judgment. They're alive. We can—"

"I'm afraid we do need to rush," Jeff interrupted. The first forty-eight hours were critical to successfully solving any case. Stats backed him up on that. "We have a fatality."

A long second passed. Then another. "Visitor or villager?"

Jeff's voice cracked. He cleared his throat. No way was he identifying this victim over the phone. Word would sweep through Seagrove like wildfire. "A villager." He moved over to the cake, snapped a shot. A curled edge of paper was half buried in the frosting. "Whoever did this left a message. It's attached to the bride buried in the cake."

"Can you read it without disturbing it?"

Jeff moved around, positioned at an angle and the bold black print became clear. "I can read one word." Chills slammed through his chest, spread like fingers to his limbs. He jerked away, stiffened.

"What does it say?"

"Boom."

2

&

T he ink hasn't dried on our last arrest report and the jerks are at it again." Ken Matheson slid into the cruiser and passed his partner, Bill Conlee, a giant-sized foam cup of sweet tea. "Which jerks? NINA?"

Nihilists in Anarchy were on everyone's watch list since it had been active for the second time in a year down south in Seagrove Village. Detective Jeff Meyers had personally briefed the adjacent east and west panhandle counties on two separate incidents—one smuggling bioterrorists into the country and one human-trafficking women out of the country—but nothing on any of their current cases linked to NINA. Yet with NINA expanding its activities, who knew for sure?

Ken shivered. Butting heads with NINA was way out of his league, and he was smart enough to know it. First sign, he'd suggest Bill contact Detective Meyers. With help, he'd battled and beat NINA twice.

Calmer with his mind settled on the matter, Ken parked his own cup between his legs and clicked his safety belt into place. Warranted or not, Bill drove like a demon was on his heels and woe be to his younger partner if he complained. Their first time out, Ken had learned to buckle up, hang on, and keep his mouth shut.

"Maybe NINA." Bill took a sip of tea. "I meant the pornographers we arrested up off 126 and old Magnolia Branch Road—in that rusty abandoned shed down from Race Miller's."

Race Miller's place was a fifty-acre plot north of Nilge Reservation out in the middle of nowhere. After Hurricane Ivan ripped through, it had taken two years to get electricity back out to Race—a fact he'd reported to the sheriff's office every day, knowing they couldn't do a thing but report it to the co-op. That whole northeast corner of the county was just about uninhabited, which meant it was prime real estate for dopers, transients, and, apparently, now for pornographers.

"Told you we should've shot 'em. We had just cause. The jerks pulled weapons on us."

Bill laid a glare on Ken and without a word left the Pac-a-Sack convenience store's gravel-and-dirt parking lot, swinging wide to miss a pothole large enough to swallow a truck, and then pulled onto Highway 90.

"Okay, okay." Ken looked out onto the road. It was twilight and the scent of rain hung heavy in the air. "Lighten up, Deacon. I didn't shoot a soul." He sipped at his sweet tea. "But I could've and it would've been totally legal."

Bill spared him a sidelong glance that made his forehead look even wider and his jaw disappear into his double chin. "Your professional ethics and morals need work, partner."

"I'm all over it," Ken said, though they both knew he wasn't and the well-intended reprimand wouldn't do a bit of good. He was doomed for life to float in humanity's sea as pond scum. And he liked knowing where he fit.

Bill draped his wrist over the steering wheel. "After the last bust, Race sold that shed."

"Hadn't heard. To who?"

"Didn't ask. Not my concern."

"Will be if the same kind of folks bought it."

"When and if it becomes our business, we'll deal with it." Bill took the left onto Tyner Road, which led to Gramercy down in Seagrove or up to 126, which led—directly—to the old road to Magnolia Branch, a little community that bit the dust when construction exploded on northwest Florida's Gulf Coast thirty-odd miles south and Highway 126 lost favor to 331 over in Walton County.

Skipping the back roads cut nearly a quarter hour off the trip to Tallahassee or Pensacola, and Race Miller had been in a foul mood ever since.

'Course, he'd owned most of Magnolia Branch, and not one of his businesses had survived, so a man couldn't blame him for that. At least he still had his church, even if he hadn't found a preacher to run it since the community folded, but no nevermind. Race handled Sunday services himself, and Bill acted as a deacon.

He dragged Ken along every now and again, trying to save his soul, and Ken let him, in exchange for Bill not reporting Ken's little indiscretions, like him saying they should've just shot the porno jerks and spared the county the expense of a trial.

But truth was truth, even if saying it was a professional offense Bill should report to Sheriff Dobson, and if they had shot them, then he and Bill likely wouldn't be headed out to Race's right now. It was also truth, and Ken gave credit when due, that no one preached with more vigor than Race Miller.

Pines twisted and bent from a couple bad years of hurricanes lined the road, and dense wild growth lay low to the ground beyond it; scrub, mostly, with a stray pin oak or magnolia sprouted here and there. Spiny bushes Ken couldn't name but had seen all his life sprung up everywhere, and the thick woods filled in so dense that the sandy dirt floor didn't see much sun even in noonday light. The whole place was riddled with rattlers, mostly pigmy, and cottonmouths. Aggressive as all get out, those cottonmouths. Ken hated them.

Race's wife, Aline, hated snakes too. She had called Bill and Ken more than once to come handle "an intruder," which turned out to be of the slithering variety. The last two times she'd called, she vowed if she opened the dryer door one more time and a snake was in the tub, she was moving down to the village and Race could like it or not. Bill figured the snakes were crawling in through the outside vent, plugged the hole, moved the vent up from ground level to under the house eaves, and that had been that—no more snakes in Aline's clothes dryer.

Race was still a little ticked off about that too. Aline was an accomplished harper. No doubt Race had looked forward to her village stint giving him a little peace.

They passed a couple Hank Green for Mayor signs and at least a dozen for Tack Grady. It was a Seagrove Village election, but lots of folks up north had businesses and tight connections down south so politicians campaigned in both. "Who you figure'll take mayor?"

Bill cocked his head. "Hard to say. Hank's been a good coroner, but with his brother tagged as a NINA conspirator in that terrorist-smuggling business, I figure Tack's got the edge."

"I don't know." Ken weighed the matter. "John wasn't mixed up with that—he was a God-fearing man. But Tack knows a load of people." He'd owned a diner on the harbor for years, until the economy tanked and he lost everything. Tack Grady needed the job.

"It isn't helping Hank that Darla's just out of jail."

Her being charged with John's murder had been hard on Hank. "Yeah. The gossip mill is chewing on the whole mess again, but it would be anyway with Lance shunning her in court and all." Darla was the richest woman in the county. It'd taken months to clear herself from her husband's murder, but by then her relationship with their only son, Lance, was shot. The teenager lived with Hank, and they'd gone to court to make sure Lance could stay with him. Freezing his mom out had to be hard on her, but the whole mess was hard on the boy and Hank too. "Sad situation."

"Tragic. The boy and John were close. He'll never believe his dad came down on the wrong side of the law."

Ken looked at Bill. "You don't believe it either, do you?"

"No, I don't. John Green was a good man and a good mayor."

"So you'll be voting for Hank?"

"I will."

Ken would be too—and hoping it wasn't a mistake. "I thought Tack was broke, but he's sure campaigning like he's got deep pockets."

"You said yourself he knows everybody in the county."

He did. Still…

They didn't pass a single car on the road—or on old Magnolia Branch. Bill drove down to the fork, headed left, and the pavement gave way to a red dirt washboard that was hard on the cruiser's shocks. The ice in Ken's sweet tea sloshed against the sides of his cup, and he spotted the gap in the woods marked by a rotted-out post, which probably once held a mailbox. Whoever bought the place wasn't getting mail here.

"That's it." Ken motioned left to a rutted path.

Bill turned into the ruts and headed up the mile-long trail paralleling Bear Creek. Halfway, he eased the cruiser up against the brush, stopped, then shoved the gearshift into Park. "Best walk it in from here or they'll see us coming."

Not eager to interact with nature but less inclined to complain and hear another lecture, Ken hauled himself out of the cruiser. They had walked in last time and had been successful. Maybe it'd be worth it. "Fair warning. If I get eaten up by chiggers again, I *am* gonna shoot the jerks."

Bill sent him a "grow up, boy" look and seated his black-frame glasses on his nose with a paternal sigh. "Can't tromp the woods and not run into what's natural to 'em."

Ken didn't bother responding. He respected Bill. Admired him. But on occasion, living with his righteousness and calm acceptance was a pain in the backside for a regular guy. Just once, Ken wished the deacon would raise a little sand. Of course, the odds of that happening were about as good as Ken's were of salvation and surviving Armageddon. Pond scum just couldn't quite make it from here to there without a miracle, and he hadn't seen any lately.

They moved down the trail. Twigs and dry leaves crunched underfoot. Even with twilight settling in, the humidity was heavy and it was still hot. In no time, Bill's breathing turned raspy and Ken was sweating profusely. His sleeve was soaked from swiping at his face. Heat being this bad in early June, August and September would be pure killers.

Finally the trail narrowed to a path and the rusty metal shed came into view. At one time it likely held farming equipment: combine, tractors, maybe a cotton picker. But the land was bitter, didn't welcome crops, with the exception of a little pot they came across now and then. Ken had wondered aloud once if maybe smoking a little wouldn't improve Aline's disposition. Big mistake. The deacon had taken serious exception—and Ken's backside had been parked on the front row pew for the next four Sundays.

He hadn't risked rendering many unsolicited opinions since then, or again made the mistake of commenting on Aline or her disposition.

Bill stopped at an old oak, cocked his head, and listened.

Had he sensed something? Ken hadn't picked up on a thing. Still, he waited a long minute before swatting at another mosquito buzzing his head. The pests were thick as thieves. "You want me to go round back?" he whispered, wondering when he would develop that instinct the sheriff called "cop's gut." Bill had it. Others on the force had it. But even after two years, Ken hadn't so much as sniffed a whiff of it. Would he ever?

"No sense in it." Bill pulled a folded paper napkin from his pocket, then mopped the sweat from his brow. "Shed's just got the one door."

"No cars around." Ken scanned the clearing, which was about the length of half a football field. The shed sat dead center. It looked empty, but he glanced at Bill for confirmation.

"Fresh tracks everywhere." Bill hitched his pants to shake a snagged leg loose from a briar. "Appears they've already hightailed it." He stepped out from behind the old oak's twisted trunk. "Let's take a look inside anyway."

Race Miller's place was within shooting distance. If he noticed something amiss, he'd been known to fire off a couple rounds before calling the sheriff. He could have scared 'em off.

"What for?" Ken was curious, not opposed to going inside. "They sure didn't hoof it up here, not hauling cameras and lights and all their equipment."

Bill didn't look back. "Got a feeling." He unstrapped his holster. If he needed to draw his weapon, he was ready. "Step left. Snake."

Ken grimaced at Bill's shoulders and took a couple steps left, avoiding a rattler slithering away from them. His skin crawled. "What kind of feeling—exactly?" He didn't like the sound of it.

"A bad one. A real bad one." Bill took off walking toward the shed door.

The hair stood up on Ken's neck. Bill had a decade more experience, and in the two years they'd been partners—Ken's first assignment—he had come to respect the man's cop's gut. By anyone's measure his instincts were honed razor-sharp. Tensing up, Ken thumbed the snap on his own holster and followed Bill in.

The broad shed door creaked and groaned and finally swung open. It was dark inside. Dark and hot and stuffy. "No filming going on in here today. New owners must be into something different." Ken stepped back out to grab a breath of fresh air.

Bill reached for his flashlight. "We're going in anyway."

"Why?" The place gave Ken the creeps. "It stinks to high heaven and it's empty."

"We're going in." Bill's tone didn't welcome argument.

"All right, then." Ken grabbed his flashlight and swatted at another mosquito buzzing his head. "Whatever you say." It'd take a week to get the stench out of his pores.

Moving right, Bill motioned Ken left. They walked inside, fanning their flashlights. A glint caught Bill's wedding band. His hand was on his gun. That set Ken's teeth on edge and strummed his nerves. Bill never touched his gun without reason. "What's going on, Deacon?"

He directed his beam to light up a distant spot on the floor. "That."

Ken looked over. A mattress rested on the dirt. Likely somebody had dumped it in the woods. It happened all the time. Folks not wanting to pay the fee at the landfill would toss old washing machines, refrigerators, and such in the woods. Transient probably came up on it and dragged it into the shed to get out of the rain or something.

"What's all over it?" Ken couldn't make it out from this distance. "Too bright to be mud."

"Ain't sure yet." Bill moved in close and then stopped beside the mattress. "Oh, sweet mercy." He made the sign of the cross.

The mattress was covered in blood.

Ken swallowed hard, swept the corners of the shed with light, but saw nothing, heard only his own pulse throbbing in his temples and the squishing, grumbling sounds of his stomach roiling.

"Mattress is saturated." Bill stooped to a crouch, then held his hand in a hover just above it. "Cold."

"In this heat?" Ken couldn't believe it. "Blood would be warm coming out of a body. How can it be cold? Besides, it's sweltering in here." Didn't make a bit of sense.

"Ain't sure yet." Bill slowly swept the mattress with his flashlight. "But, Lord, help 'em home. Nobody could lose this much blood and live."

Ken watched their backs, turned his light on a cluster of stuff to his right. Cracked wooden boxes stacked haphazardly and covered with inch-thick dust and cobwebs stretched between them and the wall. The boxes hadn't been moved for a while. Nearby, wadded paper, trash, and a couple kinds of cans and bottles littered the floor. And beside that—"Someone's tagged that area as a rest room."

Bill glanced over. "Chain marks in the dirt between the pole, the mattress, and the area you're talking about." His expression soured, then turned rigid and his jaw snapped tight. "Someone's been held hostage here…and died."

Ken feared Bill was right and examined the mattress closely. "There's no bullet hole."

"Could've been stabbed."

Yet another possibility occurred to Ken. "What about the porno folks? This could be fake blood. That could explain why it's cold." Stage setting.

"Yeah, it could." Bill stood, his knees snapping. He swiped his napkin over his face. Since walking into the shed, he looked as if he'd aged ten years. "Guess we ain't sure yet. Better call it in."

Ken radioed in a report to the sheriff's office and then turned to Bill. "You think that blood's human, don't you, Deacon?"

"Yeah, I do." Bill looked at his partner. "I surely do."

Ken knew that look. Bill would be chewing himself up for the next week for not getting here sooner and saving the poor slob who'd bled out on that mattress. He thought Ken didn't feel regret about such things, but he was wrong. For months to come, Ken would be kicking himself for not running a daily routine check on the shed to make sure the pornographers hadn't come back, especially since he hadn't known the property'd flipped owners.

"I'm gonna look around outside before dark falls." As bad as snakes and mosquitoes were out there, what was in here was worse. "See if they dumped a body anywhere close."

⊘⊙

Bill watched Ken go. When he disappeared outside, Bill tapped the transmit button on the radio attached to his collar. "Millie, get Sheriff Dobson for me, will you?"

"Roger that, Deacon."

A short minute later, the sheriff's voice sounded through the radio. "Yeah, Bill. What'd you find up there?"

"Ain't sure yet, but you better get us some forensics help." Even breathing shallow, the stench rattled his stomach and set off his gag reflex. He fought it and kept fighting it.

"What do you see?"

"Blood." Bill rubbed his thumb over his .45's soft rubber Hogue grip. "Could be movie props, but it don't smell like it." He hesitated. "Sheriff, I got a bad feeling about this one. Might want to call Jeff Meyers to come take a look." He and his friends had experience. There hadn't been a murder in Oakton County in ten years. "Who owns this place now?" That might prove important.

"SaBe bought it from Race."

Everyone in the tricounty area knew about SaBe. Beth Dawson and Sara Jones-Tayton started out with nothing and made a fortune. They were a real hometown success story, and neither of them forgot where they came from. Both did a lot to help out locals. "I can't see them mixed up in something like this."

"Me either. I'll call Jeff." The sheriff's respect for those instincts came through loud and clear. "Protect the scene."

"Yes sir." Something glinted on the mattress like a glass shard and Bill took a closer look. It disappeared before his eyes. Must've been a trick of the light.

"Fatalities?"

"None located yet." Bill blocked the overwhelming stench with a finger to his nose. "But if the blood I'm seeing is human, yeah. At least, one." Sweet mercy, outside of car accidents—bad ones—he'd never seen so much blood. "Maybe more…"

3

Seagrove Village, Florida

Clyde Parker was dead.

Nora sat in the grass weeping, holding his hand, her free arm wrapped around an also weeping Kelly Walker, who'd become like his adopted daughter. Dr. Lisa Harper had tried everything, but there was no reviving him. Clyde Parker had gone home.

Beth Dawson's heart ached. She loved Nora like a second mother and seeing her in pain had Beth's eyes stinging. Nora's twin, Nathara, on the other hand, woke up complaining and had hardly paused to draw breath. Beth had to restrain herself not to gag the woman.

"Come on, Nora. Let them do their work and get Clyde out of this heat." Nathara tried to forcibly lift her sister.

Mark Taylor didn't take it kindly. Lisa shot out an arm to keep him from interceding.

"Leave me be." Nora slapped at her sister's hand, her eyes as red as her lipstick.

Nathara tried again. Beth stepped forward before Mark could. "Nathara, Kyle, that officer near the arch, needs to take your statement."

Frowning, she straightened her askew hat and then followed Beth. "What's wrong with her? My sister's acting like an emotional fool." Nathara cast a reprimanding look back at Nora. "The man's had a good life. It's done now, and that's that."

Beth bit her lip to keep quiet and delivered Nathara and her attitude to Kyle. Once, when Lisa's mom, Annie, was in the hospital, Nora had warned everyone that her twin sister was there in a pinch but as mean as a snake. She was, bless her heart.

Hazmat set up a safe area, and everyone had to step behind makeshift screens, remove their clothing and put it in special biohazard bags, then get showered down head to toe in small, shallow swimming pools where the water was retained for safe disposal. They were given scrubs to put on—all blue ones—and paper socks.

When everyone else was done, Beth signaled Kelly, who nodded.

"Nora, we have to go shower now. They need our clothes."

"For what?" Nora looked up at her, her eyes red rimmed and weepy.

"To run some tests to find out what was done to us. It can help them figure this out." Kelly stood and offered Nora her hand.

"Jeff'll find 'em." Nora sniffed, took Kelly's hand, and tried to lift herself but couldn't. Ben and Mark stepped in and got her to her feet. "My knees are mushy, my boy," she told Mark. "Can you help me over to the kiddie pool? Annie? Where's Annie?"

"I'm right here, Nora." Lisa's mother rushed to get to her roommate.

Nora clasped her arm. "You tell Hank we'll be planning Clyde's funeral for Tuesday. I know what he wants and I won't have it not done right."

"I'll tell him, hon." Annie patted Nora's shoulder. "Don't you worry. We'll do exactly what Clyde wanted."

Jeff Meyers walked past. Nora snagged him. "You were late. I'd blister your ears, but considering somebody gassed us, I'm thinking it's a blessing you weren't here."

"There was a problem down at Ruby's—"

She cut him off. "Beth told me." Nora leaned hard on Mark, wagged a warning finger. "I don't care if the whole village erupts in a war, you'd best not be late for Clyde's funeral."

"No ma'am. I won't."

Her clouded eyes burned bright and her voice cracked. "You find 'em, Jeff. They took my Clyde." She shuddered, stiffened, and hiked her chin. "I'll have your word on it."

"Yes ma'am. I promise." Jeff slid Beth a help-me look.

"He'll be on time and he'll find them, Nora. Mark and Ben will help." *That should ease Nora's mind.* "They've stopped NINA twice." *First with Kelly Walker and then with Dr. Lisa Harper.* "They surely can get whoever did this."

"Could be them. That Karl Masson is still on the loose," Nora said. "Kelly and Lisa can identify him."

Masson was the latest NINA operative they'd battled and he'd escaped. His boss, Raven, had been tagged as existing, but despite enormous efforts by all resources, she remained a mystery. Nora's observation about Masson had Jeff frowning. He'd spent many a night awake in a cold sweat.

Mark dipped his dark head, his expression stern. "We'll handle it, Nora."

"I know you will." She reached up and patted his angular face.

"Definitely." Beth said it, and prayed it proved true. "You get cleaned up now, Nora. We've got things to do."

Mark and Ben walked Nora over. She tottered, still unsteady on her feet.

Annie scanned the clusters of people in the courtyard. "I need to find Hank."

"He's over with Clyde," Beth said. Now why was Sara staring at the cake, as still as a statue? That "boom" message and the strings being tied to their fingers had scared her socks off. Beth's too, but Sara seemed...worse. *Why?* Beth walked over. "You okay?"

"Robert still has his phone turned off." Tall and svelte, Sara lifted her blond head, her voice as vacant as her blue eyes. Her chignon had half fallen; strands of long blond hair brushed her shoulders.

Right now, Beth couldn't care less about Robert Tayton. "He'll turn up." *Bad pennies always do.* "I asked about you." Sara didn't look unreasonably anxious, but her reassurance would be welcome. Anxiety really complicated her lifelong medical challenges. "You okay?"

"No, I'm not." Sara craned her neck and looked Beth straight in the eye. "I doubt I'll ever be okay again."

Sara wasn't being melodramatic. She always had been fragile. "You can't fall apart right now. Honest, Sara, you're going to have to cope like the rest of us. Nora's a wreck, Nathara's grating on everyone's last nerve, and there isn't a soul who doesn't think NINA's behind this attack. We do *not* need you getting wound up and triggering an attack that lands you in the hospital, so just don't go there."

"NINA *is* involved." Sara blinked hard, her eyes full of fear.

Beth stilled. The way Sara said that...she wasn't speculating, she knew. But how could she? "What aren't you telling me?"

For a second, Sara looked as if she might say, but then a shield slid down over her face and she disappeared behind it. "Nothing. Everyone says NINA's involved."

Her general remark sure felt specific—and it probably was, but Sara could be bullheaded. She always did things in her own time. Apparently whatever she might share she wasn't going to—yet. "For me, the question isn't *if* but *why.* They didn't take anything or hurt anyone except Clyde, but I doubt they expected to kill him. So why attack this at all? What did NINA want to prove?"

Sara stiffened. "That they're in control. That they can kill us all, or specific ones of us, any time they choose."

Knocking them all out and tying fishing line to those women with NINA connections proved that. "Granted, but why the warning? We knew they could get to us. They've done it. Kidnapping Lisa, hunting down Kelly Walker. So why attack here now?"

A tear leaked out of Sara's eye. "Because they can."

"No." Beth frowned. "There's a specific reason. NINA's disciplined and always specific. It never makes general statements. There's more to this."

Sara looked away. Her phone rang. "Maybe that's Robert."

Bad pennies. Giving Sara privacy, Beth joined Mark, Jeff, Ben, Harvey, and

Roxy, huddling with Hank. First break in the conversation, she asked, "What did they do to us?"

"Anesthetic." Hank looked at Beth. "Used for surgery all the time. Not harmful."

"Not harmful?" She lifted a hand. "So Clyde is dead because…?"

"*Typically* not harmful," Hank said. "Clyde had complications due to other medical issues."

Nora wouldn't take comfort in that. As soon as the initial shock wore off, she'd be spittin' mad—and poor Roxy looked equally devastated. She had looked forward to this day for months and now attackers had ruined it. Forfeiting three years of her marriage in a divorce she didn't want but needed to keep her husband alive and safe… Hadn't she sacrificed enough? Beth's chest went tight. It just wasn't right. "How can I help?"

"Anything you can run down on similar attacks would be great," Mark said.

"Wait," Jeff objected. "I'm not authorized to ask you to do that, Beth."

"They knocked us all out." She slid Jeff a loaded look. "I don't need to be asked."

Relief flashed across his face. He wanted to ask her to share what she found; she saw it in his eyes, but he wouldn't. Tight budget.

And she wouldn't make him. "I'll courtesy copy you and Mark on everything—in case somebody catches me digging and takes exception." Bending, she hugged Roxy and then Harvey Talbot. "I'm sorry these jerks messed up your special day."

"Me too." Roxy blinked hard. "But everyone else is okay, we have tomorrow, and that's what most matters—except for Clyde."

And Nora. Beth's heart wrenched. Clyde had been Nora's companion for a lot of years, ever since he'd been widowed. She'd feel his loss most, and that she had to infuriated Beth. She owed Nora more than anyone knew and was determined to find out who had done this.

Sara came over. "We can go now, right?"

Jeff nodded. "All the cars in the lot have been swept and everything's fine."

Sara's expression said it all. Her jerk husband, Robert Tayton III, was still missing.

Head down and shoulders slumped, Sara departed.

"Is she okay?" Roxy asked. "She looks ready to jump out of her skin."

She did. Something was definitely amiss. They were all upset, but Sara carried some extra burden. For some reason, she seemed to be blaming herself for this incident. Why?

Hank answered Roxy. "Sara's always been high strung. But if she made it through this without an attack, she'll be fine."

He was right about that.

"You calling in your old team?" Jeff asked Mark.

Mark had been in Special Operations. His team had all been in the village to help when Lisa had been abducted. Beth liked them all, but one team member was special. *Joe.* Her breath hitched. She'd love to see him—he'd planned to be here today for the ceremony—but something he wasn't free to discuss had come up.

That was often the case for the former Shadow Watchers. Spies who once spied on spies had a lot of things they weren't free to discuss, even after they left the intelligence community and just consulted on special assignments. Having consulted often with Quantico, Beth fully understood. It's impossible to take out of a person's head what you've put into it. Once in, to some extent, you were in for life.

"The team's tied up right now," Mark told Jeff.

Disappointment bit Beth hard. She tucked her chin-length hair behind her ear. This ordeal rattled her in a way she'd rarely been rattled. Joe had a soothing effect on her and others. Tall and broad-shouldered, he had a calm and confident air that made him serene even in crises. With eyes somewhere between blue and green and thick blond hair that curled low on his neck, the man was a woman magnet and just plain cool too, which is why she'd had coffee and dinner with him dozens of times but hadn't allowed herself to fall for him.

He'd break her heart just like Max had, no doubt about it.

Max had been cool too—and he'd humiliated her, ditching her very publicly for a glamour girl. The same kind of glamour girl that gravitated to Joe and clung.

"Sorry, Beth. You're too…ordinary."

Even now, Max's words stung. Everyday average couldn't hold up to glamour. Never did, never would—which is why Joe, no matter how sincere he seemed or how charming, had to be kept at arm's length.

Still, his skills would be helpful. He'd been on the front line and instrumental in resolving Lisa's abduction. If this was about NINA, the villagers needed Joe. Beth did too. He subtly invited her to lean on him, and she could…but only just a little. Another broken heart she did not need.

Not that she was the same woman now she'd been with Max. Now, she was a successful businesswoman, rich, and confident in her skin—and that skin was slimmer now due to her daily beach runs, but it was still ordinary and everyday average. *Once burned, twice shy.*

Annie stood near Nora's shower screen, waiting patiently. Beth looked at Lisa. "You'll get your mom and Nora home, right?" They shared an apartment at the Towers, next door to Beth's beach house.

"Mark and I will handle it." Lisa nodded. "Don't worry, Beth. Mom's good at comforting the grieving. She'll take care of Nora."

Annie would. Beth started walking away, stopped, and looked at Mark. "If you hear from Joe, have him call me when he can." Her insides twisted. She needed a little of Joe's calm, even if it was from a distance.

Knowing glinted in Mark's gray eyes. "He'll like that."

Unable to miss Jeff's disappointment, Beth walked out toward her car. Jeff was a good man. He was also still half in love with her. If she had half a brain, she'd jump at him, but her heart wouldn't let her. He deserved someone to love him back, and she just didn't. So every day of her life, she prayed he'd find a woman who would. So far, it hadn't happened, but like Nora always said: "In God's own sweet time."

Ironic that Beth felt the same way about Joe. And even more ironic was, despite Mark's comment, Joe was about as apt to be genuinely interested in her as she was in Jeff. Oh, Joe said he wanted a home and a family, one day—and he said it in a way that made her think he'd never really had either one—but she wasn't a fool. She was fine for coffee and conversation, but Joe would build that life with an extraordinary woman.

Beth sighed. *Love's fickle. That's that.*

Fire trucks lined the front of the parking lot. Every patrol car in the tri-county area seemed to be on site. From the cameras and lights, a ton of reporters had gathered just outside the police blockade. Their shouted questions garbled but one snagged her ear. *"Was it NINA?"*

The media all thought NINA was responsible too. Why?

Beth didn't know—yet.

4

ᘓᐧᘒ

W e've got a problem."

Joe recognized his former Shadow Watcher teammate's voice in his Bluetooth. After taking down NINA's human-trafficking operation and rescuing Mark's Lisa, the team decided it best to keep their distance for a while. *Broader target.* Fortunately they had secure phones to stay in touch.

"What's up, bro?" Joe slid on his stomach through the grass and held up his night-vision goggles.

Nearly nine thirty, long past dark, and still no sign of Karl Masson. Joe's sources had been adamant that the escaped NINA operative was in this state park. His RV and the car he towed behind it hadn't moved in two days, but the man was a no-show.

Mark filled Joe in on the club attack.

Joe's stomach clutched. "Are Beth and Lisa okay?"

"Lisa's safe. Beth's rattled but fine. She's why I'm calling."

She's safe. She's safe. Breathe, Joe. Breathe. "Oh?"

"Yeah. She's looking into the incident, Joe."

"Dangerous work." If NINA was behind it, deadly.

"And then some. She wants you to call her." Mark sighed. "She's like you."

"What do you mean?"

"Always the strong one holding up everybody else."

"You're subtle as mud, bro." Mark had overhead one too many calls from Joe's wayward brothers, hitting him up for bail money. "It's different. She's different."

"I don't think it's different."

"Taking care of everybody is her nature." Joe loved that about her. As a kid, he'd longed for someone to take care of him and his brothers. But with his parents, that was a pipe dream. They'd rather drink than feed their kids. With Beth, caring was just there. As natural to her as breathing. Was it encoded in her DNA or something? He wondered. Often. The woman was gorgeous—slim, brown shiny hair with gold streaks and bright brown eyes—and got Joe's attention, but her nurturing everyone—even him… That snagged his heart and reeled him in like a fish. Where she stood toward him was anyone's guess.

"Not to change the subject, but you need to know. We had a fatality—Clyde Parker."

Joe recalled the arthritic senior he'd first mistaken for Nora's husband and his stomach clutched again. "I'm sorry, bro. He was a good man." Joe skidded back to a tree and sat up behind it. "How's Nora taking it?"

"About like you'd expect."

"Yeah." Joe let his gaze drift. "You summoning the team?" Mark would get the indirect question. *Do you think NINA pulled the attack?*

"Considered it, but things here are too hot. FBI is handling it."

And Homeland Security. "I'm there if you need me."

"I'm not officially in the loop. Anything changes, I'll let you know."

"Understood." Beth wanted him to call. She confused Joe, and he couldn't get her out of his head. She seemed interested in him, but his charm didn't work on her. Figured. The one woman he wished it would work on was immune. "Did Beth say why she wanted me to call?" Was it personal or professional?

"No."

"Care to speculate?" Joe couldn't tamp his interest.

"Could be she's shaky. Seeing everyone blacked out like that and Nora losing Clyde—you know Beth's really close to Nora, right?"

"Yeah, I know." There wasn't much Beth and he hadn't discussed except those parts of their work that neither of them could discuss with anyone.

"She might want to talk about Sara's husband."

Beth and Robert Tayton had a longstanding feud. She didn't trust him and he hated her for it. Sara was stuck in the middle, playing peacemaker, and Beth hated that most of all. "What's the snake-oil salesman done now?"

"I don't know. He didn't show up today. Sara couldn't reach him. She was worried."

That'd send Beth into a tailspin. Back in college, she'd promised Sara's mom she'd watch over Sara, and since Sara's parents' deaths, Beth had kept her word. "I'll call her."

"Anybody phone home?"

The team. "Sam's neck-deep in the annual Civil War battle reenactment." Mark would know that was in Alabama. "Tim's down in the Keys."

"Still nursing a broken heart?"

"Oh yeah." Joe frowned and swatted a mosquito buzzing his face. "Mandy was supposed to marry the guy she dumped Tim for today."

"Did she do it?"

All the guys had hoped she'd come to her senses. "I haven't heard, so I guess she did."

"Tim'll be a wreck for a while then."

"Yeah." Tim and Mandy had been engaged for nearly a year when she met Mr. Wonderful and kicked Tim to the curb like a piece of trash. Foolish move she'd one day regret. Tim had it all: looks, personality, money, and class. Joe didn't get it—and he liked women and understood most of them better than they understood themselves. But he'd never understood Mandy. The woman had secrets; Joe would bank on it.

He swiped at the sweat on his forehead with his shirt-sleeve and glanced over. Light from a pole splayed over Karl Masson's RV and the rear windshield of his car. Nothing stirring. "I haven't talked to Nick."

"Special assignment. Madagascar, I think."

Joe deciphered the code. *Middle East. One of the oil-producing countries.*

"Where are you?"

"Following up a lead on Karl Masson."

"Without backup?" Mark's voice elevated a full octave.

"Just some recon, bro. No interdiction."

After the human-trafficking incident, the FBI put out word that Masson had died in a fishing camp explosion in Louisiana. As long as NINA continued to think that, Masson would live. Yet something was going on, or headquarters wouldn't have requested Joe take on a special assignment monitoring Masson's RV.

"Watch your back."

"Will do." Joe checked again. Still no activity. It'd been nearly forty-eight hours. Where was he? Had to be on an extended rafting trip. That's the only thing that made sense. "When's Clyde's funeral?"

"Tuesday. But don't come. Like I said, things are too hot here right now."

Typical Mark. Always trying to protect everyone else. But if things were that hot, someone needed to watch his back and Beth's. "Understood."

"I mean it, Joe. NINA would love to kill us both. Lay low."

"Got it, bro." Joe would radio in the RV's GPS coordinates and leave immediately for Seagrove Village. Mark knew Joe would; had known it when he called. One of those strings had been tied to Lisa's finger. No way would Mark stay out of it—officially or unofficially—and for the same reason, neither would Joe.

Beth Dawson might not yet realize she mattered much to Joe, but he realized it. She was sporting one of those strings *and* looking into the incident? Wild horses couldn't keep him away.

"Get creative."

Very creative. "Yeah."

"And check with your sources on Robert Tayton III. Something's off with that guy."

Of the team, Joe had the broadest reach on connections. His team depended on that to survive. "Any idea what?"

"No. But it's something."

Mark's instincts were legend. "All over it." Joe locked in the GPS coordinates and crawled on his belly and elbows through the woods to his bike. He'd call Sam on his way down to the village and have him run a background on Tay-ton. Nick was sharper on computers, but Sam had a bloodhound's nose. If there was anything to find, Sam would find it. "Karl Masson's been MIA from his gear for forty-eight hours. He could be your man."

"You think NINA knows he's alive and brought him back into the organization?"

"Do we have proof NINA ever considered him dead?"

Mark grunted. "Valid point."

Joe slid over an oak's protruding roots, scraping his stomach and thighs. "Get me a secure line to talk to Beth."

"I need a couple hours."

"Fine." A rock dug into Joe's elbow. He winced. "Who's handling the club attack?"

"Roxy."

It was her event—she was the bride—and the FBI assigned her? She was good, very good and gutsy, but the personal interest made assigning her a questionable move. "She's way too close, bro."

"She can handle it. She's the top authority on NINA and motivated."

So Homeland Security made the call and pegged NINA as its primary suspect. With Karl Masson on the loose, this didn't look good. "You need the team."

"No. Not this time."

"Understood." They could best assist from a distance—and maybe stay alive.

Joe walked the last twenty yards to his Harley, then drove off into the night, dialing Sam.

ᏣᎤ

From behind a twisted oak, Karl Masson watched Joe go. When he was out of sight, Karl fished out his own phone and hit speed dial.

A woman answered. "Yes?"

"Raven?" It sounded like her, but he couldn't be sure.

"Who is this?"

"Gray Ghost." He studied the spiderweb tattoo on his right hand between his forefinger and thumb.

"Mission?"

"Dead Game."

"Code?"

"A72777."

"You're late reporting in."

It was Raven. "Yes ma'am. Unavoidable."

"They've picked up on you, then."

"Yes ma'am." How high up the chain, he wasn't sure. But having a Shadow Watcher on his back for two days proved word he was active was no longer secret. Masson broke into a sweat. With Raven, the truth or a lie could get an operative killed—even if he was the best go-to cleaner in the entire organization. Truthfully, she worried him more than Homeland Security or the Shadow Watchers. They weren't ruthless. "He's departed the fix, which means he's probably en route to Seagrove Village."

"We're ready."

Her local operatives were in jail, tied up, or campaigning for mayor. She needed someone stealthy who could actually do her some good. "What are my orders?"

"Leave the car and RV in place and get down here as soon as you can."

Great. Just great. Mark Taylor and Benjamin Brandt would be looking for him on every corner. Their women, Lisa Harper and Kelly Walker, would be too. Raven knew that, so why was she bringing him—a possibility struck hard. "You're not suffering any ill effects?" He started walking. It was six miles to the nearest town.

"No, I'm fine. Having me at the club during the attack was a stroke of genius."

"Thank you." His idea and, since it was successful, his glory. What better cover for Raven than to be one of the victims? "Where should I go when I get there?"

"Call half an hour before arrival for further instructions. Raven out."

The line went dead.

Masson shivered. When he'd contacted Raven about Harvey and Roxy's ceremony and suggested the Dead Game operation, he figured his odds were fifty-fifty. Raven would either welcome him back or kill him. She had bought into the FBI claim he was dead. He tried, but he couldn't stay hidden. Not with authorities turning over every rock to find him. They'd gotten too close to his kids. That's when he had to move, take the risk, and hope Raven brought him back into the fold. Fortunately, she liked his plan.

It was brilliant.

But whether or not it was brilliant enough to keep him alive, Raven alone would decide. And what she decided, he suspected, would depend on that nosy computer whiz at SaBe.

5

⊘✿⊙

t was a hard night to be alone.

A few hours before midnight, Beth sat on the back porch of her Gulf-front home with her laptop balanced on her knees and ran an update on NINA and today's incident. Waiting for her security clearance to kick in, she looked over at the Towers. Nora's apartment was still lit up. Poor thing likely wouldn't sleep a wink tonight.

Few knew Nora worked as a housekeeper for Ben because he needed her and not because she needed the job. She and Nathara had learned business at their dad's knee, and on Nora's eighteenth birthday, she'd bought her first store. Over the next fifty years, she built an empire. Beth hadn't known that—few did—until she'd started SaBe with Sara, and Nora made it her mission to help Beth successfully navigate business's shark-infested waters. She'd saved Beth's hide a million times, celebrated her every accomplishment, and somehow always knew SaBe's exact status.

Sara and Beth had been born to average middle-class families, spent four years as roommates in college, and after graduation started SaBe Inc. They'd worked hard, built a sterling reputation, and in a gutsy move had formed a strategic business alliance to do the software for the patent owner of a semi-conductor doping process that revolutionized electronic devices. In five years, their little software business had exploded. They had licensing agreements for their software with every major electronics firm and thousands of feeder firms—enough that SaBe was up to twenty-eight employees, most of whom were attorneys, security, and support staff. They were well paid, and Beth and Sara were beyond rich. Robert Tayton III wanted a big piece of that—Sara's piece of that.

For nearly a year, Nora suggested Beth hire a new software developer, but since the lab was Sara's domain and the one place she seemed like the woman she was before marrying Robert, Beth hadn't done it. The look in Nora's eye proved she knew exactly why, and she never uttered a single reprimand. Beth loved that. She was too soft for cutthroat business, but Nora was tough. It took a secure woman to be that comfortable and confident being tough, and no one understood that better than Clyde Parker. How many times had Beth told him if she could find him in a thirty-year-old model, she'd marry him? Dozens. Beth choked up. So hard to believe he was gone.

He and Nora were there when Max humiliated Beth. They'd nudged her toward Jeff, but when Beth said the x factor just wasn't there, that was that. They trusted her judgment—even after the Max debacle. That meant a lot to her—and she considered having them lecture her parents. They'd been bad after Max, but after Sara married, they'd been single-minded in their goal to get Beth married so they could live their dream of moving to Europe for a few years. Her mom denied that, of course. *"You can take care of yourself, but life gets lonely. It's nice to have a partner to ride out the storms."*

Nora's take was more Beth's style. *"Ain't but one reason to get married, dearie. Because the idea of not marrying the man makes you want to crawl in a hole and die. Don't fret. God'll send the right man to you. Just watch for the signs he's arrived."*

That resonated. So until he arrived, Beth was hanging on to single life without remorse, and if Joe made her feel a little wistful, well, she'd just get over it. She didn't even know his last name—or any of the Shadow Watchers' last names, except for Mark Taylor's. Was Joe even Joe? She had no idea. But he was gorgeous and had an easy, laid-back charm that made Beth melt. Frankly, that was too reminiscent of Max—unnerving. Not even a stand-up guy like Joe should have that kind of power over her. Was that a sign? Or just chemistry?

All in all, if Sara hadn't issued that bizarre warning to Beth a week ago— *"No matter what happens, don't trust me. I can't and won't explain. Just promise me you'll protect yourself from me—and if you can, protect me from myself"*—Beth would love her life. But when your best friend puts that kind of monkey on your back…well, who could love life lugging that around?

Her phone rang.

Who'd be calling this late? She checked caller ID. *Sara.* "Hey, what's wrong?"

"Robert still hasn't called home. He's not at the hotel, not answering his phone—Beth, something bad must have happened." Her voice cracked. "Can you come over?"

No attacks. Please, no attacks. Beth shut down the computer and slipped inside. "I'm grabbing my purse."

"I'm scared."

And likely reliving her parents' deaths again. "It'll be okay. He's resourceful, Sara."

"Just hurry over, okay?"

"I'm on my way." Beth hung up, grabbed her purse, and locked the door behind her.

Twenty minutes later at Sara's kitchen table, Beth focused on Sara's crisis—because to have a friend you have to be one. "You haven't eaten?"

"First the attack, now Robert. Who can think about food?"

Beth made them a salad and pulled out the crackers. "Eat."

Sara frowned but picked up her fork.

On the phone, Sara had sounded frantic. Now she shoved lettuce around on her plate in silence. Beth debated. She should keep her mouth shut but didn't. "You took your meds, right?" When Sara nodded, Beth added, "Then you better eat so you don't get sick."

"My stomach's going to have to fend for itself." Parking her elbow on the table's polished edge, Sara wiped her face with her hand and covered her eyes. "I can't swallow." She looked over at Beth from between her fingers. "How can I eat when I can't swallow?"

"Sounding really stressed there." Tension had been building in Sara since she spotted the cake-topper bride with the groom ripped away. It didn't take much imagination to link that groom and Sara's both being missing. "Stress kills" wasn't an overstatement for Sara. She'd landed in the ER three times in the last year alone—and that was during a time she was supposedly well and happy. Asthma was a merciless wretch. Add anxiety attacks and being high-strung to it, and then toss in other medical complications Sara never discussed, and it made one wicked recipe for disaster.

Rocking her head back, Sara sought solace at some point beyond the ceiling and clearly didn't find it. "Where is he?"

Robert. A smooth talker who had shown up at an electronics conference in Atlanta last year and swept Sara off her feet. He was handsome and suave. She was naive and sheltered—a vulnerable recluse whose first love was her work.

Sara and Beth's differences made them perfect partners. Beth loved illogical and messy people, Sara loved creative computing, and they both had vision, drive, and more ambition than sense. They knew enough to risk anything and not so much that they feared failing. It was a recipe for success, and that they trusted each other implicitly gave them a little extra kick that impacted everything they touched in thousands of ways that couldn't be measured or charted.

Stealing Sara's heart had been disgustingly easy for Robert Tayton. He'd caught her up in a whirlwind relationship and a scant month later, he'd whisked Sara off to Las Vegas and married her.

You should have taken her to a remote cabin and nailed her feet to the floor until she got her head out of the clouds and her sense back. You knew Sara lacked experience—she had never been that close to a man in her life. She might have listened. Okay, maybe she would have listened. All right, all right. Odds were she wouldn't have heard a word, but at least you would have tried. You should have tried.

Oh, if only she could go back. Warn Sara away from him right off the bat. In the hotel lobby that night, *before* he sank his grubby manicured claws into her heart. Why hadn't Beth done that? Why? Why? Why…?

Remorse turned her salad bitter, and Beth pushed her plate away. In Atlanta, she had been sure he was out for a diversion. But when he followed them back to Seagrove Village, claiming he lived in Destin and had fallen in love with Sara at first sight, Beth had seen right through him, and she assumed Sara would know the truth at gut level—in that way women do, especially when they wished they didn't.

Unfortunately, Sara hadn't seen or known spit.

Logic had floated right out of her body and she'd bought into his bait—hook, line, and sinker. Robert Tayton III had fallen in love, all right—with Sara's assets. And letting him know Beth knew it had been the first of Beth's many mistakes. Sara paid the bill for that, which added interest to Beth's guilt that had her minding her p's and q's and keeping her mouth shut when she really wanted to just smack Sara and say, "Girl, he's using you. Grow a spine and kick him out on his social-climbing rump."

Of course, southern women didn't talk that way to southern women. It simply wasn't done, and if it were, it would open a great divide between them that neither woman would ever cross much less close. The rules of friendship were finite when it came to their men. If he's a louse, he's her louse. Never forget it, or else forget her.

Trying not to sigh, Beth cast a sidelong look at the sheaf of papers tucked into the side pocket of her briefcase propped against the edge of the counter near the door. She and Sara had planned to sign the agreement today, but there was no way she could hand it to her with Robert missing. Not even if Beth wouldn't enjoy a restful night's sleep until the documents were duly executed and turned back in to Nick Pope in Legal. Only after he and then Henry Baines, who headed SaBe's legal department, signed off on them would she be assured that if something happened to Sara, Robert wouldn't be sticking his nose into SaBe's business. Given a choice, Beth would exile the man to another planet, but since Sara loved him, banning him from SaBe would do.

"Where do you think he is, Beth?"

"I don't know."

"Maybe he's lost his wallet or his phone was stolen or something."

He could call home from any phone. "He'll get in touch when he can." *If not before, certainly when his money runs out.*

"You're right." Sara took a bite of salad and slowly chewed. "It's not just where he is, though. It's what he might be doing."

"What do you mean?" Beth frowned. "What do you think he's doing?"

"If I could answer that, I wouldn't be so worried."

"Are you afraid he's with another woman?"

Sara grunted. "Wouldn't it be wonderful if it were that simple?"

Odd response. Sara would be devastated. Puzzled, Beth pushed. "Would it?"

Before Sara could answer, someone rapped on the back door.

Eleven o'clock—who'd drop by? "I'll get it." Beth walked over and peeked out. Mark Taylor. What was he doing here? She opened the door. "Hi, Mark. Come on in."

"Can't. Lisa's working the graveyard shift at Crossroads. I need to get some food over to her." He passed a phone to Beth, and his sparkling eyes sobered. "Don't let anyone else know you've got this. When it rings, answer it."

"Okay." Beth took the phone and put it in her pocket. "Can I ask why?"

"Sure," he said, then turned and walked away.

You can ask. Just don't expect any answers. "Thanks," she called after him, unsure if it was warranted.

He didn't wave, slow down, or even look back.

A chill raced through Beth. She closed the door and, for some reason, locked it.

"Who was that?" Sara asked.

"Mark."

"What's he doing here?"

"Just checking in. He does that for Joe now and then." The phone had to be about Joe. Nothing else made sense. "I'm not sure why." She wasn't, though she'd wondered plenty.

"You know, I don't think Joe is as out of your reach as you believe." Sara left the sleek glass-top table and then paced between it and the long granite breakfast bar.

"I'm not reaching."

Sara frowned. "He's not Max, Beth."

"No, but they share traits I'd have to be a fool to ignore." Joe was totally out of her reach. Cool hooked up with glamorous, not with ordinary. One Max was plenty. Sara's reflection shone in the countertop's surface. Why was she tottering? "New shoes?"

"What?"

"You're hobbling." Why did she wear heels at home anyway? Beth shed her shoes the second she hit the entryway. Sara had never been the barefoot kind, but at home she used to wear flats or on rare occasions slippers. Now she probably wore heels to shower. Had to be to please Robert. "Take the things off." Was her instep bruised? Hard to tell with her black hose, but her ankles were definitely swollen.

"They're new. I need to break them in." Sara looked down at the black pumps, then shut her eyes a brief second. "I'm going to call the hotel again." She strode around the counter, listing heavily to the right, then snagged the wall phone near the gourmet center. "Surely he's gotten there by now."

On returning from the hairdresser, Sara had found a note. Robert had gone to New Orleans to meet an editor interested in publishing his novel. After he and Sara married, he had quit his job in the pharmaceutical industry to pursue his dream of being a novelist.

"The concierge said he would have Robert call the moment he arrived," Beth reminded her, knowing it wouldn't stop her from calling the poor man yet again.

"I know." She rubbed at her throat. "But something could have happened to the rental. He could be broken down on the road in a dead zone. That'd explain his phone not working."

Or he could be dead in a ditch somewhere. That kind of thinking was reminiscent of Beth's mother's. Anything that frightened her she reduced to the morbid, and Sara was becoming more and more like her. *Programmed negative.* Beth held back another sigh, wishing someone—anyone—in her immediate circle besides Nora wasn't dysfunctional.

"His e-mail said the Hummer had a 'check engine light,' but the dealer wouldn't let him take a loaner out of state, so he—"

The cherry-red Hummer, a wedding gift from Sara. "Went to your regular shop where they could handle the repair and he could get a rental. He also promised he'd call as soon as he checked into the hotel." Beth had no illusions Sara would listen.

"The trip should have taken him a little over four hours." Sara checked her watch. "It's eleven fifteen. He's seriously late—and his phone is out of order."

"I know." Beth plucked a bite of ripe tomato from her plate. Robert knew Sara would be worried sick and having fits. He knew what this kind of worrying did to her, and he was putting her through it anyway. So much for being her devoted, besotted husband. He faked it with his high-society friends but didn't bother with Beth. *Ordinary.*

Sara dialed the phone. A pause, then, "This is Sara Tayton again." Her voice trembled. She smoothed her hand down her slim black skirt. "I'm sorry to keep bothering you, but—"

She'd called Beth to come over *and* dressed in black—Sara was already in mourning. Now she gripped a hank of long blond hair near her scalp and shook it. The gesture was too familiar to miss: a bad, bad sign. He wasn't there.

"Thank you." Blinking hard and fast, Sara braced her hand on the countertop for support. It was shaking. "Yes, I will. Sorry to trouble you again." She hung up, took a deep breath, then again lifted the receiver and punched in a number.

His cell. Beth rinsed their plates. Sara's housekeeper, Maria, was devoted to Sara and locked in mutual disdain with Robert. She left early most days to give him a wide berth. Beth loaded the dishwasher, her concern escalating. When Sara hadn't heard from Robert by lunch, she was a wreck—after the incident at the club, a walking catastrophe. Watching her slide down the slippery slope to one of her debilitating attacks knotted Beth's insides. Hopefully the jerk would show up before Sara tumbled into a full-fledged breakdown.

Could either of them survive that again?

Unsure, Beth shuddered. "Still no answer?"

"No." Sara cradled the phone and limped back to the table, twisting a rope of pearls hanging from her neck. "This isn't like him."

Beth hated pearls as much as Sara loved them. They suited her pale, delicate features and her quiet personality. Beth was not quiet or delicate. Her dark hair and eyes and olive skin required bolder accessories, ones that made a statement.

Sara was content to purr.

Beth naturally roared.

"No, it isn't." Robert typically stuck closer to Sara than glue on a stamp, terrified that something Beth said would sink in and Sara would ditch him. Oh, how Beth wished she had that kind of influence. But she didn't. Resigned, she snagged a paper towel from the roll and then dabbed at a water spot on the front of her bright red blouse.

Anger simmered in Sara's eyes. "Don't pretend to be concerned. You hate him."

"I don't hate him." Here it came. An anger dump. Scared women acted angry. It was one of the mysteries of life right up there with crying when happy. Beth shored up for it.

"You and Robert have been at war for six months. I know. I've been caught between the rock and the hard place, trying to keep you from killing each other."

"It hasn't been that bad." It could have been, but Beth had bitten her tongue until it bled to keep Sara from having to choose between them. Not that Beth had a single doubt what Sara would do. The man was her husband.

"It has been that bad. Maybe worse."

Okay, so Beth and Robert had been at war. Well, an undeclared war. When they couldn't avoid each other, they were civil but clearly on hostile ground. Robert had brought that on, systematically undercutting Beth and Sara's friendship and causing friction at SaBe. Sara couldn't see it; she was in love with the jerk. But Beth's vision was crystal-clear.

Treading on dangerous ground, she carefully framed her response. "I am concerned. Everything that matters to you concerns me."

Sara's anger drained. "I'm sorry I snapped at you." Sara cupped her head with her hands, squeezed her eyes shut, and then slowly reopened them. "I know you're concerned—at least, for me. But I know how you feel about Robert too. You say you don't hate him, yet…"

"I don't like him?" Beth suggested, keeping it real. Sara nodded and Beth stopped sponging the tabletop. "I don't lie to you—never have and not starting now. I don't like Robert, I never did and frankly I never will. But we're family, Sara. I love you, and you love him. So there it is."

"When I grow up, I want to be just like you." Sara gave her a watery smile. "My marriage has been hard on us and SaBe, but…" Her voice faded. A strange sadness filled her face. "I wish this had never happened." She lowered her gaze. "I wish everything had stayed the same. If I could go back…"

What was *that* about? Go back to before Robert? Or to before Sara and Beth had gotten off on the wrong foot about Robert? "Forget it, okay?" No good could come of going down that road. "Family is family. No man can change that." On Robert, the lines in the sand had been drawn and neither of them would ever cross over to the other's side. "We're fine. No matter what, we'll always be fine. That's a promise, okay?"

"Okay." Tears had Sara blinking hard. She wanted to say something, nearly did, but then fell back and regrouped. "I'm sorry. You aren't to blame for any of this. I'm—I'm just…"

Terrified. Reliving the worst tragedy in your life, the death of your parents. "You're worried. First the club attack and now this—sure, you're worried."

Sara dropped her gaze. "Yes."

Beth drank from her glass and then shrugged. She could afford to be gracious; the anger dump was behind them and Sara had been reassured. Considering everything, that was the best Beth could offer. "No problem. We help each other through hard times."

"In ways you can't imagine. God willing, you'll never be able to imagine them."

Beth stilled. "What does that mean?"

She waved a hand. "Nothing. Just…nothing."

"You've been dropping cryptic bombs on me for a week. When are you going to tell me what's going on?"

"Not now. I…can't. When I can, I will." Sara slumped, spotted a card on the counter and snagged it. "Oh no. The fund-raiser's tonight."

"Tonight? It's midnight."

"No, tomorrow—Sunday night." Sara wrung her hands. "I can't do it, Beth. It's Robert's group."

Beth supported the charities, but socials with Robert's snooty friends left her cold. "One day you're going to knock this off and stay away from them. You give in to panic and it just gets stronger. Pray on it instead. Have you prayed on it?"

"I can't pray on this."

"Of course you can. You can pray on anything."

"Not on this," she snapped. "You don't understand."

Sara rarely snapped. Beth studied her. "Then explain it to me."

"It's best that I don't." With a trembling hand, she shoved her hair back from her face. "Just go in my place." She passed the card. "It's for the moms."

Something weird was going on that terrified Sara a lot more than the attack. NINA, and yet this was worse? Fear slithered down to Beth's bones. "Is the reason you can't pray connected to the warning you gave me—about protecting myself from you, and you from yourself?"

Sara didn't answer.

It did connect. Whatever it was, it was worse than bad, and there was no way Sara was going to talk about it. Beth tugged at her sleeves. "Okay, I'll go."

In the past year, Sara had taken an intense interest in domestic violence and single moms. It started eight months ago with a case at the crisis center, which often took roll-over 911 calls when the department was short staffed. A four-year-old boy had phoned in and said, "My daddy killed my mommy." Sara had taken the call, and on learning most stayed in violent situations because they lacked the means to get out of them, she began a fund-raising blitz that she was still on. She wanted to adopt that little boy, but Robert wasn't ready for kids. Sara had seen the child placed with a good family and kept tabs on him, and so far she had raised nearly a quarter million dollars for victims of domestic violence. "Where is the fund-raiser?"

"At the club." Sara shot Beth an apology. "Sorry. I know it's the last place you want to go, and I wouldn't ask, but it's important. We need rent-subsidy money and the kids need fun stuff—swing sets, bikes, and—"

"I'll donate a million if I can skip it," Beth seriously bargained.

"I'll take your million, but the goal for tonight is to raise two million. I need you there to guilt them into it—and to work on Darla Green to donate that Airport Road property. It's perfect for rent-subsidized apartments for women with kids, trying to get on their feet."

"I thought that's why we bought that land up north from Race Miller."

"We did, but it's so far out and there's no public transportation."

Both of which they knew before buying it. "So get them a bus or something."

"No, it's too remote." Sara looked guilty. "Race's wife, Aline, said the average response time on 911 calls is about twenty-five minutes. That's just too long."

"Mark Taylor could put in a great security system, Sara. Like he did at Ben's house."

"I know—and the one at Three Gables is great. But I—I just don't want them there."

Odd. She'd been wild about the idea. Settled on it before she'd even told Beth about it. Why the big change? Boy, a whole lot of things with her lately just weren't making sense. "Okay, I'll work on Darla. What are we gonna do with the land we got from Race?"

"I don't know yet. But Airport Road would be perfect for the moms."

"You are remembering airports have planes and they make noise, right?" Beth caught Sara's glare. "I'm just saying."

"It's a grass strip and rarely used." Sara stilled. "Please, Beth. It's Robert's friends and I don't want to disappoint—"

Robert's friends, Darla Green aside. "Is anyone normal going to be there?" Status. Money. Social standing. Robert's group thrived on all that rot.

"One or two. Maybe. Please, Beth. For the moms."

Beth grabbed a banana from the fruit bowl and began peeling its skin. "I hate it when you pull that guilt-trip stuff on me." She chomped down on a bite.

"I know. But I'm desperate."

"You do it because it works."

"That too," Sara said.

Beth sighed. "Okay. I'll stomach them long enough to take their money." At least it would be used for something constructive. "Does Darla know she's donating this property?"

"She knows I'm after it."

"Well, if she comes back to the club after today, odds are she's giving it to you."

"She hinted she was. That's why it's critical for you to be there. Darla would move mountains for you."

She would. On two commercial acquisitions, Beth's tips had saved Darla a fortune. It had to be hard for her, losing John, being arrested for his murder, and spending months proving her innocence. Then her own son disowned her—that had to cut to the core. "All right, I'll go."

"Thanks. Nine o'clock. Darla is handling the details. You'll just need to speak a few words—and it'll help if you don't snarl at them."

"Cute." Sara obviously didn't expect this problem with Robert to resolve quickly. Now what should Beth think of that? "I need to check on Nora. Hey, maybe she'll come along." Beth dialed her cell phone. "She could squeeze blood from a turnip."

"It's late. Don't call her now."

"With Clyde passing...she's not sleeping."

"Don't ask. She won't be comfortable with Robert's friends."

"Nora's comfortable anywhere. Robert's friends won't be comfortable seeing themselves through her eyes. Maybe they'll donate more to make themselves feel better."

Nora answered on the first ring. "Do you realize it's after midnight, Beth Dawson?" Some game show played on Nora's television. "Who else is dead?"

"Nobody. I just knew you'd be up." Beth walked out into the yard, looked beyond the grass onto the calm cove water bathed in moonlight.

"Ah. Quit fretting, dearie, I'm fine. You should be catching a wee wink."

Beth filled Nora in on what was going on at Sara's.

"He's up to no good, that one."

Nora was not a Robert fan either. "I'm afraid so too," Beth admitted, glad she didn't have to guard her words. Jasmine bushes lined the edge of the yard and their scent hung heavy in the air, blending with the salt-tinged breeze blowing in off the water.

"You watch her, Beth. Our Sara puts on a fine face, but she's had a time with that one."

Did Nora know anything about that cryptic warning? "Why do you think so?"

"It's in her eyes, dearie. She ain't happy, and that's that. Sara's a troubled soul."

Beth swallowed hard. "Do you know why?"

"Girl, God gave you sense. Use it. She's married to a shyster, bless her heart."

"Point taken." A fish jumped and moonlight sparkled on the ripples. "So will you go with me to the fund-raiser? It's at the club. If you don't want to be there after today, it's—"

"I'm mourning my Clyde, true enough, but I got enough of my wits to stay away from that club and so should you. NINA was there. It ain't safe and that's a fact."

Beth had considered that. "They'll stay away because we know they were there."

"Your call, of course, but I don't like it and I ain't going. Annie and I are making arrangements for Clyde's funeral. It's Tuesday. Two o'clock. Reverend Brown's doing a graveside service. Don't be late."

"I won't. I'm so sorry about Clyde, Nora." Beth swallowed a knot of tears. "I'll miss him."

"Me too. Something fierce, my girl." She sniffed. "I'll send money for the moms and kids. You know I ain't tight-fisted like Nathara, but I can't abide Robert's friends. They scrape my nerves. With Nathara here, ain't much left to scrape."

They scraped Beth's nerves too, though it shamed her to think it. "Want me to invite Nathara and give you a break?" She had to ask, but after Nathara's acidic attitude today, Beth was weary. *Please decline. Please…*

Nora cackled. "She'd fit right in with that bunch, but no need to make you suffer. Darla invited her. Spare your nerves and go on your own. Shame Joe won't be there, but maybe you'll meet a nice young man like him—and be sure security walks you to your car."

"Me meet a nice man in Robert's crowd?" Beth grunted. "Don't hold your breath."

"Smart woman. Just go take their money for the moms and run."

"As fast as my feet can carry me." Beth grinned. "We are so bad, Nora."

"Decadent, dearie."

"See you at church in the morning."

"Keep me posted on the truant husband. Nathara says she hopes he stays gone." Nora sighed. "Hate to agree with her on anything, but Sara could use the peace."

"She could." Beth should feel awful for saying that but didn't. "Try to sleep. 'Night." She hung up the phone and went back into the kitchen.

Pacing the floor, Sara sneezed three times, took a few steps, and sneezed twice more. Something had triggered her allergies. Frazzled and barely able to conceal it, she stopped beside the sink. "Do you think he's all right?" She made circles at her temples. "Really?"

NOT THIS TIME   49

What in the world? Sara was fragile but not obsessed. She looked ready to crawl out of her skin. "I'm sure he's fine." If Beth could get her hands on him right now, she'd pull a Nora and blister Robert Tayton's ears. "He probably got to New Orleans late and met with the editor before going to his hotel, or something simple like that."

Beth sat across the table, thumbed the edge of a soft green silk place mat. "Honestly, if he were hurt, you'd have heard by now, you know? This is a time when no news is good. He's just doing stuff men do when they're out on their own." *Hopefully that didn't include anything he shouldn't be doing.* Beth would rip out her own vocal cords without anesthetic before saying that to Sara.

Still rubbing at her temple, which was obviously pounding, Sara cast her a doubtful look. "If he'd just turn on his mobile…"

Next Sara would be wishing they had agreed to Robert's suggestion to have locator chips implanted in their necks—a suggestion he made the day he supposedly found out just how wealthy Sara and Beth's little company had made them. Beth had refused, of course, though she had wished a hundred times then that she'd had a chip implanted in her digital recorder. She'd kept everything loaded on it and when it disappeared, she lost a month's worth of work, not to mention hundreds of notes on different projects that could never be recovered. "He will when he gets around to it," she told Sara for the hundredth time. "Let's get some rest, okay?"

"You're not going home now, are you?"

"No, I'll rest in the den. You go to bed for a while. If the phone rings, I'll answer it right away and get you."

"Okay. I do need to get off my feet." Sara went down the hallway to the master suite.

How could she actually believe Robert had no idea about her money? He'd probably run financial histories on both of them before they even left Atlanta—and if not then, certainly he had after he visited Sara's home.

Her mansion on the cove was impressive by anyone's standards—even if they had redecorated it to make it "theirs" in a sophisticated, minimalist style that was totally Robert and so not Sara. The house used to be beautiful and charming, warm and friendly—more like Beth's. Now it was palatial and glacial and lacked any evidence of its owners sharing a real life in it. That manipulation of image was probably a strategic move on Robert's part to make him seem warmer. Not that it did.

Beth stretched out on the den sofa and stared at the phone Mark brought her. Had to be for Joe. But why did he need a separate phone? He had her cell.

Clearly, he didn't want to use it.

Which, with Joe, could mean anything at all. Her glance stole ceilingward. *Keep him safe. He might be out of my reach, but he's not out of Yours, and I do worry about him.*

Where was he?

⊙✕⊙

The phone ringing awakened Beth. She reached for her cell. It was silent—*the special phone.* Jerking it up, she pushed the Talk button. "Hello."

"Hi, gorgeous. You okay?"

Joe. "Not really."

"I'm sorry about Clyde. Mark says Nora's holding up. Is she?"

"Yeah, but it ripped my heart out to see her weeping." Beth swiped at her eyes. "Did Mark tell you Robert's missing?"

"Not missing, no. Just that he hadn't yet called home."

"He should have called in before we left the club. Still no word, so Sara's a basket case."

"Which means you're one too."

"I've had calmer days." Beth scrunched a throw pillow under her head. "But I'm feeling better now that you've called."

"Really?"

Clueless man had no idea what he did to her. "I'm not sure why but you have that effect on me."

"Glad to hear you're not totally immune to me."

She laughed. "I wish."

"Now that's just mean."

"It's not." She tested the truth. "I just never compete for a man's attention." Didn't he realize how many women were after him?

"Ah, you're being compassionate to other women."

"Excuse me?"

"They can't measure up."

That was a different take than intended or expected, but no way was she
taking that comment seriously. "See? Calming."

"Did you want to talk about anything specific, or just talk?"

"Honestly, I just needed to hear your voice."

"Careful, gorgeous. I might just start believing you care about me."

"I'm a caring person."

"Yes, you are, or you'd be at home and not at Sara's."

She stilled. "How do you know I'm at Sara's?"

"She's in crisis. Where else would you be?"

"Joseph."

"Okay, okay. You caught me. I called Crossroads to check on Nora, and Lisa
told me you were at Sara's. But I already knew you would be, and that's the truth."

Beth's lips twitched, wanting to smile. "You're kind of adorable."

"Hold that thought a minute, and tell me about the missing Robert."

She filled him in and answered his questions as best she could. "Are you
coming for Clyde's funeral Tuesday?"

"I wish I could be there now."

He couldn't. A pang of disappointment rippled through her. "Me too."

You're being stupid, Beth. He's gonna break your heart.

*Maybe my heart needs breaking. Maybe I need to know I've still got a heart
capable of breaking. Otherwise, isn't Max defining my life? Shouldn't I define my
life?* "Why did I need this phone?"

"So we can communicate in a way no one else knows exists."

"Okay." Was that important on his end or hers? Probably both. "So you're still tied up?"

"More or less. But I'm only a phone call away from you. Remember that."

Odd conversation. "All right."

"I haven't forgotten you wanted coffee. Next time you see me, I'll bring you a cup."

There was a message there. What it meant, she had no idea. "I'll hold you to it. Two sugars, one cream."

He laughed. "I remember, gorgeous."

Gorgeous. It sounded so natural coming from him, tugged her into baring her soul. "Joe, I'm scared."

"I know. But that's not a bad thing considering the circumstances. Fear can be healthy. It keeps you on your toes. But you can't give in to it, or your enemy's already won."

"How do you fight it?"

"Think steel. Just focus on the solution and think steel."

Shadow Watchers. They used that phrase; she'd heard it. "Do you think NINA attacked us at the club?"

"Yeah, but I can't prove it."

"I think I'm even more scared of whatever's going on with Robert."

"Why?"

"I've got a bad feeling he's up to something. I feel it." Down to the marrow of her bones. "I don't know what, but I'm worried it'll hurt Sara. She's acting totally weird."

"Totally weird—how?"

Beth told him about Sara's warning, about the hundred unusual things she'd said and done in the past week, and especially the odd tidbits relayed tonight. "But you know what scares me most?"

"What, *sha?*"

Sha. A Cajun endearment for "sweetheart" or "darling." *Heart, don't you dare leap. He probably uses it all the time.* "The way she looked at that cake topper. The bride and groom had been torn apart, and the groom was missing. Sara's reaction was bizarre."

"With Robert missing, her reaction seems pretty normal."

"It wasn't normal for Sara. She wasn't devastated, Joe, she was angry. Unnerved and scared, but really angry…and I think a little relieved."

"Now that's interesting. Why would she be angry or relieved?"

Beth slid down on the sofa and checked the darkened hallway to be sure she was still alone. "I don't know, but tonight she told me she wished she could go back. It wasn't clear if she meant back to before Robert, but that's how it came across."

"Maybe she regrets marrying him."

"See? Totally weird. Since day one, she's been besotted with him."

"Put your bias aside and tell me what your gut says about him."

"I can't." She squeezed a throw pillow, half ashamed of that truth. "It runs too deep."

"Try."

Her mouth went dry. "He's dangerous. That's the first thing that always comes to mind. I don't know why."

"God gave us instincts for a purpose. You don't have to understand, just listen."

Joe's tone carried a warning. Did he know something she didn't about Robert? NINA?

Before she could ask, he went on. "I want you to know that I care about you, Beth."

"We've become good friends."

"That too, but this is different." He paused, then added, "Man-to-woman different."

"Why?"

"I have no idea. Women usually love me. I'm crazy about you, and you treat me like a kid brother. It's demeaning—and don't tell me you didn't know it. That would make it worse."

"You're crazy about me?" Her heart beat hard and fast, then harder. "Seriously?"

"Seriously. Laugh and I'll put salt in your coffee instead of sugar."

"I'm not laughing." Her jaw was on the floor. He was crazy about her? *Her?* Impossible. Couldn't be. "I just…had no idea." She didn't dare believe it.

"Maybe I'm just crazy."

Guard your heart. Guard your heart. He'll break it. You know he will. "That's far more likely." Guys like him didn't hang their hearts on women like her. They went for models and beauty queens. The women who at sixty were still stunning. "You genuinely like all women. I've seen it in the way they react to you."

"It is genuine. I think they react to that, but Nick says—"

Another Shadow Watcher. "What does your mother say?"

"We don't talk much. We never did."

That had been hard for him to admit. "She was immune?"

"Mostly pickled."

"Guess that was hard on you and your dad."

"On me and my brothers. Dad was pickled too." He sighed. "I really don't want to talk about the family, Beth."

He never did. But only now was she getting a grip on why. "I'm trying to figure you out, Joe. You say you're crazy about me."

"Yeah, I did say that."

"Did you mean it?"

"I always mean what I say. Otherwise, scars can cut deep, and you know it."

She'd never told him about Max, but it sure sounded as if someone else had. "Then let me know you so I know what to make of your craziness. You like most women. Are you crazy about all of them?"

"Of course not. I respect them all. Not that I don't respect you too, I do. Very much."

"Because I'm a decent businesswoman?"

"You're an amazing businesswoman, but no, that's not why."

"What is then?"

"Do we have to talk about this?"

"No." She worried her lip. "But if you're really crazy about me you will."

"I'm not liking this, sha."

Warm. Endearing. A hint of his Cajun accent. She loved that. "Me either." Closing down was just stage setting. Max set those stages well. "Would you rather I ask Mark about you and your family? What it was like when you were a kid?"

"Go ahead."

"He can't tell me, can he?" A strange sadness swelled in her. "You haven't told him?" She didn't wait for an answer. "Why not? You guys seem so close."

"We are close."

"Well?" She let silence fall. And stretch. And yawn.

Finally, he sighed. "It's not pretty, okay? I didn't have your kind of childhood."

"Both of your parents drank. I understand that." What had they done to him?

"No, you don't. They ran out of money before buying food, but there was always vodka in the house—when we had a house, or a barn, or a tent. Vodka was their poison of choice."

"You went hungry?" Her stomach knotted.

"I really don't want to talk about this, Beth."

"I know, Joe. But I think you need to." Not idle chat, this. "Is that why you're charming?"

"You think I'm charming?"

"I'm serious, Joseph."

"I can hear that you are. So am I."

"Are you going to talk straight?"

"Trust me. You don't want that."

"I do, Joe. I really do. I'll even admit I need it."

Another sigh. Deeper. "Fine. I grew up on the wrong side of town. Two brothers, both younger. Parents who didn't just drink but stayed drunk. They didn't know what planet they were on much less which one we were on. It was a small town. I had to prove I wasn't like them. So I worked at being a good listener, at picking up on other people's moods. I learned to be what I needed to be to get by."

"What do you mean, to get by?"

"Food comes to mind first. I'd target large families—they always had extra food because they didn't know who'd be home or extra hungry at a given meal. I'd show up. I was polite, I was appreciative, and I'd get to eat."

"And you'd bring home food to your brothers?"

No answer.

"Did you, Joe?" He'd never let them go hungry, would he?

"Always. My childhood prepared me well for my later work."

As a Shadow Watcher. Chameleon. Infiltrating hostiles. Doing what needed done. Thinking steel to get through hard times. "It did."

"God has a way of giving us what we need, even when we don't want it at the time."

He was ashamed. That's why he didn't talk about his childhood in Louisiana. "Yes, He does." Beth hugged the pillow tighter, her heart aching for the boy who'd had a man's worries in feeding his brothers. "It probably saved your neck a time or two."

"It has." He cleared his throat. "I've never told anyone about that. Not even Mark."

Yet he'd told her. "You trust me."

"So far."

"You won't regret it. That's a promise."

"You keep your promises?"

"Absolutely. It's my nature."

"Your nature is to nurture. You'd bite your tongue to spare feelings."

"True, but I won't lie."

"I have a question."

"Okay?" She braced.

"Why do you do that—nurture everyone?"

"Boy, don't I wish I knew. I worry about everybody."

"I noticed. Nora, Sara, Clyde—I'm really sorry about Clyde, Beth."

"Me too. He was a remarkable man."

"You loved him."

"I did." Her eyes burned. "To him, I was special." Not ordinary. Not average.

"You are special."

"He thought I was." And he'd thought so at the time she most needed to feel special and didn't even know it. After Max's grand exodus.

A phone rang in the background. "Gotta go, gorgeous. Info coming in I need now. I'll call again as soon as I can."

"Just one thing, Joe."

"What?"

"I want to be clear. You didn't call just because I asked you to. You would have called me anyway?"

"Beth, you were attacked. I just told you I'm crazy about you. Whether or not you want to believe it, I needed to know you were okay. Worry is part of the crazy-about-you package."

She smiled, her emotions in riot. "In that case, and because you trusted me, I'm going to take you at your word, so if you're joking around, knock it off."

"I'm not joking around."

A little thrill raced through her. "It'll last maybe a week."

"Live dangerously and let's find out. Gonna risk it?"

She laughed. "You break my heart, Joseph, and I'll have to sic Nora on you—and Peggy Crane." The Crossroads director was as tenacious as Nora.

"Woman, you're a piece of work. I tell you you're gorgeous, I'm crazy about you, and you threaten to unleash Rambo and Cupid on me. Sha, you need to ease up and just be. You'll get used to me."

That was the problem. She could get used to him so easily, and then he'd recover from this insane but temporary interest in her and return to his usual kind of woman. "I am used to you." But she hadn't yet answered how much he was like Max. "I'm okay short-term. But long-term, you need someone more your type."

"I have a type?" His voice took on a hard edge. "Is this your way of saying I'm not good enough for you, Beth?"

Shame. "Don't be absurd. You're amazing."

"So my type isn't someone like you. It's…what?"

"Your phone is ringing again."

"I asked you a question."

"Some gorgeous superwoman."

"If I weren't relieved, I think I'd be insulted, but forget about that. Honey, the truth is, I have to stretch to touch the soles of your feet."

Tears stung her eyes. Was that genuine? Sincere? "Now you're baiting me."

"I bait for fish. I never play games with anyone's heart. It's bad form." He paused while the phone rang yet again. "Bad timing, but I really have to go now. Be careful—and don't tell anyone about this phone. Not even Sara."

"Why?"

"Trust me."

"Me? Trust a woman magnet?"

"You're clearly immune to the magnet. Trust the man."

Oh, but she wasn't immune. She so wasn't immune. "Okay, but I wouldn't mind if you finished up fast and got your body down here."

"Are you coming unglued?"

"I don't come unglued." Why had she said that? She'd lost her mind and her dignity.

"'Course not. You miss me, eh?"

"Like a sore tooth. The truth is, I haven't gotten a decent cup of coffee at Ruby's since you were here. The waitress doesn't fawn over me." She'd loved their conversations at Ruby's. He was a wonderful listener and told fascinating stories. And bluntly put, she needed a hug. Strong arms around her, a solid chest to lean against. She could stand on her own, she could hold up others, but it'd sure be nice to lean on Joe just for a while.

"No risk of getting an overinflated ego around you. It's always about the coffee." He feigned a sigh. "I'll do what I can. Keep the phone on your body at all times. Promise."

"I promise."

"Not in your purse, on you. I'm always just on the other end."

"On me. Got it." His calm seeped to her. Grateful for it, she smiled. "Same here."

෨෬

The doorbell rang.

It wasn't yet dawn. Before Beth could drag herself awake, Sara bolted past her to the door. With her hand on the knob, she stopped cold and shot Beth a terrified look.

"What?" Beth made a mental note to insist that Sara throw those stupid shoes away. They were crippling her.

"It's going to be bad news. Good news would be a phone call from him." Sara's eyes went wild. "Oh, mercy. I can't open the door, Beth. I—I can't..."

Beth walked over and clasped Sara's shoulder. "Step back a little and I'll open it." Beth moved her enough so the door wouldn't bang her shoulder. "You've got to get a grip."

"Please, don't let it be bad." Her staggered breath hitched her chest.

"Sara, quit. Enough trouble finds us on its own. Don't go looking for extra."

"I feel it, Beth." She pressed a hand to her stomach. "I have all day."

All day. She hadn't been to bed. Still dressed as she had been last night. Beth sent her a warning look. "You know what will happen if you don't calm down."

Shaking hard, Sara squeezed her hands until her knuckles went white. "Lecture me later. Answer the door."

Beth swung it open. Jeff Meyers and the rookie, Kyle, stood on the porch.

Beth automatically looked at Jeff. His pug nose was red from rubbing, and he'd ruffled his brown hair. He did that when he was upset. "What are you doing here before the crack of dawn?"

"We need to talk." Same suit he'd worn to the club. A bit more rumpled but a good fit on his broad shoulders. "Destin police asked me to drop by."

Destin police? "What for?"

"Is Robert home?" Jeff asked.

"No." Jeff had no idea how much Beth resented that.

Sara burst into tears. Beth frowned. "He left on a business trip yesterday morning, e-mailed from his phone that he'd call when he got to the hotel, but he ran into car trouble and called to say he was getting a rental and that he'd call when he got to the hotel. That's it. He hasn't been heard from since. Sara is…worried."

Compassion rippled over Jeff's face. Dread chased it. He shot a concerned glance at Kyle.

Sara sniffed, dabbed at her nose. "Is he dead, Jeff?"

The detective blinked. "What?"

"Robert," she spat at him as if he were a dimwit. "Is he dead?"

"Not so far as we know." Jeff's gaze skidded past Kyle to look at Beth, and then settled back on Sara. "We were hoping he'd be here and we could talk to him."

"Come in." Beth waved them into the grand entry and on to the living room.

Sara wadded bits of her skirt in her fists, crushing the raw-silk fabric. "I'm sorry." Her apologetic little laugh sounded hollow and never touched her eyes. "I just… I was terrified."

What Sara feared Jeff had come to tell her was only too clear. But if anything, Jeff looked more serious. He had something else to say, and it wasn't good news. "Sit down, Sara."

Beth turned her toward the pristine white sofa. Sara perched on its edge, looking brittle enough to snap.

Jeff and Kyle sat on chairs near the bank of windows separated by long glass tables. Both looked as if they'd rather be anywhere else.

What has Robert gotten into now? "Why exactly are you looking for Robert?"

Kyle ignored Beth's question and asked his own. "So Mr. Tayton phoned yesterday morning when getting a rental car. When was that, Mrs. Tayton?"

"About ten o'clock. I wasn't in but he left a voice mail message. He was at the auto shop, waiting for someone to bring him a rental car."

Beth hurried things along. "He paused during the message to answer some-one—it sounded like he took delivery on the rental."

Sara nodded. "I took it that way too."

Kyle's eyes turned hawkish. "He said he'd call from the hotel, but you haven't seen or heard from him since?"

The hair on Beth's neck stood on edge. Something was *seriously* wrong.

"Not a word." Tears welled in Sara's eyes. "His cell isn't working."

Jeff rubbed at his ear. "You're sure he's not at the hotel now?"

Dread might as well have been scrawled on Jeff's face in red ink. "She's checked several times. He hasn't called home. What's going on, Jeff?"

He leaned forward and laced his hands at his knee. "Robert's rental car was found abandoned in a local subdivision."

"Abandoned?" Sara looked confused. "In the village?"

"No, in Destin."

"But that's east of here. New Orleans is west."

"Yes." Jeff twisted his academy ring on his finger, his face flushing. "Some kids were playing, and a boy chased the ball over to the car. He saw something inside and told his mother. She'd noticed the car parked there at about eleven thirty yesterday morning but hadn't thought much of it until her boy came to her. When night fell and no one came for the car, she figured she should check the car herself. So she did, then called police."

Sara just stared at him.

Why wasn't she asking the obvious question? Beth stiffened. What had the boy seen? What alarmed his mother into phoning the police?

Jeff waited but Sara still didn't utter a sound, so he went on. "We knew from the tag that the car was a rental, but it took time to determine who had possession of it."

Sara didn't blink or glance away; she'd zoned out. Bad news was coming and she was delaying its delivery to give it time to change to something not painful—or so Beth thought until Sara did a one-eighty that worried her even more.

Her face lit up in a wondrous smile. "So the Destin police *did* find Robert."

"No." Jeff shot Beth a silent plea for help. "They've canvassed the neighborhood, but no one saw him."

Sara frowned. "But you just said—"

Another pleading look from Jeff. This one, Beth answered. "They found the car. Robert wasn't in it." Beth looked back at Jeff and asked the burning question. "What did the boy and his mother see in the car?"

Kyle fidgeted. It took a lot to make a cop fidget, even a rookie. Jeff pounded out dread. "Jeff?" Adrenaline surged through Beth. "What did he see?"

He leaned back, distancing himself from them and the situation. "Blood."

"No!" Sara gasped, mangled a shrill keen. "No. I-I—" She stammered, gasped, then gasped again. "I…can't…breathe…"

"Yes, you can," Beth said. "Calm down, focus, and slowly inhale. There's plenty of air. Breathe it in, and then let it out." Sara's doubt flooded her eyes. Beth firmed her voice and expression even more. "I said, you're fine. Just breathe."

Kyle scooted, ready to bolt. Jeff dropped his gaze to the floor and his face flushed. He hated delivering this news and upsetting Sara. "So the boy saw blood and no one saw Robert?"

Attuned to Sara's precarious condition, Jeff quickly clarified. "A very small amount of blood, and this." He passed Beth a shiny object in a little plastic bag. "Don't open it."

Beth held the bag in her palm. Inside it was a plain gold wedding band.

Sara gasped again. "Robert's..."

It looked like any other plain gold band to Beth. The slick package crinkled between her fingertips and thumb. "There are millions of gold bands. You're sure?"

Sara nodded wildly. "It's his, I'm telling you. Look at the inside."

Beth stretched the plastic smooth, looked inside the ring, and saw the engraving: their names and wedding date. Her chest tightened. "It's his." She passed the bag back to Jeff, her stomach twisting into knots. *The rental car abandoned. No Robert. Blood. His wedding band. What does all this mean?* Beth looked over at Sara. She'd probably had about all she could stand. "Do you need your medicine?"

"No." Sheet white, she shook her head. "I'm okay."

"Asthma," Jeff mouthed to Kyle. "Severely complicated by other medical issues."

Nearly everyone in the village knew about Sara's attacks. They knocked her to her knees, then nailed her even more. Medicine given too soon wouldn't be effective when she most needed it. Too late, and her airways would lock down. Fast action was required or Sara could lose her life.

Kyle nodded.

Jeff cleared his throat. "Police checked the trunk and found something else. I couldn't bring it with me. It's being examined."

Sara's breathing was leveling out. Almost normal. Beth was thankful for that. At the dorm the night her parents died, Sara had coded. They'd fought hard to get her back, and it'd taken two long days and nights to get her stable and another two days before she'd been released from the hospital. Beth had never been so scared.

In the years since, Sara had seven severe attacks; three in the last year, all when she had been overly tired, upset, or excited. That's when Beth had learned that good news could be stressful too. For the most part, Sara's attacks had been medically controlled, though the tension over Robert had triggered multiple mild attacks in the past six months. Keeping them mild and not life threatening had required Beth to tolerate more jabs and stabs from him than she typically would have tolerated from anyone.

This attack could be as rough as the one at the dorm. Anxiety had been building all day, an attack seemed inevitable, but hopefully—*please, God, don't be napping*—not one as bad as that. "What else did you find?"

"A note," he said.

Like him, Beth waited a long minute, giving Sara time to absorb before setting her off again. "What kind of note?"

"From Robert?" Sara held her hand at her throat, gently massaging her skin in what looked like an absent gesture, but Sara was attempting to stop muscle spasms.

"No, it wasn't from him." Jeff shot Kyle a look that he ignored by focusing on a vase of white lilies on the table between two long, arched windows.

Not good. Oh, definitely not good. Beth braced. Kyle didn't want to be one to deliver this news to Sara, and that more than prepared Beth. She excused herself, snagged Sara's inhaler, shoved it into her pocket, then returned to the living room.

"What…about…the…note?" Sara struggled to get the question out.

Jeff tried, but he just couldn't seem to bring himself to look at Sara. "It said…" He shot Kyle another silent nudge to take over.

Kyle grimaced and took up the banner. "It said, 'Answer the phone tonight. Kidnapped for ransom.'"

Sara's face contorted in horror. She shrieked a wail so shrill it nearly made Beth's eardrums bleed.

"Call 911!" Scrambling, Beth shoved the inhaler into Sara's gaping mouth.

Robert? Kidnapped for ransom?

6

Anyone's world can change on a dime.

Beth's grandmother had told her so a million times, and Beth thought she had understood. After Sara's parents had died and she'd become another Dawson child in Beth's family, their worlds had changed drastically. When SaBe had rocketed and their worrying about rent money had become history, their lives had changed radically again. But those changes didn't prepare a person to fight for survival.

Robert had been kidnapped, and regardless of his outcome, the event had thrown Sara into a life-threatening situation. So only in the past two hours had Beth really come to understand her grandmother's saying. Sara's world had turned topsy-turvy and then collapsed around her ears. The impact had been so jarring that she had to be flown to Sacred Heart Hospital in Pensacola, where she now lay in ICU with a team of doctors trying to keep her throat open, her lungs functioning, her bronchial tubes out of lockdown, and her blood pressure low enough to keep her heart from exploding. Her medical condition was worse than she'd told Beth. Sara had a weak heart.

Peggy Crane and Harvey Talbot were on their way to Sacred Heart. They'd watch over her. Beth was forced to stay put—in case the kidnappers called.

She sat woodenly on Sara's sofa. A flurry of police and FBI agents coordinated, setting up and testing their equipment. Kyle Perry had left as soon as the FBI had arrived, but Jeff stayed with Beth. When he refused to let her board the helicopter with Sara, she'd nearly lost it. But he had made points she couldn't dispute. The hospital was over an hour away, and if there, then she wouldn't be positioned to respond to the kidnappers' demands. That could create lethal challenges for Robert, which could create lethal challenges for Sara. Beth best served her friend here. Oh, but seeing her go through that attack…watching them load her onto the Life Flight alone…

Beth's eyes burned and her throat constricted. She blinked fast and swallowed hard, a snippet of conversation with an EMT replaying in her mind.

"What happened to her feet?"

"New shoes."

He gave her an odd look and started to comment, but his partner whispered something about patient privacy and he'd whispered back, *"Women cripple themselves just so their legs look good. It's insane. Look at her feet, man."* Then they'd boarded the chopper and taken off.

A sheet covered Sara on the gurney; Beth hadn't seen her feet. But he'd gotten *that* bent over a couple blisters and swollen ankles? In his line of work? Weird.

"When the kidnapper calls, you've got to take it," Jeff said. "They could want information you have that we don't."

"I won't have it either. You know Robert and I don't get along. My concern is Sara."

Surprise and suspicion flickered through Jeff's eyes. Beth buried her emotions to think. "You know what I mean."

"Are you involved with Robert's disappearance?" Jeff frowned. "I have to ask…"

"You're kidding, right?"

"No, I'm not. You have motive."

Beth's jaw fell slack. "I don't like him. That's a long way from harming him. Would I do that to Sara?"

Jeff looked her in the eye. "That's what I'm asking you."

"No." Anger roiled in her stomach. "I'm not involved in Robert's disappearance or his kidnapping."

"So your concern for Sara is because…"

"She's fighting for her life. She's been my best friend all my adult life."

Suspicion burned in his eyes.

Beth resented it and wished Joe were here. He'd tell Jeff a thing or two…wouldn't he? Or would he be suspicious of her too? Unsure, she fell silent.

Around her the world went on, people working, sleeping, eating, and she hung in this horrific limbo waiting for her cell phone to ring, afraid when it did she'd be told bad news about Sara. *God, please let her live. Please.* From Jeff's behavior, she feared no matter what happened to Robert, she'd be blamed. *Joe, please break away and get here.*

The phone looked so innocuous sitting on the coffee table next to a free-form sculpture simulating the circle of life, but every time Beth looked at it, the note ran through her mind. *Answer the phone tonight. Kidnapped for ransom.* It terrified her. What if she messed up? What if the kidnapper asked her something she didn't know? She could get Robert killed. Sara would forever believe Beth messed up intentionally to get Robert out of her life and never forgive her. And Jeff would think Beth had goofed up on purpose. If he didn't, he'd be unsure. He wore his doubt just as he wore his shirt. It was so unfair.

She was afraid to leave the room long enough to call Joe. She wanted to pray. Her whole life, whenever crisis struck, she always prayed. But what did she pray for? Sara's life, of course. But pray for Robert's safe return? That'd be total hypocrisy. Beth didn't want him to return. Yet she didn't want him dead either, and if he was, she didn't want to be blamed for it. No one had more issues with Robert. Naturally Jeff saw that as motive—Kyle sure did and made no bones about it. Maybe she should pray for Robert's safety… But if he was safe and he'd worried Sara intentionally… Oh, how Beth wished she believed he had more character than to do that. But she didn't. *God, forgive me. Let Sara survive.*

You're terrible, Beth Dawson. How can you think these things?

I can't help it. I try, I really do. But I know he's bad the way one knows the sun rises. I wish I didn't. For Sara, I wish I could adore him. But I…don't.

"Greater good."

The words formed clearly in her mind. Peace followed. She grasped them, welcomed it. She could pray for the greater good of everyone concerned. *Thank You!*

Beth excused herself, went into the empty kitchen, and prayed hard.

Then she called to update Nora.

"I'll come over. Nathara can drive me," Nora said. "Should I call your parents?"

"No, you stay put. They're in Alaska on a cruise. Peggy and Harvey are on their way to Sacred Heart."

"Peggy's likely alerted the prayer warriors."

"They've been at the Crossroads chapel since the club attack."

"Nathara and I can come wait with you."

"No offense, Nora, but I can't take Nathara or her attitude right now. I'm frazzled."

"Don't fret, my girl, I understand."

Beth made sure no one else was within earshot, then dropped her voice. "Robert's been kidnapped. The FBI's here. They think it's notable that the cake-topper groom and Robert are both missing."

"They think they're connected?"

"Maybe, though no one's saying how." Beth's hand shook. "Jeff asked if I was involved with Robert's kidnapping."

"I'm going to blister that boy's ears."

Relief washed through Beth. Nora believed in her. "He's just doing his job."

"Being ridiculous?"

"He won't be the only one who looks my way, Nora. You know it."

"Sorry to say that's true." She sighed. "Be careful who you trust and keep your mouth shut. I'm thinking, this ain't good for Sara or you—or for SaBe."

"I haven't thought about SaBe. Too scared for Sara. There was blood in Robert's car."

Nora repeated that and then told Beth, "Mark says the FBI should be involved in both, so there you have it."

Her boy was the final authority. "What should I do to protect SaBe?"

"Get your Margaret to respond to press inquires."

The personal assistant she and Sara shared. "No comment?"

"Absolutely not. Ask for prayers for Sara and her husband—*if* word's out she's in the hospital. Just a second." A pause and then, "Nathara says nothing about Sara's been on the news, so keep mum about that for now. No sense giving anybody more to chew on."

Sensing movement, Beth glanced back, but the kitchen was still empty. Just the whir of the fridge motor and the clink of the icemaker dumping ice into the bin broke the silence. "The agent in charge should be here any time."

"Maybe it'll be somebody Roxy knows," Nora said. "I'll give her a call."

"No, it's two in the morning and she's had a really bad day."

"Didn't notice the time. I'm thinking you're right, but if things ain't suiting you, let me know. I'll get the boys busy."

Mark, Ben, and maybe Mark's old team. "All right. Thanks, Nora." NINA attacking the club. Of course her boys were already busy. *Joe, I wish you were here.*

"Did you talk to Peggy or Ben? I'm thinking some private help finding Robert would be a good thing."

"I'm scared to do anything. If I jump through hoops for Robert, the FBI is going to assume I have something to hide. Jeff really is suspicious. Now, for Sara, everyone knows I'd jump through anything."

"A better friend ain't been born."

"A better friend would have kept her away from the skunk, knowing he was a skunk."

"Ain't none of us perfect, and Sara is a grown woman. You have to respect her choices, even if they're bad ones." Nora harrumphed. "Just a second, Beth... Nathara, you ain't in this conversation, so kindly shush yourself. Okay, Beth. I'm back."

Beth rubbed at the knots in her neck. "I can't think right now. Sara—"

"Is in God's hands. The best thing you can do for her is to be there when those kidnappers call and go to that fund-raiser and get her the money for the moms. She'll be upset as all get out if you don't."

"Seriously?" Beth groaned. "I hadn't even thought about going."

"Of course you should go. It's important to Sara." Nora's tone turned sad. "We do for those we love because we love them. What's important to them is important to us." She cleared her throat. "I learned that too late, dearie. My Clyde is gone home now, but don't be tromping through that mud hole first-hand. Learn from my trip through it. Get Sara her money. The moms and their kids being safe will make her happy."

If Nora felt that strongly about it... "I'll go." Jeff wouldn't like it, but she'd go anyway. Why hadn't the kidnapper called?

"That's my girl." Nora sounded relieved. "You let me know how it goes, eh? And keep me posted on Sara."

"I will. Do you think the authorities have let the club reopen?"

"Let me ask Mark. He's staying close tonight since Lisa's on duty at the crisis center and can't be here herself."

Likely Mark and Lisa didn't want Nathara driving Nora over the edge when she was already so upset about Clyde, and Lisa's mom, Annie, had maxed out on patience. Mark would make a good buffer.

"He says the all clear came through about half an hour ago, so it'll be fine for Sara's fund-raiser tonight."

"Thanks." Beth stared at a slat on the shutter on the window above the sink. "Nora, I'm grateful for you." Her eyes stung and her throat swelled. "I—I just wanted you to know."

"I know, my girl." Tenderness filled her tone. "Me too."

Beth sniffed and hung up the phone, then reached in her pocket for her special phone to call Joe, but Kyle walked into the kitchen. She kept it in her pocket and went back into the living room, where Jeff stood apart from the FBI team as if he wasn't quite sure what to do. "Any word?"

"Not yet." He looked rumpled and as bone weary as Beth felt. "Some-times they delay to play mind games—to ratchet up the tension."

"The club. Sara. Now this." Beth let out a staggered sigh. "There's plenty of tension."

"Get some rest, Beth. If the phone rings, I'll wake you."

She was dead on her feet and worried sick. Sleep was as out of reach as Joe.

"The sofa in the den is a whole lot more comfortable than this marble slab they call a sofa."

Beth attempted a smile. "The concrete porch is more comfortable than that slab." Quiet would be good. Calm would be good.

She went to the den and curled up on the sofa. Every muscle in her body ached from tension and knots of fear. *God, help Sara. Help…* She couldn't say it. Couldn't. Shame slid through her. *Forgive me my flaws. I have a ton of them, and I know I'm a disappointment. Sorry about that. I know You'll do what You know is for the greater good of all anyway. Thank You for everything, but especially for that. I know sometimes I test Your patience and I'm really hard to love.*

Her special phone rang.

Joe.

She answered and began filling him in on Sara. "She's critical, Joe."

"She's in God's hands. Are you all right?"

"No. Jeff asked if I had anything to do with Robert's kidnapping."

"That's routine."

"It didn't feel routine, and the way he looks at me isn't routine either."

"The man's half in love with you."

"Was. We're just friends, not that he looked at me like one. He's suspicious."

"He's scared. Finding everyone out cold, Clyde dead, Sara critical, and Robert kidnapped. Jeff's got a lot on his plate."

Hardly the response she wanted, but not the one she feared. The question burning in her mind was different. She did fear his answer to it, but she had to ask. "Aren't you going to ask me if I had anything to do with it?"

He laughed, soft and melodic. "No, sha. You might slug Robert Tayton, but you'd never have him kidnapped."

Slug him? "I've never hit another human being in my life, but your belief in me… I adore you, Joe."

"Ah, progress."

"Don't let it go to your head. I adore puppies and kittens too."

He laughed. "Adore the man, gorgeous, but not for believing in you. You'd never do anything to hurt Sara, and harming Robert would. If Jeff were thinking clearly, he'd remember that and that it'd be a violation of your faith. Not happening."

Exactly what she needed. Exactly. Was that one of Nora's signs? Had to be, for goodness' sake. "Can you come?" Her voice came out weak. She resented that but couldn't seem to stop herself.

"I'm doing everything I can to help. I'll fill you in on what that is when I can. But I can't get down there immediately. Wish I could, but I—I just can't."

"It's okay. I understand." In his job, he couldn't call in someone to take over.

"You do, but you're upset anyway, and I don't blame you. Beth, believe me when I tell you that you want me where I am right now."

Doing all he could already. She processed that. "You're looking for Robert."

"Mark told me you were a smart woman. I knew it from our talks, but I think you might be smart and intuitive. I love your mind, sha, but I'm going to have to remember that."

Her heart fluttered. *Don't feel special. Don't you dare.* "What you need to remember is to be careful."

"I will. You too—and watch what you say. It's amazing how twisted up things get."

"That's what Nora said. Well, actually, she told me to keep my mouth shut."

"Wise woman."

"Yes, she is. I'll work on it. Holding my tongue isn't easy." She paused. "Joe, what if Karl Masson did this? He could be working with NINA again, or on his own."

"Factoring that."

A cold chill swept through her. Joe was working on that too. "Be very careful." They knew only too well NINA's capabilities and Masson's specifically.

"I will."

"And smart."

"I'll try."

"And—"

He chuckled. "Careful or I'm going to think you adore me more than puppies."

Maybe she did. "If I were as smart as you say, I'd toss out a pithy comeback, but I don't have it in me right now. I want you safe. So don't mess up my already awful day by getting yourself hurt. I don't need the added stress."

He laughed. "I'll do my best not to inconvenience you."

"I appreciate it." Jeff came in. Grim and solemn. "I have to go."

"Soon, sha."

Beth hung up and held the phone in her hand rather than making a production of stuffing it into her pocket, praying Jeff wouldn't notice it. "What's up?"

"An update on Sara."

Beth jumped to her feet. "Is she—?"

"Peggy and Harvey are with her. She's fighting hard."

"She's still critical?"

"She had a secondary attack, Beth. She survived it, but it's taken a toll."

Beth sagged down on the sofa. "Will she make it?"

"It's too soon to tell." Jeff rubbed his fingers at his side. "Harvey says you need to be prepared…"

◯╳◯

Karl Masson had done all he could to prepare. The kids were with his mother-in-law and tucked away where they'd never be found. They had money, a nice house, and college funds—everything he could do from a distance in case Raven decided to kill him. That she was having him drive to Seagrove Village wasn't a good sign, and knowing it didn't offer any alternative choices. That irritated him.

Driving the red rental sedan down Highway 98, he passed the spot where he'd worked over Annie Harper during the Lisa Harper operation.

He'd done few things in his life he could feel good about, but giving Annie CPR that day was one of them. Though if he'd known her daughter, Lisa, was going to wreck the entire NINA trafficking operation, he'd have let Annie die. "Lesson learned. Show no mercy." In the green glow from the dash, he grabbed his phone and dialed Raven.

She answered on the third ring. "Yes?"

Two in the morning and she sounded fully alert. Did the woman ever sleep? As high up as she was in the organization, probably just power-napped her way through life. Only in the last few months had he heard the name of one higher up than Raven—Jackal—though there had to be a host of honchos; NINA was international. For their own protection, even those on the inside were briefed just on their immediate chain of command. "Gray Ghost. Dead Game. A72777."

"Are you in position?"

He passed a white Honda with a dented rear panel, then swung back into the right lane. "Yes ma'am."

"Go to Darla Green's house."

"New or old?" The new one she'd bought off the government, who'd seized it from an arrested NINA operative. The old one was the former mayor's residence.

"New."

NINA had gotten Darla out of jail for killing John Green, which meant she owed NINA for her freedom. It would collect a hundredfold. But Tack Grady was a caretaker there—at least until NINA got him elected mayor. They'd spent a fortune to see to it he won; though whether or not Tack knew who was bankrolling him, Karl had no idea. Best he could tell, the total reason NINA cared who was mayor in Seagrove Village ended with Raven. She wanted to control it. Probably because the people here had destroyed two NINA operations. NINA couldn't let that stand. Others would test NINA's resolve too, and that Raven couldn't tolerate.

"You'll be expected."

"Yes ma'am." By whom? Darla or Tack? Masson's position with NINA was too precarious to ask, but apparently Raven had taken one of them into her confidence.

Question was, which one?

7

A bell sounded.
At the desk in his Magnolia Branch hotel room, Joe leaned back from the laptop's screen, checked his phone, then read the text message. *Call home.*

Omega One, a trusted source still active in Intel. Joe called in on a secure line. When someone answered, Joe said, "It's me." Ten seconds and the voiceprint recognition system would flash in the operations center and his face and bio would be front and center on Omega One's computer screen.

"You asked about Robert Tayton. There's an interesting case we believe could be connected. Draft is waiting in your 6719 account."

"On my way. Thanks." They never e-mailed. Saving a draft didn't create a transmission to intercept or track. Much safer.

"Good luck."

"If you pick up anything, let me know." Joe stared at the reflection in the television. "I need all the help I can get on this."

"You're in the loop."

Exactly what he'd hoped to hear.

The line went dead and Joe opened the draft, scanned it, but nothing that could be related jumped out at him. Slowing down, he started working their list of encryption codes. Using the third one revealed an embedded message. "Oh, man. This is so not good."

Processing, he stood, rubbed his jaw, the back of his neck. If this was the connection, then showing his face in Seagrove Village was a suicide mission. But how could he not go? *Beth. Mark, Lisa, and all the Crossroads people.* Joe had ties there now…

Showing his face.

Mark hadn't yet unearthed this potential connection or he'd have told Joe. Still, his *get creative* instincts had been right on target.

Joe stretched to set down the phone and Beth called. "Woman, why are you still up?"

"Robert's kidnappers never called and Sara had a second attack. Why are you still up?"

"Thinking about you, gorgeous. Is Sara going to be okay?"

"She's critical. Harvey says I'd better prepare myself for the worst."

"And you reacted to that…how?"

"Honestly? I'm a wreck, but I'm still going to Sara's fund-raiser at the club."

"Why?" He thought a second. Considering security there now, she was probably safer at the club than at Sara's.

"I'm standing in for her." Beth told him about the moms, about Darla's Airport Road property. "This kind of event isn't my thing on a good day, much less today."

Should he warn her? No, that'd increase jeopardy. Alternative measures were necessary. "You'll handle it."

"I will, but it'd be easier if it weren't with all Robert's friends."

Joe grunted. "They'll be too busy trying to find out what you know that isn't being reported in the press to give you much grief."

"True." She sighed. "Okay, you've worked your charm. I'm calm."

"At least I'm good for something. You like my voice."

"You're good for lots of things and I love your voice. There's a hint of an accent in it that soothes me."

"You picked up on that?"

"Obviously, Joseph. I just said I did."

"You did, but…it's Cajun. I've worked hard to get rid of it. I had to—critical in my job. For some reason, around you it surfaces."

"I think I like that. I take you to a different place."

"You do, sha. But don't try to sidetrack me. You said you loved my voice."

"I did."

"Women never use the love word about anything except shoes or dessert unless—you really do care about me."

She covered a laugh with a cough. "I told you, I'm a caring person."

Protecting her heart. She was amazing—beautiful, brilliant, kind, and good. And nurturing. So nurturing. The kind that was faked annoyed him. But Beth's brand was genuine, potent and powerful, and it made her irresistible to him. Didn't she know how special that made her? Apparently not, or she knew but didn't trust it. "You're a paradox."

"Excuse me."

"You're open and caring but also guarded—at least, with me. Or is it with men? Did someone hurt you, Beth?"

"I don't want to talk about this."

"I'm sure you don't. But when I didn't want to talk, you insisted. I'm insisting."

"Why does it matter?"

"It matters."

"You're forcing me to make a choice I don't want to make, Joe."

"What choice? It's a simple question."

"Do I live a life someone else defined for me, or do I define it?"

"Good question. How will you answer it?"

"Honestly." She paused. "Does anyone reach adulthood without having her heart broken at least once?"

"But yours wasn't just broken. It was shattered."

"How do you know that?"

"In a thousand ways, sha. Who was the jerk, and why were you hung up on someone so shortsighted?"

"Shortsighted?"

"You're a treasure. A man with sense would know it."

"Thank you, Joe."

"It wasn't a compliment. Just stating the facts."

"That's even better. Let's say he hid the truth about himself well. We dated six months. It was serious. Very serious—for me."

"You loved him?"

"I did. I don't anymore."

"Fine line."

"Yeah. Crossing it's pretty easy when you're with a guy at a New Year's Ball, surrounded by all your family and friends, and a glamorous woman catches your guy's eye and he dumps you on the spot."

"He dumped you at the ball? In front of everyone?"

"Yes."

"He humiliated you." Fury seeped through Joe's voice.

"It was quite the chatter—and a real shocker. Everyone thought he was so perfect. Handsome, charming—you know, like you—not that you'd humiliate a woman… You wouldn't, would you, Joe?"

"I can't believe you have to ask. I'm definitely insulted."

"I didn't think you would, but I didn't think he would either. So naturally I have issues with my judgment."

"Gorgeous, it's his judgment that should be questioned. Not yours."

"I'd agree, but until that happened, I thought he was a good man."

"He was shortsighted and shallow—and he lacked compassion and respect."

"Now you're getting the hang of how I felt. But I'm over it now."

"No, sha. Not yet. But you will be. All you need is a man who appreciates you for the treasure you are." He grunted. "Was Nora there when this happened?"

"She was."

"How'd she react?"

"Her face was the color of an apple."

"She was embarrassed?"

"Nora? No way. She was outraged. Everyone was. I was embarrassed."

She'd been devastated. "I'm sorry I brought it up. But it's done, and you can bet he's regretting it now."

"Funny, it never occurred to me that he might regret it, though I'm sure he regretted letting everyone else see his true colors."

Joe groaned. "You going to be finding out if he did?"

"I think not. One collision with that kind of humiliation was more than enough."

"Glad to hear it."

"Why?"

"Men like that seldom change, and if he hurt you again, I'd have to take exception."

She laughed. "You gonna beat him up, Joe?"

"Might." He sighed. "He sure is costing me a lot of extra work, trying to convince you I'm crazy about you."

"Tiring of the effort already, eh?"

"Not by a long shot. I'm staying put, sha. I'll grow on you eventually." She probably feared exactly that. That she'd get used to him, and then he'd walk out on her. "Things will work out in time. For now, stay calm and get some rest."

"I will."

"If anything odd happens, let me know. See you soon."

"Soon. Is that in days? weeks? months?" She sighed. "Never mind. If you knew, you would have told me. Call me later, if you can—if you want to, that is."

He wanted to, and that she wanted him to conjured an errant smile. "Need glue, eh?"

"After a couple hours with Robert's bunch? Probably a bucketful."

"If Nora heard you say that, she'd blister your ears."

"She would. She says strength is a choice. The less choice you have, the stronger you have to be."

"Wise woman." Joe took a swig of soda. Beth wasn't herself. She was scared, weary to the bone, and worried sick about Sara. "Nora would say to rely on your faith to get through the hard stuff—and I'd agree with her on that too."

"It's keeping me upright. Still, a little human glue helps."

If what Joe saw in that draft was related to Robert Tayton III, Beth was going to need a lot more than a bucketful of glue. "Who's going with you?"

"Jeff Meyers, but he doesn't know it yet."

The pit of Joe's stomach hollowed. He stared at the lamp burning on the desk. *Jealous.* That was crazy. He should be happy that a trained guy like Jeff would be there to watch over her—and Jeff would watch. Even if she thought they were just friends, the man was still a little in love with her. "You inviting him on a date?"

"Of course not. He doubts me, Joe. Thinks I'm mixed up with Robert's kidnapping—at the moment, I'm not even sure Jeff's a friend."

Much better. Much, much better. "I'm glad it's not a date."

"Would it bother you if it were?"

He dragged his teeth over his lower lip. The answer didn't require a second's thought. Disclosing it did. "Yeah, it would bother me."

"Keep up the straight talk and you'll make me believe, Joe."

That guy clearly had burned her badly. "I'm counting on it." He rubbed at the knot of muscles in his neck. "'Night, gorgeous."

"'Night."

He hung up, grabbed a bottle of water from the minibar, and absorbed the new information into the old. First, he'd better call Jeff Meyers and give him a heads-up and maybe put him on friendly notice, in a good guy-to-good guy way that he was interested in Beth. Just notice, not a warning. Yet. Then he'd call Mark and get the lowdown on Beth's shortsighted heartbreaker.

ᏯᏭᎤ

Dawn and noon came and went, and the afternoon dragged into evening with no further news on Sara or Robert and no word from the kidnapper.

The only things that had kept Beth sane were Joe's calls, a visit by Peggy and Nora midafternoon, and one from Lisa and Kelly just before dusk. Lisa had talked to the doctors at Sacred Heart and Sara was still critical, but all the signs were good for her stabilizing. They were cautiously optimistic.

Good signs and cautious optimism gave Beth hope.

At eight o'clock Jeff returned to Sara's. Freshly showered and shaved, he looked more rested. "You hanging in there okay?"

Very protective, and seemingly less suspicious. Wondering why, Beth nodded. "I have to go to the club in forty-five minutes for a fund-raiser. It'll take a couple hours."

Jeff's jaw dropped and he lifted an opposing hand. "What if the kidnapper calls?"

"He didn't call last night—if it's a he—and who knows when or if he will?" She'd thought about this and had a solution. "We can forward Sara's calls to my mobile." With all the visitors and activity, Beth hadn't made it home for clothes to wear to the gala. She'd have to wear something of Sara's.

"It's a bad idea, Beth. The club's a crime scene."

"The FBI released it." He'd slept or he would know that—not that he appeared any less worried on hearing it. "Sara asked me to fill in for her tonight, and I'm not going to tell her she isn't getting the two million she needs for abused moms and kids because the phone *might* ring. It's a simple matter to forward the calls."

"I see your point, but anything out of the ordinary could have unintended consequences."

"Well." Beth paused, then looked up at him. "If I don't go, you'll have two million intended consequences to explain to Sara."

"She'll have a fit."

"Oh, yeah. A bad one."

His face flushed. "Okay, you'll go, but I'm going with you."

"Fine." That had been easier than expected. "I'll be ready in a few minutes."

Joe never would have caved so easily—not that it was fair to compare the men. But maybe it wasn't about her. Jeff had looked really grim about having to tell Sara…

Odd, but then again, why wouldn't he want to avoid that? She was clinging to life by a thread.

Beth went upstairs into a guest room closet where Sara kept her formals, grabbed a black dress that was vintage conservative Sara, and put it on. It didn't look half bad, though with its high neck and empire waist it wasn't a style Beth would have bought. Would Joe have liked it?

What's the difference? He's charming. Crazy about you at the moment, but he's probably crazy about puppies too. It doesn't really mean anything. She met her eyes in the mirror. *Get it through your head. No matter what he says, it wouldn't work. He's for someone special, not for an average woman like you.*

Her head had the message. It was her heart that was deaf. Deflated, she twisted her hair up and loosely pinned it into place, slid into a strappy pair of heels, smeared on some lip gloss, and then headed for the door.

Jeff stood waiting near the front entryway. "You look pretty."

"Thanks." She wrinkled her nose. "You too."

"Ready?"

No. Absolutely not. If she never set foot in the club again it'd be too soon for her. "Yes, I'm ready." Beth took in a steadying breath and walked out.

☙❧

Beth pumped up the group to open their wallets, praying the phone wouldn't ring. Afterward, she fielded and sidestepped a few questions about Robert and then talked with Darla Green. Stunning in red, she wore her hair darker, short and jet black, and her bright green eyes gleamed.

"You need some good news." Darla hooked their arms and led her to a quiet corner. "When you talk to Sara, tell her she can have the property on Airport Road. I know she wants it. I'll even contribute a hundred thousand dollars toward a building. That will motivate her to get well."

"It will." Beth smiled. "She'll be thrilled, Darla. Thank you."

"Glad to do it." Worry creased her arched brow. "Anything new on her condition?"

"Still in ICU, but Jeff checked on our way over. She's stabilizing."

"That's good news."

"Every minute she breathes is good news."

Darla clasped Beth's hands. "She's lucky to have you for a friend, Beth. We should all be so blessed."

Clearly she was thinking about her son, Lance, shunning her. "Things work out. Keep hoping."

"I'm beyond hope for myself. Too many skeletons." Sadness flickered in her eyes. "But I'll hope for Sara."

"No one is skeleton free. You only lose if you give up. Keep hoping anyway."

"No sense in it. Not for me."

"Darla Green. I never pegged you as a coward."

Darla sobered, her lips drawing tight. "Excuse me?"

"Hope when you have reason to hope is easy. It's when you can't see a reason and hope anyway—"

Darla's expression softened and her eyes misted. "I hear you, but I'm beyond that too. I've made too many mistakes."

"Need a superhero, huh?"

Darla laughed, but there was no mirth in it. "At least a superhero."

Beth clasped her arm. "I'll lend you mine."

"Joe? Honey, you're crazy. I'd never lend him to any woman."

Joe. Everyone came back to Joe. Mr. Unreachable. He wasn't even hers to lend. "I was talking about God."

She sputtered. "Trust me, hon. God doesn't want me."

"He already has you. He's just waiting for you to remember it and welcome Him," Beth countered. "But enough said. Some things you have to realize on your own."

"Pray for that then, will you? Because after all I've done, I can't see God ever being anything but disgusted with me."

"You're wrong about that, and I will pray for you." Beth gave Darla's arm a pat. She was thawing. Opening up to the idea. Maybe eventually she'd open up to Him.

"Just encourage her as you have been. Ultimately, it's her choice."

Free will. I'm not exactly a shining example. Her feelings about Robert proved it. *I'd hate to fall short and disappoint You or mess up her chances for finding You.*

"You're My choice."

Beth smiled. Loved. Warts and all.

"Beth, do you really think a person can't get past the point of redemption?" Darla asked.

"I know it." Through Christ all things are possible.

"Interesting. I'll have to muddle on that." Darla blinked hard. "I don't believe I've ever thanked you for supporting me—during the hard times. I know it wasn't easy. John was beloved here, and…and…"

"You've done a lot of good here too, Darla. Don't forget that. There weren't many who believed you would do…what they said you did." Killing John? It was absurd. He adored Darla and she adored him.

"Very few thought I was smart enough to kill John." She shrugged, and a whiff of her cologne breezed Beth's way. "It's okay. I know most of the villagers think I'm an airhead."

"You're not an airhead."

"I know, but they believe I am. Anyway, I appreciate your kindnesses. They helped me through some dark days."

"Those days are behind you now."

"Yes." Darla sniffed. "Now, have you reached Sara's fund-raising goal?"

"Not yet." Beth hated to admit it, but Sara would get the money even if Beth had to cover it herself.

"How much more do you need?"

"Five hundred thousand or so."

Darla tapped her cheek with her fingertip. "Well, I'd better get busy then. You know, I'm pretty good at fund-raising. I did it for John every campaign."

She still missed him, and likely the social life that came with his office. "You were a great Mrs. Mayor."

"I enjoyed it." Darla lifted her chin. "Don't worry. I'll get Sara her money. I know everyone's secrets—and they know I know them." She wiggled her eyebrows, then laughed. "Oh, don't look so worried. I won't blackmail anyone. I'll charm them."

Relieved, Beth seized the opportunity. "Work on Ben Nelson about financing the construction on the mom apartments?"

"Already done, dear. Miranda Kent and I visited him at the bank yesterday morning. If you or Sara will stand behind the loan, he'll do it."

Beth had no idea what Sara would or could do. Robert had been playing some bizarre financial games that worried the SaBe accountants. But Beth did know her own position. "What's the projected cost?"

"Seven million, more or less. Mark Taylor told Sara cottages would be safer than a traditional apartment building, but either way she goes, seven should cover costs." Darla hiked her brows. "Reduced, of course, by however much I can wrangle out of these stuffed shirts."

Seven million was a lot of money. Butterflies swarmed in Beth's stomach. "I'm in."

"Then I'd best get busy."

Some of the tension lifted from Beth's shoulders. "I appreciate it, Darla."

"It's a good cause," she said with a little grin.

"Good for the soul too," Beth said as Darla stepped away.

Nathara tapped Beth's arm. "Don't you love it when the two go hand in hand?"

"Excuse me?"

"Soul work and good causes. When they come together."

She'd overheard their conversation. "Yes, I do." Even Nathara had left her mean streak at home tonight. *Thank You!* "Glad you could come. How's Nora doing?"

"She's fine. Finally dozed off just before I left. Annie's fluttering around, making sure no one disturbs her, and that Mark is like a personal bodyguard."

Envy etched into Nathara's tone. It didn't look good on anyone, but it seemed doubly odd coming from a woman who looked so much like Nora. Identical twins could be so different. "They love her and she's mourning. She and Clyde were inseparable."

"They're separate now." Nathara cocked her head. "Darla's an excellent ally, but I have to say I'm surprised you associate, considering she was jailed for her husband's murder."

"She was found innocent, Nathara." Beth put a bite in her tone.

"After she was convicted, little one. Everyone knows her partner took the blame." Nathara grunted, leaned closer. "Bet that set her back a pretty penny."

Anger roiled in Beth. She paused a second to let it pass. "Can you prove that?"

"No need. Common sense says nothing else could have happened."

"Without proof, we'll have to agree to disagree on that." Beth sent Nathara a frosty smile. "If you'll excuse me." Beth had to get outside away from Nathara or her head would explode. Some villagers speculated that what Nathara suspected was exactly what had happened, Hank among them. But there wasn't any proof of it. Going around saying horrible things about someone without proof was just wrong. And it wasn't lost on Beth that if things ended badly with Robert, she could be next in line as a victim of sharp tongues.

Beth slipped through the french doors onto a terrace that overlooked a Mardi Gras fountain. From beneath the water's surface, gold, green, and purple lights shone up on the cascading water. The night air was calm, and quiet surrounded her. Nora was right about her coming. The ground gained for the moms would make Sara happy. Beth breathed in deeply, satisfied, and listened to the frogs croak.

"Don't turn around," a man said from behind her.

Startled, Beth stiffened. Her heart pounded a rapid tattoo and the hairs on her neck stood on end.

"I have a message for you."

Beth didn't utter a sound. His voice didn't sound threatening; his tone was actually gentle, and though she should be terrified, for some reason she wasn't. *He could be NINA. Robert's kidnapper.*

"Are you listening?" he whispered close to her ear.

His breath warm on her neck, she nodded.

"Sara has been to the hospital three times in the last six months."

True, but not what Beth had expected. "Yes?"

"Not for asthma or mild attacks."

He was wrong about that. Beth instinctively started to turn to tell him so and to ask his purpose for passing this message to her. Who was he? What was this about?

He grabbed her shoulders, held her firmly in place. "Not for asthma or mild attacks."

She didn't understand. His words were clear, but his message wasn't. "What are you telling me?"

"Sara's in deep trouble. She needs your help."

Her cryptic messages to protect herself from Sara…to protect Sara from herself, if Beth could…Sara's odd reactions to the club attack…her wanting to go back to a time before Robert… What was really happening here? Did Sara's trouble tie to Robert's abduction? Did it tie to the club attack? Beth fisted her hands at her sides. "Then what put her in the hospital?" Each of the three times, she'd told Beth it was a mild attack.

"Find out." He uttered a throaty growl, released his grip on her shoulders.

She waited but he added nothing else, his body heat at her back disappeared, and then the scent of his cologne faded. He was gone. She knew it, yet her knees shook so badly she couldn't make herself turn around to verify it.

A long minute later, a man called out to her. "Beth?"

Jeff. Had he seen the messenger? He walked across the stones toward her, skirting decorative urns overflowing with lush blossoms. "Yes?"

He searched her face. "Are you all right?"

Worried sick about Sara's health, terrified she'd mess up and get Robert killed, being treated with suspicion and watched by Jeff and Kyle and virtually all of Robert's friends, and now a strange man scared her with yet another cryptic message that Sara was in trouble and needed help—no, Beth wasn't all right. She was anything but all right. "I'm fine." What was the point in saying anything else when the man asking considered her suspect? If Joe had asked... No point going there. For reasons only known to him, he couldn't be here. "Did you see a man standing behind me?"

"No, just you." Jeff scanned the terrace. "Is something wrong?"

Keep your mouth shut. It's amazing how twisted up things get. She couldn't share what had happened. The messenger could have been a crackpot. If she sent Jeff on a wild-goose chase, it could wreck what was left of her credibility. Nora and Joe's warning echoed in her mind yet again. These were Robert's friends. Their distaste for each other was their main topic of conversation. Besides, there was something going on with Sara that she didn't want even Beth to know. Revealing that to Jeff would be betrayal.

"Everything's fine." *Someone* needed to know about this. Someone...Peggy. Beth could tell Peggy Crane. The director of Crossroads Crisis Center could be trusted with anything.

"Can we leave now?" Jeff tried not to sound hopeful.

He felt as uncomfortable as Beth in this group. "Yes." She turned for the french doors. "Just need to do the farewell tour, then we can go."

She said her good-byes, thanked Darla again, and then went to the car. Who was the messenger? What had he meant? And what drove him to tell Beth about Sara?

No way could Beth dismiss it. He'd been blunt, not cryptic. Sara was in deep trouble and needed help.

What kind of trouble? With whom? And if not mild attacks, then what had sent her to the hospital three times this year?

And what kind of friend was Beth that she didn't know?

∽

Half an hour later, Beth was back in her own clothes and sitting on Sara's beautiful-but-comfortable-as-a-concrete-slab sofa, tuning out the activity buzzing around her. Men and electronics were everywhere. She checked with Peggy and Harvey at Sacred Heart—no change on Sara—then called Nora with a fund-raiser update. Beth debated telling her about the terrace messenger, but she'd had enough shocks. Beth hadn't told Peggy either. To talk to either of them about it, Beth needed privacy and she just didn't have it.

With her permission, the FBI tapped her phone in case the kidnapper knew Sara was critical and called Beth instead. With the history between Robert and her, Beth couldn't see that happening, but she'd rather be safe than sorry—even if she suspected tapping her phone was Jeff's way of keeping tabs on her and her activities. His suspicion hurt. It shouldn't; Joe was right. Jeff was just doing his job. But he was her friend, and his doubt about her character hurt.

She steeled against it, leaned back on the sofa, then adjusted a throw pillow under her head. In the morning, she would go to Crossroads and talk to Peggy. Working closely with the hospitals, odds were good she could find out the facts on Sara's hospitalizations.

Beth's mind reeled. Fuzzy snippets on a myriad of things flashed through her thoughts. To think clearly, she needed to rest.

"Beth?"

She opened her eyes and looked at Jeff, silhouetted in the soft lamplight. "Yes?"

"The FBI has assigned Roxy Talbot to Robert's case. She's finishing up her club attack analysis so others can take over. Until she's freed up, I'm overseeing operations here and reporting them to her. You okay with that?"

"I'm fine with it." So Homeland Security was taking over the club incident. Not good, not good. "Surprised the FBI assigned her. She's involved."

"I'm sure they have their reasons."

"They do. She's the utmost authority on NINA." Beth waited, but Jeff just gave her a blank look that frustrated. "She worked the NINA cases, Jeff. Good grief, we were both there on Kelly and Lisa's cases, working with her."

He didn't respond.

Someone had gagged Jeff on the matter.

"Can I sit with you for a second?" When she nodded, Jeff sat beside her. "It might be good to discuss handling the ransom call."

Thank heaven. Doing this without getting Robert killed would be fantastic. "Good idea—provided we get a ransom call."

"They're proving they're in control and we're not, but they went to too much trouble to snatch him not to call." Jeff tugged at his left earlobe. "When they do, we want to maximize our odds for success."

"You keep saying *they.* Do you have reason to believe it's more than one person?"

"The profilers say it's rarely one person. Logistics are harder, so if the stakes are high enough, it's usually two or even a group."

"The intent is to soak Robert and Sara, then?"

"We don't know until they tell us, but prevailing thought is Sara's vulnerable."

She was, and the protective look in Jeff's eyes took the edge off Beth's annoyance with him. She nodded. "So we maximize our odds for success…how?"

"Without Sara, it'll be tough. You're most familiar with her and Robert, but with the bad blood between you and him, Roxy's team thinks our best chance is for you to pose as Sara with the kidnappers."

Surprise ruffled through her. "You're kidding me."

"I'm not." He lifted his eyebrows. "The kidnappers' objective is to get money. If you're not Sara, they'll doubt getting it."

"Especially from me," she conceded. "I could tell them to just keep him. Is that what the team thinks?"

"It believes the kidnappers might, and that wouldn't be good for Robert."

It irked her, but Beth saw the wisdom in the team's thoughts. "What if they know Sara, or they know she's in the hospital?"

"Then they won't call her. But they won't want to just give up. They'll call you."

"But you just said—"

"You and Robert don't get along, but you and Sara have been close most of your lives. You'll protect him for her." He laced his hands on his knees. "It depends on whether they call you or call her. If they call you, and there is a connection between the club attack and his kidnapping, NINA will know that too."

Beth hated having her back shoved against this particular wall, but what choice did she have? "I don't know much about him." She shifted on her seat. "Robert is a private person, but he's even more private with me."

"So I've heard," Jeff admitted. "That's created tension between you and Sara."

Beth stilled. He was interrogating her. Gently, but still interrogating her. And he'd clearly been talking to someone to know that much. Should she call a lawyer? She blinked, thought, blinked again. Why bother? Truth was truth. *Keep your mouth shut. Watch what you say. It's amazing how twisted up things get.* "Yes." More tension than the law should allow. "But Sara loves him."

Understanding lit in his eyes. "What we endure for those we love is shocking, isn't it?"

"Mmm."

Sara's home phone rang.

"Everybody pipe down. This could be it." Jeff snatched up the receiver off the coffee table and checked his watch. "Monday, June seventh. Ten thirty a.m.," he shouted out, then passed the receiver to Beth. "Wait until I tell you to answer." He looked back over his shoulder to the desk where Kyle sat in front of a computer screen. "Say when, Kyle."

Kyle keyed in something and then signaled with a lifted finger. "Go."

Beth took the phone in both hands, shaking hard. *Please, don't let me mess this up.*

It rang again and Jeff dipped his chin toward the phone. "Answer it, Beth."

Blowing out a hard breath, she pushed the button to open the connection. "Hello."

"Sara Tayton?"

The voice sounded mechanical. Definitely voice altered. Man or woman? She couldn't tell. "Who is this?"

"You received the note?"

Beth's skin crawled. Staring at Jeff, she went clammy. "Yes."

"Then the FBI is there with you."

Afraid of saying the wrong thing, she stayed silent.

"Insignificant. Go to the marina. Alone, Sara. On the lot west of it is a Dumpster. At its front right corner, dig down in the sand."

Jeff signaled Kyle with a finger loop above his head to get people positioned there immediately. Beth was confused. "Dig for what?"

"Further instructions. If you want to see Robert alive again, follow them exactly."

When something like this happened in a movie, Beth considered it melodramatic. But when it was real and happening to you, the threat chilled, rippled layers of fear through your whole body. "I want to talk to him. How do I know you have him or he's not already dead? There was blood in his car."

Silence.

Had she blown it? New fear heaped onto the old. Her heart slammed against her chest wall. It was a reasonable request. Who wouldn't want proof? "Are you still there?"

No answer.

Oh God, please. Please tell me I didn't blow this. Please. She squeezed her eyes shut. "Listen to me. Are you listening to me? I need to know he's okay."

Still no answer.

She cast a worried look at Jeff, who gave her a reassuring nod and motioned her to keep talking. "I'll do what you want, but first I have to talk to Robert."

"Sara? Sara, it's me."

Robert. Angst-ridden and clearly terrified, but definitely Robert. Awash in relief, Beth silently mouthed, *It's him.* "Robert, are you hurt?"

He hesitated.

"Robert? Robert, are you there? Have they hurt you?"

"Do what they tell you," he said in a rush. "I know you're upset with me, Sara, but these people will kill me. Do what they say. You hear me? Do what they—"

The line went dead.

"Hey, bro."

"Joe? Where are you?" Mark Taylor asked. "I've been trying to reach you for hours."

"Best if you don't know." Joe looked up at Sacred Heart hospital. "What's up?"

"Checking out a lead."

He draped a hand over his Harley's handlebars. "The missing groom clue is too obvious to miss."

"How did you know? I didn't tell you about that— Ah, Beth."

"Yeah, but why didn't you tell me?"

"Not convenient. Later." Mark's expelled sigh whistled his relief, crackling in Joe's ear. "Spot your man yet?"

"Not yet." And Joe wasn't apt to spot him here—unless Masson had let NINA know he hadn't expired in Louisiana at that fishing camp in Lisa's human-trafficking case. If so, interesting strategic move. Could save his neck or get him killed. With NINA, Joe wouldn't bet a nickel either way. "How's Beth holding up?"

"So you haven't kept in touch?"

Joe shifted on his Harley's seat, chewed a fresh piece of gum. "I have. She says she's fine, but she'd say it regardless."

"You've got her nailed. More than a passing interest…?"

"She's the one. She doesn't know it yet, but that's for later. Is she okay?"

"Seems to be holding up. I haven't seen her since the kidnapper called. They gave *Sara* more instructions about ten thirty this morning."

Beth posed as Sara. What was Roxy thinking? Jeff? Had they lost it, putting Beth in that danger? Fear streaked through Joe. That was it. He needed to infiltrate. Beth had no idea what she was facing. "She says Jeff suspects she's involved in Tayton's kidnapping."

"Yeah. Roxy talked to him, but he says he had to hear it straight from Beth himself. I'm not sure why he'd consider her a person of interest, but…"

"Could be personal."

"What do you mean?"

"Making her rely on him. He has a thing for her."

"That's been over for a long time."

A muscle in Joe's neck seized up. He rolled it to work out the kink. "For Beth, but what about for him?"

"I'll mention it to Roxy, provided you're sure she's clean."

Joe didn't take offense. They'd both known too many who'd turned. "She's clean." Two nurses wearing scrubs crossed the parking lot and entered the hospital. "I'll check in later, bro. Got to go."

"Later."

Joe disconnected the call and fired up the Harley. He should stop and change clothes. Riding his bike in formalwear at eleven in the morning wasn't cool. But changing clothes could wait. Beth couldn't.

He took off toward Seagrove Village.

∽⌇∾

Karl Masson arrived at Darla Green's house on the cove and rang the doorbell with no idea what to expect.

A woman in her late fifties opened the door. She was squat with graying dark hair pulled back in a bun so tight it tugged the skin on her face taut. "Mr. Masson, come in, please."

The woman's Scottish brogue was thick and easily recognizable from his years in Europe. Karl nodded, a little disappointed. He'd hoped to know the identity of his ally in this house by who answered the door. Obviously that wasn't happening.

He followed the maid straight through the heart of the grand house to the terrace. "Herself is expecting you. I've prepared a light lunch. If you'd rather have something else, just let me know."

Herself? Definitely not Tack Grady. Did the woman mean Darla or Raven? "That was thoughtful. Thank you."

She opened a glass door that led outside. "To the right, sir."

Karl walked outside, heard her footsteps behind him. It was a stellar view. A broad expanse of lawn and beyond it, the glistening cove water. The terrace table came into view. It was set for three with fine china—and empty of diners.

He turned back to the maid. "There's no one here."

"Ah, but there is. You just don't see what's before your eyes." She turned aside, then back to face him.

"Darla?" Why was she posing as the maid? She'd gained some weight in jail—a gun in her hand snagged his full attention. He stiffened, reached for his shoulder holster, but before his arm cleared his suit jacket, she aimed and fired.

The force of the bullet knocked him back, off his feet. He landed on his back on the concrete, half-surprised he wasn't already dead. He lifted his shaking hand and touched the area of his abdomen that burned like fire. *Bad. Gut wound.* He'd die here.

"Why?" He'd been devoted to NINA all his adult life. Taken the jobs no one else wanted, been Raven's go-to guy. Spots formed before his eyes. *Weakening.*

She harrumphed. "You dare to let me think you were dead and then try to buy your way back in the organization with a mission?" Her voice sounded cold. Ruthless.

His children. He'd never again see his children…

"Dead Game is a good mission." She sniffed. "So I took it. But I will not take you."

"You—you're Raven." He couldn't believe it. *Bleeding out.* His head went fuzzy. Darla, the airhead, couldn't be Raven. But she was. She'd done what he'd done as a cleaner his whole career: she'd hidden in plain sight.

Pain exploded in his chest. Dying. Life seeping away. Two minutes, maybe less, and he'd be dead. Dead and gone. His kids wouldn't even know. No one would mourn.

"Yes, I'm Raven—and you dared to cross me." Her eyes burned fire. "Gray Ghost, your services are no longer required." She pulled the trigger again.

Masson heard the bullet. They always said if you were going to die, you never heard the bullet.

They lied.

8

⨍

ou okay?" Jeff took the phone from Beth and set it on Sara's coffee table. Who with a brain could be okay? When Kyle and Jeff had first arrived with news of Robert's kidnapping, Beth's insides had crumbled. She'd gone downhill from there. "I'm fine."

"Good." Jeff dismissed her, focused on Kyle. "Do we have a location?"

He swiveled his chair at the electronics table. "Highway 98 in Destin. Congested area. Info on the number is coming in now…" His look of anticipation soured. "Phone's a throwaway."

"What's that?" Sara's housekeeper, Maria, asked.

Jeff seemed as disgusted as Kyle. "A prepaid disposable. No records on ownership, no service contract, no paper trail to follow. A dead end."

Beth wadded a tissue to dry her damp palms. "So much for getting lucky."

Jeff let her see his worry. "Can you handle the drive to the marina? Other people are on the road, so if not, say so and I'll inform Roxy. She should stand in anyway."

Roxy was six inches shorter than Sara and a redhead. Even wearing a blond wig and a hood, no one would take her for Sara, and if Robert died, Sara wouldn't blame Roxy, she'd blame Beth. "I won't give her permission to drive Sara's car." Beth put the onus on herself. "I can do it." Sara was five-seven; Beth was an inch taller, but no one would notice that. The wig under a hood, tips hanging out to be seen, and dim light from the storm—Beth could pull it off. Her hands were freezing. She rubbed, warming them. "I'll sign whatever you need signed."

"Why?" Jeff looked surprised. "This is dangerous, Beth, and you and Sara don't look any more alike than she and Roxy."

"We're about the same height, weight, and age, and Sara's got a blond wig. I can wear it and a hood." They were both knocking at the door of thirty. Sara was naturally lean and svelte, but Beth's daily beach runs had slimmed her. She couldn't do a thing about her olive skin, but with the storm coming, light would be poor at best. It could work. It had to work.

"I didn't mean to offend you."

"You didn't. I'm scared. I get mean when I'm scared. Sorry." She waited for his nod then added, "I have to do what I can so this ends with Robert safe— for Sara. We're family."

Understanding lit in his eyes. "Okay, then."

"I don't think Roxy will approve Beth stepping in—"

Jeff silenced Kyle with a warning look and stood. "Beth, you drive Sara's car. We'll position people to protect you but you have to appear to be alone, so don't look for them. The kidnapper could be watching." He tugged at his ear-lobe. "Probably will be."

Fear curdled in Beth's stomach. Queasy, she got Sara's keys. "I'm taking my cell phone. If you hear anything on Sara—"

"I'll call," he promised. "Your number's on speed dial and I'll be close."

That made her feel better, though it shouldn't. Anyone sane would be scared out of her skin. Beth was no hero. She was plenty scared and considered calling her mother and Nora. But both would pitch a fit at her doing this. Joe would understand, but flaunting him in Jeff's face would just be mean.

Disappointment bit. This time, God aside, Beth was isolated and on her own. *Fewer choices, greater strength.*

Unfamiliar with the feeling, she stilled. How many times had Sara felt this way?

Parched, Beth drank some water. It sloshed onto her shaking hand and she set the glass down. What was it Joe and the guys on his team said in tough times? He'd reminded her—*think steel.* That was it. That's what she needed to do.

"Bad storm moving in," Kyle said. "Best get moving."

Think steel. "I'm ready."

Beth said it, and prayed it proved true.

⊙⊙⊙

The wig itched.

Beth wore it anyway, and forty minutes later she parked Sara's black Saab in the marina parking lot. Thunder crackled in the distance and heavy, black clouds blanketed the sky, blocking the sun. It was nearly noon but dark outside. Pole lights were on in the parking lot.

Jeff had fitted her with a communications earpiece. Sure it was properly seated, Beth grabbed the garden shovel she'd snitched out of Sara's garage. "On my way." She headed west across the parking lot toward the Dumpster.

"Wait. We need a second. Tie your shoe."

She had on slides—no laces. Pausing at the front fender of a tan pickup, she wiggled her heel. Security lights spilled little halos of amber light over the cars. *Empty.* The coming rain had everyone indoors. A restaurant/bar on the corner lit up J. Ray's flamingo-pink, neon sign. Muffled soft rock music from inside the beach-shack club sounded dull and distant. The band must be practicing for tonight. In the adjoining lot, she spotted the Dumpster.

Seconds later, Jeff said, "Okay, go."

Beth walked on, out of the asphalt parking lot, then across the cool sand toward the Dumpster. Waves crashing against the shore scraped her frayed nerves. She pulled her hooded sweatshirt close around her face. The stiff breeze blowing in off the Gulf was hot enough—or she was nervous enough—that she was breaking a sweat. She could mimic Sara's carriage, and Sara's wig should convince any spotter.

Between the water and the street, the wooden frame of a new building jutted up like a wooden maze from a concrete foundation. The Dumpster stood beside it. *Don't look around. They're watching.*

Her shoes filled with sand that grated against her feet. If she walked much more, she'd be hobbling as bad as Sara. She stopped. Which side of the Dumpster did the kidnapper consider the front—the side facing the street or the water?

The water, she decided. In the village, everything was about the water. In position, she looked down. The sand had been freshly turned. Looking straight down so the hood would shield her lip movements, she whispered, "There are footprints down here."

"Are they fresh?"

She grimaced. "Probably. The machine's been by to smooth, but rain is pitting the sand now. They're on the hard pack, walking away from the burial site." She looked around. "I don't see anything to protect them from the rain."

"Try not to disturb them. Get the instructions and vacate. We'll check them out later."

They were watching. Not just Jeff but the evil people who'd done this too. Away from the prints, she dropped to her knees, then started digging. "If Robert's buried here, I'm going to be sick."

"You talked to him."

"Did I? If they can do all they've done…" A foot down, her shovel pinged against something…*glass.* Glass was forbidden on the beach.

She carefully dug out around it. Trembling, she fumbled the shovel twice. *Get a grip, Beth.* What kidnapper worried about getting fined for bringing glass on the beach? What if the kidnapper and the FBI started shooting at each other? They could kill her. They could shoot her on purpose.

"Think steel," Joe's voice whispered inside her mind.

Surprised, she listened. Spoke back to it. *I need a bigger shovel so I can get out of here faster.*

"Panic later. Focus, sha."

Maybe she deserved Jeff's condescension. She sounded neurotic even to herself.

"Dig, gorgeous. Just dig."

The glass was a mayonnaise jar. She dusted at the damp sand clinging to it, realized she could be wrecking evidence, and stopped. A rolled piece of paper was inside. "Do I open it?" She didn't see anyone watching, but that included the FBI agents.

"Take it back to the car," Jeff said. "Try not to touch more than you must."

Fingerprints—and perhaps immediate instructions. Beth stepped around the footprints.

The sky split open. Fat raindrops pelted down, stinging her skin, soaking her clothes. She shielded the jar and hustled back to Sara's Saab, eager to get out of the open.

Drenched, she climbed in, locked the doors, and cranked the engine. Brushing a tissue over her face, she hid her mouth. "Okay, I'm in the car."

"Let's see what the kidnapper has to say."

Rain beat on the car like a thousand drums. Lightning cut jagged streaks across the sky and thunder vibrated through the car, through Beth. She clicked on the overhead light and carefully removed the paper, its edges clamped between her nails. "Two million. Waterproof bag. Insert in inner tube and drop in Blackwater River at Jay's Place. Dawn tomorrow. Will recover then phone directions to RT."

"Two million? By dawn?" Jeff sounded surprised and worried.

"That's it." Beth put the paper back into the jar and placed it in a small ice chest Jeff had put on the passenger-side floorboard. "How is Sara supposed to get two million together by dawn?" Even if she weren't in ICU, getting that kind of money to the village that fast? Could it be done?

"Drive back to Sara's," Jeff said. "We'll coordinate there."

Even more worried than before, Beth ground the starter. On her second try, the engine cranked. "Are we private, Jeff? Or is everyone listening in?"

"I'll call you right back."

A long three minutes later, her cell phone chirped. Had he forgotten it was tapped too? She depressed the button and listened. "Hello."

"You have something private to say?"

"Several things, but I'll wait to say them in person. Anything on Sara?"

"Some good news from Harvey Talbot via Peggy Crane. Sara's off the critical list. She's stable."

The back of Beth's nose burned. "She's out of danger?"

"Yes."

Beth squeezed her eyes shut and let it settle. *Thank You, God.*

"She's out of ICU. If she's still stable in the morning, they'll release her. Peggy and Dr. Talbot are staying with her, so you're not to worry. Peggy said to be sure to tell you that."

Of course Peggy was staying with Sara. But Harvey too? If she was stable, then why? Odd message.

Quit borrowing trouble, Beth. You have enough. Just be grateful.

She was grateful. But Clyde Parker dying, NINA, and Robert and Sara…a lot had happened and all of it was spooky stuff. Of course she'd be apprehensive, look for hidden meanings. "I'm glad."

Hanging a right off Highway 90, she headed to Sara's, letting hot, healing tears wash away her fear for her friend. Beth was the youngest of four kids and always the odd one out. The others were replicas of their father—she didn't understand them any better than she understood him. Sara was different. She was the one family member on Beth's wavelength. If anything happened to her, Beth just couldn't stand it.

Parked in the garage, she grabbed the ice chest, then crawled out of the car, bumping her knee on the steering wheel. Pain shot up her leg. "Yeow!"

"You okay?" Jeff walked up behind her.

"I'm fine." Wincing, she rubbed at her knee. "My SUV sits a lot higher." She felt as if she'd ridden the entire way dragging her seat on the pavement.

Jeff took the ice chest. "We'll get this to the lab. Maybe we'll get something."

"I dusted the jar a bit before I thought about fingerprints."

"My fault. I should have said something." He rubbed at his ear. "Actually, I never should have let you go. Protocol breach, but Roxy couldn't pass for Sara at midnight on a moonless night much less on a rainy day. My back was against the wall."

"I wouldn't let her drive Sara's car. My responsibility." Beth reminded him of the cover he needed to stay out of the FBI doghouse. She swung open the kitchen door.

Jeff stopped at the bar near the sink. "Is Robert really as bad as you say, or is it just the change—him being in the picture that bugs you? I need to know, Beth."

She waffled between honesty, diplomacy, and silence—she couldn't offer all. Setting her purse next to a crystal bowl of fruit, she shrugged. "Robert is a miserable person. Sorry, but that's the nicest thing I can say about him." No blinking light on the answering machine.

"He's miserable because he's married to Sara?"

"'Course not. Sara adores him. He's just miserable. But because he's married to Sara, it makes me sick to have to say it." Beth tugged off the wet hooded parka and itchy wig then draped them on hooks near the back door. "I wish things had been different, but…"

"Family peace is nothing to sneeze at." Jeff glanced at notes stuck to the fridge with matching vegetable magnets. "It's been rough between you guys— more than you first said."

"No secret there. Everyone in the village knows we're oil and water." She looked him right in the eye. "Since Robert blasted into our lives, I've had on my party manners—for Sara. It's been beyond wicked." Beth leaned against the bar. "But Sara is a family member I picked, not one I got stuck with because of genetics. She's worth the effort."

"Your business partner and best friend," Jeff said. "Also free will choices."

She nodded.

"Why?" Jeff did look at her then. "You're nothing alike. She's so…fragile."

"We've been through everything together. It's hard to explain those kinds of bonds."

"Yet you couldn't protect her from Robert?"

"Sara doesn't open up to people easily, and I thought he was harmless."

Boy, had she been wrong about that. "By the time I realized he wasn't, it was too late." Beth checked her cell phone, then set it on the bar. "I couldn't protect her." Admitting that grated. "What can I say? She fell in love."

Jeff looked away, clearly assimilating. If he could figure out a cohabitable peace for the three of them, no one would rejoice more than Beth. But Robert didn't grasp the rudiments of compromise and he had no interest in peace. Control was his weapon. His way, or no way.

"So what happens now?"

Jeff darted his gaze as if mentally shifting gears, and worry dragged at his face. "We figure out how to get two million in cash in the next"—he checked his watch—"fourteen hours."

Dawn. Beth grabbed a soda from the fridge. "Want one?"

Jeff nodded. She passed him a drink, then flipped the top open on her own. It clicked, then hissed. "Obviously we can't bother Sara with this. So what do you recommend?"

"She's stable." He hiked a shoulder. "I thought I'd have an agent go to the hospital—"

"No." Beth's can clanked against the bar. "She's stable compared to being dead. You tell her about this demand, and she'll slide right into another attack. I guarantee it."

"But, Beth—"

"No. We are not taking that risk."

He held up his hands. "Look, this is my job and my responsibility."

Ego? Surely not. "If you want to be responsible for her death, then do it your way."

"What's our alternative?" He slid a hip against the cabinet and leaned toward her. "We're talking two million. If not from Sara, where are we supposed to get it?"

"It's a lot of money. Give me a second to think." Pacing between the bar and sink, Beth dragged her teeth over her lower lip. She couldn't take the money from SaBe. Henry Baines would have a fit, and with good behavior it would probably take him a decade to recover. No, messing with Henry wasn't worth the fallout. SaBe funds were out. She paced some more.

"Well?" Jeff leaned back, folded his arms and stretched out his legs, then crossed them at his ankles.

Near the wine cellar door, Beth stopped. "I'll have to fund it." That was the path of least resistance and the most expedient solution. Since it was for Robert, it chilled her blood, but it was the right thing to do.

"You'll fund it for Robert?" Jeff looked taken back, and even more suspicious.

"Absolutely not. I'll fund it for Sara."

"Can't you draw it from her funds?"

"I have several powers of attorney for her but not for anything like a kidnapping. I suppose I could use one under our emergency clause. I'd have to check with Nick Pope in Legal, but it probably wouldn't be wise to do it."

"Why not?"

Keep your mouth shut. Things get twisted. "I'd rather not say."

He frowned. "Under the circumstances, I have to insist."

She worried at her lip with her teeth. If he thought she was willing to fund this because she'd had Robert kidnapped and would get her money back, then that could be really bad. She'd better nip that notion in the bud. Still, she hated revealing what she must to do it. "Robert moves her money. Sara nearly had a check bounce because he didn't bother telling her where he'd moved it. Fortunately, she'd been a good customer, so the bank called her to cover it."

"And he's still breathing?" Jeff grunted. "Bet she threatened to rip his heart out."

"Sara doesn't do rip your heart out," Beth said with a little sniff. "She was embarrassed—humiliated, actually—but all she said was that they'd had a serious discussion about it." Serious discussion. What *exactly* did that mean?

"I'm sure they did." Jeff's lip curled. "What would you have done?"

"Removed his power of the pen on everything financial, and then threatened to rip out his heart and feed it to the fish."

Jeff didn't look surprised. "That's what I'm talking about. A woman with true compassion."

"I've got tons of compassion, just no patience with people who put me in embarrassing situations." Beth took a swig of her drink. Max taught her well.

"I hear you." Jeff straightened the pale blue tie pressed against his once-crisp white shirt. "Why not use SaBe funds?"

"It'd take too long to do the paperwork. Our senior attorney is a hybrid accountant—corporate law. He's as brilliant as Churchill but a stickler about paperwork. Way too cumbersome for our purposes."

"Are you saying he wouldn't do it—for Sara?"

"Henry Baines would die for Sara. He adores her." Beth leveled a look that spoke volumes. "But this isn't for her."

"Ah, so Henry doesn't like Robert either."

"I don't speak for anyone but me."

"But off the record?"

"I suspect with constant nagging, Henry would round up the cash for Robert in about two weeks."

Jeff rubbed at his jaw. His beard stubble made a light scratching noise. "That's a little past the dawn deadline."

"Just a tad." Resignation settling into her bones, Beth grabbed the phone off its cradle. "That leaves the funding to me."

"I'm sure Sara will appreciate it."

Punching in numbers by rote, she glanced over at Jeff. "She'd expect it. And if I didn't do it, she'd never forgive me."

"So you're doing it to keep the peace with her?"

"No," Beth said. "I'm doing it to keep you from putting Sara back in ICU by asking her for it. She might not recover next time." Beth paused. "I know her, Jeff. No matter what the doc says, she won't be stable until Robert's safe at home." Beth stilled, then added, "And because she'd do it for me."

"The money could be lost. You should know that up front."

"I figured." Beth crooked the receiver at her ear. "No guarantees and all that." The idea of losing two million for Robert made her queasy, but the idea of having to tell Sara she wouldn't risk it was worse. The guilt of wishing Robert gone a million times didn't help. But it was her words to Darla that most haunted her. Refusing was cowardly. She could be obedient and pleasing or not. It was that simple, and that complex.

A woman answered the phone. "Green Enterprises."

"Beth Dawson for Darla Green, please."

Kyle came in and Jeff passed him the ice chest. "Lab's ready and waiting. Tell the others Beth's working on getting the money."

"Yes sir." Kyle lingered to listen to Beth's call, unabashedly curious.

"Hi, Beth," Darla said. "I didn't want to bother you, but I'm glad you called. We not only met but exceeded Sara's fund-raising goal. Tell her we raised $2.7 million."

"That's great news. Thank you, Darla."

"So I heard down at Ruby's that Sara's out of ICU."

Gossip grapevine was fast today. Probably because the rain had everyone inside. "She is." Beth rubbed her pounding forehead. "Don't shoot me, but I need another favor."

"Sure. What's up?"

"An emergency, but please don't ask its nature." All any of them needed was for a society rag to get a hold of this information. Or worse, Robert's friends. The repercussions to SaBe could be significant.

"Can I help resolve it?"

"Indirectly." Beth rolled her gaze toward the ceiling and got down to business. "I need two million dollars in cash in twelve hours. I have the assets, but I can't liquidate that quickly."

"Hold on." Music flowed through the phone. A long minute later, Darla came back on the line. "Dennis Porter's conferenced in with us, Beth. Dennis, Beth needs two million in cash in twelve hours. As VP of Community Bank, will you please handle that?"

"Twelve hours?" He stammered. "Is that what you said, Darla?"

"Yes."

"But—but I can't get two million to the village bank in twelve hours. I need a couple days."

"Beth doesn't have a couple days. If she did, I wouldn't be asking for it in twelve hours."

"Darla's right, Dennis," Beth interrupted. "I know making this happen won't be easy."

"Beth, allow me," Darla said. "Dennis, Beth is up to her earlobes in alligators. This isn't a debate. She has the money. We both know it, so get her the cash."

"It's not that simple, Darla."

"If it were simple, I'd handle it myself. Now, I have every confidence that when Beth steps up to the bank's front door at three o'clock in the morning, you will be there with the money, ready and waiting for her. I'll be there to see it. Have I made myself clear?"

"I—I can wire it out of your STAR fund immediately, Beth," he suggested.

That was her mad money, and the kidnappers wouldn't take a wire. "It has to be from my personal accounts, and no wire or cashier's check. I need real money. Cash."

"You can't walk around with that kind of money in cash."

"I need cash."

"I don't have that much on hand."

"Dennis," Darla cut in again. "You're not hearing me. Handle it—and never tell a woman what she can and can't do with her own money. It's offensive."

"I was just trying— She has no protection, Darla."

"A fact she surely knows since she was bright enough to earn every penny."

"But—but—"

"Twelve hours, Dennis. Front door. Cash. Good-bye." A click sounded, then Darla added, "Sorry about that, Beth. He's protective."

He was right. "Will he have it?"

"Definitely. Dennis would never disappoint me."

He wouldn't. She'd buy the bank and fire him. "Thanks for the assist."

"Any time."

Beth hung up, then looked at Jeff. "Okay, that's done. What's next?"

He frowned. "It isn't done. No bank in the village has that kind of money in its vault. Porter will have to get—"

"Dennis Porter will have the money at the bank's front door at three o'clock."

"He'll want to, he'll try, but there's no way he can do it." Jeff raised his hands and clasped his face, dragged his fingertips down to his chin. "You've asked the impossible."

"No, I didn't. Darla did."

"You're not hearing me, Beth. He can't do it."

"He can and will. Dennis Porter was John's best friend his whole life. He'll find a way."

"That's why you called Darla. Widow of his best friend had better odds of success."

"Yes." Beth brushed off his impatience, studied him closely. "You don't have much faith in people, do you?" The reserve would deliver to the local banks in the morning. Porter and the other banks worked together, and if he had to wake every banker in town, he'd get the money. Jeff was right. No village bank vaulted that much cash, but competitors—especially those in small towns—helped each other because next time they might be the one needing help. Jeff didn't seem to get that.

Well, it was a little opportunity for him to grow as a person. For something good to come from all this bad stuff.

No answer.

"I said, you don't have a lot of faith in people, do you?" she repeated.

He looked exasperated but kept his tone civil. "What's that got to do with this?"

"Everything." Her soda was warm. She filled a glass with ice and drained the can into it. It fizzed and the ice cubes crackled. "I have faith in some people, and Darla Green is one of them. Dennis will get the money. Not for me, but for her."

"He can't perform miracles. Neither can she."

"We'll see how it works out at three o'clock."

Jeff frowned. "You know I arrested her for John's murder. I mean, you do understand that Darla's guilty and her former sidekick Johnson's taking blame covering for her, right?"

"I've heard the gossip." The village grapevine hadn't missed a thing.

"It's a lot more than gossip."

"Then why isn't she in jail?"

"I'm not a lawyer or a judge. Maybe they know she killed the mayor but can't prove it. Or maybe they botched the prosecution and with Johnson's confession the conviction wouldn't hold up on appeal. Or maybe they cut her loose to see what she would do, who she knows, and if she was acting with just Johnson or with a larger group. Maybe with NINA."

"Oh, please. You think Darla-the-Airhead-Green works with NINA?"

"She's not an airhead, Beth. She's shrewd and ruthless."

She wasn't an airhead. "She was John's trophy wife. And she can't be that shrewd or ruthless or she'd go to someone a lot smarter than me for business advice."

"You've done well."

"With computers. Business is a maze I crawl through on my knees."

"Think, Beth. Who better to sting you than someone you never see coming?"

Roxy and Lisa, Mark—Joe—none of them shunned Darla. "I don't believe it. Those in a position to know welcome her in their circle. Roxy invited her to the ceremony, for pity's sake. They're not stupid."

"No, they're not stupid. They're watchful."

Someone would have told Beth, unless they didn't trust her either. She couldn't accept that; she had access to all of the Crossroads computers. That required a high level of trust. Still… "You may have a point." Beth sighed. "But Darla's been kicked hard. If the evidence proves she's guilty, okay. Just don't ask me to condemn her without it. I won't do that." Doubt seeped in. Giving Sara the property on Airport Road and making a sizable donation could have been a manipulative move to get back into the villagers' good graces. It wasn't impossible. Oh, Beth hated doubting Darla. They weren't close friends, but it was just unfair.

"I was involved in that investigation. I saw. Just keep what I said in mind." Jeff tossed his empty can in the trash with a little extra force. "Meantime, we need a backup plan. We can't go to that river empty-handed."

"Will you quit and move on to whatever comes next? The money issue is resolved." She spoke more sharply than she intended, but Jeff kept pushing, knowing she was frazzled and worn-out. Dennis Porter would handle it. Why couldn't Jeff give her credit for knowing it?

He shoved a fisted hand into his pocket. "You're asking a lot—and betting someone else's life on it. A man you dislike."

"Now you're crossing the line. I know cops have to be suspicious, but you're insulting me." Her temper flashed. She struggled to leash it. "I've done what needs doing, which means I'm asking very little. Why is trusting me difficult?" That raised her hackles. "I've done nothing to earn your doubt."

"You hate the victim." Jeff looked away. "Bottom line, this is about saving his hide."

"Disliking a man is not hating him or wishing him dead." Jeff should know that. "But whatever. Just wait and see what happens. Dennis Porter will be on the bank steps with the money." Beth tilted her glass toward Jeff. "You're forgetting that to me this isn't about *your* victim, it's about Sara. I thought I knew you. I thought your priorities were in order. But I don't know you at all. That's fine. I don't need to know you. I know me. And I never take unnecessary risks with *my* family."

"Don't make this personal." A muscle in his jaw ticked.

"I didn't. You did."

"I can't afford the luxury of waiting and seeing. It'll be too late to do anything else."

"It's already too late to do anything else. That's the kicker. Whether you don't see it or won't admit it doesn't matter—though, I have to say, both tick me off. But here's a deal you'll love. If I'm wrong and Dennis is a no-show, then just shoot me." What else could he possibly want from her? "That'll make us even."

"Don't tempt me." His face burned red and he clamped his jaw.

"Save your outrage for later," she said, taking a tip from Joe. "Right now, we need to address a couple concerns, if you don't mind." Putting up two million to get Robert back should buy her that much goodwill. If Sara made it through this ordeal, she'd reimburse Beth. Robert wouldn't even consider it.

"Fine."

Beth backed up to the bar and snagged an apple. "First, your concerns."

"Okay." Jeff circled around to the table, then clasped the back of a chair. "When the kidnapper put Robert on the phone, he said he knew Sara was upset with him. Was that upset about the bounced check?"

"Doubtful. The check incident happened months ago." Beth washed the wax from the apple at the sink, snagged a napkin, then sat at the table and took a crunchy bite. Her stomach was full of acid and rumbling.

Jeff sat opposite her. "Then why was Sara upset with him?"

"I don't know." Beth recalled the nagging feeling she'd had earlier. "But something was off with her all day yesterday. If she and Robert were at odds, that could have been it."

"You guys are close. If there was trouble, wouldn't she have told you?"

"We talk about everything *but* him. Sara knows I tolerate him for her. That's not a sympathetic ear for airing your troubles."

"Reasonable." Jeff pulled a peppermint from his pocket and unwrapped it. The cellophane crinkled in his hand. "So who would she talk to about him?"

Beth chewed an apple bite and thought. "Maybe Margaret."

"Who?"

"Our personal assistant, Margaret McCloud. Though that'd be a stretch."

"Let me guess." Jeff slid Beth a deadpan look. "Margaret doesn't like Robert either."

"Actually, she doesn't, but that's not why. Margaret lives in a world of her own and just kind of drops out of the clouds to work for us. She's an excellent assistant, don't get me wrong, but she has her own brand of relationship reality."

He popped the mint into his mouth. "I don't understand."

He couldn't, could he? Beth squirmed. She didn't like talking about Margaret this way, but the last thing she wanted was for Jeff to get it in his head that Margaret could be a suspect. "Let me give you an example," Beth said. "Three years ago, Margaret married a musician. He danced to his own drum—you know what I mean." When Jeff nodded, Beth went on. "When she got tired of supporting him and his habits, she moved him out. A few months later she fell in love with this mechanic and married him."

Jeff shrugged. "What's odd about that? People remarry all the time."

"They usually get a divorce or an annulment first. Margaret didn't." Beth cocked her head and shrugged. "That's how Margaret thinks. If she wants to get married, she gets married. She doesn't bother with the details, like divorcing her current spouse first."

He nearly choked on his mint. "So she's a bigamist?"

"You're getting sidetracked," Beth warned him. "My point is that Margaret loves being a bride but she's not crazy about being married. She might have a dozen husbands out there. I don't know. But there hasn't been any trouble. Every now and then one of them shows up at SaBe. She's glad to see him, and he's glad to see her. It's weird, but it works for Margaret. I've tried and tried to get her to go to Crossroads for counseling, but so far, she's not interested. At the office, she's a powerhouse—great work, totally trustworthy, and no trouble. I can't make her personal choices for her."

"Is that a woman thing, or what?"

"It's a faith thing." Beth frowned. "I'm a work-in-progress, especially where Robert's concerned. I'm not fit to judge anyone. Margaret's stuff is between her and God."

Jeff thumbed the place mat. "Sara wouldn't go to her. No common ground."

"That was my thinking, but you make your own call." Relieved that he got it, Beth sifted through other possibilities. "Sara used to come home for dinner once a week—Robert nixed that—but she and Mom had lunch fairly often."

"What do they talk about?"

"Probably all the things girls and their mothers discuss that is of no interest to anyone else; you know, the mundane and significant."

"They're that close?"

"Closer." Beth nodded. "But don't waste your time there. Their chats are private. Neither will tell you a thing. There just isn't anyone else." Sara had lots of acquaintances but only one really close friend. If Beth could have been thrilled about Robert, it would have meant the world to Sara. Things should have been so different. Guilt swam through her, settled in her heart. It wasn't warranted—he was a user. But she regretted the situation for Sara.

"What's troubling you?"

"It'd be easier to answer what isn't." Beth bit the apple, enjoyed its tart crunch, and focused on what she would next say. "During the kidnapper's call, something odd happened." Surely Jeff had noticed. It was his job to notice things like that, but he hadn't said anything. "It's nagging at me."

"What?"

Keep your mouth shut. Things get twisted… "You know, it was probably nothing. Forget—"

"No." He lifted a hand, still holding the wadded mint wrapper. "Tell me."

"Robert called me Sara."

"So?"

"So the man talks to his wife a dozen times a day. He's terrified anyone else will influence her."

"What's your point?"

Palms on the table, she leaned toward him. "My point is a question, Jeff." She almost regretted bringing this up. Almost. But something warned her not to drop it, that it was significant. "Things important to women don't always register with men."

"Granted, though we do have other redeeming qualities."

Clyde Parker would have belly laughed at that one. "You do."

"So there is a *but* in that comment," Jeff said. "What is it?"

Doubt left Beth. "How can a man talk to his own wife on the phone that often for that long and still not recognize her voice?"

∞

"Nathara, what are you doing here?"

Darla Green closed her front door and stared at Nathara and Tack, standing in the middle of her entry hall.

"Running an errand for Nora." Her floppy hat had a wide green brim that shadowed her eyes. "I thought you were at Crossroads, manning the phones."

"I was. Every crazy in the tricounty area is calling in sniff reports."

"Sniff reports?"

"Smell something funny—because of the club attack."

Tack harrumphed. "Seeing the Hazmat teams on the news, I expect."

"Probably, Tack. Things are finally settling down." Darla laid her purse on the entry table, then dropped her keys on a silver tray. "So what does Nora need, Nathara?" Tack hadn't moved. Why was he staying put? And what was that on his shoes. It looked dry—and it'd better be. If he soiled her new white carpet, she would be upset.

"Nothing from you. She wants Tack to be a pallbearer at Clyde's funeral tomorrow. It's at two o'clock."

That "nothing from you" stung, but Darla ignored it. "How's she doing?"

"It's silly." Nathara sniffed. "Such a fuss over her and a man who lived a long life."

Darla bit her tongue. She wasn't fond of Nathara, but what Beth said at the club about Darla not being beyond redemption had stuck with her. She didn't want to put it to the test. Her mistakes were bad ones, and there were a lot of them. She'd mulled over Beth's words—especially that coward remark—and figured she had nothing to lose by praying. That's why she'd gone to Crossroads. All those people prayed a lot in its little chapel and God heard them. Darla figured if she prayed there, maybe He'd hear her too. So she gave it a try. But if God had heard her, He hadn't let her know it. Still, she wasn't giving up. She wasn't a coward and something had to change. No mere mortal could do what needed doing to help her. She'd hit rock bottom and parked there. It was God or nothing.

"I'd better get back." Nathara walked past Darla to the door. "Don't be late for Clyde's funeral. Nora's reminding everyone. Why that's so important to her, I have no idea."

Tack tipped his hat. "I'll be there early."

Nathara frowned, looked down her nose at Darla. "Will you be there?"

"Of course. I've known Clyde for years." That she wasn't wanted didn't escape her; Nathara's expression made it abundantly clear.

"Then you need to know he's not being buried at the village cemetery but at Race Miller's old place in Magnolia Branch. Nora says everybody knows where it is."

Darla did. "Why is he being buried there?" Surely he could afford a cemetery plot.

"Apparently Clyde was born on that property and he wanted to be buried on it."

"But it's private property," Darla told Nathara. "Race Miller sold it to SaBe."

"So I've been told."

"Then Beth's given permission to bury Clyde there?"

"You'd have to ask Beth that. All I know is what Clyde wants, Nora will get." Nathara walked out and closed the door behind her.

Darla turned to Tack. "Did you know Clyde's family once owned that property?"

"Yeah." Tack's weathered face looked pinched. "For a couple generations. Then Clyde fell on hard times—back when his wife got sick—and he got a mortgage from Race. The community went bust about the same time. Poor Clyde lost his wife and the land. Race left it vacant until some pornographers trespassed to make movies and got arrested on it. He was beside himself about that and sold it to SaBe."

Tack lifted his cap then set it back on his head. "I heard at Ruby's that Beth bought it and tried to give it to Clyde, but he wouldn't take it. Said them putting a safe house on it was a fine thing."

Beth adored Clyde. Her offering it to him didn't surprise Darla a bit. "How awful for Clyde to lose his family's land."

"He was holding on to it for sentimental value. Ain't lived up there since he was a kid."

"Sad. I just hate that." Darla was genuinely touched. "Family is important." She'd had one and lost it. John to death, her son to guilt. She deserved the loss, but she still regretted it.

"Well, I need to get back to work." He moved to the back of the house, toward the door to the terrace. "I'm bleaching the terrace to kill any mold. Best let it dry before coming out."

Being so close to the water, everything outside molded or rusted. "Didn't you do that last week?"

"Yep, but with all the rain, it needs doing again."

Usually the deep cleaning lasted a lot longer than a week. Strange. "Don't you have a campaign debate with Hank tonight at the high school?" The polls had them neck and neck.

"Not until six." Tack went outside.

Something on the floor caught Darla's eye. It looked almost as if it had been tucked behind the sofa's rear leg. She bent down and picked it up. Soft. Rubbery. Skin colored. "What in the world?"

She flipped it over—*a mask*—and saw a nose.

A nose that looked remarkably like her own.

9

Someone shook her shoulder.

Beth startled awake, blinked rapidly to clear her vision.

Jeff stood beside the sofa. "Sorry, but it's time to go to the bank."

She shoved off the velvet throw, stiffened against the sudden chill and then stood, dragging herself from grogginess. "Give me five minutes."

"No problem." He checked his watch.

Probably freaking out at them relying on Darla when he believed she killed John. Beth couldn't hold that against him. In his work, he saw the worst in people a lot more often than he saw the best. That could make a man cynical. Maybe Dennis Porter getting the money would restore a little of Jeff's faith— providing, of course, he did get it.

Beth climbed into Jeff's black Tahoe, closed the door, then clicked her seat belt. With only the odd porch light on, it was inky dark in Sara's housing development. Jeff cranked the engine. It pierced the still silence, loud and obnoxious.

His jaw set, his knuckles shone in the green dash lights. "Which bank branch?"

Silently, she prayed Dennis wouldn't let Darla and her down. "Community on Highway 98, just past Home Depot."

Traffic was light, but the ride over was tense. It set Beth's teeth on edge and a dull ache started in her head. If Dennis failed, Jeff would believe that failure was intentional and nothing would convince him otherwise. That strengthened the temple thud and put knots in her neck.

He tapped the turn signal. Its click kept time with the thud. When he turned into the parking lot, she strained to see the bank—and nearly wept with relief.

Darla stood just behind the glass front door and Dennis Porter, bless his heart, stood beside her wearing a frown, a three-piece gray suit, and a lemon-yellow tie.

"Well, he's here." Jeff wove through the lot, which was empty except for two cars. "Not that being here means he has the money."

Beth bit back a smile. "What do you think is in the black case at his feet?"

"I don't believe it." Jeff's jaw went slack. He stopped at the curb in front of the bank.

"Miracles happen, Jeff. You just have to have faith in people."

"Miracle? More like a felony." He shoved the gearshift into Park. "To pull this off, Porter had to commit a bunch of them."

Now that ticked Beth off. "What an unfair thing for you to assume about any of us. I'm not stupid enough to do business with a banker who'd commit felonies."

"This isn't working. You're trying to make this about you, but—"

"I'm trying to pay the ransom." She wasn't taking one more insult. Not one more.

He frowned and held it. "I *am* going to ask how he managed this."

Dennis would tell him too, but Jeff wouldn't learn a thing about having faith in people. "If you do, I'll tell him to forget it and put the money back in the bank."

"What?" Jeff looked at her as if she'd lost her mind.

"You heard me." She hiked her chin. "I have no legal obligation to do this or to be involved at all. I choose to help, but I have ethics and personal lines in the sand, and you're crossing them. Maybe you insult people who move mountains to help you, but you're not going to insult them for moving one for me." She clenched her jaws. "That's just the most ungrateful thing I've ever heard of in my life, and I won't be a party to it."

He stiffened and let out a sigh that could propel a boat halfway across the Gulf. "Fine." He cut the engine and jerked the key from the ignition.

"Fine." She wanted to clam up, but couldn't risk him accusing Dennis of anything illegal. "You seem so enlightened at times, it's hard to believe you have such a lack of faith in people." Amazing. He was so close to Peggy Crane and the Crossroads bunch. Beth opened the door and delivered the final blow. "If Peggy Crane knew this, she'd have the prayer warriors going around the clock for you—and Nora would be devastated."

To his credit he held his tongue.

Hoping she wouldn't regret her outburst, Beth walked up the steps of the bank.

◌

Beth and Jeff were back at Sara's with the money. Kyle scanned the bills to capture the serial numbers, Mark put the bills into a black waterproof bag, and Roxy verified them as included.

Jeff hadn't said a word to Beth in the half hour they had been at Sara's. That was fine with Beth. She was tense, chiding self-indulgence in giving in to her temper, bone tired, out of patience and irked because she still had so far to go on her spiritual journey. Would she be stuck forever as a work-in-progress?

The front door opened.

Everyone alerted.

Sara walked in and stopped suddenly, startled by all the activity in her home. "Beth?"

Peggy circled around Sara, her chunky iridescent necklace winking in the light. "We tried to make her stay put, but if Harvey and I hadn't driven her home, she would have walked."

"I understand." Beth frowned at Sara. "She's stubborn."

"She's determined." Sara lifted her chin. "And she's fine."

"Did Dr. Franklin and Harvey say that, or just you?" Beth hugged her. "He didn't release you, did he?"

No answer.

"You left without him releasing you? Sara, what are you doing?" Beth backed away. "You'd better really be okay, or I'll take you back to the hospital myself."

Sara put down her purse. "Quit worrying. Dr. Franklin authorized my release."

"In the morning." Peggy guffawed. "Not that she gave him much choice."

"It is morning." Sara glared at Peggy for outing her, then looked at Beth. "I was going crazy, wondering what was happening here."

"All right." How could Beth object? She'd feel the same way. "But any sign of trouble—and you're going right back or else I'm going to Nora."

Sara groaned. "That's so unfair. You know how she gets."

"Yes, I do."

"I told her the same thing, Beth." Peggy crossed her arms. "But, bless her heart, she's as hardheaded as you, and that's saying something."

The FBI agents watched closely, and that comment seemed to please Jeff a tad too much. He was still smarting from her dressing down, so Beth let it slide.

Sara nodded a greeting to the agents and looked around the living room, noting the assembly line and all the equipment. "Roxy, what is all this?"

"Beth will explain. We're a little short on time."

"Time for what?"

"I'll explain that too," Beth said. "Peggy, how about you put on a pot of tea while I catch Sara up?"

"Of course." Peggy looked at the agents. "Would you like tea or coffee? A snack?"

Beth led Sara into the family room, sat her down on the sofa, and then briefed her on the major developments. No sense in bothering her with minutia; the less strain the better.

"You put up the money for Robert, didn't you?"

Beth's face burned. "For you, not him."

Sara squeezed her hands. "Thank you."

"You're my family." Their gazes locked, and Beth turned the subject. "Are you really okay?" Surely Harvey Talbot wouldn't bring her home unless he was sure she could handle it.

"I really am," Sara assured her.

Peggy walked in. "Any signs of stress and Harvey is waiting for her at Crossroads." She sat on the other end of the sofa with a grunt. "Gracious." She winced at Sara. "Not to be critical, dear, but this sofa is as hard as a rock."

It was. There wasn't a comfortable seat in the entire house.

"Sorry," Sara said. "I don't like it either, but Robert loves the thing, so what can I do?"

"I understand. My Frank has a twenty-year-old recliner I'd love to toss on the trash heap, but he refuses to give it up."

"Men. You gotta love 'em." Sara turned to Beth, regret in her eyes. "I'm sorry I wigged out on you. I tried to hold it together but I couldn't do it."

"You don't have to apologize, but you've got to quit scaring me. Your body can't take it, and neither can my heart." Beth considered telling her about the messenger at the fund-raiser and asking her about the hospital visits that according to him weren't for mild attacks, but the timing wasn't right. Sara had kept that private and, like it or not, Beth had to respect that.

Peggy stood. "I'm going home to shower and change clothes. If you need me, Beth, call. And do be careful, Sara." With a gentle hand, she touched Sara's cheek. "No more medical emergencies." When Sara nodded, Peggy looked at Beth. "And no more unnecessary risks. I heard about you retrieving the instructions." She huffed. "I'll be speaking to Jeff."

"Don't, Peggy. Somebody had to pose as Sara. It was Roxy or me. I'm taller."

"I see." That she really did shone in her eyes. "Lisa and Harvey are at the center if you need them." Peggy passed Sara two prescription bottles. "One of each every six hours. First hint of a symptom, you go to the center. No debate."

Sara nodded. "Thanks for everything."

"Of course, hon." Peggy walked out of the room and into the entryway.

When she was out of earshot, Sara asked, "You posed as me?"

Beth gave Sara a brief overview, trying not to throw her into overload.

"You've done everything possible on every front. I'm grateful, Beth."

Beth shrugged and words tumbled out of her mouth she never intended to speak. "Jeff asked me if I was involved in Robert's kidnapping."

Sara stiffened and stared, silent.

Uneasiness settled between them. Beth hated it. "I'm not."

"Why did he ask?"

Beth tried not to be hurt. Tried not to resent Sara's failure to object, to state her certainty Beth would never do such a thing. But this was Robert. Beth understood, yet letting go of the disappointment was going to take work and a little time. "He said he had to."

"Jeff always has been very conscientious." Sara touched a fingertip to her chin. "Maybe you should appreciate him a little more for that."

"I appreciate him doing his job; I just don't love him."

"He gets to you. I know he does, and since Max showed his true tacky self, few men get to you, Beth."

Max had made her gun-shy and she wouldn't deny it. She survived that humiliation once, but she never wanted to go through it again. Still, Sara was almost right. Wrong man. Joe got to her, but she didn't want him to get to her. "Jeff doesn't get to me in a good way. Honestly, there are times I have to work at it to like him at all."

Sadness flashed through Sara's eyes. "Love can do that too."

"It's not love." She'd considered them friends, but now? Lacking faith in people left a gaping hole in their friendship. Joe didn't doubt her. He hadn't hesitated for a second. Her heart skipped a beat. He'd break her heart, regardless of what he said, but he believed in her.

"Well, that's that on Jeff, then. Pity. I always liked him."

Something in her voice alerted Beth. "You had a thing for Jeff?"

"I did," Sara confessed in hushed tones. "A bad one."

"But you never said a word."

"He only had eyes for you."

"We only dated a couple times, Sara. Why didn't you—?"

"It would have been awkward. Then I met Robert, and everything changed."

Boy, had it. "I can't believe this. I had no idea."

"Let it go. Life's moved way beyond that now." Sara let out a wistful sigh. "Tell me about the ransom. What happens next?"

Beth shifted on her seat. "We're to drop the money at Jay's Place at dawn. Put it in an inner tube and set it afloat in the Blackwater River. That's all I know." Beth checked her watch. "Jeff will be in any second. It's time to go."

"What's Jay's Place?" Sara stood. "I've never heard of it."

"I hadn't either. It's near the Blackwater River State Park. There's a picnic area on the river and they rent canoes. People float down the river in them or in inner tubes, then someone from Jay's retrieves them and returns them back to their cars."

"Did Jeff think this was odd—in this kind of case, I mean?"

"If he did, he didn't say so. Roxy either."

Sara rubbed her hands. They were shaking. "Let's go, then."

"Oh no." Vintage Sara. Ignoring Dr. Franklin's orders already. "You stay here and rest. I'll handle it."

"No." Sara's expression changed to steel. "The kidnapper said I was to drop the money off and I'm going to do it."

"What's the difference?" Beth tried to reason with her. "So long as the money is set afloat, do you think they really care who puts it in the water?"

"Maybe. Maybe not." Sara's fear and worry showed in every tense line on her face. "But if something goes wrong—God forbid—I'd care forever."

Guilt, Beth understood. And sitting here worrying would make Sara a nervous wreck. If she went along, at least Beth could watch over her. "I would too."

"I'm doped to the gills on antianxiety meds. Very relaxed but not out of my head goofy. Can't drive." Sara coughed. "I just hope this is enough to save Robert's life."

Looking into Sara's fearful face, Beth said the only thing she could say. "I hope so too."

◎

Civil twilight would begin at 5:47 a.m. Official sunrise would be at 6:12.

At 5:00, Jeff seated Beth behind the wheel of Sara's Saab, Sara in the backseat with the waterproof bag of money, and then he climbed into his Tahoe. Mark Taylor, Roxy, and Crossroads owner, Ben Brandt, piled into Mark's SUV. Beth's insides quivered. Backing out of the garage, she glanced at Sara. She had to be a basket case, but she looked as serene as she did in the SaBe lab. Strange.

About ten minutes out from Jay's Place, Beth fought to focus. Her nerves jangled.

"Beth?"

"Yes?" She glanced at Sara in the rearview. Her eyes were droopy, but she hadn't dozed.

"What happened when the kidnappers called? They expected me to be there—"

"They thought I was you."

"That's absurd." Sara met her gaze in the mirror. "No one would mistake your voice for mine."

Beth agreed—her voice was at least an octave lower—and that they hadn't known the difference troubled her. "I faked it. Even Robert thought I was you."

Sara gasped. "You spoke to Robert? You didn't tell me."

Must be the medication. "Yes, I did." Beth passed a white Honda and a rusty pickup, then veered back into the right lane behind Jeff. "He sounded okay." Terrified, but okay. "They didn't let him talk long." Should she bring up that bit about Sara being upset with him? The messenger from the terrace fund-raiser? Not with Jeff hearing every word. Thwarted again, Beth added, "He just said for you to do whatever they want." Beth deliberately omitted his "They'll kill me." Sara did not need to hear that.

She shifted. The moneybag crackled. "Odd. I can't believe he mistook you for me."

Beth replied honestly; otherwise, Sara would know immediately. "I thought it odd too."

Through the earpiece, Jeff jumped in. "Robert was in a hypertense situation. Maybe he was too afraid to notice."

"Jeff says in tense situations sometimes people don't notice," Beth relayed to Sara. "That makes sense to me."

"I don't believe it," Sara insisted. "He knows my voice—and he knows your voice too."

Also true. "Maybe he faked it so the kidnapper wouldn't know I wasn't you."

"Plausible." Jeff grunted approvingly. "And probable."

Still stinging because of his attitude toward her, Darla, and Dennis, Beth ignored Jeff.

"If he talked to you as if you were me, he did it intentionally."

Beth agreed. She couldn't ask about the terrace messenger in front of anyone else, but it was only a matter of time before Jeff asked about it. "Robert did say something I didn't understand."

"What?" Sara sounded wary and disturbed.

Another strange reaction. "He said he knew you were upset with him, but to please do what the kidnapper said." Beth looked back in the mirror for Sara's unguarded reaction. "Were you upset with him?"

"No." Sara stared out the side window into the darkness. "He was letting you know he knew who he was really talking to—you stay upset with him, Beth."

Sara had lied. *Lied to Beth.* Stunned, her skin prickled. She stared down the road, out at the hurricane bent and twisted trees lining it. Why would Sara lie to her? She hated lying.

"Makes sense." Jeff tossed in his observation.

It did, but it was still a lie. Beth's stomach soured. If Robert thought Sara would refuse the kidnappers' instructions and let him die, she had to have been deeply upset with him. That he had doubts about her proved it.

Again the terrace messenger's warning replayed in Beth's mind. Again she felt his warm minty breath fan across her neck and shoulder. Who had he been? Dr. Franklin had been there. She thought back to her days in his office, talking to him about Sara's condition. His office. Dimly lit, bookshelves lining the walls. Stack of files on his desk and a banker's lamp. A leather blotter—and a little crystal bowl of ice-blue mints!

He would certainly know why Sara had been hospitalized. Even at the fund-raiser, he had been phone-consulting with the ICU personnel and the doctors with Sara. Maybe he wanted Beth to know something else was up with Sara's hospitalizations but couldn't tell her without violating confidentiality. Privacy rights had hushed the EMT guys about Sara's feet, whatever that was about.

But the ice-blue mints weren't the right mints.

The messenger's breath was the same peppermint scent as the one Jeff had at Sara's kitchen table. Beth sat up a little straighter in her seat. He was on the terrace afterward, and he could get access to Sara's medical information. She frowned. But judging by his comments, he would assume Beth knew why Sara had been hospitalized three times. And considering her a suspect, he wouldn't tell her anything. If she ever got two seconds alone, she'd ask Margaret to look into the reason for Sara's hospitalizations. She handled the insurance claims. They'd disclose the truth.

But the messenger had to be someone else. Dr. Franklin was the better bet. She tried to recall his cologne. The terrace messenger had worn a subtle citrus scent. One Beth never had noticed on Dr. Franklin. And she would have noticed it. The fragrance pulled at something low in her stomach. She definitely would have noticed—if she'd been close enough to catch the scent. She couldn't honestly ever remember being that close to Dr. Franklin...

Worthless speculation.

It was. She needed to focus on the moment. Sara could answer the questions and end Beth's internal debate. And she would, probably, when Beth asked. But that really didn't worry her. What put knots in her stomach and hurt in her heart hit far closer to home.

Why did Sara lie to her?

☙☙

Jay's Place was at a bend in the river.

FBI agents and local authorities had coordinated and well before dawn had dug in at various points up and downstream. The current was swift at the bend and lazy after it—a great place to launch a canoe or a tube for floaters. Here, the river was only about the width of a dozen cars placed end to end, and thick woods flanked both sides—alpine cedars, more twisted pines, and stray oaks and magnolias, which stood out because of their bright green, waxy leaves. A narrow sandy beach jutted out on Jay's side of the river. The opposite side had a steep, six-foot drop to the water, scrubby and natural with plants and roots helping hold the sand in place. A short distance around the bend, the river widened up again to twice its bend width and the current slowed substantially. It was easy to imagine a group of people in tubes laughing and floating down it, towing a rope-tied tube holding an ice chest full of cold drinks.

A single tube lay in the sandy beach near the water's edge, no doubt placed there by one of Jeff's agents for Sara to put the money in and set it afloat. Later in the day, little kids would be playing there, digging with shovels and filling buckets, building sand castles, but at this early hour, the beach—all of Jay's— was deserted except for their group.

"Let's get this done." Sara crawled out of the car, hauling the moneybag with her.

She had on flats—practical but amazing considering her position on heels these days—and black pants, not shorts. She'd be roasting by eight o'clock, but hopefully they'd be long gone before then. She was already staggering. "Let me help." Beth clasped her arm. "I'll carry it."

"No. I need to do it myself."

"Okay." Beth didn't argue. Too much was outside Sara's control in all this, and carrying the bag was something she could choose. Using it to hold herself together, she leaned heavily on Beth. By the time they made it down to the tube on the beach at the water's edge, Beth's arm muscles burned.

"The tube has a bottom." Sara bent down and stuffed the bag into the tube's center hole.

"Lots of them do. Keeps stuff dry."

"Oh." Sara glanced back at her. "Hand me that cord, will you?"

Beth passed the bungee cord, but Sara's coordination was severely impaired and within seconds she muttered, "I can't do it."

Scooting around, Beth attached the cord to a loop handle on the tube, then stretched the cord across the hole, snagged the second loop, and secured the bag.

"It won't fall out?" Sara asked. "You're sure?"

Beth tugged it. "It's not going anywhere until someone removes those cords."

Sara dragged the tube toward the water. "It's heavy."

Two million in bills did pack some weight. Beth worked with her and they twisted the tube over to the water, its bottom scraping the grating sand. Finally, the edge of it glided into little curls of water. Sara got into position to set it afloat and bent down to give it a shove.

A horrific sense of dread slammed into Beth. She grabbed Sara's arm. "Wait." When Sara looked back at her, Beth shared the warning. "Don't let go. Something's not right, Sara. Don't let go."

"I have to let go," Sara insisted, thick-tongued and slurring her words. "They'll kill him." Her expression twisted, crumbled. "If they kill him, things could be so awful. Everything will be destroyed. *Everything.*"

Certainty rippled through Beth. Sara meant far more than her marriage and, if she weren't medicated to the rafters, she wouldn't have said as much as she did. A horrific sense of catastrophe settled in, knotted Beth's stomach. Confused and torn, she scanned the shoreline, the dense woods that crept down the far riverbank, but nothing struck her as out of place. Still, she couldn't shake the dread. It was crushing.

"Sara, listen to me. Something is wrong." Beth shoved her damp hair back from her face. "Remember that feeling I got when you were going to ride from the canteen to the dorm with Trevor Mason? You were already in the car, and I made you get out? Remember?"

Sara shuddered. "He got in a wreck a few blocks away."

"Everyone in the car was killed."

Sara frowned. "What does that have to do with this?"

"I have no idea," Beth admitted. "But I've got that same feeling right this minute. Don't let go of that money."

That remark clearly had Sara at war with herself. "What? Do you think they've already killed Robert or they're going to, or something like that?"

"I don't know," Beth spat out, more frustrated with herself than Sara could possibly be. The dread started the minute she'd stepped into the water and had intensified every second since. "I couldn't explain on campus, and I can't explain now. But I know this is the wrong thing to do. It's going to trigger something awful, Sara."

In soft sand with water soaking her slacks to her calves, Sara stilled and stared down.

"Sara, don't. Please, don't."

Worrying her lip with her teeth, Sara shoved the tube.

"Sara!" Beth let out a sigh of pure frustration. "Why did you do it? Why?"

"I heard you." She turned her back to the river. "But there are things you don't know that I do. Not doing this will definitely trigger something more awful than you can imagine." Sara dusted the sand from her palms and stumbled up the shallow incline to the parking lot.

Beth followed her. "What are you talking about?"

"It's better for you not to know."

Exasperated, Beth asked, "Not to know *what*?"

"Look, I'm doing what I have to do." Sara lifted a hand to stay Beth's protest. "I hear you, okay? But I can't afford to listen. Not this time."

What had Robert gotten Sara into? Whatever it was, it was bad. Would it hurt her? Hurt SaBe? *"Sara's in deep trouble. She needs your help..."* the man on the terrace had told her. Beth folded her arms over her chest. "Are you going to explain this to me?"

Sara calmly turned and looked her right in the eye. "No."

Shock pumped through Beth. Nothing but cold resolve shone in Sara's eyes. "Is SaBe going to be hurt?"

"Not if I can prevent it."

"I might be able to help, Sara. If it impacts SaBe, then I deserve to know."

"I said, no. No is a complete sentence, Beth." Sara walked on.

Jeff's voice sounded through the Bluetooth. "Beth, what is going on between you two?"

Beth kicked at the sand. "I wish I knew."

"You have no idea?"

"None." Beth pivoted and watched the tube float down the river. The dread knotted in her stomach sank under a deluge of inevitable doom.

10

ara wouldn't talk straight. Trying not to huff up about it, Beth followed Sara to Jeff's Tahoe. She still wasn't steady on her feet and for some reason she elected not to remove her water-soaked flats. They squished with her every step.

Beth crawled into the backseat beside Sara and waited. Sara never said the first word.

Dawn went and morning arrived with the full force of hot sun and high humidity. The silence was deafening. Beth glanced at Jeff, sitting behind the wheel. Tension radiated off him and he paled; he'd heard something on his earpiece that disturbed him. "What now?"

"Message from Roxy. As soon as Sara launched the tube, we got an e-mail from the kidnapper. The two of you are to wait here. They're calling in Robert's location on that pay phone." Jeff pointed through the windshield to the phone mounted on Jay's cedar-shake wall just beyond the picnic area.

"They're going to call," Beth said, glad the wait was over. "This is good, right?"

"They're watching us, Beth." He looked at her in the rearview mirror. "And we haven't spotted them."

Beth's stomach flipped.

"Are we keeping people off the phone?" Sara craned to see around Jeff. "Should we be over there?"

"No," Jeff said. "Stay put."

Sara grabbed the door handle. "We should keep anyone off that phone."

Beth touched her arm. "We shouldn't be out in the open. He's scared we'll be shot."

"Seriously?"

"They have the money in sight, Sara. They don't need you anymore."

Suddenly this was all too real, too frightening, and Beth's fear reflected in Sara's eyes. Sara, who had secrets that could hurt her, Beth, and SaBe. Shivers rippled over Beth's skin.

A dull roar from the river grew loud, then louder. *Engines.*

Two Jet Skis zoomed into view from the north, screamed past the launch site to the bend, then down the river and out of sight.

"Is that them?" Sara squeezed Beth's hand hard enough to crack bones.

Jeff barked orders into his headset; acronyms and codes alien to Beth.

"Can we see if that's them?" Sara's voice shrilled and she shook like a leaf tossed by a gust of wind. "They'll take the money and not tell us where to find Robert."

Jeff spared Sara a glance over his shoulder. "No one can get close to the money without us knowing it."

Her breathing went ragged. "Don't do it, Sara," Beth warned. Another attack now could kill her. "Your body can't take any more. Keep it together or—"

"I'm fine," Sara snipped back.

"Shh, I can't hear." Jeff glared back at them. "They've stopped. Approaching the tube."

Tension thickened, almost palpable. Beth fisted her hands and held her tongue. *Joe, why aren't you here? I need you here.*

"Think steel, sha. Think steel…"

"They're checking out the bag." Jeff twisted his lip mic. "Hold your positions until they take possession and start to depart. Can you hear what they're saying? If so, relay."

They'd put a listening device in the bag, a tracking device on the tube. Jeff should be able to hear every word. But if not, then surely his men could. The river was narrow here—maybe twenty feet wide—their voices would carry over the water to the agents hiding in the woods on the banks.

Seconds passed. Then more. And when Beth was certain every nerve in her body was about to snap, Jeff muttered.

"What?" Sara reached forward and clasped his shoulder. "Tell me."

"They opened the bag and saw the cash. Now they're debating whether or not to take it," Jeff told Sara. "One wants to; the other says it's got to be drug money and taking it will get them killed."

"Logical deduction." That's exactly what Beth would have thought.

"They're not taking it." Jeff dabbed at his damp forehead with a napkin. "Now they're discussing reporting it to the cops."

Beth grunted. "No way is that going to happen."

Jeff looked back at her.

"What? Would you call?" She shrugged. "I'm just saying…"

Sara chimed in. "File a report and identify yourself to drug dealers? Welcome to running from them the rest of your life—which won't be long. I'd want to call; I'm just not sure I'd actually do it. Maybe anonymously."

"A caller wouldn't discuss calling," Beth said. "He'd dial the phone." Somebody had to stand up, but it wouldn't be the skiers. "They'll let it float and forget they saw it."

Long minutes passed. Then Jeff grunted. "You got it, Beth. They closed the bag and left it to float." He looked back at her. "So much for having faith in people."

She resented the dig. "Different criteria, different standards." She wrinkled her nose at Sara. "No one wants a drug dealer after him—or one coming after his wife or kids. Taking or reporting the money carries risks, and others pay them too. You don't know these men or what their lives are like, Jeff. Don't judge them."

"Two million dollars is a lot of temptation," Sara said. "Greed is strong."

Home to corruption too. Beth blew her hair back from her face. Sweat-slick, it was stuck to her cheek. "True, but dead men don't need cash."

"They're gone." Jeff sighed. "Our near-hit was a dud."

Beth slumped on the seat, both relieved and disappointed.

Sara closed her eyes and let out a shuddering breath.

"What now?" Beth checked her watch. Nearly nine. "Clyde's funeral is at two. If we're late, Nora will flip out."

"We can't leave." Sara took a drink from her water bottle.

Jeff draped an arm on the steering wheel. "We wait for the phone and watch the money."

⚬⚬

By ten o'clock, the heat in the Tahoe was stifling. Sara was dozing, no doubt due to the antianxiety drugs and sheer exhaustion. Thanks to the attack and continued stress, her stamina was shot. Beth was going stir-crazy, grumpy, and sticking to the leather seats. "Do you think it's safe to step outside, Jeff?" She blew her hair back from her face. "I need air." Even more, she needed to talk to Joe.

"Stay on this side of the building. We've got it covered. Everywhere else is vulnerable."

Beth grabbed a bottle of water and her special phone, got out, and left the door cracked open to let fresh air inside. Hot and humid, the outside air still felt cool on her skin. She walked across the narrow parking lot to the little picnic area. Only the guy handling the rentals and a half-dozen tubers were around.

She sat on the table under the shade of an ancient oak and rested her feet on its concrete bench. A hot breeze feathering across her skin, she dialed Joe, hoping more than she wanted to admit to herself that he answered.

"Hi, gorgeous."

Tension ebbed from her body. Excitement replaced it. "I wish you were here."

"Tense, huh?"

"Beyond tense, but the meds have Sara dozing, so that's good."

"Have they picked up the money yet?"

"No." She twisted the cap off the water bottle and took a drink. "This whole money-drop thing and waiting—it all feels wrong. I got an awful feeling and asked Sara not to let go of the tube. She said if she didn't, something awful would happen."

"Did she say what?"

Beth's frustration bubbled. "No. But she knows more than she's saying and whatever it is scares her socks off. She had that same look as at the club, staring at the wedding cake."

"Its groom was missing and so was hers. That had to hit her hard."

"You think they're connected." Beth sat straighter.

"Don't you?"

Did she? Beth worried her lip with her teeth. Cryptic warnings. Lying to her. Acting strange. Wishing she could go back to before Robert. "Yeah. Yeah, I do."

"Mark says the abductor's having you wait for a pay-phone call."

"Isn't that weird? They have our cell phones. Why do they want us here? It doesn't make sense."

"I don't know, but I don't like it. If you didn't have Class-A protection, I'd suggest you leave." He shifted subjects. "Did you ask Sara about the hospital visits?"

The terrace messenger popped into her mind. She should tell Joe about him, and she would shortly. "Not yet. There's always someone around. Since she didn't tell me the truth about them, she obviously wants them kept private. I'm trying to respect that but, Joe, she did lie to me. I couldn't believe it."

"That's significant. About what?"

"I'm not sure exactly, but Robert was in the middle of it. She was evasive—she's been cryptic a lot lately." She paused, then told him about the terrace messenger. "I think whatever is going on involves her and me and even SaBe. I've been racking my brain, but I can't figure out what she could be hiding."

"I'm looking on this end. I'll keep that in mind too." He hesitated. "Do you think Sara's breached confidentiality on classified information? With her work at Quantico, she has access—"

"She'd die first." About that Beth had no doubt.

"Would she let Robert die?" Joe's voice went husky.

Beth felt sucker-punched. Uncertainty crept in. "I—I don't think I can answer—"

"Never mind, gorgeous. I understand."

Torn between loyalty and certainty, Beth stilled, swallowed a lump from her throat. Jeff and Sara had doubted her, and now she doubted Sara. Now she better understood. She didn't like it, but she understood it. "You'll look at everything on this yourself, right?"

"I will."

Relief washed through her. He and his former Shadow Watcher team would find whatever there was to find. After working with them on Lisa's abduction case, Beth didn't doubt it. "Thank you, Joe." Her throat went thick. "I'm overwhelmed right now." A tear leaked out, fell down her cheek. "I know I'm supposed to be strong—I'm always the strong one, but..."

"Nobody can be strong all the time, sha. We're human, we have limits— even you."

"Shameful, but I think I hit mine." Nora would cut out her tongue for admitting that. *"Never admit weakness to anyone but God."* She'd said it a million times.

"Then you're positioned to get stronger."

"What?"

"When you exceed your limit and endure, you get stronger. Next time, your limit is more. Surely you've heard a sermon or two on that."

Beth cringed. "Looking ahead to more trials and tests is supposed to make me feel better?"

"It's supposed to reassure you that you can handle whatever comes."

"Like faith."

"You go as far as you can. God carries you the rest of the way."

"Is that experience or faith in the abstract?"

"In my job? You tell me."

Experience. He'd specialized in scrapes his entire career. She paused, sighed. "Do you think they'll really release Robert unharmed?"

"It could go either way. Hard to hear, I know, but honest."

"If they pick up the money, maybe. If not, I can't see it."

"They could be letting it float for a couple hours hoping the FBI agents get lazy and drop their guard. The current's slow right now. It could take a couple days before the tube hits the bay and then longer to get to the Gulf."

How did he know all that? Beth dusted a leaf from her knee. "A pickup in the Gulf sounds safer for them. They could use subs. NINA funneled in terrorists with minisubs. It's not like they're watching the clock."

"Possibly. They have Robert and they're watching you and Sara. You can bet they're watching the money too. I'd say they're more apt to retrieve it at night than in broad daylight."

"It's creepy, them watching us and yet we can't spot them." Squinting against the harsh sunlight glaring off anything shiny in the parking lot, Beth took a long drink of water, then poured a little in her hand and smoothed it over her face and throat to cool her heated skin. The temperature had to be hovering near a hundred. "That rattled Jeff."

"I don't like it either. Makes me wonder if someone supposedly on our side is reporting back to them."

Beth frowned at a stone on the ground. "Seriously?"

"It's possible. Roxy assures me they've run extensive checks on everyone out there—and I have to say, you look a little cooler on the bench than you did in Jeff's Tahoe."

Shock pumped through her. "You can see me?" He was here?

"Do you really think I'd let you come out here and not watch over you?"

He'd come. He'd dropped everything and come. Her eyes burned. A smile tickled her lips. "Why don't you show yourself? Frankly, I could use a hug."

"Later. Right now, that's not a good idea."

"Why not?" She casually looked around, seeking a glimpse of him.

"I'd put you in more danger. I'm on NINA's hit list."

Her stomach knotted. NINA wanted to kill him? "Because of Lisa's kidnapping case?"

"Among other things."

Beth fixed her gaze on the Tahoe. "Then go away. You shouldn't be here."

"I have no choice, sha. You're here."

Her heart filled and some strange tenderness she hadn't felt before settled inside it. "You really do care about me."

"I've been telling you that for months, when you weren't telling me I was being ridiculous."

He had. But she hadn't dared to believe it. *Max defining, even now.* Her mouth went dry and she forced the words out of her throat. "I really care about you too, Joe."

"Finally."

She squeezed her eyes shut. "Yeah."

"Now that makes the risks worth it." His smile sounded in his voice. "I'm hanging up."

"Why?"

"Sara's coming your way. Hide your phone."

"Be careful, Joe."

"You too, gorgeous."

Beth thumbed the button and stuffed the phone in her pocket, then watched Sara approach. Her feet were still sore, gauging by her awkward gait.

"Anything new?" Sara sat primly on the bench next to Beth's feet.

"Afraid not." An uncomfortable silence settled between them. "Sara, we need to talk."

"I know. But I can't do it now." She glanced out at the water, back at the pay phone. "Just know that if I could change things, I would. I can't, so I'm doing what I can do."

More obscure and cryptic. "Like what?"

"I talked to Dennis Porter. He's put your money back into a holding account. You need to let him know where you want it." Tears filled Sara's eyes. "Thank you for doing that, Beth."

"You don't have to thank me. I told you, we're family."

"Yes. We're family." She squeezed Beth's hand. "Without you I wouldn't know what that means. I owe you and your folks so much."

"You give as much as you've gotten and always have."

"You didn't have to take me into your circle. I'm grateful you did. I know it's been hard—all the tension and everything—but don't think for a minute that being part of the family hasn't meant the world to me. It has." She released Beth's hand. "Just remember what I told you." She swerved her gaze and looked Beth in the eyes. "Protect yourself from me."

An awful feeling slithered through Beth, left a bitter taste on her tongue. "What are you doing to me that requires protection?"

Sara sank her teeth into her lip, blinked hard, and shook her head no.

"I'd have better odds for success if you'd just tell me the truth. Maybe together we could save us both and SaBe. We've always been a strong team." She'd said all three were at risk.

"That would hurt you more."

"Sara, that makes no sense. Would you please just talk to me? Whatever this is all about, we can figure it out."

"Not this time."

Beth bit back her disappointment. "Then at least tell me why you were in the hospital three times this year."

"I had attacks. You know that."

"I know that's what you told me. Is it the truth?"

Sara clamped her lips and remained silent.

⚏

Shortly after noon, Jeff came over with a bag of burgers and fries. The wind shook the old oak's leaves overhead and tugged at his damp hair. He had to be burning up in that suit, and with everyone else in swimsuits, shorts, T-shirts, and sandals, he stuck out like a sore thumb.

He passed the bag and two cups of soda with red straws. "We're eyes-on and in position. The money is still floating."

"Thanks." Beth unwrapped a burger and took a bite. The tang of onion and tomato burned her tongue.

Ten minutes after eating, Sara started fretting. By twelve thirty, she was agonizing, and by twelve forty-five, tears flowed freely down her face. Terrified that she was setting herself up for another attack, Beth frowned at her. "Stop it. Just stop it."

"I can't help it." Sara swept a hand over her forehead. "You don't know—"

"That's right; I don't because you won't tell me. If you don't care about yourself enough to nix this, fine. Do it for me. Don't put me through another attack. Frankly, I can't take it."

Sara looked at her as if she'd lost her mind. "What?"

"I'm worn to a frazzle and I can't take any more. So woman up." Close to losing her temper, Beth got down from the table. "I told you Joe said they were more apt to retrieve the money after dark. It's a long time until dark. I'm going to the rest room. Get it together, Sara. For both our sakes." Beth walked away without looking back.

When she stepped back outside, Jeff stood waiting. "Sara's looking pretty frail. I've put an ambulance on standby."

Beth nodded. "I spoke to her about it. Not sure how much good it did. She knows she won't survive another attack right now." While in the rest room, Beth had prayed hard, then called and asked the Crossroads prayer warriors to pray for Sara too. Now it was up to God and Sara. "I don't know what else to do."

"Being out here isn't helping." Walking back to the table, he joined Sara, still seated on the bench. "We're forwarding the pay-phone calls to your cell, Sara. It's time to go."

"Has something happened?"

"We've deemed it too dangerous for you two to remain out here. We can't continue to justify this kind of manpower without some kind of contact or development."

She wouldn't like that. Beth cringed. "We have to leave now for Clyde's funeral."

Sara squared her shoulders and didn't move. "I'm not leaving."

Beth lifted a hand. "You'll get the call wherever you are."

"Listen to me," Jeff said. "They're taking their time. It's a delay tactic. You can't be out here after dark, and that's when we all think they'll move in."

Sara folded her arms over her chest. "I'm *not* leaving."

"Sara, you're not staying." Jeff's tone was sharp. "There are no security lights. Anyone could come through the woods from nearly any direction and kill you."

Couldn't argue that, and truth be told, Beth didn't want to argue it. "He's right, Sara. Let's go."

She still didn't move.

Jeff's face burned red. "Are you going to make me physically—?"

"Excuse us a second, Jeff." Beth interrupted. The last thing they needed was Sara digging in her heels, and his was a surefire way to assure it.

Irritation flashed in his eyes. He nodded and walked out of earshot.

"He's conscientious, remember? He will carry you out of here," Beth warned Sara. "Spare your dignity. Get up off the bench and let's go."

Sara glared up at her and didn't move.

"Look, maybe for Robert you're ready to fight the professionals and risk your neck. But risking the necks of those protecting you is just plain selfish. These officers have risked plenty already, and I've risked all I'm going to. You can't stay out here by yourself, you can't drive if they should call, so get up and get in the car or I'll help Jeff drag you, and I mean it."

"I can't believe you're doing this to me."

"I'm talking and not just leaving you here because we're family." Beth didn't give an inch. "Staying and making everyone else a target is just plain stupid. Do you think Jeff, Roxy, and the agents should guard us or find Robert?"

Sara digested that, got up off the bench, glaring at Beth, and then joined Jeff. "Promise me if anything happens you'll inform me immediately."

Relief slid over his face. "I promise, Sara." Sincerity shone in his eyes.

Beth might just forgive him his earlier transgressions for that. Liking and not liking him didn't make a lot of sense, but since when did any relationship make sense to anyone?

At the car, Sara got in on the passenger's side.

"Will she go to the funeral?" Jeff asked about Sara.

"She will or I'll have Nora send Nathara over to keep her company."

"That's cold, Beth." Jeff shuddered. "You telling Sara that?"

It was cold. But justified. "If the need arises."

"She'll be at the funeral then. Makes my life a lot easier. I promised Nora I wouldn't be late." He rubbed at his earlobe. "You're an effective negotiator."

Something had changed. Did he not consider her a suspect anymore? "I have my moments." No one wanted to disappoint Nora or to endure Nathara's acidic attitude.

"I'll follow you back, then to the funeral." Jeff glanced at Sara's car. "Her medical condition scares me, and frankly, I wouldn't know what to do for her."

"I know what you mean." Beth had never felt so helpless as in Sara's first attack. The memory of it still curdled her blood. "Harvey and Lisa will be there." They were both fine docs and familiar with Sara's condition.

"Mark and Ben will be at the service too. You'll be well protected." Jeff motioned to a second Tahoe parked three cars beyond his. "Roxy's team will stay with the money."

Beth nodded. "How long will you let it float?"

He urged her toward Sara's car. "Until we're convinced it's a failed attempt."

At least overnight. "Cover of darkness and all that."

"We're prepared for it."

Everyone knew technologically the US ruled the night. "Be safe." She slid into the Saab. Sara had reclined her seat and closed her eyes. Obviously, she was ticked and freezing Beth out. Needing the break, Beth grabbed the wheel, turned the key. The engine roared to life and the air-conditioning blast on her face was a slice of pure joy.

Sara slept—or pretended to sleep—all the way back to her house.

Avoiding you. Avoiding questions she doesn't want to answer.

Beth pulled into the garage. *God, if You could help me out here, I'd appreciate it. She says to protect myself—from her. What's this about? Protect myself how? I need clarity, guidance—something.*

Without it, she didn't just fear for her business. She feared for her life.

⸎

"It's no wonder Clyde left this land. It's a snake pit."

Sitting behind Nora under the white tent top, Beth heard Nathara's comment and inwardly groaned.

Nora patted her twin's knee. "You should feel right at home, then, dearie."

She was sad but still Nora, and not a soul sputtered. Peggy winked at Beth. Sara stared at Clyde's coffin, her stony expression unchanged. Where was her mind?

Everyone from Crossroads was there—Mark and Lisa, Harvey and Roxy, Ben and Kelly, and Mel. Miranda Kent, the columnist, and the prayer warriors were manning the phones at the center.

Reverend Brown performed the service, and Beth learned a lot about Clyde Parker she hadn't known. Wasn't that just a shame? Someone she thought she knew well, she knew so little. *Learn from that.*

He'd been a vet, won a Purple Heart. Married his wife when they were teenagers, and he'd buried her and all three of their sons. Beth could only imagine that kind of pain.

The bugler played "Taps."

Nora accepted the flag offered by a soldier in uniform. "…on behalf of a grateful nation…"

Nora stiffened.

Nathara sighed.

Tears flowed freely down Kelly Walker's face. She'd become a daughter to Clyde. Seeing raw pain in her got to Beth. She sniffled, swatted at her nose with a tissue.

Clyde's coffin was lowered into the ground. Nora, supported by Kelly and Ben, dropped in the first handful of dirt. Rose petals were mixed with it. Annie, Lisa, and Mark followed. Then one by one, the others paid their last respects.

Nathara didn't leave her seat. Neither did Darla Green or Tack Grady.

Not sure what to make of that, Beth shot a glance at Jeff, who was looking at Mark. They too had noticed. It meant something to them; that was obvious. But what escaped Beth.

She swiveled her gaze to the rusty tin shed. Nathara was cold. But Darla and Tack? Their reasons could be personal, but Beth doubted it. Clyde was a good man who hadn't held a grudge his whole life. Even Race Miller, who had foreclosed on Clyde's property in Magnolia Branch, stood red-eyed, paying his respects.

That sense of dread and doom at the river washed through Beth again.

Something significant had just been revealed.

Something that carried steep consequences.

But what? And to whom?

11

❦

Wednesday came and went.

No news. Nothing remarkable.

At eight o'clock on Thursday morning, more than forty-eight hours after the drop, the money still floated in the river with no retrieval attempts. The pay phone still sat silent with no incoming calls. And there had been no further contact from the kidnappers. Robert's disposition and location remained unknown. Sara hung on by a thread so thin that Beth put Harvey Talbot and Dr. Franklin on speed dial, and Beth wasn't feeling far behind her.

Haggard but freshly showered, Jeff showed up at Sara's breakfast table with a bit of news. "While you were in the hospital," he nodded, thanking Maria for the cup of coffee she placed near him, "we sent a sample of Robert's hair from his brush in for DNA tests."

"Why?"

"To cross-check against the blood found in the rental car." Jeff gave her a second to absorb. "The results are in. They matched."

Sara twisted her pearls. "We expected that, what with his wedding band in there and the ransom demand."

"Yes, we did." Jeff agreed. "But now it's confirmed as fact."

Maria flipped pancakes at the stove. Why did she seem so nervous? And why wouldn't she meet Beth's eyes? Strange. In the three years she'd been with Sara, they had been close.

"Sometimes we have to slow down to prove what we already know. Speculation is risky, and we can't afford unnecessary mistakes."

Sara set down her teacup. "No, we can't."

Beth sensed Jeff building up to more news. "So what now? Do we just keep waiting for them to make contact?"

"We don't have any choice." He sipped from his cup. "They've got Robert and they could be anywhere now. We're investigating all the usual—transportation, credit card purchases—but the possibilities are limited and limitless."

Shaking, Sara nicked her cup. It scraped against its saucer. "Can't we do something? It's taking way too long."

Jeff didn't say anything.

What could he say? They were doing what they could do. "Listen." Beth shifted on her seat. "We've kept this low key and out of the press. Maybe it's time to change that."

Sara frowned. "We agreed it was safest not to bring in the media. If NINA's connected, they could want to push their ideology. That's the last thing we want."

"We did agree, but things have changed." Beth waited for Maria to set a platter of pancakes on the table. "Then, they were going to fish the money from the river and call with Robert's location, but it's been two days and that hasn't happened. They've had two nights. If they were going to retrieve it, they would have by now." There. She'd finally said what they'd all been thinking and hadn't wanted to be the first to say.

In her mind, the visions had played out. In the dead of night, guys wearing diving suits, slipping into the river and away with the money while agents watched from the bank and saw nothing. But that's not what happened. *Nothing* happened.

"Something scared them off, or happened on their end—I don't know what, but it's clear they're not picking up the money." When Beth had talked to Nora yesterday, she'd agreed that it was time to force them to act. Her honed instincts were sharper, and she had the emotional objectivity Beth lacked.

"We don't know that." Sara stabbed a pancake.

"The odds are with Beth, Sara. The money's in the Gulf and they haven't moved." Jeff thumbed the rim of his coffee cup, watched the steam rise from it. "Historically, the more time that passes, the less the odds of a safe return." Regret laced his voice.

Tears welled in Sara's eyes. She set down her fork.

"That proves we need a game-changer."

"This is my husband's life, Beth. Not a game."

"We can't just wait and let the odds stack up against him. We need to act."

Sara dragged a hand over her hair, clasped in a barrette at her nape. "What can we do that isn't already being done?"

Beth had mulled over that very question with Joe on the phone just after dawn. No matter what scenario they spun out, being stuck on terminal hold was worse. "We can hold a press conference and appeal for Robert's safe return." Beth lifted a hand. "You know whoever abducted him is monitoring the news. Maybe someone's seen Robert and will call in."

"He is high profile," Jeff said. "The kidnapper knows that. He's probably secured at a remote location."

"So it's a long shot." Beth shrugged. Nora and Joe agreed, yet they also agreed with Beth's suggestion, which hopefully Sara and Jeff would too. "But, Sara, you two have been plastered on society pages for a year—you're celebrities. That might be beneficial now."

"Robert's the celebrity," Sara said around a bite of fresh raspberries. "I've participated because he insisted." She glanced at Jeff without apology or emotion. "I'm a recluse—well, almost. I don't like to socialize."

"Why didn't you tell him no?" Jeff asked.

Maria coughed. Beth looked over and Maria turned away. *Something* was up there.

"Why doesn't any wife or husband just say no? I wanted peace in my home."

A sad empathy lit his eyes. Jeff glanced to Beth. "Celebrity status means we'll get ten times the usual crank calls—and that's a lot."

"So if not this, then what do we do?" Beth asked. "Last I checked, no problems resolved by solutions appearing out of thin air. We didn't build SaBe that way."

"No, we did the seek-and-you-will-find method," Sara admitted. "You've been thinking about this for a while. Did you run it by our secret weapon?"

"What's your secret weapon?" Jeff asked.

"Sorry." Beth wrinkled her nose. "Secret means secret."

"So did you?" Sara snatched more raspberries, then spooned yogurt over them.

"Earlier, yes."

"Update and ask for suggestions." Sara shoved at the berries with her spoon. "We're too close and this is too gnarly. We need a fresh perspective and I trust her judgment."

"Your secret weapon is a woman?" Jeff asked.

"I'm on it." Beth stepped away from the table, snagged Maria, and pulled her into the butler's pantry. "What's up with you?"

"Nothing."

"Maria, I know something's worrying you. What is it?"

She compressed her lips, refused to speak.

"Do you think I did this to Robert?"

"Did you?"

"No. Did you?"

"No, but I wanted to."

"Why?"

"He—he's not nice to Sara."

No news there. "How not nice wasn't he?"

"I don't know. But she hasn't been happy with him for a long time, Beth."

That was news. "Was he…mean to her?" No way could she make herself be any more specific than that.

"I never saw him do or say anything mean," Maria said, but she didn't look at Beth when she said it.

"You suspect he was mean to her."

"I only know she wasn't happy, and she should be happy."

Beth digested that. "Do you know anything you're not sharing that could help?"

"No."

"Then why are you acting so distant? You've never been that way with me."

She dipped her chin. "I feel guilty."

"Why?"

Maria forced herself to meet Beth's gaze. "Because I'm glad he's gone and I hope he never comes back."

Beth wished she didn't feel the same way. She squeezed Maria's arm lightly and let her empathy show in her eyes. "I understand."

"You'd better make your call. I don't want Sara upset anymore. She'll know we're talking about her."

Beth grabbed her cell and dialed, walking back to within Sara's line of vision. When Nora answered, Beth filled her in on the latest and ended with, "Sara asked for your advice."

Sara sat staring at her. Beth backed against the kitchen counter and listened, but Jeff's expression was most telling. Stunned.

"Have some berries and pancakes." Sara shoved an empty bowl his way. "This could take a minute. They get into details, which is probably why the advice is so good."

"No thanks." Jeff sipped at his coffee. "I'm a little…well, surprised."

"About what?" Sara dabbed at the corner of her mouth with a napkin.

He shrugged. "You two are megabusinesswomen."

"Ah." She set her napkin back in her lap. "So we shouldn't need or seek advice—especially not from older or wiser ones who've successfully negotiated business trenches longer than we've been alive?" She smiled. "Jeff, our mentor is a business genius. It's in her genes. She's also a good and honest woman willing to share her wisdom with us. We're good at computers and software, but business is a mean maze."

"You're both so smart."

"Smart enough to know there's way too much we don't know, and far too smart not to seek help when it's there for the asking. We have no illusions about our strengths and weaknesses."

"But—"

"Look," Sara interrupted him. "We created some dynamite software. We hired some very sharp lawyers to create really good licensing agreements, but we're not the brightest business brains on the block. We're just good enough to seek advice, hire smart people, and trust trustworthy people. We deal straight, do business with people who deal straight, and we've been blessed."

"You've made a lot of money."

"A whole lot of money—because we know our limitations."

He took that in and swallowed another sip of coffee before responding. "That's why having faith in people is so important to Beth."

"No, that's a God-thing. How do you love one another if you lack faith in one another? But it is why knowing we *should* have faith in people is important to us both. We've experienced its value firsthand."

"I haven't had that experience, but I learned a hard lesson on it from Darla Green." Jeff flushed, obviously speaking before thinking and wishing he hadn't. He looked away.

"Don't beat yourself up about Darla. We experience what we experience for reasons." Sara waited until Jeff looked back at her. "Here's the thing. Lessons about faith can come at any time from any direction. So one day you didn't know you couldn't trust her, and a different day you do know it. Knowing the truth is good, right?"

"I guess. But if I'd known earlier, then John might be alive."

"He wouldn't. When it's time, it's time."

"So you think Darla killed him too?"

"Beth doesn't."

Jeff sent her a level look. "Darla killed John Green, Sara. I know it."

"I think so too, but I don't know it. Until I do, I'll believe the best."

"Why? She's dangerous. She could be with NINA."

"Or not, and then she'd be falsely accused. Believing the worst is easiest but cowardly." Sara covered his hand on the table and gently squeezed. "I know you're no coward, Jeff. Thinking the worst carries no risk of being disappointed. Who needs faith to think the worst?"

"I see what you mean, but she is guilty, so be prepared for the fall."

Sara smiled, bittersweet. "You're a good man. It's nice to be around a good man."

That snagged Beth's ear and she nearly dropped the phone. "Nora, hold on a second."

"'Course, dearie."

Beth focused on Jeff and Sara. There were sparks between them. Good sparks. The *I'm interested in you* kind of sparks. What was going on here? Sara might be upset with Robert, but even if she hated him, she wouldn't cheat—and he'd been kidnapped.

So many weird actions and reactions, Sara was making Beth dizzy. Everything was upside down.

Jeff smiled at Sara. It touched his eyes. "I could say I shouldn't have brought it up. It wasn't professional. But I can't regret it when good came from it. Instead I'll apologize for the professionalism lapse."

"No," Sara said. "You are a professional—a very good one. There's nothing wrong with letting people see that you're human. It's reassuring, and I'm ashamed to admit how badly I need reassurance right now."

"I'm sorry for all you're going through, Sara."

"Me too." A sad smile touched her lips, shone in her eyes. "Thank you for caring."

Beth glanced at Maria. Tears were in her eyes. Tender, happy tears. She approved of what was happening between Sara and Jeff? Had she forgotten Sara was married?

No way. She and Robert were oil and water too. "Maria?"

She turned and fled the kitchen.

"Beth?" Nora said through the phone. "You there, girl?"

"I'm here. Sorry to keep you holding so long, Nora."

"Did you need anything else, dearie? I've got to go. Nathara is harping at Kelly about Clyde not really being her family. If you find her bound and gagged, I did it. Have my boys come bail me out."

Beth half hoped she'd do it, then shamed herself for it. "I'll bail you out myself. Thanks for the help." Beth hung up the phone, snagged the coffeepot, and refilled her cup at the table. "Our secret weapon says this is war."

Sara set her napkin on the table. "Empty the arsenal?"

Beth nodded and they shared a look they had shared before. "Full assault."

"All right, then," Sara said. "Jeff, any better ideas?"

"No. I can't see other options."

Now he was thinking. "We have to flush them out. Make them want to talk to us."

"It'll be a frenzy," Jeff warned Sara. "You up for that medically?"

It would be frantic. On arrival in the village, Robert had jumped into the social world with both feet, and because he was married to Sara, locals welcomed him with open arms. The media would be relentless.

"Absolutely," Sara said with a conviction that surprised Beth.

Jeff nodded and scooted his chair back from the table. "I'll arrange it."

"I'm sure Peggy and the Crossroads folks will help field the calls."

"Counting on that." He looked at Sara. "Will Beth be speaking for you?"

"No, I'll do it myself. It'll be more effective, the frantic wife and all that."

That comment shocked Beth, and it must have showed.

"You know what I mean, Beth." Sara lifted a more determined gaze than Beth had ever before seen on her face. "Set it up for noon, Jeff." Sara refilled her cup from the teapot. "We'll catch the lunch crowd."

"That might be kind of tight for the networks," Beth said. *Who is this woman? She seems nothing like Sara.*

"They'll get it before the evening news. That's most significant." Sara stopped pouring, the pot in hand, spout above her cup. "Tell me this is caffeine-free Earl Grey."

"It's unleaded," Beth assured her. "Drink at will."

12

ara handled the press conference like a pro.

She pleaded earnestly, shed the requisite tears to capture the attention of even the hardhearted, and eloquently conveyed her fear for her husband that made it all too easy for any wife watching to imagine herself in Sara's shoes—at least, that's what Mark Taylor whispered to Ben, Roxy, and Jeff, and Beth pretended not to overhear.

Later that night, Mark proved accurate. The story had played over and again on the local news and was picked up by the networks, and the coverage had been constant on all the cable news channels. Sara's phone rang nonstop, and at ten thirty that night, Beth insisted Sara stop answering it, take Dr. Franklin's pills, and go to bed. Beth unplugged the bedroom phone and set it on the kitchen counter. For once, Sara hadn't complained about being handled.

Roxy assigned Mark to supervise the leads coming in from the Crossroads phone bank, and from his reports, it was hopping. At midnight, they were averaging two hundred calls per hour. Most weren't reporting sightings, just wishing Sara and Robert well and offering prayers and assurances that they were keeping an eye out.

Sara's voice mail box had filled and been emptied three times—Robert's friends calling to see if there was any news. Maria took care of those. They irked Beth. Not one caller asked about Sara. Maria had summed it up well. *They each want to be first to get the scoop and tell the others.*

Beth checked on Nora, who had taken refuge in her room to get a break from Nathara. She talked about Clyde with such tenderness it put a lump in

Beth's throat. She couldn't ease Nora's pain. She could listen. And so she did until well after one.

After hanging up, Beth showered and changed into blue jersey shorts and a T-shirt and headed to Sara's family room sofa. Too exhausted to sleep, she snagged her special phone in case Joe called, stretched out and muted the sound on the television. A clip from Sara's press conference was on the screen. With a sigh, Beth glanced away, to the window. Through the sheers, she saw a small cluster of people just beyond the security gate, holding vigil with burning candles.

Earlier, they'd startled Sara, but Jeff said they were people from different churches and local organizations Sara had supported. She had been moved to tears and clasped Jeff's arm, staring out through hungry eyes. She didn't know them, but their support was genuine and heartfelt. It meant a lot to Sara.

And Beth was grateful for it, though it put a little ache in her heart. Sara was beloved by strangers. She knew Robert's friends were exactly that—*his* friends. Sara was still an outsider.

That had to sting. Beth sniffed. Seduced by the swine, they ignored the pearl.

Staring at the ceiling, Beth thought heavy thoughts about people and the way they behaved. Some people were in your life for your whole life, but most were there just for a season. When it ended, they moved on and so did you. Of those people, some were blessings, some gave you something you needed, and some took something they needed. Most did both, gave and took, depending on their situation at the time.

Beth scrunched a pillow to her chest. All that was normal. Human. Expected. The people she didn't understand were the takers who didn't move off the dime. The ones who took and took and kept on taking. No matter how much you gave, it was never enough. People like Robert and Max.

I wish I understood him. I really do. I just…don't.

Hours later, Beth still drifted in twilight, neither asleep nor awake, pondering. What kind of person had she been?

"He's made the front page." Roxy's voice carried to Beth from the living room.

"Local or national?" one of the male agents asked.

"All of them." Roxy sounded happy.

A little shiver raced through Beth. Had going to the media been the right thing? Suddenly, she wasn't sure. *Please, don't let me regret it.* She swallowed hard. *More important, don't let Sara regret it.*

⚮

Morning came and went without news.

The living room and study were hubs of activity, people chasing down promising leads that, so far, had all been dead ends. Sara spoke with reporters again at one o'clock and, to her credit, sincerely tried to stay serene, upbeat, and positive.

With the lack of news, it couldn't be easy. But Sara was hanging in there in ways Beth wouldn't have believed possible just days ago. Beth was glad to see it, even if she worried that the reason was the result of quiet talks between Sara and Jeff. *Dangerous ground.* The sparks between them were just one of many bizarre reactions from Sara since all this started. She'd never been flighty or made a vow she didn't keep. She knew fear and isolation and loneliness and loss. She understood grief and had survived its ravages, rebuilt a life from its remnants. Her medical condition made her seem fragile, but could a person endure all Sara had and really be fragile?

Beth now doubted it. So Sara was in trouble and it impacted others, but what was its source? How did it impact Beth and others? Had Robert done something? Sara done something? Had they done something together? Did that—whatever it was—somehow connect to the club attack? That missing groom on the cake, Robert missing? Maybe Jeff and Roxy were right. Joe thought it was connected too, and maybe it was—

"Beth?"

She turned to look at Jeff. "Yes?"

"A man is here to talk with Sara about Robert." Jeff's forehead creased. He seemed wary. "She agreed, but she doesn't know him. I'm sitting in. Thought you'd want to know."

He feared an attack. Somewhere along the way, he'd stopped being suspicious, but he didn't trust her. He needed her. She didn't bother being irked. In his shoes, she'd probably consider herself a suspect too. Beth stood. "Why did Sara agree to speak with him?"

"I'm not sure." Jeff shrugged. "Hungry for news?"

Probably. She was desperate. "Where are they?"

"In the study." Jeff stepped back so Beth could pass through the doorway. "She has her inhaler. I saw her pick it up off the counter."

Praying Sara wouldn't need it, Beth brushed past him. She walked into the study that was as cold and unwelcoming as the rest of the house. Everything in it was monotone gray with not a single splash of color anywhere. Steel desk, minimalist chairs, and not a single personal item in sight. That was the problem with the whole house. It was filled with beautiful, impersonal things and nothing that reflected the people who lived in it. Beth had been in warmer, more personal hotel rooms.

Jeff stopped at the door, just outside Sara's and the visitor's line of sight. Beth expected him to direct the conversation, but Jeff, being Jeff, had his own agenda.

Dressed in black, which said all that needed saying about her emotional state, Sara sat stiffly behind the desk. A man sat in the visitor's chair across from her, his back to Beth. On the edge of the desk in front of him was a cup of coffee from Ruby's. Beth recognized the cup. "Sara?" Beth walked around, stopped beside her, and then looked at the man. "What's up?"

"I'm not sure." Sara's face was the color of ice and her hand was in her pocket, no doubt wrapped around her inhaler.

Sara feared him or what he would tell her. Beth shifted her gaze to him. Well dressed in a good-quality navy suit. Broad shoulders, tiptop shape, about thirty-two or -three, black hair cropped close, and she guessed, as he was seated, well over six feet tall. He shouldn't be at all attractive; his facial features were sharp and angular—broad forehead and square jaw, blunt nose and wide eyes. Singularly, they shouldn't fit together into a compelling package, but they did. Compelling and oddly striking.

"Hello." She stepped over and offered her hand. "I'm Beth Dawson."

"Thomas Boudin." He stood, clasped her hand, and firmly shook. "I'm sorry to intrude, but I saw Mr. Tayton's photo and I had to follow up."

"On what?" His cologne smelled vaguely familiar. Subtle and understated like the man. Beth backed away to get a clearer read on him. Jeff looked as invested as a presidential bodyguard.

Boudin set out to put her at ease. "I'm a former military member, Ms. Dawson. OSI—Office of Special Investigations. Two years ago, I became a private consultant."

Was he a friend of Joe's offering to help? If so, what could he do that the others weren't? She couldn't imagine. A little warning went off inside her. She darted a covert gaze at Jeff, who nodded to press on. "Private consultant covers a lot of territory."

"Yes, it does," he admitted, but didn't offer further clarification.

Sara curled her fingers into the chair's arms. Her knuckles bleached. *Definitely scared.* "So what do you want, Mr. Boudin?"

"I'm looking into a case for a friend. Mr. Tayton's photograph in the paper this morning…he might be connected."

"What kind of case?" Beth grew more uneasy with his every word.

He glanced at Sara. Her hands were trembling. "At this time, I'm not at liberty to say."

That surprised Beth and clearly worried Sara. Was he trying to upset her more?

"Mr. Boudin, what do you want from me?" A sharp breath hitched Sara's chest.

"Answers." He gentled his voice. "So I can determine whether or not Mr. Tayton is connected to my case—"

Sara pulled out her inhaler, nodded at Beth.

She needed a moment. Beth stiffened her voice. "Mr. Boudin, join me for a second."

Confusion riddled his expression. "Excuse me?"

"In the hallway," Beth said from between her teeth. "Right now, please." She ushered him past Jeff and into the hall.

"Ms. Dawson—," he began.

"Don't you *Ms. Dawson* me. You come here knowing Sara is half crazy with worry and suggest her missing husband could be hooked into some other case you won't discuss, and you honestly expect cooperation? She's just been released from the hospital. Did you see her pull out that inhaler?"

"I did see it. That's why I was trying not to add to her distress." Boudin's neck and face flushed. "I didn't withhold information to be cruel; I was trying to protect her."

Beth didn't believe it. From Jeff's stony expression, he was still on the fence.

Boudin lifted an arm. "Until I ask the questions, I can't know if Mr. Tayton is involved in my case. If he is, and Mrs. Tayton can take hearing the truth without injury, I'll tell her what she needs to know. If he's not involved, then I'll be sorry I wasted her time and mine and be glad I spared her from hearing unpleasant things that weren't relevant." His gaze turned intense, riddled with a warning. "Believe me, Ms. Dawson, you do not want Mr. Tayton to be involved in my case, and unless I must, you definitely do not want me to tell his wife about it."

That set Beth back on her heels. Fear swirled with curiosity. Beth believed him. Worse, if Boudin's case was bad, no matter what it was about, she could imagine Robert involved up to his slimy eyeballs in it. Still, she couldn't permit a fishing expedition that negatively impacted Sara. The lack of news had her brittle. This was no time to risk something unrelated making her snap.

"Sara's medical issues are complicated. She hasn't sufficiently recovered to survive another attack."

"I'm sorry." He paused a thoughtful moment.

His sincerity stopped Beth cold. Sara's attack and hospitalization had remained out of the press for fear the kidnappers would use it to sensationalize the case. "No, I'm sorry, Mr. Boudin. I overreacted. You couldn't have known about Sara's medical condition."

Jeff looked shocked that Beth took responsibility for her mistake. *Why?*

"I understand." Boudin seemed to mean it. "You're trying to protect her."

Beth let him see the truth in her eyes and noted something oddly familiar in his. "I am worried." Terrified would be more honest. "About her and what else this could cause to happen."

"Understandable. I read the report about the attack at the country club."

There was something about him. Something…known. SaBe maybe? Or one of her trips to Quantico? Where? "Do you really think Robert might be connected to your case?"

"If I didn't, I wouldn't be here." Boudin pulled a mint from his pocket, offered one to Beth.

The scent struck a chord and a chill crept up her back. *The terrace messenger.* "Um, no. Thank you." She searched her memory. She didn't know his face, but she knew that scent and she knew those eyes. Yet if Thomas Boudin had been at the fund-raiser, she definitely would have noticed and remembered him.

"For Mrs. Tayton's sake, I hope her husband isn't involved."

That comment struck fear in Beth's heart. "If he is, will Sara be hurt?"

"I don't know yet, but it's possible." He dropped his shoulders, crooked his neck. "I'm not being evasive. Based on what I know now, that's as accurate as I can be."

She liked him. Direct. Compassionate. Honest. "Okay, Mr. Boudin. I'm going to take a leap of faith on you. Don't make me regret it. Ask Sara your questions, but if I touch my nose," she said for his and Jeff's benefit, "then it's over. You reassure Sara, thank her, and end it. No more questions and no delays. Agreed?"

"Agreed. The questions really are routine and harmless. They shouldn't distress her."

"Just keep your promise—and if he is your guy, you still reassure her, thank her, and end it. Then you privately tell me."

Jeff sent her a suspicious look.

So did Boudin. "I'm uncomfortable with the ethics—"

"It's not negotiable, and it has nothing to do with ethics." Beth's tone went flat. "If what you discover could upset her, then I need time to prepare."

"Prepare?"

Beth nodded. "Arrange conditions to minimize the impact. Get her calm, get her doctor here. If the news warrants it, get an ambulance on standby."

"Oh, I see." His doubt faded. "One touch of the nose, and we're done."

A decent judge of character, she decided Thomas Boudin's word might just be worth something. "All right, then." She walked back into the study with him following her. Sara did not look pleased.

"Pretty lengthy sojourn in the hallway." Sara laced her hands atop the desk, tapped her fingertips, signaling she expected an explanation.

"Sorry." Beth shrugged. "There was a parking jam in the driveway. A couple cars needed shuffling."

Sara shifted her gaze to Boudin. "You'll have to forgive Beth, Mr. Boudin. She's a lousy liar, but she's my family and she loves me."

Beth didn't complain. She'd earned the smack. But if Robert was involved in Boudin's case, then this definitely was going to be one of those protective times.

"I have a family myself, Mrs. Tayton. Unlike yours, mine is riddled with thugs, thieves, and outlaws, but they're mine." His smile put a twinkle in his eyes. "I protect them."

Beth harrumphed because it was expected. So long as the inhaler was back in Sara's pocket, either of them could say anything.

Sara leaned back in her chair. "So what do you want to ask me?"

"May I?" He held up a digital recorder similar to Beth's that had disappeared. "It's the only way I can be sure to keep everything straight."

"I have the same problem," Sara said. "You have my permission to record."

"Thank you." He entered the date and time and those present. "How long have you known Robert Tayton?"

"Almost a year. We met at a conference in Atlanta on July third."

"And you married—"

"August eighth. I know," Sara said with a little smile. "It was a whirlwind relationship."

Jeff pulled a pad from his pocket and jotted notes. It made Beth uneasy.

Boudin withheld comment and asked his next question. "Do you get along with Mr. Tayton's family?"

Sadness crept across Sara's face. "Unfortunately, we've never met. They've been estranged for many years."

"How many years?"

Sara started to answer but her expression went blank and she flushed. "I don't know."

Now she'd chew herself up for not knowing and for not realizing she hadn't known. Great. Viewing a sculpture, Beth dragged a fingertip over its sleek metal surface. A circle with four tails? *Weird.*

"Is it just his parents Mr. Tayton avoids, or is it his sisters and brothers too?"

Surprise flickered across Sara's face. "Robert has siblings?"

That she didn't know surprised Beth and Jeff.

"I don't know, Mrs. Tayton." Boudin glanced at Beth. "I was asking, not informing."

"Oh, I see." She let out a nervous little laugh. "He's never mentioned siblings, so I don't believe there are any. I'm not sure his parents are still alive. I don't think he even knows." She glanced away. "Talking about them upsets him so I don't ask questions. Whatever happened is painful for him. He refuses to speak their names."

Beth pretended to be dispassionate and stone deaf, but what Sara didn't know shocked her. Her husband could be anyone—and Boudin's next question proved he thought so too.

"Did Mr. Tayton change his name because of the estrangement?"

"Robert changed his name?" Sara shuddered, putting Beth on alert. "Are you serious?"

"Again, I'm asking, not informing." Boudin lifted a hand to halt her. "Has he ever gone by any other name?"

"Not to my knowledge." Her tone stiffened, turned formal.

Beth understood her discomfort. They were rudimentary questions she should be able to answer and couldn't.

"These questions seem very...strange." Sara's breathing grew labored and she visibly struggled to regain control.

Gauging by Jeff's expression, he agreed. Beth cleared her throat and touched her nose.

Boudin caught the signal. "I believe that'll do it, Mrs. Tayton. I don't see any irrefutable similarities in the cases at this time. Thank you for talking to me." He reached across the desk to shake her hand. "I hope Mr. Tayton soon returns safely."

"Thank you." She nodded and swiped at her brow, her hand shaking hard. "Jeff, would you walk me to my room? I'm not steady and I need to rest for a while."

"Sure." He extended an arm. "Lean on me, Sara. I've got you."

What was going on? Sara should be calmer but she looked ready to shatter.

Boudin stood beside Beth, waited until Sara and Jeff were out of earshot, then said, "She thinks Robert is involved."

"She does, and it scares her." Beth looked up into his face. "So what do you think?"

"What I think isn't significant."

Beth frowned. "No games, Mr. Boudin. I took a leap of faith and trusted you."

"I kept my word." He clicked off his recorder and tucked it into his jacket's inside pocket. "I did exactly what I said I would."

"You did," she agreed because it was true. "Trust me."

"If trust were the issue, I would." He lifted a hand to his chest and dipped his chin. "But it isn't. This case is ultrasensitive to innocent people. I can't bring you or anyone else into it unless I'm certain you need to be there."

He was protecting his client. Unable to blame him for that, Beth crossed her arms and pushed anyway. "You think Robert is someone else. What has he done?"

"I don't know that he's done anything. That's what I'm trying to determine."

Boudin wasn't going to tell her a thing. But he had a hidden agenda, and hidden agendas involving Robert usually related to Sara's money. "Well, since you're unwilling to be open with me, I'd say we're done."

Boudin started to object, looked her in the eye, and smiled.

She knew that smile. Knew that scent, those eyes. Who was he? The answer was right there on the fringe of her mind, fuzzy and unfocused. She tugged at the memory all the way to the front door.

Boudin started through it, then passed her his business card. He dropped his voice so only she could hear. "Does anyone you know have a full-face photo of Robert Tayton?"

"Why?"

"On the news, the photo was of him kissing Mrs. Tayton at some social event. In the newspaper photo, his face was obscured." Boudin dipped his head. "This is a hunch. If no one has a full-face photo of Robert Tayton, then the odds that he's the man I'm seeking increase significantly." Boudin glanced over at the agents, then whispered. "The Robert I'm looking for has good reason to not want to be identified."

That disclosure sent chills racing up her spine. "Why? Give me something."

The look in his eyes spoke volumes. "If no one has a picture that clearly shows Tayton's face, then guard his wife, Beth. This Robert is lethally dangerous."

Beth's stomach dropped. She pushed Boudin outside, stepped out, and shut the door behind her. "He *killed* somebody?"

"I'm not saying that," Boudin said quickly. "In fact, I'm not saying anything more." He pulled his car keys out of his pocket. "I don't know if the two men are one and the same, I'm just warning you—in case. That's all."

What did she do with that? Especially when it was clear that if they were the same man, Robert was lethal. Whether Boudin meant that literally or figuratively, she wasn't sure. He seemed bent on dropping bombs, leaving whether or not they could detonate up in the air. She tucked his card in her pocket and nodded. "Thank you, Thomas."

"If I find evidence linking the two, I'll contact your office and we'll discuss how to tell Mrs. Tayton."

"Use my cell. I have it with me all the time," Beth said. "Do you have a pen?"

He pulled out one of his cards, wrote her name on its back, then added the number. "Until I know for sure, keep a watchful eye. Warn Jeff too."

Jeff, not Detective Meyers. She hadn't told him Jeff's first name. Had Sara? "I will. Thank you." Beth nodded again. To her shame, she half hoped Boudin proved right about Robert and half hoped the lethally dangerous Robert remained a stranger. *Major work-in-progress, Beth. God has to be weeping.*

"Oh, I forgot my coffee. You have it. I haven't touched it." Thomas Boudin walked down the sidewalk to the street.

Her drink his coffee? That'd be insane. She didn't know him—wait. Joe. Joe promised to bring her coffee. The eyes, the smile...of course. He was Joe—or was he? She wasn't sure. Wouldn't Joe reveal himself to her? He could be in disguise. NINA was after him, and he suspected someone was taking back information to NINA from their group.

No. No, she had to be wrong. She'd told Joe about the terrace messenger, and he hadn't admitted being him. That had been Boudin. His voice, scent, and those mints. Definitely Boudin.

Beth watched him go, admiring his confident gait, the square of his shoulders. He was gorgeous, no doubt about it, in a totally nonclassical, unique way. She liked his style—and that he'd kept his word. Admirable, that. She also respected him. It would have been easy to come in and just let the chips fall where they may, but he'd been compassionate toward Sara. Still, he couldn't be Joe. Joe made her heart flutter, her awareness ratchet up. No disguise could fool her. She would know Joe. She was crazy about him.

Boudin's walk intrigued her. Captivated… An elusive memory snapped into place. *Joe!*

She gasped. Recalled his eyes, Boudin's eyes. His walk, Boudin's walk. His… Oh, it was him. Boudin was Joe. What on earth was he doing?

She whipped out her special phone, dialed—and hung up.

He'd come because she was in danger. Just as he'd been somewhere at Jay's Place. But when they were alone, why hadn't he told her?

She couldn't imagine. Until she could, revealing she was aware wasn't the thing to do. Men like Joe—former Shadow Watchers—rarely did anything without a reason.

With a regretful sigh, she went back inside and closed the front door. Jeff magically appeared in her path. "Nothing noteworthy," she said before he could even ask.

"Are you sure?"

"Unfortunately, I am." She walked into the study and lifted the coffee cup, walked through the house and up the stairs, then down the hall to the spare bedroom. For some reason, Sara wouldn't sleep in the master suite.

Beth cracked open the door and peeked into the bedroom. Sara lay curled up atop the covers, a throw over her legs and feet, clutching a pillow to her chest. Relief and disappointment shafted through Beth. She'd hoped to glimpse Sara's feet to see if there was bruising along with the ankle swelling. New shoes hadn't caused that swelling, but Sara might have tripped or stumbled, and that certainly could have. But for now Sara rested peacefully. *Fantastic.*

Beth pulled the door closed. Moving down the hall, she passed a long and narrow table. Its surface gleamed. This house was just plain unnatural, perfect and lifeless and totally without character or charm. It used to have both. It used to feel…happy.

Beth grabbed the handrail and started down the wide staircase. There was no denying that Sara had been worried, sad, afraid, and tense. She deeply feared the kidnappers and what they might do to Robert. But in the last twenty-four hours something else had come to light. Something unexpected and as strange as anything on the growing, lengthy list of recent oddities: Sara was angry.

Angry.

Baffling.

Outsiders would peg that anger as fear, and fear was there, naturally, but it was rooted in anger. An anger so atypical of Sara that Beth didn't understand it.

Who was Sara angry with? God? Her parents for dying and leaving her? Robert for allowing himself to be kidnapped? Or was her anger directed at herself because she hadn't prevented those things? From the work at Crossroads Crisis Center, Beth knew that was a common reaction. Or was Sara angry because she didn't know simple things about her spouse?

Beth let her hand glide down the banister. It could be any or all or none of those things. Fear was never rational, and it was mean. It didn't matter whether or not you deserved it. If fear got its claws in you, it would sink them in deep, shred your heart, and rip out your soul—all just because it could.

Stepping down to the foot of the stairs, she returned to the living room to get an update on the leads being checked out. They needed a break in this case in the worst kind of way. They needed contact from the kidnappers.

Roxy was seated at her electronics table doing something on the computer and looked up when Beth walked in. "Any news?" Beth asked.

"Nothing." She tried to mask her frustration, but Beth saw it in her eyes.

"Can I get you anything?"

"I'm good." Roxy nodded to a stainless-steel thermos on the end of the table. Of all them—Roxy, Mark, Ben, and Jeff—only Jeff would accept even a cup of coffee from Maria, Sara, or Beth. Must be some kind of rule.

Beth crossed the hall. As she passed the study, she heard Mark on the phone. His deep voice carried out to her, though his tone told her he wasn't having any better luck at chasing down phone leads than Ben was having checking transportation, credit card usage, or ATM withdrawals.

Soul-weary, Beth went on into the kitchen and poured herself some lemonade. She sat down at the table and placed the glass alongside Boudin's coffee cup. What she wouldn't give now for some of Nora's calm wisdom to come and melt her frustration. Not being disheartened when thwarted at every turn proved difficult. *Get proactive.* She grabbed her cell phone and checked in with the office.

"SaBe. How may I direct your call?"

"Margaret, why are you answering the phone?"

"Helping out. We're getting a lot of calls and e-mail support messages. I've set up folders for them. Do you want me to forward them or respond?"

"Respond to the ones that came to the office and leave the personal ones. We should respond to those ourselves, I think." Beth stared at Boudin's coffee cup and swallowed from her own glass. "Anything else going on?"

"Henry's in Dallas finalizing a feeder-firm agreement. He's scheduled back tonight. Otherwise, business is quiet."

Beth finished up the call and then set down her phone and finished her lemonade, waiting for something else—anything else—to happen. She spotted a dark scratch on the cup from Ruby's and reached for it, then examined it. Loose but small letters: *Sha.*

Joe.

She smiled but it quickly faded. He'd warned her of Sara's three hospital visits. That she was in trouble and needed help. Sara was able to speak for herself, and if she felt that reveal would do Robert any good, she would have told Jeff herself. Beth telling him would only be betraying Sara for nothing. Since she hadn't revealed recognizing Thomas Boudin, she could tell Joe and even tell him about Boudin. He didn't let her see his face on the terrace because he feared she'd recognize him. Had it disappointed him that she hadn't? Was there an actual case? Had to be. His warning about Robert had been genuine. Maybe he expected her to recognize him, or was he testing his disguise? Regardless, no one else would write *sha* on a promised cup of coffee. Jeff had heard every word between them in the hallway, but Joe could have revealed himself when they were outside and alone. Yet he hadn't said a word.

"You're confusing me, Joseph."

Beth grunted. Here she sat thinking it was odd that Sara knew so little about Robert but was crazy about him, and she was just as bad. That she hadn't married Joe brought little solace. If he asked and he was serious, she would.

That's the sign.

She gasped. It was. That was what Nora meant. Good grief, Beth was in love with the man.

Oh no. It was an awful time to even think about something as fickle as love. Especially with a man like Joe. When she'd felt attracted to Thomas Boudin, she had felt twinges of guilt for being disloyal to Joe. Boy, would he get a laugh from that. Not that she'd tell him. Well, not yet anyway. She thumbed her glass. Tilted it and watched the ice clink against its sides.

Okay, so she wouldn't tell Jeff. If Joe had wanted him to know, he'd have told him. But it wouldn't hurt to have Margaret run the insurance forms submitted and see what came up.

Wouldn't hurt? Breach Sara's privacy and her trust—on something she would have disclosed if she'd wanted you to know, and you say it wouldn't hurt?

Shame slithered through Beth. She couldn't do it. There was nothing Sara wouldn't disclose about herself to get Robert back safe.

But she's admitted she's not sharing something. How could Beth protect herself or Sara against an unknown?

Thomas Boudin—Joe—wouldn't say Robert was lethally dangerous unless he was lethally dangerous. He thought the two Roberts were the same man or he wouldn't have said they could be. He just couldn't yet prove it. Joe's warning replayed in her mind. *"If no one has a picture that clearly shows Tayton's face, then guard his wife. This Robert is lethally dangerous."*

Harsh reality set in and Beth shuddered.

Sara could be married to a killer.

13

◎⦚

Friday afternoon, Jeff approached Beth and Sara. "We're running out of time and budget."

Beth spotted three idle agents in the living room. That wasn't a good sign.

Jeff lowered his voice. "If something doesn't break soon—word from the kidnappers, an attempt to retrieve the money from the Gulf, a new lead, *something*—they'll have to assign the agents to other cases." His stomach growled.

"I understand." Sara sighed and stood. "Would you like a sandwich or something?"

"I would. I missed lunch."

Beth watched them walk out of the family room and worried. Sara was falling for him. It was evident in everything she said and every move she made. She wouldn't act, but the feelings were there and growing, and from all signs, they were there for Jeff too.

Regret squeezed inside Beth. If Robert weren't in the picture, Beth would be elated. Sara and Jeff brought out the best in each other. But Robert was in the picture, and that made what was going on, well, Beth didn't know what to think. Neither, she suspected, did Sara or Jeff. Both were honorable people who respected marriage vows. How had things gotten so messy?

Roxy and Ben came into the family room. "We've got to go, Beth. Before I leave," Roxy said, "I wanted to tell you that I expect headquarters is going to cut—"

"Jeff told Sara and me. She understood. What can you do when nothing is happening?"

"I'm sorry. We are still working on it, but frankly, we need a break."

Ben stepped forward. "We'll keep working on this privately. I remember what it was like. Not knowing who killed Susan nearly drove me out of my mind. I'd turn over every stone to spare Sara that." It'd taken years to find his wife and son's killers.

"Thanks, Ben." Mark and Joe would do everything humanly possible, and so would Roxy on her own if not through the FBI, but if Robert Tayton didn't want to be found—and that was possible if he was Joe's other Robert—then he wouldn't be found. It'd be just like Robert to leave Sara trapped in the heart-less misery of uncertainty for the rest of her life.

And because Beth had no doubt he was capable of inflicting such misery, for the first time, she didn't just not like him. She feared him.

A man who could do that could do anything.

⚭

A hard rain started after dark and persisted through the night and the next morning. By afternoon, the local weatherman dubbed it Stormy Saturday.

Grim-faced, Jeff met Beth in the hallway. "Do you have a minute?" He kept his voice down. "I need to speak to you privately."

"Sure." Beth led him to the family room. "This okay?"

"Where is Sara?" He looked back at the door as if worried she would sud-denly appear.

"In the shower." This couldn't be good news. Beth braced.

He tugged at his earlobe. "It's been seventy-six hours since we've had any contact."

Resignation slid through her. "The honchos have executed reassignment orders. That's why Roxy and the agents haven't come in today."

"Yeah." Sympathy flashed through his eyes, then stayed. "I'm sorry, Beth."

Thunder rumbled and shook the house. Rain beat hard and heavy against the windows, splattering fat drops that dripped down the glass panes. Beth smoothed her hands down her thighs. What else could they do? The agents couldn't hang around waiting for a call that didn't appear to be coming. "I expected this before you mentioned it yesterday."

"Off the record, if Robert and Sara weren't so well connected, it probably would have happened sooner. The case has gotten a lot of media attention, and the honchos don't want it to appear as if we've abandoned them. Honestly, we haven't. We've just exhausted all leads."

"If everything's been done, then there's nothing left to do." She'd heard Mark tell Ben to triple-check something yesterday, which meant they'd already double-checked everything. "Your efforts border on heroic, Jeff. Seriously." Reality had to be accepted.

"We've pulled the money from the tube. It'll be recorded and held for a time, but if nothing springs loose within a couple weeks, we can petition…"

"Sara repaid me. I doubt she'll be worried about it." Beth dragged her teeth over her lower lip. "She understands the drawdown, but she's going to take removing the money hard."

"That's why I'm telling you first." He hitched his slacks. They were wet from the rain nearly to his knees. "You think she'll be okay? Or do we prepare for another attack?"

"I think she'll be okay." The man standing in front of Beth was partially the reason.

"I hate doing this to Sara."

The tenderness in his voice tugged at her hard. He'd developed strong feelings for Sara. *Oh, but that he'd been first, before Robert.* Sara would have been happy with Jeff. Now she was unhappy, and poor Jeff was falling in love with yet another woman who couldn't love him back. It was just heartbreaking, especially considering that the emotional toll of his job was so heavy and yet he willingly put his heart out there anyway. Such a brave man. "Will anyone be here?"

"One agent," Jeff said. "But I don't know for how long."

"That sounds ominous." Beth blinked hard. "Do you think this is over now? With no resolution?" *Please, God. No. Give her some kind of closure.*

"I just don't know." Jeff frowned. "The consensus is something scared off the kidnappers. We know they were watching at the river, and they've had ample opportunity to recover the money. We've been all over the woods and in the river. Two agents have been eyes-on on the money the entire time and no one's come close. They're just gone."

"What's the consensus on Robert? What would they do with him?" Her stomach muscles clenched in a tight wad that nearly doubled her over. Jeff's sober expression darkened. She lifted a hand to her chest. "You think they killed him."

"I won't speculate." He looked away. "But I'll keep the case open until it's resolved."

She stared at her briefcase, at the paper edges of the unsigned agreement between Sara and her removing Robert from operations in SaBe. "If they abandoned the money, then he's a loose end. They wouldn't just let him go. They'd kill him, and then move on to whatever else they intend to do." A thought occurred to her and she hesitated. "May I ask a question?"

He nodded.

"What if Robert is involved in this? What if he is the same Robert in Thomas Boudin's case and this isn't about money but about disappearing?"

"I shouldn't discuss this, but Joe raised the same questions. We checked everything we could find but nothing led to Robert arranging his own kidnapping."

"You know what Thomas Boudin's case is about?"

"No, but Mark checked with some of his Intel friends. They didn't find anything."

"That doesn't mean something isn't there." *Keep your mouth shut.* Beth ignored the reminder. "Robert is capable of arranging all this, Jeff."

"You're speculating."

"Yes." She frowned, irritated that he wouldn't discuss the hypothetical. "What if speculation is all Sara ever has? Do you think they'll let him go without the money?"

He focused on that weird circle-art sculpture. "Probably not."

"Probably not?" Beth guffawed. "Good grief. Are you that unsure of what typically happens in these cases, or are you just hiding from the truth because it's easier?"

"I'm not speaking for myself. I'm speaking for the police. I can't speculate."

"Have you found a tie between Robert and the club attack?"

"Not definitively."

She hadn't expected they had, but she'd hoped. Staring off, she spun scenarios and they all ended badly. "Regardless, nothing appears to bode well for Robert."

Jeff stared at the floor. "Personally," he finally said, "I agree with that assessment."

Beth's heart twisted. Sara would draw the same conclusions.

And she would be devastated.

☙❧

By dusk, the equipment had been removed from Sara's house, Roxy had pulled the last agent to work on another case, and Mark Taylor had stepped in to fill the gap.

"If something doesn't happen soon, I guess you'll be going too." Beth tried not to sound abandoned—that would be irrational and unfair—but wasn't sure she succeeded.

"Nora would filet me like a fish." He smiled. "Ben said he'd told you Crossroads is in for the long haul."

"He did. But if nothing is happening, what do you do?"

"Something will break. Someone will make a mistake or talk out of turn and it'll get reported. It happens all the time."

"A lot of cold case files just wither, Mark."

"True, but we're going to do all we can to make sure this isn't one of them. Joe's working overtime on it. He has tons of connections, and he'll exhaust them. He knows how much Sara means to you."

"Joe is a special man."

"I'm glad to hear you say that. He's my best friend and I'd hate to see him get hurt."

"Could I hurt him?" Sounding pathetic, she tilted her head. Nora would be mortified.

"Oh, yeah."

Warmth oozed through her chest, settled in her heart. "Hard to believe."

"Why?"

"Joe is…you know. He could have any woman he wants and I'm supposed to think that's me?"

"Why not you?"

"Come on, Mark. We've always talked straight with each other. Guys like Joe go for glamorous women. I've got my assets, but I know only too well that I'm ordinary."

"That's Max's trash talk. You know better."

"I know what I've lived. Max was cruel, but that doesn't mean he was wrong."

Mark's smile turned tender. "You're not ordinary to Joe. To him you're remarkable."

Beth smiled. She couldn't help it. "Really?"

"Definitely." He reached for his thermos. "I remember the first time he saw you. It was at Lisa's party when she got her medical license. He took one look at you and was knocked off his feet."

Overwhelmed, she stilled. The warmth in her chest burned stronger. "He offered to beat up Robert for me but I refused. It'd upset Sara." She couldn't stop smiling.

"Appears he knocked you off your feet too."

"He did, but don't tell him I said that. Remember how unsure you were Lisa would ever give you a second look?"

Mark grimaced. "It was bad."

Beth nodded. "It was—and now it's my turn."

"Slightly different," Mark said. "Max messed with your head. You don't see yourself the way others see you—and you sure don't see yourself like Joe does, or you'd never think things like that."

"I'm not fishing for compliments. Honest."

"I know that. I remember the doubt and uncertainty. Man, I hated it." Mark's eyes darted back and forth like he was locked in an internal debate. "Let me ask a question. Has Joe ever called you *sha*?"

She nodded. "It's one of the few times I pick up on his Cajun accent. It's…special."

"You have no idea. He's worked hard to bury it—security purposes."

He'd have to; it'd be a dead giveaway, infiltrating on Shadow Watcher missions. "What do you mean, I have no idea?"

"You know what *sha* means, right?"

Beth nodded again. She'd looked it up. "It's an endearment."

"To Joe, it's almost sacred." Mark softened his voice. "No details—those have to come from him—but in his entire life, Joe's heart hasn't been whole. He's not into uttering endearments. When he's ready, he'll tell you why…assuming you want to know."

"Of course I want to know."

Mark dipped his square chin. "Idle curiosity?"

"More—but I don't know how much yet."

"Fair enough." Mark's expression eased. "I know the Max thing has been hard, and you need to understand. Joe isn't like you think. He's friendly and he genuinely likes women, but…"

"What?" Did he feel he was betraying Joe's confidence? No, Mark wouldn't do that. He was trying to give her insight without being explicit.

He sent her a level look. "Never, not once, have I heard Joe call any woman *sha*."

Almost sacred. Beth wasn't sure what that meant, but her heart sure did. It skipped and thudded, and she felt…treasured. Three little letters, one little word, and she felt like a rare jewel. "Thanks for telling me."

NOT THIS TIME   179

Mark's phone rang. He took the call, talked for a few minutes, and then relayed to Beth. "Peggy's setting up a schedule. People from Crossroads will be here, and members of my security staff will rotate shifts. Sara will be guarded around the clock."

Joe had apparently passed on his concern for Sara's safety. "You think that's necessary?"

"If NINA is connected, we all do. Until we know, we'd rather be safe than sorry."

"Sounds smart." Did Mark know Joe was Thomas Boudin? She wished she knew.

"I'm going to run a perimeter check on the property. I know you've got a business to run, so do what you need to do—and don't worry. We're prepared to handle medical crises as well as emergencies."

"I know you are." Sara had reacted to the force reduction by taking Dr. Franklin's pills and crashing on the family room sofa. "Tell Peggy I really appreciate this."

"She'd be insulted. You and Sara have always helped Crossroads. Of course they're all here for you." Mark went out the front door.

If he knew about Joe being Boudin, Mark wasn't saying anything. Had Joe gone rogue? It was time to call the question. She pulled out her special phone and dialed.

It rang and kept ringing. But no one answered. Disappointment bit her hard. Her questions would have to wait. Resigned to it, she linked Sara's laptop to the office and worked with Margaret. The lab was quiet, Legal was swamped, and things were moving smoothly. While listening to Margaret's rundown on specifics, Beth checked her e-mail and winced. If she worked at it steadily, she might catch up on her messages by Monday.

"I screened Sara's mailbox," Margaret said. "What needs attention, I forwarded to you. I handled the mundane."

"Anything urgent not yet handled?" Beth deleted two more messages and silently muttered at spammers for stuffing mailboxes across the Net.

"Urgent this second? Done," Margaret said. "Legal has seven new licensing agreements ready for you and Sara to sign. Nick Pope needs them back for review by noon on Monday before they go to Henry. I'm sending a messenger over with them."

"Okay." Sara wasn't in any condition to review anything, but between now and Monday surely she'd be lucid enough to read and sign them.

Beth should have her sign the agreement in her briefcase too, but with it directly preventing Robert from involvement in SaBe operations in the event of Sara's death, Beth couldn't bring herself to include it. She wanted it, SaBe needed it, but this wasn't the right time.

How long Margaret had been talking and Beth had her tuned out, she wasn't sure. "I'm sorry, Margaret. What was that?"

"I said you sound like the walking dead. Are you sleeping?"

Sleep? Define sleep. "I'm okay."

Margaret sniffed. "You're exhausted and worried sick about Sara. We all are. But she's stronger than you think. She'll make it through this."

Beth yearned to feel half as certain. "Of course she will." *God willing.* "Margaret, I need to talk to you about something, but it has to be confidential."

"All right."

"Something strange happened at the fund-raiser. It's about Sara's hospital visits—not the last one, but the three ones prior. What was she treated for?"

"I don't know."

How could Margaret not know? "Don't you have the insurance submissions?"

"If there were any, I'd have them."

"She paid cash for the hospital bills?" The hair on Beth's neck stood on end. Why would she do that? SaBe had excellent coverage.

"I'm glad you brought this up, Beth. I've been concerned but didn't want to cause any trouble. Nothing ever came through on her insurance, so Sara had to have paid the bills personally." Margaret paused. "If they were for attacks, she'd have submitted them. So what's wrong with her?"

"I don't know."

"She hasn't told you?"

"No." It hurt to admit that.

"Then Robert's got to be involved."

"That's a big leap, Margaret."

"It's not a leap at all. Sara tells you everything except when it's about him."

She did. Or Beth had thought so until this past week. Now she didn't know what to think. "Have you noticed anything else odd with her lately?"

"I feel funny mentioning this, but I know you're on her side in all things, so I'm going to say it and hope you take it the way I mean it."

"You adore her, Margaret. I know that." Beth shut down the laptop, gave Margaret her full attention. "What is it?"

"I don't know exactly. She's troubled. Quantico has called her several times in the past month, and she won't take their calls."

Quantico always had priority. Assisting was their patriotic duty. "Seriously?"

"Seriously. She said to send them to you and wouldn't even speak to the guys on the phone. I didn't understand it—still don't. There's no reason for it that I can see, but it's just, well, not Sara or SaBe policy to refuse queries from Quantico."

"Protect yourself from me—and if you can, protect me from myself..." Beth shuddered. That warning and refusing Quantico contact? Was that the connection? Sara would never do so without reason. She and Sara assisted with computer expertise. Wrote programs, reinforced firewalls and security software. What would make her refuse Quantico? "This doesn't make sense."

"At first it didn't, but then I thought of one situation where it makes perfect sense."

Beth was afraid to ask but had no choice. "What situation?"

"If she had a reason to not want to know what was going on there."

NINA. The bottom fell out of Beth's stomach. The club attack. The missing groom on the cake. Robert missing. NINA would love access to Quantico. It sold intelligence, countered missions. The lengths to which it would go to get access had Beth mentally staggering. Was that what all this was about? NINA sending Sara a message to cooperate and deliver what it wanted?

"It's the only thing that makes sense, Beth."

"Okay. Okay. We need to check this out. All future Quantico inquires come straight to me. I don't want Sara getting so much as a memo that they've been in touch. Nothing. And tell Henry Baines I need to talk to him as soon as possible."

"You got it." Margaret paused, her voice less certain. "Do you think Sara's in trouble?"

She did. She really did. "I intend to find out. For now, keep everything away from her. I don't want even a piece of spam going to her. Redirect her mailbox to one only we can access. Encrypt it." Beth's mind whirled. "I'm not shutting her out—you understand that, right?"

"You're protecting her."

"Trying, Margaret. I'm trying."

Against NINA Beth had serious doubts about her success.

∽

"What's your ETA?"

Mark Taylor's voice carried to Beth and its pitch sent a chill racing up her back. *ETA. Estimated time of arrival.* One of many familiar acronyms. Who was coming? And what was wrong? She'd tried three times to reach Joe but hadn't gotten him. And every time she started to tell Mark she might have found the connection between the club attack and Robert's kidnapping, she heard Nora's voice in her mind: *"Keep your mouth shut."* Then Joe's warning. *"Things get twisted…"*

Praying her silence wasn't a mistake, she rushed into Sara's living room. Mark stashed his mobile phone and, sober-faced, sat at the empty electronics table. "Who's coming over?"

"Jeff." Mark avoided looking at her.

The nonverbal warnings grew stronger. "When?"

"Any second now."

A scant minute later, the doorbell rang.

Jeff walked in from the pouring rain, shrugging out of his drenched raincoat. Never had she seen him look so grim. "Hi, Beth. Where's Sara?"

"Sleeping in the family room."

"Still?" Jeff hung his raincoat outside under the porch, then closed the door.

"After the reduction news this morning, Harvey prescribed two pills. He says she'll probably be out until morning."

Jeff dragged a hand through his damp hair, shaking loose clinging raindrops. "This can't wait. We have to talk." His Adam's apple bobbed in his throat. "It isn't good news."

"Is he dead?" Sara's voice sounded from behind them.

Beth turned. Sara's hair was disheveled and she was wearing black pj's, a robe, and slippers. The slippers surprised Beth, but she was glad to see good sense overriding Robert's preferences. "You shouldn't be up. The medicine—"

"Beth, stop." Sara pivoted her gaze to Jeff. "Is Robert dead?"

"We need to sit down." Jeff shot a pleading look at Beth and led Sara to the sofa. "You too, Beth."

Stone-faced and distant, Mark had disassociated—a horrible-news harbinger.

Tears gathered on Sara's lashes and her face splotched red. "Well?"

Jeff twisted toward Beth and covertly mouthed, "Inhaler?" When Beth nodded, he sat directly across from Sara. "You remember that Robert's rental car was found in Destin." Sara nodded and Jeff went on. "That same day, the sheriff's office up north requested I come up to Magnolia Branch, but I was tied up with the club attack so it wasn't mentioned to me until today."

Clyde was buried in Magnolia Branch. What did this have to do with Robert? Sara grasped Beth's hand. It was ice-cold.

"The sheriff wanted me to take a look at something their deputies found on a routine disturbance call. Bill Conlee was one of the deputies. I've known him a lot of years. He's good, Sara. He saw your press conference on the news and got a hunch. So he acted on it."

She nodded but held her silence.

Jeff cleared his throat. "Race Miller from up north also saw the newspaper article about Robert and called in about the same disturbance."

"I know Race," Sara said. "His wife, Aline, too." She looked at Beth. "We bought Clyde's property for the moms from him."

"Right." Jeff looked at Beth, then back to Sara. "Race sold you that property because a porn ring had been filming on it in an old abandoned shed."

"He told me. He's the pastor of the local church," Sara told Beth.

Beth stilled. Were pornographers the connection and not NINA? Was that what was troubling Sara? Possible, but it didn't feel right. They wouldn't have Sara refusing calls from Quantico. "Why didn't I know about this?"

"It was over and had nothing to do with anything." Sara returned her attention to Jeff. "So…?"

"So Race's call was a complaint that they were back." Jeff swiped his pug nose. "When the officers got there, the shed was empty except for a bloody mattress."

"Robert!" Sara's face bleached and she gasped. "Oh no." She clasped her throat but shoved away the inhaler Beth offered. "I don't need that. Go—go ahead, Jeff."

"The amount of blood on the mattress was significant." He paused but she didn't utter a sound. Didn't blink, didn't breathe. "There was no body—the deputies searched extensively."

"But…what? I hear a *but* in your voice, Jeff."

"Bill Conlee felt no one could sustain that substantial a blood loss and survive."

Her jaw parted and Sara hissed in shallow, staggered breaths. "But there was no body. He could be wrong. Maybe it was someone else. It could be someone else. Robert could still be alive."

Beth looked at the hope in Sara's face and nearly cried. Only a desperate woman could look at and hear Jeff and deny the evidence to back up his bad news was coming.

"When they failed to find a body and no one was reported missing, they thought the mattress could be a prop used in filming the, uh, movie. But when Bill learned Robert's kidnapper didn't retrieve the money, he had the lab test the mattress blood. That was the hunch he followed."

Oh, God. Beth clasped Sara's arm tighter. *Help her. Please, help her.*

"DNA tests were done, just like on the rental car. It was human, Sara," Jeff said slowly. "The lab compared the sample to the one we tested from Robert's brush." Jeff blinked, then blinked again. "All the results are in now."

Sara's face twisted in agony. "They match."

Jeff nodded. "I'm so sorry. The blood on the mattress is Robert's."

A knot lodged in Beth's throat and her eyes stung.

"So he was injured," Sara said. "That doesn't mean he's—"

"Hank Green examined the mattress and confirmed Bill's opinion. Robert couldn't have sustained that substantial a blood loss and lived."

"But there's no body." Sara shook her head. "If there's no body…"

"Hank estimated the blood loss at six pints, Sara. There's no doubt," Jeff said firmly but with compassion. "I'm very sorry, but your husband is dead."

Sara crumpled like a broken doll, collapsing into Beth's arms. Beth held her, felt her whole body heave and ebb in heart-wrenching sobs that speared through Beth's soul.

"Use your inhaler." Beth looked over at Jeff. "Call Harvey Talbot."

Mark asked, "Do you need an ambulance?"

"No. No." Sara pulled away from Beth. "No doctor, no ambulance. Just let me think. I need to think."

Odd. Beth passed her a tissue from the box. "You need to *think*?"

"I meant mourn. I need to mourn." Sara flushed. "Don't worry. I'm okay."

Beth studied her. Sara looked okay, but how could she be? Beth didn't dare to trust her eyes. "Let Harvey check. Please."

"I said I'm okay. There'll be no attack." Determination fired in her. "Not this time."

Beth stared a long moment. There was sadness but no grief. Nothing of a woman being told the love of her life was gone. She had loved Robert; Beth knew she had. But Sara didn't look much like she loved him right now. She looked...something else. Something Beth couldn't tag but was strange. Very strange.

Bits of Sara's cryptic messages flashed through Beth's mind. *"Protect yourself from me—and if you can, protect me from myself."* Her intimate conversations with Jeff—the sparks and signs of a developing relationship. The terrace messenger. Joe as Thomas Boudin with his *"Sara's in trouble...not hospitalized for mild attacks."*

The club attack and missing groom. Robert's kidnapping. Joe's Boudin case— *"This Robert is lethally dangerous."* And now, Sara's strangest reaction yet.

Robert's dead and Sara's...relieved?

Thomas Boudin had some explaining to do.

☙❧

Beth spent the weekend slipping out into Sara's backyard to call Joe on their special phone.

He didn't answer. Not the first or fifth or twenty-fifth time she tried reaching him.

She plucked a leaf off a jasmine bush and tossed it to the ground. Should she be angry? Or scared stiff NINA had found him? Unsure, she alternated between the two. "Let him be safe." She looked skyward. "At least until I know whether I should slap or hug him."

"Beth?" Peggy Crane called out to her. "You okay?"

She turned away from the cove toward the house, walked toward Peggy. "I'm fine."

"He still isn't answering?"

"Not yet." Beth was half sorry she'd told Mark she'd been unable to reach Joe, but she thought maybe he should know in case Joe had run into trouble. Peggy had overheard and now knew the reason Beth eased outside every chance she got. "I'm worried, Peg. He said he'd be at the other end of the phone whenever I needed him."

Peggy hooked their arms, patted Beth's. "You know how his work is, hon. He'll call when he can."

"NINA's after him." Beth spoke her deepest fear. "What if—?"

"Mark would know. The whole team would know."

So they all were working behind the scenes—Sam, Nick, and Tim, as well as Mark and Joe. "Then why hasn't he called?"

"I don't know. I wish I did. I'm rather fond of your Joe. Of all the team, really."

So was Beth.

They went back inside. The crush of people had thinned out a little. Sara spoke to everyone and looked less fragile than Beth ever recalled. Beth was glad; she just wished she understood it.

"I've got to get back to the center to relieve Lisa." Peggy hooked her purse over her arm. "If you need me, yell."

"Thank you, Peggy."

Beth watched her go, pretended not to hear Nathara complaining about spending her entire vacation surrounded by people in mourning, and located Nora—sitting on the sofa, quiet, watchful, and unseeing, her sadness reaching across the space between them. Missing Clyde was etched into her face. Sara didn't have that look. When had she stopped loving Robert?

The thought stunned Beth. She shooed it away as nonsense, but it refused to go.

"If I could go back…"

Beth stood statue still and let the truth sink in. Sara *had* stopped loving Robert.

And that raised a whole new crop of questions.

Questions Beth couldn't answer.

14

The rest of the weekend was as hard as only times of grief and mourning can be—and as busy, with a steady stream of people dropping by with condolences, flowers, plants, and food. Maria was overwhelmed, but Mel, Lisa, Annie, and the others from Crossroads stepped in and managed the crush.

Predictably, not one of Robert's friends came to see Sara.

On Monday Maria made two trips to the local mission to drop off carloads of food and still had more than would fit in Sara's fridge.

Nora and Annie sat with Sara in the family room. "Hank says you might need a little help with the funeral arrangements," Annie said.

"Thank you." Sara nodded. "No wake. Race Miller can do a simple grave-side service."

"Not Reverend Brown?" Nora sounded shocked.

"No, Race Miller."

Nora and Annie shared a look Beth fully understood. Robert would have wanted an event. Why was Sara doing this? Was it because there was no body? Was she in denial about Robert being dead after all? Race Miller. He wasn't even a real minister… Bizarre, but her call.

"Simple is best," Nora said.

"Best." Annie nodded.

Baffling, but Nora and Annie agreed with Sara. For the rest of the village, it wouldn't matter why. For Beth, it didn't matter at all. Robert was gone. Sara hadn't had another attack—grace in action, if ever Beth had seen it—and that's what mattered.

Beth's mother had flown home from her cruise. She'd been with Sara around the clock, which had given Beth an opportunity to check on things at home and at the office. If she could just reach Joe, she'd feel a whole lot better. He must be up to his neck in alligators, though Mark assured her he was fine, just tied up.

Beth understood tied up, and she wouldn't be neurotic about contact, but she needed to talk to him about the potential connection between Sara's anti-Quantico stance and NINA's attack and Robert's kidnapping. She'd thought the situation through from every angle and that they all were connected was the only way everything happening made sense.

On Tuesday morning, everyone from SaBe came to pay their respects. Nora and Nathara walked in right behind Margaret.

"Nora." Sara took one look at her and lunged into her arms. "I—I can't do any more of this. I just can't."

"Of course you can." Folding her into a hug, Nora whispered, "Stay strong, my girl. The worst of it's behind you now."

The worst of what? Beth started to ask but Darla Green sidetracked her. Aflutter, she grabbed Beth's arm. "Hank and Lance are here. What do I do?"

"Nothing." Nora and Sara disappeared into the family room. "Just stand here with me. They'll see you. If they come over, fine. If not, then just stand here."

Darla trembled, looked at Lance with hungry eyes. "He's grown so much." She swallowed hard. "Look at him, Beth. He's even more like John than I remembered."

"Inside and out." The resemblance was striking. "He's a good young man."

"Because of John. I wasn't a good mother, but he was a wonderful father." Darla's voice cracked.

Uneasy, Beth turned her gaze from Lance to Darla. "Yes, he was."

Tears glossed her eyes. "He deserved better than he got from me. They both did."

"What did he get?" Was she confessing to killing John? *Not today. Please, not today.*

"He loved me." Darla sniffed. "I should have loved him more."

"You adored him. Everyone knew it. I saw it myself."

"I should have tried harder to be the woman he saw in me." She sniffed again. "I didn't appreciate that when he was alive."

"Appreciate what?"

"The security and confidence that comes with knowing you're loved." She tore her gaze from Lance. "I took John for granted. I was the center of his world. Until he was gone, I had no idea what a privilege that was."

"John was content with you."

"He deserved more. A lot more."

Darla snagged Hank's gaze. He whispered something to Lance, who shot his mother a surprised look. Darla sucked in a sharp, hopeful breath. He hesitated a long moment, then turned away.

A soft cry garbled in Darla's throat. "Excuse me, Beth." She rushed out the back door.

Beth started after her, but Lisa caught her arm. "Give her a few minutes. She doesn't want to be seen upset."

"You sure?"

"I'm a doctor and this stuff is my business, remember?"

"It's hard, seeing her so hurt."

"It is." Lisa nodded. "Time will help them both." She tilted her head toward Lance.

He looked as devastated as Darla, and afraid. Hank wrapped a protective arm around the boy's shoulders, whispered something to him. Whatever it was, it seemed to help. Beth didn't dare to intrude, but she sure wouldn't mind knowing Hank's secret. Seemed all around her people were suffering—Nora, Sara, Darla…everyone except Nathara.

Not wanting to hear her latest tirade, Beth went to the family room door. Sitting on the sofa with tears running down her own leathery cheeks, Nora held Sara while she cried.

Beth's chest went tight. She folded her arms. The two women in the world she was closest to, and they both were mourning. Feeling small and helpless, Beth prayed. *Carry them.*

She backed away, then shut the door. They stayed in the closed room a long time. Long enough for Nathara to fray the nerves of everyone else in the house. She was now going for round two and started with Beth. "Nora always did make too much of dying."

Beth bit her tongue.

Peggy didn't. "Nora understands grief, Nathara. That's a blessing to her and others. Life holds value. It should be mourned."

"Nonsense. We live, we die, and that's that. Mourning is weakness."

"There's a time to mourn, and this is it," Peggy challenged her. "It's not weak. It's a sign of strength. Refusing to care enough to mourn. Now, that's weak."

"Nonsense, I say." Nathara shrugged. "But to each his own."

Mean as a snake. Beth squeezed her eyes shut. *So unlike Nora.* It was hard to believe they were related, much less twins.

∞

At one forty-five Sara emerged for Robert's funeral.

Dressed in a soft black dress that flowed to her ankles, black hose, and pumps, Sara straightened the broad brim on her hat. Its short veil covered her eyes. "Beth, I need a few minutes. Keep them away from me, okay?"

"Okay." Beth glanced into Sara's living room. Her entire family had come; Maria and her family; Henry Baines, Nick Pope, and Margaret from SaBe; and everyone from Crossroads, yet Mark Taylor wasn't with Lisa—and where was Jeff?

Peggy Crane came over. "Who are you looking for?"

"Mark and Jeff." Beth tried to keep her worry from her voice. "After the club and all this with Robert, I'm worried…"

"So are they. They're securing the cemetery." Peggy brushed a speck of lint from her sleeve. "We're not supposed to leave here until Mark phones with an all clear."

Relief washed through Beth. "Oh, good. Good."

"You'd better go with her." Peggy nodded toward Sara, stepping out the door into the backyard. "She thinks she needs to be alone, but she doesn't."

Beth went out the back door, but not wanting to intrude, she stopped just outside. Sara stood staring out at the cove. The sun shone brightly, spangling on the calm, rippling water.

"I know you're here." Sara didn't look back.

"Ignore me."

"I don't want to ignore you. I want…" She glanced back, sober. "What I want doesn't matter anymore."

Beth stepped closer. "It matters to me."

"I know. I love you too. You've been the best sister, Beth."

"You too."

"No. I wish I had, but…" Sara drew in a shuddered breath. "This whole funeral is just a formality. It isn't the end." She moved to the porch swing and sat down. "Without a body, it doesn't mean anything. We're just burying a coffin filled with his favorite things."

Dangerous thinking. Until Sara accepted the truth, she couldn't begin to heal. Beth sat beside her, smelled the jasmine blossoms on the light breeze. "I know this is difficult and you don't want to believe it, but it is real. Robert is dead, and as painful—"

"Not for seven years, he isn't."

"What are you talking about?"

Sara toed the ground, shoved the swing. "Henry says it's federal law. Robert can't be declared legally dead for seven years—all states respect it."

She and Henry had a long, private conversation yesterday, and it sounded as if Sara believed Robert could still be alive and she had seven years to prove it. Oh, but Beth hoped not. Neither of them had the stamina to linger in limbo for seven years. Letting her gaze slide, Beth skimmed the wooden dock, Sara's sailboat. "That's the legal declaration. But you do realize Harvey and Hank agree that Robert did die, right?"

"I know what they said."

Cagey. Evasive. Not good. Frowning, Beth tried again. "He lost over six pints of blood." No one losing six pints of blood could live.

"Yes." Sara squared her shoulders but refused to look at Beth.

Denial. "I don't know what you're doing. I don't understand, and I won't pretend I do." She wished Nora were out here. She'd know what to do. "Robert is dead. It's horrible, but it has to be accepted. He needs to rest in peace, and you need to let him."

Sara didn't say a word. Didn't so much as blink.

Beth's throat went thick. "It would break his heart to see you like this."

"Would it?" Sara frowned. "You hated him. You know nothing about him."

"I didn't hate him, and I know it'd break his heart because he loved you," Beth said. "It breaks my heart to see you like this."

That knocked the fight out of Sara. "This is so…hard. There's no easy way to work through it. The things you don't know…they make everything so twisted and complicated."

"Do you want to explain?"

"No." Resolve slid over her face, into her voice. "Not now, not ever. Just remember what I told you."

The warning. "Sara, why were you in the hospital—three times before this last attack? You told me it was mild attacks, but that's not true, is it?"

"No."

Beth's heart beat hard and fast. "You said you were in trouble. Are you still in trouble?" Had Robert's death changed that?

"Yes." A sob in her throat distorted her voice. "But—"

"No buts." Beth clasped her hand. "Just tell me the truth."

"No." Sara shook off Beth's hand. "This time, I walk alone."

It wasn't over. "Is someone pressuring you in some way?"

She shot Beth a warning. "Leave it alone. I mean it."

Frustration flooded her. "Why won't you let me help you?"

Truth burned in Sara's eyes. "Because you can't."

"Then who can? Whatever it takes, we'll get it."

"You can't get anything."

"Are you saying no one can do anything?"

"No mortal can do anything. You want to help me? Pray."

Beth prayed for all her family all the time. "Let's pray together. If we agree—"

"I don't pray anymore."

Shock pumped through Beth. "Since when? Why not?"

"I—I can't."

"Sara, that doesn't make sense. Of course you can pray."

"No, I really can't."

Beth sensed pushing would only make matters worse, but she didn't have a clue why Sara would feel that way. "Then I'll pray for both of us until you can pray again."

Tears gathered in Sara's eyes. "When you do, tell God I'm sorry."

"For what?"

"He knows."

No doubt. Beth sure wished she did.

⚬✕⚬

Joe sprinted from the parking lot across the cemetery and joined Mark. "I'm here, bro."

"Ah, Thomas Boudin has arrived." Not at all surprised, Mark moved away from the canopy above the stand where Robert's coffin would be, passed the rows of chairs, and stepped out into the open. "So did Beth recognize you?"

"I don't think so, but I left a calling card." Had she noticed his message on the coffee cup? "I haven't talked to her since I was there."

"I know. She's freaking out that you're in trouble."

"Can't be helped. She'll ask me questions I can't answer right now, and that'll just tick her off."

Mark cocked his head. "Can't answer, or won't?"

"In this case, there's no difference."

"Sorry to hear it."

"Sorry to have to say it." It was exactly this—the inability to tell what you knew—that caused hardships in relationships for people like them, and there was nothing that could be done about it. Classified was classified. "I don't want to lose her, Mark. She matters."

"Understand, buddy." Mark stopped in the clearing. "So you've connected the cases."

"Not definitively, but I'm working a lead that could, if I can get past one snag."

"Can I help?"

"Sam's working on it. We're really close." Joe loosened his tie at his throat. "You think this jerk Tayton is really dead?"

"Six pints of blood on a mattress have been confirmed as his. He can't be alive."

Joe waited for a reaction in his gut, but it didn't reassure him. "I've got a bad feeling, bro." At the canopy, Jeff Meyers was nose down, walking a grid. "What's he looking for?"

"Pulling a security check. After the club attack, we're not taking any chances."

"It'd be just like NINA to double back with gas. Chatter says the club attack was a trial run."

"Considered it, but they caught us flatfooted. If they wanted to wipe out everyone at the club, they would have."

"Hurts to say it, but I agree." Trial runs weren't necessary for NINA operatives. It employed the best. "Sara a wreck?"

"Pretty much, but she hasn't landed in the hospital again, so that's good."

"Beth was really worried about her—probably more now with Robert being dead."

"She's wounded but upright. She'd be a whole lot better if she could talk to you." Mark paused a long second. "Something serious is on her mind. I've tried to get her to talk to me, but she won't."

"What is it?"

"I don't know. But it's had her slipping outside for privacy and calling you a couple times an hour."

"Didn't realize she'd called that much." Joe tapped the phone. "Think it's just worry about Sara?"

"Maybe. Beth's watched over her since college—way too long not to be hurting bad—but my gut says it's more."

Guilt shrouded Joe. He should have called her. But how could he explain not being able to explain when her clearances were so high? He couldn't. She already doubted his interest in her was sincere. Not explaining could push her right out of his life.

"Mark!" Jeff called out. "Over here."

The urgency in his voice had Mark and Joe running.

"Boudin? What are you doing here?"

Mark started to explain. Joe stopped him with a silent signal. "Trying to figure out why you're treating Beth Dawson like a suspect."

Jeff's jaw tensed. "Just doing my job."

"She hasn't done anything."

"Not that I've found yet." Jeff pulled himself upright, clearly resenting the interference.

"What made you think she did?"

"She and Tayton have been at war. He's dead. She's got motive and means."

"She's innocent."

"I think so too, but I can't prove it."

That changed Joe's perspective. "Something you should know, and maybe you do. My sources say NINA is active here on another mission and has been for a nearly year."

"While Lisa's case was going on? They were running double missions?"

Joe nodded. "That's the word in closed circles."

"On what?" Jeff asked.

Joe and Mark exchanged a glance and Mark responded. "Information gathering."

"So have you picked up anything on the club attack?"

"Not yet," Mark said.

"Actually, bro, that's not current."

"Bro?" Surprise rippled across Jeff's face. "Joe? Is that you?"

"Yeah."

"What's going on?" Jeff darted his gaze between Joe and Mark.

"We're in the middle of another operation. Intel picked up a transmission between Raven and someone named Jackal."

"Oh, man." Jeff rubbed at his ear.

"Karl Masson was active again." *Gray Ghost.* His call to Raven had been intercepted and then hers to Jackal, who was apparently her boss. The levels in the organization seemed never ending. "We don't know what the mission is, but by its name, we're confident it connects to the club attack."

"What is it?"

"Dead Game."

Jeff processed that. "Could be the club, could be Robert. Missing groom on the cake, him kidnapped."

"We can't make that leap without evidence."

"Same thought here," Jeff said.

Mark shut this down. "So what did you find here?"

Jeff pointed to the ground. "Look at this. They're all over the place."

Joe looked down. Tiny objects protruded from the ground. To an untrained eye, they'd be mistaken for mini sprinkler heads. But they weren't. "Dispersant devices."

"Call it in." Mark frowned at Joe.

Jeff whipped out his phone, hit speed dial. "Get a Hazmat team out to the cemetery—now." His voice shook. "And call Peggy Crane. She's at Sara Tayton's if you can't reach her cell. Tell Peg to keep everyone away from the cemetery until further notice." Jeff paused to listen, then added, "Yes, Kyle, I know Robert's funeral is supposed to be in thirty minutes. It's been delayed. Blockade the cemetery gates. No one comes in except Hazmat."

Mark sent Joe a knowing look. "NINA."

Joe nodded. "And more."

"What more?"

Joe lowered his voice so only Mark could hear. "Karl Masson is dead."

"Did you get official word on that?"

From his intelligence connections. Joe could give Mark details, not from Intel but from a firsthand report, yet now wasn't the time. Instead, he pointed to one of the devices. "Evidence is right there in the ground. Masson was a professional. If he were alive, we wouldn't be seeing this shoddy work, bro. Intel is ninety-nine percent sure Masson pulled the club attack. I'm not—but I'm a hundred percent sure Karl Masson didn't plan this one."

Mark rubbed at his chin. "This work isn't up to his standards. NINA doesn't typically switch operatives midmission, so you've got a point about the club attack too."

"There's your verification. After two losses here, NINA would send their best."

"That's Masson. He's been their best cleaner in the US and Europe."

"Masson didn't do this. He's dead." Joe signaled *eyes-on* with two fingers.

Mark paused. "Who?"

Jeff rejoined them, and Joe continued, "She looked like Darla Green."

"I knew it," Jeff said. "I knew that woman was a killer."

"I said, she looked like Darla Green," Joe said. "I didn't say she was Darla Green."

"Not tracking," Jeff said.

"Unless Darla has a fat suit that adds thirty pounds, it wasn't her."

"She could." Jeff folded his arms. "Lighter, not so easy, but heavier wouldn't be a problem."

"True," Mark said. "Or someone wanted Masson to think it was her."

"Maybe." Joe checked to be sure they were still alone. "Or maybe someone knew I was watching from the cove and wanted me to think Darla was Masson's shooter."

"Which is why you're here as Thomas Boudin and not Joe." For Jeff the pieces had fallen into place.

Worry creased Mark's brow. "So if NINA killed their best cleaner and he pulled the club attack, then who's working their Dead Game operation?"

"Intercepts indicate another operative is active in the village." Worry rippled through Joe. "Raven."

Fear flashed over Jeff's face, through Mark's eyes. "Now I see why you've been avoiding Beth."

"Yeah, bro."

"Whoa. Not good news." The weight of this bore down on Jeff; his shoulders slumped. "You think Raven pulled this attack herself?"

"The club attack too. We picked up nothing at the scene. Nothing at all. That's not natural. The chemicals had to be released by someone local and known and accounted for as being there, or we would have picked up a stray clue."

"Had to be one of the guests. One of us." Jeff slid Mark a look laced with horror. "Raven is one of ours."

Raven was an insider in the village. Maybe Darla. Maybe Sara. Maybe one of the others trusted by all the rest.

"Sure looks like it," Mark said.

It did. Worried, Joe didn't bother to hide it. "And we have no idea who she is."

∾

"We're late." Nora shuffled over to where Nathara, Darla, and Tack Grady stood huddled in her Towers living room. "Get your things and let's go."

"There's no rush, Nora." Nathara sniffed. "The funeral's been delayed."

"Delayed?" Nora snagged her purse, bumping her shoulder against the wall. Her eyes were steadily getting worse. "Whatever for?" Nora gasped. "Is Robert alive?"

"Peggy Crane just said to stay put. Something's not right at the cemetery."

"Did NINA do something out there too?"

The others exchanged wary glances, but it was Nathara who responded. "Nina who?"

"Oh, for pity's sake, Nathara. Are you unconscious?" Nora plopped her purse down on the edge of her kitchen table. "NINA's that bunch of cutthroat terrorists all over the news since they attacked us at the club." Honestly, sometimes her twin drove her to distraction. "Why that sorry group of thugs has to plague my village, I don't know."

"They came after Kelly Walker and Lisa Harper before the attack," Darla said.

"I remember now," Nathara said. "But what's any of it got to do with Robert's funeral?"

"Now how could I be knowing that?" Nora roosted in her favorite chair. "Put on your thinking cap, sister. It don't take a genius to know Robert's murder and the attack are related."

"Is that what the authorities are saying?"

"'Course not. They ain't talking about no active investigation." Nora frowned at her twin. "What's happened to you? You becoming slow witted?"

"'Course not." Nathara stiffened. "I just don't see how they're related. That's all."

"Then you've gone soft in the head."

"Nora Jean," Nathara warned.

"The groom on the cake was missing. Sara's groom was missing. Now he's dead and his funeral's delayed. It's common sense, sister dear."

"Maybe in your mind, but I don't see it."

Darla grunted. "Me either, Nathara. Of course, I am slow witted."

"Like a fox you are, Darla Green." Nora rocked in her chair. A thread dangling from its cushion swayed with the motion. "It's no great mystery. We were all at the club when NINA attacked. Stands to reason if they were gonna attack again, they'd need us all together, and at Robert's funeral we would be, now wouldn't we?"

"We would." Darla shuddered, rubbed her folded arms. "I hadn't thought of that."

"Dangerous time not to be thinking, dearie." Nora nodded. "They probably woulda got us too, but this time, my boys saw 'em coming and stopped 'em."

"You don't know that." Nathara sat down across the room. "Your boys." She snorted. "You're letting your imagination go crazy. Maybe the hearse broke down."

"Say what you will." Nora rocked harder. "My boys saw 'em coming and stopped 'em. I'll believe it till I'm proven wrong."

"You sound like a speculating fool." Nathara flipped a shooing hand at her twin. "Peggy didn't say a thing about any attack. There's no courtyard in the cemetery. It's wide-open space. Dispersants can't be effective in wide-open spaces. Fresh air dilutes them."

"That's true." Darla nodded. "I heard it on the news. Dispersants and fresh air aren't a good match."

"Good enough to kill my Clyde." What they both said hit her, and Nora stopped rocking. She hadn't said anything about dispersants or about them being used in an attack. Nobody had used that word but Mark, and that was in private; it hadn't been on the news. Yet Nathara and Darla used it—but from the looks they were sharing with Tack Grady, this wasn't the time to point out that fact.

Fear bit Nora hard, clutched in her chest. "Hadn't considered that." She snorted. "Guess I could be jumping at shadows. Clyde would surely say I was."

"I understand, Nora." Darla sat beside her. "After John died, I was the same way. I still miss him."

"I'm sure you do, dearie." *Guilty as sin and free as a bird. It ain't right, Lord. But surely You know what You're doing.*

Nathara and Darla. Dispersants. Nora needed to talk to her boys. "Excuse me." She retreated to her bedroom, heard the rush of their hushed voices, closed and locked her door.

She replayed every snippet of conversation she could recall since the club attack. Dread seeped in. Fear blossomed, and a disappointment so deep she couldn't tell where it started or ended set in. Staggering, she bumped her shin on the edge of her bed, let out a grunt. The sting shot up her leg. Grabbing the phone from her nightstand, she dialed Mark.

Her hands shook. Mark would know what to do. Oh, but she wished his old team was all in town. Especially Joe. He calmed everyone down, and right now, she surely needed calming. He would understand. She just knew it was going to take them all to get her out of this alive. Her eyes burned. This was just disgraceful. How did she tell her boys this? *How?*

The phone rang. Waiting for Mark to answer, she kept a wary eye on the door and made herself think. Truth was, there wasn't an easy way to put it. Best just spit it out. *Mark, my boy, I need your help. That NINA's Raven is right here in my living room.*

The phone stopped midring.

The line went dead.

⚮

The steeple snagged Joe's attention.

He turned off Highway 20 and steered his motorcycle toward it. The church was a little white clapboard, parked out in the middle of nowhere. Nilge Reservation bordered it on two sides, and the highway on the third. Yet it didn't look lonely; it looked like home.

When your parents aren't parents, and you're targeting large families for food, churches offered your best odds. Sit in on the service, behave yourself, buddy up to a kid your age, and follow him home. They'd feed you, and you could stuff enough in paper napkins to feed your younger brothers.

If not for large families and little churches, Joe and his brothers would have starved. That he'd found faith sitting through those sermons to get food surprised him more than anyone else. *God works in mysterious ways.*

He parked the Harley right out front. There were a half-dozen cars in the lot and a black Lexus turned in behind him. Leaving his helmet on the seat, he walked through the front door and into the cool air.

A petite woman in her forties with metal braces on her teeth stepped out of an office and greeted him. "Hi," she said with a smile. "Can I help you?"

Her southern twang was endearing. Definitely a lifetime local. Enchanted, Joe smiled. "Hi. I'm traveling and saw your church." He hadn't noticed the denomination. Didn't matter to him, but it might to them. "Do you mind if I go in and pray?" He motioned toward the sanctuary doors.

"Of course not." She motioned. "You go right on in and stay as long as you like."

"Thank you." He did love southern hospitality. He opened the door. "I appreciate it."

"Sure thing, Mr....?"

"Joe, please."

"Joe." She smiled again.

The door swished closed behind him. The altar was simple. Behind it on the wall hung a hand-hewn wooden cross. Red-cushioned pews, two stained-glass windows, a well-worn pulpit.

Anxiety and worry had every muscle in his body in knots. Worry about Beth—her safety and whether or not she'd ever really let him into her life—worry about Sara, about Mark and Lisa, about all the villagers and people at Crossroads. Mark loved them, which meant Joe loved them. One of the villagers was NINA.

All the guys on the team had a life bond to be there for each other. It was as tight as family bonds—and in Joe's case, a lot more pleasant. The only time he heard from his parents or either of his brothers was when they were in trouble. He could sum up their conversations quickly: *How much do you need? Which one of you is in jail?* Those two questions handled ninety-nine percent of their calls. It'd been years since any of them had even asked how Joe was doing. But the Shadow Watchers always had his back. Mark, Nick, Tim, Sam—no matter when or where, if Joe needed them, they were there. And all those they loved came in under that same umbrella.

Because they did, and because Joe had gotten close to a lot of the villagers on his own, and he'd had time to see how Beth loved others—man, he wanted that from her for himself—he wasn't just worried, he was scared to death. Would they be able to protect all these people from NINA? Again?

NINA had money, resources, and manpower they didn't have. Add no ethics, no morals, and no boundaries—it would do anything to win—and it'd take a crazy man not to be scared.

Thankfully, Joe had a secret weapon they didn't have. The source of all wisdom, strength, ability, and skill—and promises he relied on every day in every situation, not just in ones classified and too often tagged potential suicide missions. Joe had found this secret weapon long ago in a little building much like this. It had sustained him though a childhood that wasn't fit for kids, and even the times when he was stuck in one of life's dark tunnels, seeking and seeking and not spotting so much as a speck of light. *Prayer.*

Near the front pew, he dropped down on the red-padded kneeler, folded his hands, and lowered his head, eager to lose himself in prayer.

Later, awareness tugged at him. He shoved it away but it persisted. He paused, listened. A scuffle outside the big doors, a muffled voice. *The woman who'd greeted him.*

He rushed to the doors, shoved, and pushed through.

She lay motionless on the floor.

Joe scanned, saw no one, then rushed over to her. *Breathing.* He gently turned her head to see her face. Her mouth was bleeding. Someone had punched her in the mouth. Her braces had sliced her flesh. Anger exploded inside him.

Something in his periphery flashed. He ducked, turned, and saw a masked man with a gun aiming for his head. His training kicked in; he swiped with his leg and knocked the man off his feet. The gun flew from his hand, and Joe attacked.

They fought hard. The man was no novice. He was a pro, as trained as Joe. "NINA."

"Phoenix," the man spat. "Know the man who kills you."

"In a church?" Joe crowded him, let fly a series of rabbit punches.

"Wood and nails are for fools. I believe in me."

Phoenix parried, landed a right jab to Joe's ribs that stole his breath. He doubled back with a hard left hook that lifted the guy off his feet and shot pain up Joe's arm to his shoulder.

A gunshot fired.

Joe went down and they fought no more...

15

❧

"Sara, it's time."

From the swing facing the cove, she looked up at Beth. "I don't want to go."

Beth didn't either. "It's one of those have-to-do things."

Sara rocked the swing harder. "It'll be easier for you."

"Nothing that hurts you is easy for me."

"I didn't say easy. I said easier."

"Well, of course." Beth shrugged. "He was your husband. But you'll get through it."

Sara choked on a low, mewling sound. "I don't want to get through it. I— I can't stand all that could come now—and I don't want you to have to stand it either."

Fear crept through Beth. The warning. The hospital visits. Sara holding back on what she knew about Robert's abduction and murder. "Grief is hard."

"This time is different." Sara stared at a flag on the back end of the docked boat. Wind-teased, it unfurled. "Things could happen." She looked back at Beth. "And hurt in new ways."

"I expect it will hurt in new ways. You haven't lost a husband before." Was she telling Beth the truth or just seeing grief differently? "But the very thing that makes you dread this is your weapon to get through it, Sara. You know something grief rookies don't. Survival *is* possible. That's half the battle, don't you think?"

"Maybe." Sara thought a second, sniffed, then dried her eyes. "When my parents died, I wasn't sure a body could hold that much pain and live. But I did."

So this was about grief and not revealing secrets. Beth bit back her disappointment. The delay was best for Sara. She had plenty on her shoulders today. "And you will again."

"Knowing you'll live through it should help. But when you're so deep in the grief abyss, it doesn't. All you can think is, what's the difference?"

Beth remembered those terrifying days. The hopelessness, the seeing no value or sense in living or in life. The bleak emptiness—oh, that awful, awful bleak emptiness—so strong and powerful and consuming it gnawed at the marrow of your bones and made everything seem insignificant. It had sorely tested Beth's soul.

When you're in the abyss and nothing matters, there aren't any tools to help you crawl out. It's scratch and claw every inch of the way—until you turn to God. Beth had, and finally so had Sara. It was hard enough to get out of that dark place with Him, but without Him? *"I don't pray anymore."* How would Sara make it?

"You know the difference. There's a lot of good life on the other side of grief."

Fear burned in Sara's eyes. "What if it's not just grief? What if other things are there too and it's too much? What if I can't do it again? What if I used all my strength the first time and I'm too weak to crawl out, Beth?"

"Then God will carry you out. He promised you'd never be given more than you could handle."

Sara rolled her eyes. She didn't want truth; she wanted Beth's assurance.

"Okay, look. I don't believe you can get in that deep. If you could, no one would ever say 'what doesn't kill you makes you stronger.' But if it is possible, then I'll stand in for you until you can take it on yourself. We'll get you through this."

Sara put her sunglasses back on, masking her eyes. "Even if it hurts you?"

Beth wished she'd left the glasses off. "Even then."

"Because you're my family." Sara's chin trembled.

Beth put a lilt in her voice. "You know the code."

"Whatever, whenever." Sara let out a shaky breath. "Thank God for the southern woman's take on family." She hugged Beth hard. "I love you. You know that, right?"

"Of course."

"I'm sorry we've been at odds."

"We're fine." Beth pulled back and looked into Sara's face. "We'll do what we have to do, Sara." She squeezed their clasped hands. "You'll be okay."

"I'd be lost without you." Sara stood, looped their arms, and took the first step toward the house.

"Me too," Beth confessed, certain now there had been times that even with her and the family Sara had felt lost.

Why was Sara shutting out her faith when she most needed it? What could be so bad it made her feel that unworthy? No one was worthy. Grace paved the way, and Sara knew it. So knowing she wasn't strong enough to walk alone, why turn her back? It defied reason.

At the back door, Sara sniffled. The tip of her nose was red. "Do you have my inhaler?"

"Yeah." Beth passed it over.

Sara tucked it in her handbag. "Don't worry. I asked for it because you'll be more at ease if I take it. I'm not going to need it."

"Promise?"

"Promise. I'm through worrying you." Sara tucked the crumpled tissue into her purse, then snapped it closed. "It's a new day. I'm going to deal with it without any more attacks."

What had gotten into her? Whatever it was, Beth hoped it took root. "Glad to hear it. I know I'm too protective and it gets on your nerves at times—"

"You promised my parents you'd look after me. That makes you mother and sister and friend." Sara tapped Beth's arm. "All that caring gives you lots of leeway with me."

Beth never had told Sara about that promise. "How did you know—?"

"I know my mother and I know you. It was a given." Sara's smile was faint.

"Listen, I know I'm fragile, especially compared to you, and my health issues scare you silly. I also know you'd like to slap me now and then and tell me to grow a backbone—and you would, but southern women just don't do that." Sara's eyes twinkled. "You're the consummate nurturer, Beth, and even when you disagree with me, you're supportive. Don't think I don't know how hard that is for you at times."

Beth stared at her, slack jawed. "Where's Sara? What's going on? This isn't you."

"Oh, but it is me. I'm just not hiding anymore. As close as we are, there are things about me you don't know. Things at work in all this—but I won't tell you what because I don't want you to know. Not because you'll judge me. I just want them kept private—and I don't want to talk about why either." Sara's face flushed. "If I act weird, keep your distance and trust me, okay?"

Given little choice, Beth nodded. "At least tell me what the hospital visits were for. Are you really sick?"

"I'm not sick." Resolve slid over her face, masking her expression. "What happened to me will never happen again and that's all I have to say. Please, don't ask about that again. It's over, and I don't want to think about it anymore." Sara blinked hard. "Now, let's get this funeral over with."

At the kitchen door, Sara grabbed the knob, then paused. "One more thing." She looked Beth straight in the eye. "When the funeral is over, I want you to go home and stay away from me for a while."

"What?" Inside, Beth reeled.

"I want time to myself to heal. I have to stand on my own. If you're around, I won't. I should have done this a long time ago."

"But, Sara, the next couple months will be hard—"

"Yes, and if you're around they'll be harder. You'll want to fix everything, and I'll let you. That might be what I want but it's not what I need."

"Did you talk to Nora about this?"

"I talked to me about it."

"Okay." Beth felt deflated. Betrayed and deflated, though she shouldn't feel either. She couldn't wrap her mind around this. Medical secrets, cryptic warnings, admissions of being in trouble Beth couldn't help with, shunning God, and now banning her. Just how much jeopardy was Sara in? With whom? And for what? This was about more than any Quantico and NINA connection. This was intensely personal…somehow.

Peggy met them inside the back door. One look at her pale face and Beth braced for bad news. "What's happened now?"

"Kyle called from headquarters," Peggy said. "Jeff wants us to stay here until he calls back."

Beth lifted a hand. Sara was ready so naturally the world was not. *God, could we please catch a break here?* "But everyone will be at the cemetery."

Peggy's chunky white necklace heaved against her navy dress. "No, they won't. Mark and Jeff found something out there. Something…dangerous."

"Another NINA-type something?" Beth whispered.

"Kyle didn't say, but they've requested a Hazmat team."

"Oh no." Sara's hands went to her throat. "It's begun."

"What's begun?" Beth grabbed Sara's arm. "Enough of this. It's NINA, Sara. Others are at risk. Tell me what's going on right now."

Wild-eyed, Sara gasped and fell into a full faint.

☙♡☙

"Joe, answer your stupid phone," Beth told his voice mail, angry and not bothering to hide it. Glaring at the water, she plunked down on Sara's backyard porch swing. "I'm in crisis here. I don't know what it is exactly, but it's a crisis—and I trusted you. You said you cared. Well, prove it. Call me."

She waited, and waited, but he didn't call.

"So much for counting on you."

Harvey and Lisa were in with Sara. She didn't want Beth around, but she asked for Nora. Unfortunately she wasn't answering her phone either. *Beyond odd, that.* Where was Nathara?

"Beth?" Peggy walked into view. The stiff breeze tugged at the hem of her navy dress. "Lisa says Sara's okay. No attack."

"Good." Beth let out a staggered breath. "Is she talking?"

"Yes, but she's not saying anything we want to hear. For some reason, she's clammed up on anything but her medical condition. Do you have any idea why?"

"None." Plenty of suspicions, but nothing she could share. Weary from the soul out, Beth swiped at her eyes. "Peggy, do you know what's happening with the funeral site?"

"No, I don't." Her expression sobered even more. "But it's bad or Mark wouldn't have called Roxy to the cemetery."

FBI involved again. Not a good sign. "Have you heard from Nora? I can't reach her."

"Nathara and Tack Grady are here, but Nora isn't. She wanted some time alone."

"Did Nathara say why?"

"Not really. But you know Nathara. She thinks grief lasts five minutes and it's done. Nora probably needs a break from her."

No doubt. "But she's not answering her phone." Nora never ignored Beth's calls. An uneasy feeling nagged at her. "I'm going to check on her."

"She's probably just worn out with all this coming on the heels of Clyde's passing."

"No." Beth stood. "It's more. I feel it, Peg. No matter what she's doing or where she is or what time it is, when I call, Nora answers. Something's wrong."

"I'll ride with you. If something's wrong, you shouldn't go alone."

Beth considered it. "No, you'd better play sentry for Sara. If Nathara or one of Robert's friends gets around her right now, it could get ugly. But if you could get the prayer warriors busy on Sara, I'd appreciate it."

"They've been praying for her since this started."

Tears welled in her eyes. "She told me she couldn't pray, Peg. Not that she didn't want to, but she couldn't. I said I would until she felt she could, but I don't think she believes she's ever going to have the right to pray again."

"Sara said that?"

"No, but I felt it. If you'd been there, you'd know what I mean." Beth blinked hard. To go through tragedy alone...without God...it was too painful to bear.

"Whatever her trouble is, to have her feeling that way when she knows sure as certain it isn't so seems odd to me. Grace—"

"Exactly." Lavender scent. Beth glanced over and spotted the flowers.

Peggy frowned. "I'll call Annie and Miranda Kent right away. This requires more."

"Thanks." An urgency about Nora that Beth didn't understand flooded her. She rushed into the kitchen and snagged her purse. "Don't tell anyone where I've gone. I'll be back as soon as I can."

◦◦◦

The special phone vibrated at Joe's hip. Omega One.

Joe pulled off Highway 98 and onto the shoulder. Traffic noise was still too high. He whipped into a parking lot between two cars and answered the incoming phone call. "What's up?"

"Secure?"

He checked the cars parked nearby—empty—and no one was close on foot. "Yeah." The sun streaked down on his back.

"We intercepted an interesting conversation you need to hear. The voice is altered, but the content is of extreme interest."

"Play it."

"Stand by one." A pause, and then, "Here you go."

"Phoenix, this is Raven."

"Mission?"

"Dead Game," she said. *"Code?"*

"A72777," Phoenix said.

"Verified. I just received a kill order with instructions that you're to handle it yourself."

"Who is the subject?"

"A former Shadow Watcher. Joe alias Thomas Boudin."

"But the plan... I thought he—"

"The plan has changed and he is expendable—the sooner the better. This order comes from our European associate."

"All right."

"Be careful, Phoenix."

"I'm aware of his special skills."

"You'll enjoy this, I know. Do I need to worry that your personal pleasure will outweigh your professionalism?"

"Absolutely not. You know I never get emotionally involved."

"Counting on that." She sighed. *"Execute the order immediately."*

The tape ended. Joe swallowed hard.

"Did you get it all?" Omega One asked.

"Yeah, I got it." Not surprised, but knowing you had a contract out on you and hearing it was two different things. "They've already made one attempt. I was in a church. The man said he was Phoenix."

"Fatalities?"

"No. He punched a woman, we fought, and he dropped his gun. She found it. Fired at the ceiling and he took off. I was getting some distance before reporting it." Joe gave Omega One a description of the man and his car, fed in other details, then stopped.

"Okay, then," Omega One said. "Keep your gun close and powder dry."

"Will do. Appreciate the cover."

"We're doing all we can, but you know who you're dealing with. Watch your back."

"Always."

Joe stuffed the phone in his pocket, cranked up his motorcycle, and took off.

∾

Leaving Sara's house by the back door, Beth fished out her keys and headed for her car. When she stepped into the street, a man called out from behind her. "Beth! Beth, wait!"

Her heart beat hard and fast. She stopped and turned around. Thomas Boudin jogged toward her. *Joe.* His hair was darker, inky black and absent of gloss. She met him halfway, rushed into his arms.

Surprised by the contact, he stiffened. "Are—are you all right?"

Still unwilling to reveal himself. "No. I'm not all right. Where've you been? I've called and called—"

"You got my message?"

"No. Why haven't you taken my calls?"

"I came as soon as I could."

NINA? Beth looked up at him. "Sara's banned me from being around her—something is wickedly wrong, and she's trying to protect me…I think. I know she's in trouble, but she won't tell me a thing."

He looked around. "But you think…what?"

"I think someone in NINA has been pressuring Sara for information. She won't touch a Quantico file. She told Margaret to send everything from them directly to me and not to tell her a thing about hearing from them."

"Did she have a dispute with someone there or something?"

"No. The only thing that makes sense is she doesn't want to know because what she doesn't know she can't tell."

"What exactly do you and Sara do at Quantico? I'm assuming it's computer related."

"I can't say."

"Information-type computer work?"

She didn't answer.

"That's our club-attack connection. The missing groom is Robert."

"That's what I've been trying to tell you on the phone."

"I'm sorry." He stroked her face, dropped a tender kiss to her lips. "Couldn't be helped."

"Kiss me again and I'll forgive you."

"Gladly." His lips brushed hers, testing, then settled in and caressed.

When he pulled back, Beth nearly wept. Nothing. She'd felt nothing. How could she be so attracted to Joe and feel nothing?

The hint of a smile curved his lips. "I was getting worried."

He was oblivious. Joe was never oblivious. Confused and disappointed, she wasn't sure what to say or do. "No, I'm not immune to you."

"Didn't you get the message that the funeral was delayed?"

"I did." Jerked from the disappointment haze, her worry returned with a fury. "Nora!"

"What about her?"

"She isn't answering my calls."

"Is that unusual?"

"You know it's extremely unusual." What was wrong with him? As much as they'd talked about Nora, how could he not remember that? *Men.*

Unfair. He's got a lot on his mind. Beth pushed aside a mystery of the ages and started walking. "I'm going to check on her." She thumbed the SUV's remote entry. The locks clicked and she opened the door.

"I'll ride with you. If there's trouble, you shouldn't go alone." When they were seated inside, he buckled up, then said, "Beth, I have something to tell you."

"About what happened at the cemetery?" She keyed the engine. It roared to life.

"That too."

At least he wasn't denying that something had happened out there. What else could possibly…? His case. "Did you find a connection in your case with Robert?"

He frowned, hesitated, then ignored her question and turned the subject. "A man named Paul Clement contacted me."

Beth slid the gearshift into Drive and pulled out. "Never heard of him."

"He claims he has critical information on Robert. He wants a million dollars for it."

"Scam artist?" They were coming out of the woodwork like roaches. "Mel—the receptionist at Crossroads Crisis Center—has nixed at least two extortion attempts."

"He says he has proof Robert is alive."

Braked at the stop sign, Beth stilled. Joe had a lot of contacts still active in the intelligence community—a lot more than she had from her assists at Quantico. His Thomas Boudin persona was a former OSI agent. He had contacts too. "Did you check him out?"

"Yeah. He wasn't the kidnapper. Clement was in Angola then."

"Angola? What could a guy in southwest Africa—"

"Wrong Angola. Clement was in the Louisiana State Penitentiary."

Prison. Beth hit the gas, pulled out into traffic. "He heard something there?"

"Doubtful. He was in solitary confinement." Regret shone in Joe's eyes. "I've beaten the bushes, knocked off every leaf, and come up with nothing."

"What was he in jail for?"

"Cybercrimes. He's a hacker."

Odd that Beth hadn't heard of him. Notable hackers were on her radar. "NINA related?"

Joe stilled. Blinked. Then blinked again. "No connection I can find."

"Then why do you think he could be credible?" Pulling into Nora's slot in the Towers's parking lot, Beth cut the engine, then turned in her seat to face him.

Her phone rang.

Her special phone. *Joe. Joe?*

How could that be? He was sitting right beside her.

Or was he?

She gave the man beside her an exasperated look. "I've got to take this call." She scrambled out of the car and stepped out of earshot. "Hello?" Her heart thundered.

"Hi, gorgeous."

It beat harder, pounding against her ribs, echoing in her temples. "Joe?"

"Sorry I couldn't get back to you sooner. I ran into trouble."

"Tell me in a second." Did she trust her eyes or her ears? *Help me!* "Something strange is happening." Understatement of the year. Her ear burned; trust the phone. "I'm in a pickle, Joe."

All the lightness left his voice. "What's going on?"

She looked back but didn't see Thomas. "Is your real name Thomas Boudin?"

"Why?"

"Would you just answer me? I told you, I'm in trouble—immediate trouble."

"I use it."

"And you're doing whatever you're doing in disguise because NINA is after you?"

"Yes. Beth, what is—?"

"Things are worse than I thought then." Her hand shook hard.

"Stop and tell me what's happening."

She swallowed hard. "I'm with you—well, I thought it was you in disguise, right now, at the Towers, checking on Nora. She's not answering her phone. Only it can't be you because you're on the phone with me. Robert's dead, Sara's acting like an alien's invaded her body—"

"Stop. Wait. You're with *me*?"

"I thought it was you. Obviously it's not."

"Get away. *Now, Beth.* Whoever he is, he's probably NINA."

"But Nora—"

"You can't help her if you're dead. Run. Do you see any people?"

She scanned. "No."

"Businesses? Get to a business."

"There aren't any."

"Hide!"

Parked cars. She could hide among the cars. There wasn't even a decent-sized tree or bush she could use for cover. "I need to tell you—in case."

"Hide, sha. I'm on my way, but—"

He needed to know. "Something's going on at the cemetery."

"I know that. Will you stop this and hide so I can breathe again?"

"Joe, when I thought I was talking to you, I told...whoever he is...that I found a connection between the club attack and Robert."

"What connection?"

"Sara refused to take anything from Quantico. She told Margaret to send all of it to me and not even to let her know when something came in."

"NINA's pressuring her. And they went after Robert to force her to play ball."

"That was my thought, but define play ball."

"Get them intelligence information from Quantico."

"We're on the same page. I'm glad this guy with me isn't you."

"You're making me crazy, Beth. Are you hiding?"

"I'm looking for a place. Why does everyone drive little cars these days?"

"Did he hurt you?"

"Sort of."

"Sort of? I don't understand."

"He kissed me. I felt nothing. Nothing, Joe. I thought he was you and felt nothing." That had hurt.

"But it wasn't me, so that's good news. Are you hidden yet?"

Her feet hit a hollow spot in the pavement, jamming her ankle. Pain shot up her leg. "On my way to the far end of the parking lot."

"What's wrong? Your voice sounds funny. You're hurt."

"I just hit a pothole. Turned my ankle." Adrenaline shoved through her veins. NINA. He could be NINA and he'd kissed her? She shuddered. Steaming hot and ice-cold. Nowhere to go. Nowhere!

"Think steel, sha."

Think steel. Think steel. She kept moving. "Who in NINA would pretend to be you?"

"Too many to guess."

All bad. "I recognized you at Sara's house. So when you—he—approached me outside Sara's, I assumed he was you, well, except his hair was darker." She looked around. "I don't see him now. Do you really think he could be NINA?"

"I do." His voice cracked. "I'm coming as fast as I can. If he should find you, act normal. Don't let him know you're on to him."

"I don't see—wait, he's coming back. He was inside the Towers." She shuddered. "I can't make it anywhere. I've got to get back and talk fast." She made a U-turn.

"No. Don't go back!"

"I have to if I'm going to act normal, and you're going to get him, Joe."

"No way. Forget it, Beth. You're not bait."

She ignored him. "He said a man named Paul Clement—he was in jail in Louisiana, Angola—has proof Robert's alive and he wants a million dollars for it."

"You went back. Beth, why did you go back?"

"You know why."

"We're going to have a serious discussion about this, woman."

"I look forward to it." She'd love to be alive for that. "What about Clement?"

"I don't believe it. Robert bled out. Clement's trying to hose you or Sara. Don't get back in the car with this guy. I mean it. You do, and you're as good as dead. You hear me?"

"Joe, people in Mexico can hear you."

"Then you hear and listen. Delay or stall—whatever—but don't get in that car. I'm calling Mark and Jeff now."

"He's almost here. Hurry."

"Keep the line open but don't let him know you're still on the phone."

She stuffed the phone into her pocket, so scared she could scarcely breathe.

The fake Thomas Boudin walked the last three car lengths to join her. "Nora's fine. She just needed a break from Nathara." He smiled. "She was getting into the shower and said she'd call you in fifteen minutes."

He was lying. Nora showered and dressed an hour ago, just as the rest of them had; Beth would bank on it. "Great. I'll just hang out for a bit, then run up to see her."

"She's fine, Beth. I saw her myself."

"But I'm not. I need to talk to her about Sara." As she talked, Beth inched back toward the car. "She's grieving really hard and I need tips to help her." She jerked open the car door, threw herself inside, slammed then locked the doors.

The fake Thomas yanked at the door and beat on the window. "What are you doing? Have you lost your mind?"

Beth fumbled the keys. Dove for them, then keyed the engine. He got behind her so she couldn't back up. "Move!" she shouted through the glass. "I mean it."

He stayed in place.

She blasted her horn, hoping to snag someone's attention, then popped the gas. He dove out of the way, rolling over a sidewalk and onto a patch of grass. Stomping the accelerator, Beth took off down the street, her tires screeching, churning smoke, and darted her gaze to the rearview mirror. He was chasing her car down the street.

"I'm okay, Joe, but he's coming after me on foot. I'm in the SUV," she said, not taking her special phone out of her pocket. Out of reach and shaking hard, she fumbled for her regular cell phone. "Calling Nora so she won't open her door."

The phone rang and rang, but Nora didn't answer...

‿◦‿

Darla stared at Nora's bedroom door.

Kill her.

Her throat tight, Darla scanned the apartment. There wasn't anything in it that hadn't been destroyed. Tack Grady was merciless. NINA would appreciate that.

"Kill her somewhere else, then get to Sara's before you're missed."

Those were her orders, but images of the Crossroads chapel filled her mind. She'd been so peaceful there. So sure that if there were a chance God would ever hear her, it'd be at its tiny altar. She had poured out her heart to Him but felt…nothing. Still, she knew Beth hadn't lied. She wasn't beyond redemption. Maybe her heart hadn't been right? Something? But now, now she desperately needed Him and His help. Tears blurred her eyes.

God, I meant every word I said. I'm so sorry for everything I've done. I know I don't deserve Your forgiveness, but I'm begging You for it. I'm begging You to help me. I don't know what to do. I can't undo what I've done. There's no way to make things right. If I don't kill her, they will—and they'll kill me too. Help me. Please, help me. I don't want to hurt Nora. I don't want to ever hurt anyone ever again. I want what they have—the Crossroads people. They know You, and You know them. I want to know You, and if You can forgive me, I want You to know me. To make me into someone—anyone You want. Please, God. Please…

Warmth flooded Darla's body. She closed her eyes and let it wash through her, welcoming the most unusual sensation she'd ever in her life experienced. *Love.*

Unconditional love…

Darla's knees folded. She collapsed to the floor amid the clutter and wept in earnest.

A long while later, Darla stood and rushed into Nora's bedroom on wobbly feet. Nora sat on a kitchen chair, silver duct tape over her mouth, her arms and ankles tied. Fear burned in her eyes, a fear as deep as Darla felt churning inside her. "Don't scream," Darla said. When Nora nodded, Darla removed the duct tape.

"Where's Nathara and Tack Grady, that dirty dog?"

"Sara's." Working the ropes loose, Darla helped Nora to her feet. "You okay?"

"Madder than a wet hen, I'm thinking." She shoved at the rope. "Are you gonna kill me, Darla Green?"

She stilled. Her eyes burned, blurred with tears. "I don't have any choice."

16

⚬⚭⚬

At the corner of Highway 90, a siren wailed.

Beth pulled off the road and stopped, still dialing and redialing Nora, and still getting no answer.

A motorcycle whipped in beside her car. *Boudin!* She started to take off.

"Beth, it's me, Joe!"

Joe. Lighter hair. She studied his eyes, then hopped out of the car and rushed into his arms. He pulled her close, his body shaking. She pulled back. "Kiss me. Right now, Joseph!"

Joe touched his lips to hers, and Beth's world tilted on its axis. *A sign.* They were everywhere. In his gentle hands, his quaking body, his tender lips. He was Joe. And Joe was *the one.* She forced herself to pull back, nuzzled her face at his chest, felt his heart thunder under her cheek. "It's you." The urge to weep nearly overwhelmed her.

He lifted her chin with a gentle fingertip, studied her face. "You're okay, and you're not immune."

She smiled. "I'm definitely not immune."

He smiled back. "Me either, sha. I've never been more not immune in my life."

Beth hugged him hard. "I was so scared."

"Of the fake Thomas or of kissing me?"

"Both."

His gaze passed her, scanned the street. "Where is he?"

"I don't know. He was chasing me on foot last I saw him." She pulled back to look up into his face. "I—I should have known he wasn't you. He didn't know what you do about Nora. I didn't look closely enough at his eyes. He had on contacts. I got hung up on that." She should let him go, but she couldn't make herself do it.

A black Tahoe whipped around the corner and skidded to a stop.

Joe shoved her away from him, lifted his hands. "It's me, Jeff."

The barrel of Jeff's gun glinted at the tinted window. It slid down. "Is it Joe, Beth?"

"Yes," she said on a rushed breath.

The gun disappeared from view. "Where's Nora?"

"He said she was in the shower. I—don't know. I didn't see her." Beth dragged a hand through her hair. "She's not answering the phone."

"Step away from her," he told Joe.

Beth stepped forward, toward the Tahoe. "What are you doing? I told you…"

Jeff shoved her aside, knocking her off her feet, aiming his weapon at Joe. "What's the code?"

"Think steel."

Only a select few intimate with the Shadow Watchers would know *think steel*. Beth breathed easier. Got to her feet and stepped back to Joe.

"Sorry about that. I had to be sure." Jeff lowered his weapon. "Where's the imposter?"

"I don't know, but he's wearing a suit, not jeans like Joe." She grabbed a hank of her own hair. "And his hair is a lot darker. Flat, inky black."

"Who is he?" Jeff asked Joe.

"No idea."

Jeff blew out a sharp breath. "Have you called Nora?"

She'd told him Nora wasn't answering her phone. Scared. Upset. That had to be why he was so scattered. "Can't reach her. He said she was taking a shower, then she'd call."

Joe parked his Harley in the grass off the side of the road. "Get in the car and scoot over, sha." She did and Joe slid in behind the wheel. "Go, Jeff. Nora's at risk."

Jeff pulled out, calling for backup.

At first chance, Joe whipped Beth's car around and followed Jeff. "We've got a lot of talking to do."

"Yes, we do. But not now. Focus." Beth spoke her deepest fear. "The fake Thomas has to be NINA. Maybe Karl Masson." And he'd been in her car. She shivered.

"NINA, maybe. But he's not Masson."

Something in his voice had her looking at him. "How do you know?"

"Masson is dead. That's why I've been tied up. I found his body in the cove."

Could this mess get any more twisted? "What happened to him?"

"Shot. Hank Green is examining his body now."

"Did you shoot him?"

"No."

"There's a but after that no." She sensed it. "What is it?"

"I can't say right now." He spared her a glance. "When I can, I'll tell you."

"Is he the reason the funeral was delayed?"

"No. It was another attack. Chemical dispersants. Preliminary reports are that it's the same chemical used in the club attack. No secondary confirmation yet. We caught it before they could activate."

Which meant NINA likely did both. Beth clasped Joe's hand, squeezed tight. "Why is NINA playing with us like this?" Beth thought a second. "This show of force means they want something from one of us and they're not getting it. It's an intimidation tactic to incite fear." Beth sighed. "It's Sara. I know it is. They want information she can access at Quantico."

"NINA can get to Quantico direct. It doesn't need Sara. It has operatives and tentacles everywhere."

"Some people can get to some things at Quantico. Sara and I can get to everything."

"That does make targeting either of you efficient for them."

"Yes, it does." Beth's mind reeled, trying to make all this logical. "Sara's scared. But even for Robert she wouldn't give them anything."

"So maybe these attacks are window dressing, proving they can kill anytime they choose."

"Sara said that—at the club right after the attack. It makes sense, Joe. They're driving home the point."

"Missing groom on the cake. Sara admitting she's in trouble, keeping secrets, taking herself out of Quantico. Robert murdered..." Joe rubbed at his neck. "It all fits. The thing I want to know is, which of them isn't giving NINA what it wants? Sara or Robert?"

"Could it be either?"

"It could." Joe looked up at the Towers. "Or maybe it's Nora."

"Nora?"

"Raven is active in the village, Beth. Specifically from Nora's apartment."

"Nora is not Raven," Beth said. "No way."

"I pray you're right."

Two patrol cars pulled in and stopped behind them between the two rows of parked cars. Kyle jumped out, yelled over. "Stay put. Don't want you shot by mistake." He ran into the building.

Jeff's Tahoe door stood open and he was nowhere in sight. Apparently he'd already gone into the building.

Beth felt queasy. "You don't think Nora's there, do you?"

Joe looked over. "If she were, the fake Thomas wouldn't have come out without her."

Her chest went tight. "Unless he...hurt her." She couldn't make herself think *killed* much less say it. In her mind she imagined the imposter stealing Jeff's Tahoe and taking off. "Are you armed?"

"Always."

"Watch Jeff's vehicle." Beth began filling Joe in on events, and he shared his with her.

They'd just caught up when Jeff came out and walked straight over to the driver's window of Beth's SUV.

His face was pasty white. "Nora's apartment's been trashed. Clyde's pocket watch was on the floor, and someone at some point was restrained in a chair in Nora's bedroom. Under her pillow—"

Beth couldn't help herself. "Where's Nora?"

Jeff didn't meet her eyes. "Gone."

NINA had taken her. She shot Joe a look of sheer terror. He'd known—and been right.

"Stay calm, sha. We need clear heads." Joe clasped Beth's hand, held it on his thigh, then looked back to Jeff. "What was under Nora's pillow?"

"A scrap of paper—a note." Jeff's grim expression darkened. "It said, *I'm sorry.*"

Beth frowned. "Sorry about what?" Couldn't anything be straightforward and easy?

Kyle sprinted up to Jeff. "He's nowhere around, Detective. Units are still looking, but we're coming up dry."

Joe interrupted. "He said an Angola con named Paul Clement had proof Robert is alive. He wants a million for it."

"You know anything about that?" Jeff asked.

"Nothing. I think it was bogus. Just something he could confide to Beth."

"Run it anyway, Kyle." Jeff looked at Joe. "If this guy is no longer in disguise, we could trip over him. If Clement exists, could he be testing the waters himself?"

"Possible." Joe looked back at Beth. "Did you find a full-face photo of Robert?"

"No. I searched through everything at Sara's, scoured the village, and even asked Miranda Kent if she had one on file."

"Who is she?"

"A columnist for the local newspaper," Beth said. "But nobody in Seagrove Village has a single photo of him that shows his whole face."

Joe's eyes glazed. He'd expected that; it was clear in his expression. She turned to Jeff. "What can we do about Nora?"

"I've put out an APB." Jeff rubbed at his neck. "We found something else in the apartment. A pin—the kind you wear on a coat—was stuck in Nora's pillow." He touched a fingertip to his lapel.

"Nora wears pins all the time on her coat—not that she'd need a coat in June."

Jeff's eyes sparkled. "What's on them?"

"Flowers, swirls, different things like that."

"Have you ever seen her wear one of an animal or…"

"No—wait." Beth searched her mind. "She had a dove on her hat at the club."

"You're sure it was a dove?"

"I think so. It—oh, wait. That wasn't on Nora's hat. It was on Nathara's."

"Jeff," Joe interrupted, clearly out of patience. "What was on the pin?"

Jeff hesitated as if debating whether or not to reveal that information.

Joe pushed. "It's a raven, isn't it?"

His eyes somber, Jeff nodded.

Raven. "Like NINA's Raven? But Nathara is at Sara's. It couldn't be her pin."

"It could, but either way, it doesn't mean anything other than whoever trashed the apartment used it. You're sure it's Nathara's and not Nora's?"

"Nora wouldn't wear a bird," Beth said. "When we're on the balcony and the gulls get too close, she goes inside. She's scared of birds." Beth frowned, scanned her memory. "But there was definitely a bird on Nathara's hat. I remember it."

Joe withheld comment.

He said Raven was at Nora's, and that could be true. "Nora isn't Raven." She looked to Joe and saw what she most feared in his eyes: doubt.

"Hard to imagine, but Raven is ruthless and capable of anything."

"Nora's not. Nathara, maybe, but never Nora." Beth faced Jeff. "I'd ask for your opinion, but you don't speculate."

"She took Nora, or had her taken." Regret flooded Jeff's face. "Or...worse."

Joe groaned and stared out the windshield.

That petrified Beth. "What could be worse?"

Jeff struggled to meet her gaze but didn't utter a word.

Beth pushed. "Answer me, Jeff. What could be worse? Nathara wouldn't kill her twin. She does care about Nora." She did, right? She was here to take her to an eye specialist.

Still silent, he looked away.

"Why won't you answer me, Jeff?"

Joe sighed. "Jeff thinks Nora is Raven."

⟡

Jeff barked orders into his phone, then turned to Beth and Joe. "I'll go tell Sara and Peggy about Nora. Peg and Ben will mobilize the Crossroads folks to help search. Joe, can you do anything to save time on running down this Clement? Bogus or legit, we need to know."

Joe texted someone, then said, "If he's authentic, you'll have a file with photos on your cell in a few minutes. What about Nathara?"

"We can't keep Nora's disappearance from her and run a respectable search."

"Confide in Peggy. She'll watch Nathara and keep her from causing trouble."

"Good idea. Peg can spot a liar at fifty paces. I'll brief Mark too, of course."

"Very good idea." Joe nodded. "You know that we're not going to get to the bottom of all this until we find out who Robert Tayton III really is."

"I know." Jeff sighed.

So Robert wasn't Robert—or Joe doubted he was. "How are we supposed to do that? Sara knows next to nothing about him and she knows more than anyone else." Beth looked at Joe. "Have you rattled every bush?"

"All but one. Sam turned over a lead, but Masson's murder interrupted checking it out."

Kelly Walker would be able to sleep peacefully again, knowing Masson wasn't still stalking her. That'd make life easier for Ben and her.

Jeff leaned closer to the car window. "Who do you think Robert really is?"

"He could be Robert Tayton. It'll take a fast trip to Georgia to know for sure. Beth's coming with me. We're taking Ben's plane. Be back as fast as we can."

"Wait." Beth put a hand on Joe's sleeve. "What about the funeral? Sara will need—"

Jeff interrupted. "There's little sense in having a funeral for a man who could be alive. I don't believe it—blood isn't mutable evidence. But I'll talk to Sara about postponing until we verify Clement."

"Watch her." A few days ago, this news would have elated Sara. Now Beth had no idea how Sara would react. "First sign of an attack—"

"I'll contact Harvey Talbot." Jeff slapped the car frame at the lowered window, his neck crooked so he could peer in. "Roxy's got the FBI tied up at the cemetery, but Mark and Ben will guard Sara. If she's in trouble, odds are strong it's NINA trouble. With her Quantico connections, they won't mess around—and, yes, Beth, that's a warning to you too."

"She'll be with me," Joe said again.

Jeff stared at Joe a long second, took note of Beth's hand on Joe's sleeve. "Got it."

His reaction proved he wasn't half in love with Beth anymore. Jeff had fallen—and, Beth feared, fallen hard—for Sara. Oh, but she hoped they didn't both wind up brokenhearted again. Sara was either still married or a new widow. Neither boded well for Jeff and her, and she needed a break. Time to heal and restore. Time...

Maybe she'd already had time. Her reactions had been strange for some time. She wasn't in love with Robert anymore; Beth felt certain of that. Had Sara already mourned her marriage not being what she hoped it would be? Robert not being the man he professed to be? She did wish she could go back…

Stop, Beth. You're reading too much into this. Or you could be.

"Call if you find Nora," Beth told Jeff. "I don't feel right about not staying here to search for her, but I know this is necessary." Others could do anything she could do in the search, but she had special insights that could help Joe. "We'll hurry."

"Try not to worry." Jeff backed up a step. "She means a lot to me too."

"Sara or Nora?" Beth asked.

"Both." He didn't hedge or look away.

Regret speared through Beth, and she spoke before thinking and censoring herself. "I wish Sara had married you instead of Robert."

Jeff didn't respond, but what could he say? Remorse flooded her. Jeff's face went red and Joe's lip curled. He was amused. Well, she shouldn't have done it but she had. At least it'd been honest. "I'm sorry, Jeff. I was out of line." Not perfect, as apologies go, but also honest.

"No problem. Actually, I'm flattered. When it comes to Sara, you're selective." His expression softened. "Check in when you can."

"We will," Joe said.

Jeff left in his Tahoe and Joe backed out of the parking slot. "Did you forget for a second Sara has a husband and Jeff half thinks you killed him?"

"I'm not used to being considered a suspect. I thought it and it spilled out before I could stop myself." Beth sighed. "Open mouth and insert fo—leg, actually. Up to my kneecap."

Joe's eyes twinkled. "But you meant it. Are you playing Cupid now?"

"No, that's Peggy's specialty." Beth snagged her sunglasses from their overhead holder and tapped them into place on her nose. "They're good together. That's all. Sara's different around Jeff. She talks."

"She doesn't talk otherwise?"

"Not like she does with him. She used to be crazy about him. I didn't know it until recently, but I think she still is."

"Because she talks to him?"

"Because she looks at him like I look at you."

He rewarded her with a smile. Lifted their clasped hands and planted a kiss to her knuckles. "He's a lucky man, then."

"Provided he doesn't break her heart."

Curiosity replaced Joe's smile. "Are you still worried I'm going to break your heart?"

More than worried. To the bone scared of it—and even more afraid because he could. How had he gotten that kind of power over her when she knew from the first look he was a woman magnet like Max? It didn't make sense. Actually, it did. He wasn't like Max and he was perfect for her. Her heart knew it. Her head was just having trouble catching up. "Are you?"

"No. Are you going to break mine?"

"As if I could." She resisted a snicker, biting her lower lip.

"Oh, you can, sha. Trust me on that."

Truth shone in his eyes. She let it settle in. "In that case, no, I'm not. I'll guard your heart, Joe. That's a promise."

"I believe you." The smile didn't return, but such tenderness and gratitude filled his eyes that it left Beth breathless. He needed that assurance, her assurance. He needed to feel special.

Too tender. She cleared her throat. "Where in Georgia are we going?"

"Just north of Atlanta."

Robert met Sara in Atlanta. "Who's there?"

"I don't know for sure."

"Joseph." She put a bite in her tone.

"Sorry, gorgeous. Keeping as much as possible to myself is in my genes— or I thought it was. With you, I'm different."

"It's in your training, not your genes. I'm glad I'm different, but I'm not a potential enemy, and hazarding a guess, my clearances are probably higher than yours."

They weren't, but they were close. "I think it might be Robert's parents."

"If they've been estranged from Robert for years, what can they tell us?"

"For one thing, they can positively identify their son." Joe braked for a red light and looked over at her. "And for another, if he is their son, they can tell us if they think he is capable of murder."

Beth was totally confused. Robert was purportedly a victim. They had no hard evidence he was tied to NINA. "Who do you think he killed?"

"Give me a minute and I'll tell you." Joe pulled out his ringing phone. "Yeah, bro."

Mark Taylor. He was the only person Joe called *bro.*

Beth's thoughts turned. *Robert, a murderer?* She couldn't see it. First, he'd never get his own hands dirty—literally or figuratively; too highbrow for that. Secondly, at the time of the club attack and Clyde's death, he had already been kidnapped. And he'd reportedly bled out on the mattress in Magnolia Branch before Karl Masson died. That wasn't faked. It was his blood. Too much of his blood for him to still be alive. So how did a man who'd bled out, bleed out and live? And if he had lived, who was left to be his victim in a murder?

⚬✄⚬

Jeff walked into a crowd at Sara's and approached Mark, Harvey, and Roxy huddled near the front window.

Mark nodded. "I've briefed Roxy and Harvey."

"Good." Jeff scanned the living room. Tack stood talking with Nathara in hushed tones. "Does Nathara know?" Someone had to tell Nora's twin, and he shamefully hoped it wouldn't have to be him. She wouldn't take the news well. Movement at the doorway leading to the kitchen caught his eye—Darla coming in through the back door, her phone in her hand. Must have stepped out to make a call.

"No." Mark glanced at Nathara. "We weren't sure how you wanted to handle that."

Figured. "Has to be done to get a search fully operational." He swung his gaze back to Mark. "Where's Sara?"

"In the den," Roxy said. "I don't know on what, Jeff, but she's holding back."

He respected Roxy's instincts. "Did she say something?"

Roxy shook her head no. "Cop's gut."

Jeff had felt it himself. As he and Sara had grown closer, he'd hoped she'd open up to him on whatever she was withholding, but so far she'd kept her secrets. Did she suspect Robert was still alive? Or were her secrets worse? Jeff had no idea, and he wasn't going to find out standing here. "I'd best get to it, then." He resisted the urge to go straight to Sara and stepped over to Nathara.

"You look like death warmed over, Jeff Meyers." She looked up at him. A black rose bobbed at the base of her hat where it met the brim. "What's wrong now?"

"Nora is missing." The room went quiet and everyone tuned in. "Her apartment was ransacked. Kyle will be in to get a statement from you on when you last saw her, who was there and—"

"I was there with Nathara," Tack said. "Everything was fine when we left."

"Well, things are not fine now." Jeff didn't mention the note or the fake Thomas Boudin. "The evidence is overwhelming that Nora's been abducted."

"Hogwash. Who would kidnap an old, worn-out housekeeper?"

Is that what Nathara thought of her sister? Nora was many things, but there was nothing worn-out about her. She kept a fine house and nurtured everyone who needed it. There wasn't a stray in the village she didn't watch over. If Nathara didn't know that, she didn't know her twin. Maybe she was as mean as a snake. "I'll keep you posted on developments."

She frowned. "At least tell me if there were signs she was hurt."

Finally, a humane response. "No overt signs, no." Jeff addressed the group. "An unidentified male was seen running from the Towers on foot. We'll have a description and maybe photos shortly." He frowned. "I need help on this. We have limited resources, and they're already stretched to the max."

"An unidentified male?" Nathara stared at the floor. The color leaked from her face. Nora would have been in full swing, assigning everyone duties. How different they were...

Peggy Crane stepped forward. "I'll get Crossroads ramped up. Route the calls in to us. We'll get teams organized to search. They'll be ready to go when you give us the word."

Tack rubbed at his neck. "I'll get down to Ruby's and get the word out. Peggy, fax me the description over there. I'll get us some recruits and disperse the information."

Darla stood beside Peggy. "I'll call Hank. Peggy aside, no one spreads the word as fast as Hank Green."

Darla was wrong about that. Hank was no slouch, but Megan, the waitress at Ruby's, was twice as quick as anyone else in the village. Jeff glanced at Roxy. She was already on the phone with the FBI team working the club attack and the thwarted cemetery attack.

"Jeff?" Sara stood at the den door. "What's going on?"

Mark touched Jeff's sleeve. "Go talk to her privately. I'll handle things out here."

Jeff nodded, then joined Sara. His throat was thick. Her hair was pulled up and little wisps of it trailed down her neck. "You were resting?"

"Pretending to." She stepped back into the den. "I just needed a few minutes alone."

After he told her what they'd learned, she'd need far more than a few minutes. Man, but he hated bringing her more worries. "Sit down, Sara. We need to talk."

"I heard you say Nora's been abducted." Sara sat on the edge of the sofa and clasped her hands in her lap, her back stiff. "Do you think they...hurt her?"

They, not *he*. "It doesn't appear so."

She swallowed hard. "It's NINA, Jeff."

He took a risk. "I'm leaning in that direction."

Sara looked him right in the eye. "That wasn't a question."

His heart rate sped. "Are you ready to tell me what you're keeping from me?"

Her gaze shifted to the floor. "I don't know what you're talking about."

Apparently, not yet. Disappointed, Jeff waited. Silence was a powerful tool. She'd fill it with something. Hopefully, some insight.

"Where's Beth? She and Nora are so close. She's got to be frantic."

"She's with Joe. They're checking something for me."

"I hurt her, Jeff. She's the sister of my heart, and I've hurt her badly." Tears glossed Sara's eyes. "She'll deal with whatever comes—Beth always deals with whatever comes—but I told her to stay away from me for a while. I'm not strong like her. If she's close, I'll never stand on my own feet, and I really need to do that right now."

"Because of Robert?"

Sara hesitated. "Partly, but not just because of him."

A crack. Finally. "Why, then?"

"It's time." She looked from the floor back to him, a wealth of sadness in her eyes.

He let the silence stretch between them, then tried to prepare her. Did she have her inhaler? He didn't see it. "You know Robert's dead, right? The blood—"

"I know that amount of blood loss makes survival impossible."

"Keep that in mind with what I'm about to tell you." He waited for her nod, then went on. "A man named Paul Clement claims he has proof Robert is alive. He wants a million dollars for it."

A sharp breath escaped her. There was no joy, no upset, no other visible sign of any emotion. Just the sharp breath. "Do you need your inhaler?"

"No. I'm fine." Her hands stayed folded in her lap. "Who is Clement?"

"We don't think he's credible. No one has unearthed even a remote connection."

"A scam artist." She frowned. "Do you think Robert's alive?"

Jeff didn't hesitate. "With forensics verifying the volume of blood and that it was Robert's? No, Sara, I don't." He clasped her hand. "I don't see how he could be."

She squeezed his hand tight, but her voice sounded weak. "I'm not so sure."

Her hand was ice-cold, but her breathing was steady. "Why?"

She covered their clasped hands with her free one. "I'd tell you, but then they'd probably kill you." A tear trickled down her cheek.

Beth was right. Sara was keeping secrets. Deadly ones. "Do you trust me, Sara?"

"Yes."

"Then be honest with me."

The war raging inside her showed in her swift expressions. "I can't. I want to, but… Don't you see? I'd just be replacing leaning on Beth with leaning on you. I have to lean on me."

"I understand what you're saying, but this isn't the time to stand alone." She was wrong. "We're dealing with NINA. You know more about that organization than I do. I shouldn't have to remind you what they're capable of doing and how far they'll go to get what they want. Villagers have been put in lethal jeopardy twice in the past week. Nora's missing and Clyde Parker is dead."

"Don't you think I know that?" She let out a charged sigh. "They could have killed everyone at Roxy and Harvey's ceremony—and, I suspect, at Robert's funeral, if you and Mark hadn't intervened. I know what they're capable of doing. Believe me."

The truth slammed into Jeff and he stilled. "What have they done to you?"

No answer.

"Sara?" He clasped her hand. "I can help. But I need to know the truth. Nora's life could depend on it."

Sara slumped, seemed about to reveal what she'd hidden, but a second later stiffened, eased her hand from his and said…nothing.

Jeff prodded, tried every technique in law enforcement and in his personal repertoire. He pleaded, coerced, and even begged, but Sara still held her silence…and took off her shoes.

Jeff looked down at her feet. Swollen. Bruised and battered. Shock pumped through his chest and fell to outrage. He took a moment to reign in his temper, another to bury it, and then finally looked up at her. "Who?" He didn't trust himself to say more.

Tears spilled down her face. "Robert."

Jeff opened his arms. She leaned into them and wept.

17

இ௬

idflight, Beth looked over from the right seat to Joe, piloting the plane. "This trip—Robert's parents—it's the other case you were talking about when you came to see Sara as Boudin."

"Yes."

"Are you going to tell me about it?"

"I am, but first I need processing perspective."

"What are you talking about?"

"Sara. I need to get inside her head."

"Good luck." Beth sighed.

"Just give me your impressions on her behavior lately."

"I've told you most of it already," Beth said. "In a word, she's acted bizarre."

"In what way?"

"You know about the terrace messenger."

"I do?"

"No games, Joe. I know he was you."

"How? You never saw me."

He was worried his disguise had failed. "Smell. Your skin has a distinct smell. Your cologne has a distinct smell and your mints have a distinct smell."

"I can't do anything about the skin, but the cologne and mints—I'm as hooked on the mints as I used to be on cigarettes."

It was chewing gum, then mints. "Might consider letting them go. You don't need them anymore."

"Could be dangerous, all right." He fished a couple from his shirt pocket and put them in a pouch near his hip. "Guess it's time."

Beth smiled and stroked his arm. "You know Sara warned me to protect myself and SaBe from her, and to protect her from herself, if I could." When he nodded, Beth went on, hoping to convey everything in some semblance of order he could grasp. "The really bizarre stuff started at the river, when we were making the money drop for Robert's abduction. She admitted she was hiding something but wouldn't talk about it. I tried everything, even guilt, but she's nothing if not stubborn. Still, I got the feeling she was trying to protect me and SaBe."

"From what?"

"I don't know for sure. But she worked too hard at keeping whatever this is to herself for it to be about anyone but Robert. We talk about everything but him."

"Robert?"

"I know. I was shocked too. I didn't know it then, but Henry Baines—SaBe's senior legal advisor—called me after the mattress blood matched Robert's. I said I hadn't gotten Sara to sign the agreement to keep Robert out of SaBe, and I was glad I hadn't had to have that conversation with her. He was surprised."

"Why?"

"I don't know exactly—yet."

"He wouldn't tell you?"

"Couldn't, legally."

"Did you ask Sara?"

"No, too much happened. I had the agreement with me, and I was going to ask her to sign it, but then Robert got abducted and—"

"I get it. Lousy timing."

"Exactly." Her seat belt dug into her side. Beth adjusted it. "Then Sara started saying such odd things, like she wished she could go back to the way things were—"

"Were, when?"

"In context, I'd have to say to a time before Robert."

Joe spoke to the tower and made an altitude adjustment. "So was she plan-ning on leaving him?"

"I didn't think so, and neither did Henry, but now, I don't know."

"What's changed?"

Beth wished she could avoid sharing this, but holding back anything from Joe could do more harm than good. Nora could pay the price. "Remember the bad check incident I told you about? Where Robert had moved Sara's money and she didn't know it?"

"Yes." Joe grimaced. "Frankly, I'm surprised she'd give him control."

"I was too. Sara and I respect our money. We've worked hard to earn it." Beth thought a second. Stilled. *Money. Of course.* "Can I make a phone call from here?"

"Sure." He passed her his red phone. "Use this one. It's secure."

"Not a security violation, right?"

"No, I've got global clearance." He grinned. "I don't do space."

"Glad to hear it." She dialed Henry Baines's cell.

"Baines."

"Henry, it's Beth." She waited for him to stop fluttering. He'd heard about the near-miss cemetery attack. "Henry, listen to me. I need information now."

"But Nora is missing. She's a village institution. People are swarming the streets."

"She'll be okay." Beth prayed it was true. "Mark, Ben, and Jeff are search-ing and the Crossroads staff is helping."

"Sara won't take my calls."

"She's a bit out of sorts, Henry. Considering everything, I'm sure you under-stand." Beth was losing patience. *Help me.* Henry chattered on, talking about everything and everyone at once. "Henry, stop."

Silence.

"I need to know something that's none of my business but it could help solve all of this."

"All right. Just don't ask me to violate my ethics."

"You know I admire your ethics, but right now, my concern is saving Nora's life. So bear that in mind."

"I understand."

"After the check incident at the bank, did Sara take precautions to protect her assets from Robert?"

He hesitated. "What kind of precautions?"

"Financial ones?" She took a stab at where Robert would be most apt to strike.

"Yes."

Beth's heart beat hard and fast. "What precautions did she take?"

"I can't answer that. It's definitely a violation—"

"Henry, Sara's in trouble and I'm trying to save her life as well as Nora's. If I fail because of what you didn't tell me…"

"She signed an agreement to keep Robert out of SaBe."

"Why'd you prepare another at my request then?"

"Because clearly she hadn't told you she'd done it, and I hoped maybe she would."

An opportunity to be honest with Beth. "Did she do anything else?"

"She moved all her money—I don't know where—and she put Robert on an allowance. It goes directly into an account that is only in his name. There is a POD listed on it, however."

"What's a POD?"

"Payable on death."

"Who is the beneficiary? Sara?"

"Actually, no. You are, Beth."

"Me?" Shock pumped through her body. "Why would Sara put me on Robert's account?"

"She didn't, he did."

"Why?" She was the last person Robert would want to have anything from him—unless…

"I don't know. I assumed the two of you had some agreement."

"No, we don't have an agreement. I didn't know it."

"Then his actions are irrational."

Apparently, not to Robert. "Does Sara know this?"

"It's doubtful. His money is automatically deposited on the first of each month. The statements go directly to him. Sara provides the funds but is in no way personally involved. Margaret monitors the transfers and his financial activity. She might be able to tell you more."

"Just so I'm clear," Beth said. "Sara hid her assets from Robert."

"That's correct. And she wrote him out of her will, though he doesn't know that."

"Are you sure?"

"Positive. I'm holding the original, and if Robert Tayton knew he wasn't getting a dime, he'd be pounding on my desk and making Sara miserable."

He would. "Was she divorcing him?"

"Sara?" He harrumphed. "Sara would never divorce. You know that."

Poor Sara. All her dreams of a family of her own again shattered. "I didn't think so."

"I have to say though, she created as much distance between them as possible."

"Is there anything else—anything at all—that might be important to know?"

"Not to my knowledge. But talk to Margaret. She might know things I don't."

"I will. Thank you, Henry." Beth ended the call and looked at Joe. "Sara cut Robert off. She put him on an allowance."

"Ouch." Joe winced. "I'm sure that didn't go over well. Not with his lifestyle."

"She changed her will and hid her assets. Even Henry doesn't know where she put anything." Beth's stomach fluttered. "Sara mentally divorced him. Why would she do that? Family means everything to her, so she had a strong reason." Beth dialed the phone.

"Who are you calling now?"

"Margaret."

"Sara's not going to tell the cloud queen things she wouldn't tell you."

"No, but the cloud queen is sharp and she does things Sara needs doing as part of her job. She might have picked up on something."

"Make it quick. It's nearly time to descend."

Margaret answered the phone. "SaBe."

"It's Beth, Margaret. I'm pressed for time and I need information fast. What do you know about Sara's financial relationship with Robert?"

"Beth, that's private."

"I'm trying to keep her alive."

"Literally or figuratively?"

"Two attacks and who knows what else. There's nothing figurative about it."

"He's tried everything under the sun to find out where her money is, but he hasn't done it. She put him on a fixed income, and he is raging about it. That's why he went to New Orleans to talk to a publisher about his book. He's trying to earn some cash. Novel concept, eh? To work for a living like the rest of us?"

For Robert it was novel. "Do you know there's a POD on his account?"

"Yes. But I don't know who it is."

"I just found out that it's me. Why would he do that?"

"I don't know. Maybe punishing Sara for cutting him off? She's done a lot of strange things lately, Beth. It's hard to say what she's thinking."

"What kind of strange things?"

"I've told you most of this. For months she's refused to talk to anyone from Quantico. She has me screen her e-mail and forward her personal stuff to a separate account—she won't check any of the other accounts—and anything from Quantico is rerouted to you. She won't take their calls either—no contact whatsoever."

"She's been hiding from Quantico for months?" Afraid, Beth looked at Joe, saw her reaction reflected in his eyes. "I thought that had just started since the club attack."

"Months. She's not hiding exactly. More like disassociating. We never say no to any government entity, of course, but everything goes to you. She specifically instructed me that she didn't want to know anything on anything about any of it—not Quantico, not our clients, or even SaBe business. She hasn't been in the lab in weeks."

"She's been there. I've seen her."

"You've seen her in her office, not in the lab. She stays holed up there." Margaret sounded so worried. "And, Beth, she gave me some documents too."

Sara avoiding the lab? She had to be miserable to do that. "What kind of documents?"

"Ones giving you and Henry her full authorization to do whatever you want with the company."

Beth shoved her hair back from her face. "Why didn't you tell me?"

"Sara wouldn't let me. She said if anything came up where you needed them, then I was supposed to give them to you and Henry together—so you'd be witnesses for each other that the documents were authentic. She had me notarize them."

The more Beth heard, the more afraid she became. "Anything else?"

"Just that I talked to your mother. She tried to reach you earlier but couldn't. I haven't been able to either, and I've tried every fifteen minutes since I got off the phone with her."

Every fifteen minutes. What was so urgent? "Sorry. About what?"

"Your mother is really worried, Beth. She's convinced Sara's in some kind of trouble."

"Does she think it's personal or professional?"

"She thinks Sara's bent on keeping you out of it. That's all she knows."

Now her mother had picked up on this too? Definitely confirmation. "If you find out anything else, let me know."

Joe touched her arm. "You need to end the call, sha."

Descent time. "I'll call back when I can," Beth told Margaret. "Grill my mom a little. Tell her it's vital."

"I will."

Beth passed the phone back to Joe, told him all she'd learned.

"Avoiding Quantico for months." He rubbed his neck. "Confirmation someone's trying to force her to share what she knows."

Beth's heart thundered. "NINA is after Sara and using Robert to get to her."

"Maybe." Joe mulled a moment. "Or maybe Robert is working with NINA and they're both after info from her."

"You think Robert's hooked in with NINA too?" A shudder rippled through Beth.

"I don't know—yet. If Sara's nipped his fiscal wings, he could be an outsider wanting to have something to sell. NINA would certainly buy."

He'd do that. Beth didn't doubt it for a second. "Oh, Joe. Either way, Sara's in a world of hurt. We need to warn Jeff."

"As soon as we land."

Beth reeled. "They'll kill her. She's resisted them, but they have to know if abducting Robert didn't work, nothing will. They'll kill her and use him to get what they want."

"How? He's disinherited and out of SaBe." Joe adjusted the controls. The plane's nose dipped. "He won't get access to anything."

"He doesn't know he's been disinherited or cut out. Henry's sure of it."

Joe processed that and seemed to relax. "Then we have a plan, sha." He smiled. "One that could work."

How could he smile? Relax? A plan? "I missed a step. What plan?"

"There's only one way to keep Sara alive." Joe looked at Beth, steely resolve in his eyes. "She has to die."

"Have you lost your mind?"

He tapped his temple. "If she's dead, my love, then two things happen. They can't kill her and…"

Beth drew a sharp breath. "If Robert is alive, he'll return to claim Sara's money."

"And the information NINA wants." Joe winked.

He'd called her *my love*. Her heart banged against her ribs. "You're a lot smarter than you pretend to be, Joseph. More devious too."

"I prefer *resourceful*." The plane touched down. "Sometimes my wits are all I've had."

That put knots in Beth's stomach. NINA wasn't just after Sara and what she knew. It had to be responsible for Nora's disappearance, though only the Good Lord knew why. And if NINA couldn't get what it wanted from Sara, and Robert returned and it couldn't get what it wanted from him, then there'd be only one person left for them to target.

Beth.

☙❧

The ring tone was distinct. The red phone.

Raven stepped outside through Sara's back door, then walked beyond the patio to a patch of grass where her privacy was assured. "Hello."

"Raven, it's me."

Jackal. She checked her watch. Her Swiss boss was worried. Otherwise he'd never be calling her at this hour. Contrary at being forced to choose between NINA and Nora, she sniffed. "Verification, please."

"Jackal."

"Mission?"

"Dead Game. Code A72777."

"Verified. What can I do for you?"

"You can tell me the assets have been acquired."

The intelligence Sara had on breaching Quantico's computer. The stupid woman was being stubborn. For a fragile little snip, she was standing firm. Raven had been confident Robert's kidnapping would break her, but the idiot woman hadn't budged. "Still in progress. We've experienced an unexpected development."

"I heard about the failed attack at the cemetery. Has Gray Ghost lost his touch?"

"I'm afraid Gray Ghost was the development. He's dead."

"Who killed him?"

Raven didn't dare admit the truth. "It'll be in the out-briefing. Initial indications are one of our own went rogue." Raven hadn't put a fall girl in place for nothing. If someone went down, it wouldn't be her. The way things were shaping up, it seemed that preparation was wiser than originally anticipated. In fact, she could kill two birds with one stone. *You're nobody's fool.* Raven had to move up or out in the organization, and Jackal and Phoenix clearly were angling to position Phoenix as Raven's replacement. That was not going to happen. Raven's future would be secured.

"Can you use Tack Grady?"

"He's fine for political purposes but incompetent at this type of thing." She checked the yard; she was still alone. "I'm handling it myself."

"Are you telling me there's jeopardy of a compromise?"

Foolish question. There were always risks of compromise. "Mine or the mission's?"

"Either."

Her position with the locals guaranteed her acceptance; none suspected she was Raven. If not for Nora, she could have remained active here indefinitely. Doubt niggled. Had Nora told anyone her suspicions? Unlikely, though she had been about to. She clearly deduced the truth at her apartment, but when Tack snipped the phone line, it had been ringing; no one had answered. Nora tried to out her. That infuriated Raven. "I have no immediate compromise concerns, but delivering the target alive is no longer an option." She was in too tight with Jeff.

"Eliminate her then." He switched subjects. "Has Phoenix emerged?"

"Not yet. He didn't retrieve the money from the river or the Gulf." She didn't like having to report anything less than a hundred percent success on one of her missions, but considering she wanted Phoenix to fail to ruin his credibility, it wasn't completely painful.

"This mission is taking too long, Raven. The board is increasingly concerned…"

"Everything is under control. I just need a little time."

"How much time?"

"Ten days." Far more than she needed.

"Whatever is unresolved in a week, destroy, and shut Dead Game down."

"Shut it down?" In twenty years, she'd never shut down an operation.

"Yes." He grunted. "That village has become a bane to us—and one more thing."

"Yes sir?" If she shut down Dead Game, her future couldn't be bleaker.

"Do not disappoint me again."

"No sir." She knew that tone for the warning it was. She'd used it herself many times. Fail and she'd be terminated. "Raven out."

18

A bad feeling dragged at Beth's stomach.

She sat silently as Joe drove to Marietta, following Sam's e-mail draft directions to the estate he believed belonged to Robert's parents. Looking out the window, she saw nothing that should incite dread. The Martins' was an exclusive, old-money neighborhood filled with huge magnolia trees, manicured lawns, and stately old houses. Calm and serene.

"If Robert's parents live here, he had to be a silver-spoon kid." Beth removed her sunglasses and looked more closely at the gracious homes.

"Looks like." Joe pulled close to the curb. "This is it."

Beth took a deep breath. "Are we walking into the lions' den?"

"Maybe." Joe removed the keys. "You take the lead and I'll back you up as needed."

"You're the pro."

"Yes, I am. And we're dealing with southern parents about their child. Woman to woman is our best bet for getting maximum information. You relate on a whole different level."

"Better than a pro?"

"Frankly, no. This is just more expedient." He wrinkled his nose. "You're fretting. Don't. Just be yourself. I'm here and I'll do my part, but we'll get what we need sooner through you."

"Is that an attempt to avoid emotion?" When he frowned, she added, "Just curious, not judging."

"Sha, I'm all about emotion with you. This is logic based on scientific study—and not knowing if the Martins are ordinary people or in with NINA."

"Ah, the whole truth dawns."

If he used interrogation techniques on them and they were NINA, they'd spot them immediately. He was good—had an amazing dossier—but he was human.

"Gorgeous and bright. Heady combination." He squeezed her arm. "Takes my breath away."

"Focus, Joseph." She admonished him but couldn't muster any heat. "Remember the lions' den."

"Right." His expression sobered and a distant look replaced the warmth in his eyes.

They could be NINA? Beth tried to calm down and left the car. At Joe's side, she walked up the old brick walkway, circled a fountain in its center, then stepped under the covered porch to the front door and rang the bell.

A maid answered, wearing a traditional black-and-white starched uniform. "Good evening. May I help you?"

Joe told her who they were, then asked, "May we have a word with Linda or James Martin?"

Beth hid her surprise.

The maid asked them to wait, then closed the door.

"Martin?" she whispered to Joe. "I thought this was Robert's parents."

"It is." He looked at her, about to explain, but the door opened.

"I'm sorry," the maid said. "Neither Mr. nor Mrs. Martin are available." She started to close the door.

Martin. That had to have come from his intelligence sources. Beth stretched out a hand, stopped her. "Wait. Please. Just five minutes." She let the woman see her worry. "I'm begging them. We've come all the way from Florida. It's so important." She fished a business card from her purse. "Here, give them my card. They can check me out online or I can give them Detective Meyers's phone number. He's a police detective in Seagrove Village, Florida. That's where we're from." She shoved the card into the woman's hand. Maybe with all that, with her website and the *ichthus* symbol on her card, they'd at least give them a chance. "I could be killed. Tell them that. It's true, I swear it."

The maid's eyes stretched wide. She glanced at the card, measured Beth, and then nodded. "I'll tell them. You wait here."

The door closed and the lock clicked into place. Beth's heart sank.

"She isn't sure if we're honest, criminals, or just crazy."

Beth frowned at Joe. "Do you blame her? It's what we'd think."

Minutes ticked by. Three, then five. Finally the door opened and the maid showed them in. "They're in the library. This way, please."

The turn-of-the-century mansion was in pristine condition, and the architectural details were gorgeous. Beth turned into the library, a masculine room filled with shelves of books lining all the walls. In the center of the open space, two sofas faced each other, and on the east and west stood leather wingback chairs. A third that matched sat near a window, and from its worn patina reflecting in the lamplight, it was someone's favorite and had been for many years.

Beth skirted a bust of Shakespeare on a bronze column and saw the Martins. Robert's resemblance was striking; James and Linda Martin were definitely his parents. In twenty years, Robert would look exactly like his father. His mother was tiny, a fragile-looking woman with silver hair and tender blue eyes, but Robert was clearly her son.

"Thank you for seeing us." Beth extended her hand. "I'm Beth Dawson and this is—"

"Jared Blanchard," Joe said.

Beth wasn't prepared for that name but didn't dare let it show.

"Please, sit down." Mr. Martin's tone was formal and stiff, his gray hair freshly clipped and neat. He wore a tan summer sweater that should be yet wasn't rumpled, as if it knew he wouldn't tolerate a crease.

"May Selina get you a beverage?"

"No, thank you, Mrs. Martin," Beth said. "We apologize for intruding, but it's critical to my well-being that we talk with you about your son, Robert."

Her composure melted, Linda Martin shot a worried look at her husband. He went to her side, stood with a protective hand on her shoulder. "Robert is no longer mentioned in our home, Miss Dawson." Mrs. Martin telegraphed how hard that loss was for her.

"I'm sorry. Please, may I explain the necessity?"

Beth waited for their approval. Joe seemed uncertain they would agree. That instilled doubt in her. If they refused, then what?

The Martins shared a look. Mr. Martin nodded. "Very well, Miss Dawson."

Any hope for cooperation rested with total honesty. Otherwise, they wouldn't reveal a thing. She hated the pain the truth about Robert would inflict. *The facts, as objectively as possible.* Resolved, Beth began with Robert meeting Sara in Atlanta.

When she was done, Mr. Martin stared at the floor for a long moment. "Our son is capable of great evil, Miss Dawson. He is driven by money—it's what divided us. He took advantage of a woman whose husband was terminally ill. The police came here looking for him. When he phoned, we told him to stay away from us."

Mrs. Martin wrung her hands. "You must understand. Robert has always been in trouble. We tried everything, but nothing worked. When we refused to help him evade police, he threatened us."

"Did he escape?" Joe asked.

"As far as we know." Mr. Martin stuffed a hand in his pocket. "We haven't heard from him again. For a few years, we had no idea where he was, but then my wife saw a photograph of him in the society page with your friend Sara Jones."

Sara Jones-Tayton. Why were they refusing to acknowledge Sara? Even if their son was a slug, she was their daughter-in-law. Mrs. Martin projected a strong, controlled image, but her son's heinous acts broke her heart; it showed in every weary line on her face.

"We heard about the kidnapping, of course—Sara was on the news all day—and then that Robert was…dead." Fat tears rolled down Mrs. Martin's cheeks.

Her husband pretended not to see them and Beth and Joe followed his lead. Mr. Martin sat on the sofa across from them, as if Robert's death had physically knocked his legs out from under him. Their raw pain choked Beth up. *Help them, Lord. They're so hurt…*

Silence fell. Long recuperative minutes were needed and taken.

"How long has it been since you've seen him?" Joe asked.

Mr. Martin sucked in a ragged breath, his agony in his eyes, in the slump of his shoulders. "Over three years." He blew out a staggered breath. "Our son disappointed us in many ways, but after hearing about this current situation, I'm convinced we never really knew him. Even at his worst, we never considered him capable of anything like…this."

"James," his wife said, "we tried everything."

"Yes." Anger seeped into Mr. Martin's voice. He focused on Joe. "Robert had everything and appreciated nothing. In his eyes, the world belonged to him and having it all was his right."

"I'm afraid he clung to that arrogance," Joe said.

"I'm sorry to hear that." Mr. Martin looked beyond the wall and into the past. "We taught him privilege carries responsibility, but he refused to learn that and much more."

Mrs. Martin entered the conversation. "It wasn't a matter of intellect. Robert was very bright. We insisted he do something worthy to help the community. He was wonderful with the patients."

The patients? Beth alerted.

Mrs. Martin went on before she could ask. "With him, it was always a lack of character. Robert consistently made unwise choices that hurt others. He hurt himself as well—we have no idea why, though we've spent many hours speculating." She tilted her head. Her silver hair gleamed in the light. "He was a medical student, you know."

"I didn't know," Beth said, seizing the opening to return to this. "He's very private."

Mrs. Martin lifted her eyebrows. "For good reason, considering his crimes."

"That was the crux in his fall from grace." Mr. Martin sat back, lifted his glasses, then pinched the bridge of his nose. "Robert thought he was above having to do the work required of him as a student. His attitude was arrogant and ironic. Of all the students in his class, he was one of a precious few not working his way through medical school. We handed it to him, so he had more time to do the work and study than most in his class. Instead, he cheated."

"It was an absolute disgrace." Mrs. Martin sniffed.

"To him, Linda, not to us," Mr. Martin reminded his wife. "Robert followed the path of least resistance. It was easier to cheat than to study, so he cheated. In his mind, he was above the rules. They only applied to others."

Beth glanced at Joe. A medical student could draw blood. A shiver crept up her spine.

"So he was caught cheating?" Joe asked.

"Yes. During that ordeal we discovered he was taking advantage of an elderly woman." Mr. Martin frowned, his brows meeting in the center of his forehead. "That's when we realized how serious a problem his arrogance had become."

"It ruined him." Mrs. Martin pulled a hanky out of her pocket and dabbed at her eyes. "We just couldn't believe it."

They were unassuming. It wouldn't occur to them to think as Robert did. He'd devastated them. Still devastated them.

Mr. Martin stood and paced behind the sofa, the discussion cutting too close to the bone. "We could have donated a new building and the dean would have allowed Robert to stay in medical school. I'm ashamed to say Linda and I discussed it."

"The acts of a brash young man shouldn't destroy his life," Linda said.

"Robert nixed that notion, however," Mr. Martin said. "He fully expected us to donate the building and to do whatever we must to make the problem go away. That's when we knew…"

"Knew what?" Joe asked.

"That it was time for our son to stand or fall on his own." Mrs. Martin sniffed again. "It was the hardest thing we've ever done, but we stepped back and let Robert be thrown out of school. He was livid."

"Outraged—and he demanded we allow him to return home," Mr. Martin elaborated, the agony of their decisions ravaging his face. "We had to hire a team of security guards to keep him out, but we did it."

"He retaliated, of course," Mrs. Martin said.

Beth laid a hand at her throat. "He didn't hurt you?"

"He threatened to, but no. The security people disabused him of that idea," she said. "He stole a great deal of money from us." Even now, she seemed unable to really believe that had happened. "And then he left us that awful note."

"What did it say?" Joe asked.

Mr. Martin answered. "Not this time."

"What did he mean?" Beth set her purse on the floor at her feet.

"That we had opposed him and he'd still succeeded. He'd gotten our money and then took even more of it, stealing checks and forging our signatures."

"I'm so sorry." The words rushed from Beth's heart and out of her mouth. Robert hadn't just been a disappointment; he had shamed them and shattered their hearts.

"He refused professional help, insisting he didn't need it," Mrs. Martin said. "He wanted what he wanted: a lot of money and the time to spend it doing exactly as he pleased."

That set Mr. Martin off. "No responsibility, no obligations, and not one snippet of remorse for anyone he hurt along the way. It was appalling."

"And why we banned him from our lives." Mrs. Martin blinked, owl-eyed. "Our only son…"

Mr. Martin sat back down beside his wife, taking her frail hand in his.

Beth wanted to smack Robert. What was wrong with him that he could be so self-absorbed and selfish when he had two people who obviously loved him dearly? Sara would have adored them, and they her. "For your sakes, I wish with all my heart I was wrong about him. But I'm not." Beth teared up. She blinked hard to hide it, but their expressions revealed they'd seen her turmoil. "I'm so sorry."

Beth glanced at the photographs littering the top of the piano—and stopped short. "May I look at those?" She nodded to the pictures.

Mr. Martin lifted a hand. "Of course."

Beth lifted the one that had stopped her cold. Joe moved to her side and she tilted the frame so he could see what she did. Robert, Darla Green, Tack Grady, and Nathara.

"When was this taken?" Joe asked.

"Five years ago," Mrs. Martin said. "Robert invited some of his friends for lunch in the garden. Nora loved the garden. She was fond of heather."

"Nora?" Beth looked closely. That was definitely not Nora. It was Nathara. She signaled Joe to snap pictures of the photograph with his phone.

"An adorable woman, Nora. I so enjoyed her."

Joe and Beth exchanged a loaded glance and reached the same conclusion. Enough harm had been done to the Martins. For now, they thought their son was dead, and it was best they continued to think it until his fate was fact.

"Thank you for talking with us."

"I wish we could have been more help." Mr. Martin sighed. "Take care, Miss Dawson."

"I will."

"Take care of Sara too." Mrs. Martin blinked hard. "She seems like a lovely woman."

"She is."

Joe and Mr. Martin shook hands. "I wish the news had been better, Mr. Martin."

"Me too."

Beth and Joe left the library and Selina showed them out. When Beth heard both of the Martins collapse into sobs, she shot a worried look at their maid. "Will they be okay?"

"I'll take care of them," she whispered. "If you get a chance, spit on that ungrateful boy's grave. The pain he's caused his parents is unforgivable."

Selina had heard every word. "Keep close watch on them," Joe said. "Security for a time might be a good idea. Robert had some bad friends."

"I'll call right away."

Beth patted her arm and then walked outside. Joe's eyes were shining overly bright. "You okay?"

"Yeah. Just looking for justice where there isn't any." He opened the car door. "What I would have done for parents like that. They love that heartless wreck more than life itself, and he's too warped to appreciate them. People like that make me crazy, Beth."

"I know. Me too." She meant it sincerely. "They seem like such good people. How did he become such a rat?"

"Choice. Every day when we get out of bed, we decide what kind of people we're going to be, a blessing or a curse. He chose to be a curse—every day."

Beth liked Joe's armchair wisdom, and his appreciation for family. "Did you get the pictures?"

He pulled away from the curb, dialing his phone. "Sending them ahead now."

She didn't ask where. Didn't have to; Jeff, and his friends still in the inner circle in Intel. Seconds later, he dialed again, paused, then said, "Jeff, it's Joe. We're on our way back to the plane. Robert Tayton III is definitely Robert T. Martin." He paused. "Yeah, and we saw a photo of him with Darla Green, Tack Grady, and Nathara. Already e-mailed it to you." A pause, then, "I agree. He's NINA." Another pause. "No, no way. He's not Jackal. But he's in the middle of all this." Another long pause. "We'll talk with her when we get back. We need them loose to see what they do. Just keep all three on a short leash—and tell Mark to get extra security on Sara. If what we're thinking is right, she's in lethal jeopardy."

Those words hit Beth like a punch to the stomach. She closed her eyes, forced her muscles to relax. Things were finally starting to make sense.

"Beth and I will talk to them first thing in the morning." He tilted the receiver. "Sha, write this down, will you?"

She grabbed a pen and wrote on the back of a deposit slip from her checkbook. "Ken Matheson and Bill Conlee. Call Bill 'Deacon.' Millie, the dispatcher, will locate them for us." Joe yielded to traffic and pulled into the right lane on the interstate, heading for the airport. "I won't tell you not to worry, Jeff. But I've got a plan. After we talk to the officers, we'll conference on it. Make sure Mark, Ben, and Roxy are briefed." Soon, Joe pocketed his phone.

Beth clipped the pen to the slip of paper and set it in the console. "Ken and Bill. Why are we going to see the officers up north who found the mattress?"

"We need to get their impressions—the things that don't make it into reports."

Beth jotted another note. "We also need the original lab tests on that mattress."

Joe glanced over. "Why? I'm ninety percent sure Robert's alive. It's a moot point."

Her mind raced ahead. "Because it's possible that the combination of the officers' impressions and the lab test results prove Robert choreographed everything that's happened."

"How?"

Beth dipped her chin. "The truth is in his blood."

19

Tack drained his glass, then looked at Darla. Uncertainty flickered in his eyes. "This Plan B isn't a positive development."

He wasn't ordered to kill anyone. He had nothing to complain about. "Why is that?"

"I was supposed to be mayor. This new plan puts Phoenix in my slot."

"So they have other plans for you." Darla had known Tack Grady a long time and hadn't been surprised to learn from Jackal he was a NINA operative. She was surprised Tack didn't expect NINA to use and dispose of him.

"That's what worries me." He tugged a baseball cap down, shading his eyes.

"Don't do anything stupid." Darla felt compelled to warn him. "Jackal will kill you."

"Don't you get it?" Tack tilted his chin. "We're both already dead."

Chills seized her body. Darla watched him walk away, knowing he was right.

"Trust Me."

God. If he hadn't already abandoned her, He wasn't going to. *Okay. What do I do? Tell me. What do I do?*

"Plan C."

And it was there, fully blown inside her mind. She knew exactly what to do.

Hurrying inside, she fished her car keys from her handbag. Tack would follow her, of course. Or run for his life—which would be the human thing to do but also wasted effort. No one outran NINA. Darla learned that firsthand. She'd tried and tried. With John, she'd been content if not happy. For a woman like her, content was more than enough. Yet she'd been issued her orders: *"Kill John or Karl Masson will kill John and Lance and you'll watch."*

She drove toward Sara Tayton's, doubled back, and stopped at Wal-Mart. Darla hadn't spotted Tack but developed a cover story in case he followed and confronted her. Hopefully he was too worried about saving his own hide to worry about what she was doing.

She bought a prepaid mobile phone, activated it, returned to her car, and then dialed Jeff.

"Detective Meyers."

"It's Darla. Is your phone clean?"

"Secure, why?" Surprise rippled in his voice.

"Get Beth, Sara, Joe, Mark, Ben, Peggy, and Roxy to Sara's now. It's an emergency."

"What emergency?"

"I'll explain later. Just do it, Jeff."

"Joe and Beth aren't available right now."

"Everyone else then—and hide their cars so they can't be seen from the street."

"Darla, this isn't a time for games. I'm up to my eyeballs in alligators."

"If you don't meet me, odds are good Sara's going to be dead."

"Sara?"

"Yes." That was Plan B. Clearing the deck for Phoenix required getting rid of Sara. Darla pulled out onto the highway and raced toward Sara's. "If Tack Grady sees any of you there, I'm dead. You understand what I'm saying, Jeff?"

"NINA."

He understood. And any chance for her fresh start was gone. But the only death staining her new soul would be her own. A tear slipped to her cheek. *Let me die quickly, okay?*

That's all she had the right to ask, yet her deepest regret tore at her heart, demanding she ask one thing more. *Protect my son. Let Lance be the kind of man his father was, good and kind and loving and strong. Let him be nothing like me.*

CXO

Joe turned the Highlander onto Highway 90, heading north toward Magnolia Branch community. When he got off the phone with the Walton County sheriff's office, Beth asked, "Where are they meeting us?"

"On the property, at the rusty shed."

"I should have brought flowers for Clyde's grave."

"Next time." Joe squeezed her hand. "We'd better get sharp on their report."

She pulled out their findings notes and read aloud the report Ken Matheson and Bill Conlee, the officers who'd found the bloody mattress, had filed. When she was done, she glanced over at Joe. "Hear anything unusual?"

"No, but didn't expect to. Their impressions don't get into the reports."

Again, a worry nagged at Beth. "Do you think we can trust them? So many are in with NINA—people we didn't think could be." Doubt about Darla speared her, and she hoped her instincts were wrong.

"Jeff says we can."

"That's hedging." Beth dipped her sunglasses down on her nose. "What do you say?"

"We'll see."

"That's what I thought."

He smiled. "You know me too well, sha."

That thought should have scared her right out of her shoes. Instead, it comforted her. She smiled back. "I do, don't I?"

"Ah, she loves me. I can see it."

"Don't tease me, Joseph. I might be falling in love with you just a little, but that doesn't mean I trust you."

"You trust me, gorgeous." He kissed her wrist. "It's yourself you don't trust."

She opened her mouth to protest, but before a word left her mouth, she realized he was right. "I hate it when you do that."

"What?"

"Know my mind before I know my mind." She frowned. "It's just wrong."

"Blame it on love. It makes me look harder, notice more. It makes me eager to know everything."

Any second her heart was going to rocket right out of her chest. "Even the bad stuff?"

"Especially the bad stuff."

She looked out the window, insanely content. A man who knew the bad stuff and loved her anyway. *Amazing—and nothing at all like Max.* Spotting the mailbox post, she pointed. "Is that it?"

He checked the GPS coordinates on his phone app. "Looks like."

The washboard dirt road had dust lifting into a cloud behind them. Joe drove on and the rusty shed came into view, looming like the remains of a life. With all the weeds and twisted trees, knowing what was found in that shed and what had been done there had Beth's skin crawling.

"You okay?" Joe scanned her face.

"Creeped out, but fine."

"Considering the history here, being creeped out is sensible." He parked near the rusty shed beside Bill and Ken's police cruiser.

"Owning it is worse. We're ditching it. I might burn this shed down."

"Couldn't blame you." He winked. "Ready?"

She nodded and they got out of the SUV, then greeted Ken Matheson and Bill Conlee. Both were in uniform. Matheson was young and brash, and Bill carried the weariness of a more seasoned cop. She liked him immediately and in their discussion pegged him as a teddy bear of a man: respectful and very careful to be precise and accurate. Matheson called him Deacon, and Joe asked how he'd gotten the moniker.

Ken gave Joe an odd look. "He's a deacon."

Beth bit back a smile and listened to all they had to say about the discovery and everything that had happened afterward. When they were done, Beth still wasn't convinced. "Bill, how could Robert Tayton, med student or no, lose all that blood and survive?"

Squinting against the late afternoon sun, he seemed lost in thought. "That's troubled me too. The heat in the shed that day stole my breath away."

"What the heat didn't take, the stench did." Ken scrunched his face. "It would've gagged maggots."

Bill shot him a look to keep his comments to himself. "Yet the blood was cold. I still haven't figured that out."

Joe's eyes narrowed. "Cold? In that heat?"

"In that heat." Bill nodded. "Figured the blood might be stage props because of it, but forensics don't lie. It was Mr. Tayton's blood."

Joe rubbed at his temple. "I don't remember cold blood being in your report."

Bill looked to his partner.

Ken shrugged. "My fault if it's not. I wrote it up."

"Better check it again and if it isn't, file a supplemental correcting that."

"Will do, Deacon."

Bill remained thoughtful. "I remember stooping down by the mattress—it was pretty disconcerting to see that much blood, you know—and spotting a glint. Looked like a glass shard until it disappeared right before my eyes." He shrugged. "I put it down to a trick of the light, but now, I wonder."

"Mind if I take a look in the shed?" Joe asked.

"No reason not to. Coroner's released it and Beth owns it." Bill cocked his head. "The lock's busted…"

"Thank you, Bill." Joe extended his hand.

He clasped and shook. "You thinking that blood was on ice?"

Joe nodded. "It's the only thing that makes sense."

"Could be right." The deputies retreated to their cruiser, then headed to the highway.

"You can wait out here," Joe said. "I won't be long."

Gathering his own impressions. Beth's instincts hummed. "Thoughtful, but I'm coming. Just stay close."

"For as long as you like, sha."

They walked through the dark shed with flashlights. "Ugh. Ken wasn't joking about the stench." She gagged.

"Go back outside." Joe looked closely. "I'll be just a second."

Not waiting to be told twice, Beth stepped out the door and gulped in fresh air. *Horrible place. Definitely razing it.*

When Joe came outside, he looked green. "Man, that's raunchy." He kept walking toward the Highlander.

Beth stepped lively to catch up, slid into the car, and as soon as Joe started it, she turned up the air full blast to blow off the stink and cool down. "We need to look hard at the forensics report on that mattress." She reached for the findings file.

"What are you thinking?"

From his expression, he knew exactly what she was thinking. He was testing her, pure and simple. "That I was even more right than I originally thought. The truth really is in Robert's blood." She flipped open the file. "Forensics estimated the loss at six pints. That's more than enough to kill a man and end any further investigation."

"Not without a body." Joe glanced her way. "They had to prepare to go before a judge and declare no doubt that the man was dead."

Hope sparked. "So they ran other tests immediately, while the blood was fresh and accurate results could be obtained?"

"A variety of them." Joe glanced at Beth. "What are you looking for?"

Another test. Hand to her face, she admitted, "I don't know." Obviously Robert hadn't lost all that blood at one time or he'd be dead. "Did you personally review the report?"

"He was dead—case closed." Joe shrugged. "Come drive and I'll look at it now."

They switched seats and he dove into the report. Several page flips, then suddenly he stopped. "Whoa."

"What?"

"The samples tested from different areas of the mattress have different glucose results."

"Sugar levels change, depending what you eat or drink, whether or not you're exercising—all kinds of things affect that."

"Yeah, but not this substantially, this short-term," Joe said.

"Which proves…"

Joe's expression flattened. "The blood came out of Robert but over time. Not in a single, violent bleed-out incident."

The little hairs on her neck lifted. "I hoped you'd say that." Beth signaled a left turn back onto Highway 331. "A med student could draw blood. If he did it over time, then he had to preserve it." She glanced at Joe. "Freeze it?"

"Thaw it at one time, it decomposes at one time." Joe nodded. "Forensics was first interested in quantity to see if they were looking for a wounded or dead man. Once they determined he was dead, they'd run the battery of tests, but why bother with more than a cursory review of the results? The guy had to be dead."

"Bill Conlee said the blood was cold—and that disappearing glint he thought was glass could have been ice." She reached for her phone. "I'm calling Jeff to search Sara's freezer."

"He's already checked hers and Darla Green's and Nora's."

"You've already thought of all this."

He smiled.

"Why are you testing me?"

"You're smart, Beth. It's helpful to know how smart."

"So how am I doing?"

"Great." He gave her a dreamy smile. "I'm enchanted."

She snorted and smacked his thigh. "Focus, Joseph."

"I am, sha."

"Not on me. On where else Robert would hide frozen blood and the stuff he needed to draw it." Beth tapped the steering wheel. "He's taken extreme measures to point blame elsewhere. If he's alive, he had to know someone would look into how he dropped six pints of blood and lived. He'd be prepared."

"What aren't you saying?"

He read her like a book. "It's a game to Robert and he means to win. He'd blame me."

"For control of SaBe, he might."

"Then NINA gets what it wants—whether he's with them or their victim—and he gets what he wants. Me out of his way." Beth continued thinking aloud. "Sara pulled the financial plug on him. He'd kill her for that. Doing what he did to his parents, do you doubt he'd do it to Sara?"

"No." Joe grunted his disgust. "He couldn't get to her money through her anymore, so it's logical he'd steal Sara's power to access it. But then you still stood in his way."

Beth nodded. "But if he got me out of the way and drove Sara into an attack that killed her, then he'd have free reign with her money and at SaBe."

"Not if she died. If she died, he didn't get a dime."

"He doesn't know that."

"Maybe he does." Joe frowned. "What if he did know and he wanted her alive? He forces her to bend to his will, you're out of the way, and he has free reign personally and at SaBe." Joe stilled. "Robert didn't set you up for his kidnapping, sha. He set up Sara. If she's alive and in jail for kidnapping him, he gets access to her money and SaBe, including whatever NINA wants to know—unless Sara countered that move and he knows that too."

"Okay, it could turn out to be any or all of those things. Regardless, Robert covers his bases. If he didn't know he'd been disinherited, it makes sense. If he did, it still makes sense. Either way, he neutralizes Sara and me and he's running everything unfettered except my personal funds."

Joe chewed a stick of gum.

"Craving a cigarette?"

"For the first time in months." His frown deepened.

"It'll pass."

He wadded up the wrapper. "Yeah."

"So weighing it all, which of us do you think he set up, Joe?" Beth felt torn. "I can see it either way."

"I think both, but I'm still working through it." He chewed slowly. "So say Robert knew Sara had cut him out of her will. If he got her arrested for his abduction, then she's on ice in prison and he can spend at will."

"Just her personal funds. Not SaBe's." Beth nodded. "But that only works if Sara's alive. He had to figure all this stress would cause an attack with high odds of killing her. He's too sharp not to realize that."

"Yes. Which makes setting you up the better choice because SaBe is where the real money is." Joe stuffed the gum into the wadded paper. "Robert might not have known what Sara had done, but he had to suspect she might. If he's alive, he'd keep as many options as possible open to blame her or you. Give himself maximum flexibility."

"If he's alive."

"Or if NINA brought him into Dead Game, got rid of him, and stepped into his place."

Robert might have started all this on his own and then NINA forced its way in. He could join them or die. "That's possible too." Beth looked over. "Did you find out anything on Clement?" He supposedly had proof Robert was alive.

"He's disappeared."

"NINA?"

"Maybe." Joe didn't spare her a glance. "My sources don't expect him to surface."

Someone had gotten to the man. Beth's stomach soured. "So where did

Robert freeze and store the blood?" Beth searched her mind, blinked and then blinked again. The answer was so obvious she'd looked right past it. "At the one place Sara and I frequently accessed and he rarely showed up. SaBe."

"That could implicate anyone who works there." Joe blew out a breath. "Maximum flexibility. But wouldn't someone notice blood in the freezer?"

"Doubtful," Beth said. "No one uses the freezer. I've never opened it. The fridge has a door dispenser for water and ice—and I'll bet no one else has opened the freezer part either."

Joe shot her a questioning look. "Robert has a key to SaBe offices?"

"Sara's." Beth shrugged. "He snitches it, copies it, returns the original, and he's in. No one is around on the weekends except one security guard. He could go in and pull the blood. He'd have all the privacy in the world."

"That's motive, means, and opportunity. But if he was setting up Sara, what would her motive be for kidnapping him?"

"Other than him blowing through her money, bouncing checks, and causing her a lot of grief? Her housekeeper said Sara's been really unhappy. Robert could use that against her."

"He could definitely make that work." Joe glanced over. "We're on target, sha. Let's force his hand."

"How?"

"We'll run this by Jeff. If it holds up, then we leak to the press that you and Sara have been cleared in Robert's case, we have two persons of interest, and, if things go as we expect, we'll be making an arrest shortly."

"If he is alive, that'll freak him out." A little bolt of pleasure rippled through her.

"It'll have him ready to commit murder. Yours and Sara's." Joe looked at Beth, a frown settling deep on his face. "It'll freak out NINA too. I'm not so comfortable with that."

"Neither am I. But it could be the only way we'll ever know if he's acting with NINA or in spite of them." Beth mulled it over and then made the call, grateful Joe would be there, watching her back. And—no small thing—she wouldn't have to be strong alone. If she needed to, she could lean on him, and he'd be there for her. A little shiver raced through her. *Definitely a sign.* It warmed her inside, down deep.

"Talk to Jeff. Let's flush Robert out and find out how he and NINA connect." She shoved her hair back from her face. "But first let's go to SaBe and check the freezer."

Joe's phone rang. "Jeff," he told Beth, then put him on speaker.

"When will you guys be back?"

"Fifteen minutes," Beth estimated.

"Go straight to Sara's and park around back so your car can't be seen from the street."

"Why? What's happened now?" Her heart skipped a full beat. "Oh no. Is it Nora?"

"No word on Nora," Jeff said. "Darla Green's called an emergency meeting and those were her instructions."

"What for?" Joe asked.

"I don't know, but she wants Mark and Roxy and Peggy here too, and she said it was a matter of life and death."

"Whose?" Beth cast a worried look that Joe returned.

"At this point," Jeff said, "who knows?"

20

A ll those summoned sat grim faced at Sara's kitchen table.

"They don't look happy," Joe whispered from beside her.

They didn't. Beth braced for more bad news. "Darla?" She'd called the meeting, and she'd be quickest to cut to the chase.

She shot a dread-laced look at Jeff. "I can't tell her this. I—I can't."

Beth stepped into her line of vision. "You can tell me anything," she spoke softly.

"Not this." Darla's eyes filled with tears and she blinked hard. "I thought I could. I found God, Beth, and I thought that would make it easier, but it's not. It's just not." She took a tissue Sara offered her. "Thanks."

Jeff vacated his chair, stood by Joe, and Beth sat beside Darla. "God doesn't make the bad things in your life go away. He just gives you the strength to deal with them. You have to do the dealing with them."

"You'll hate me." Darla stiffened. "You really will."

"I know you're working with NINA. I know you have been for a long time."

"But you believed…"

"I did believe you. But a lot's happened. What I want to know is what you've done. Are you Raven?"

"No. I'm not Raven. I swear it."

Beth covertly looked at Peggy. She could spot a lie in a heartbeat and signaled Darla was being honest. "Who is?"

"Nathara. She ordered me to kill Nora."

Everyone around Beth gasped. She didn't. "You didn't kill Nora."

"How do you know what I did or didn't do?"

"I just know. Where's Nora?"

✣

Looking into Beth's eyes, Darla relived what had happened at Nora's after she'd gotten Nora into her car…

"I told you back at the apartment." Darla looked over to Nora, buckled into the passenger's seat of her car. "If I don't kill you, they'll kill me."

Nora clamped her jaw. "I know you ain't thinking I'm gonna help you kill me, Darla Green."

"I don't want to kill you. If you're gone, they'll think I did what I was told. You live, I live—at least until they find out you're alive. Then we're both in trouble."

"Could you slow down? You're driving like a maniac." Nora grabbed the dashboard and frowned. "Where are you taking me?"

It took all Darla's willpower not to stomp the gas pedal and pray for wings to fly. "The one place I know you'll be safe. But if you let anyone know you're there, we're both dead. You understand what I'm telling you?"

"'Course I understand, dearie. I didn't just fall off the turnip truck. We're dealing with NINA. They play hardball. I just didn't know they'd be playing it in my house. Now I see why my village is plagued by NINA. It's not us messing up their plans. It's me."

"I'd say it's a fair share of both."

"My sister. Raven. Killing her own kin—or having it done. She's a coward."

"She's jealous. Envious." Nathara hated Nora for being beloved.

"God will deal with her." Nora grabbed the dash again. Her wrists were red and raw from the adhesive on the duct tape. "Where's this safe place you're stashing me?"

"Three Gables. The security there is the best money can buy. But even Mark or Ben can't know you're there."

Nora sighed her relief. "Take me to the back fence, then. I can cut through the grounds and get to the cottage."

"Can you see well enough to do that?"

"I ain't blind yet."

That was debatable, but they didn't have much choice. "What about security? They'll see you."

"I got my ways, dearie."

Darla drove around the edge of the Towers and saw Jeff's black Tahoe. "Oh no. We took too long. The police are already here. There's no way out, Nora." Panic burned in Darla.

"Quit your hissy fit and take the alley, dearie. Cut through over there." She pointed to a sand-covered alleyway paralleling the beach. "Just go where I say. I'll get us out of here."

And she did.

Fifteen minutes later they pulled up to the street alongside Three Gables, and when Darla stopped near the fence, Nora turned to her. "Why are you helping me? You were right. NINA doesn't mess around. They'll kill you, sure as spit."

"If they kill me, it's okay." She swallowed hard. "I'll be okay."

"Dead ain't exactly okay, Darla Green."

She spared Nora a glance. "I know now where I'm going."

Nora narrowed her eyes. "What's happened to you?"

"God, Nora." The back of her nose burned. "I found Him."

Nora clasped her forearm. "Dearie, He wasn't lost."

Darla let out a hushed breath. "No, but I was."

Nora squeezed her hand. "Thank you for not killing me. I'm old and worn out, but I'd like to keep my life a wee bit longer. I ain't finished with it yet."

Darla nodded. "Stay hidden until I come to get you, or you will be."

Stiffening her shoulders, Nora narrowed her gaze. "You be careful."

"Yes ma'am. I'll do my best."

"You'll need to be telling Jeff you killed John—and that my stupid sister is Raven."

"You're assuming I killed John. But that's okay. I promise I'll do the right thing." She couldn't live with lies in her life. Not ever again.

"Keep in mind that God forgives. Man ain't so kindly predisposed."

Didn't she know it? "It's going to take a little time to do what I have to do. You make sure no one sees you."

"I understand." Nora climbed out, reached around a fence post, flipped some kind of switch, then slipped through the wire fence and into the green-belt abutting Three Gables.

Darla waited for the alarm to sound, but it didn't. Apparently that switch deactivated it. Still, she watched Nora until she disappeared into the trees. "Oh, please tell me I didn't just make the biggest mistake of my life. If anything happens to her, the entire village will stand in line to lynch me."

Worry about that if you survive NINA.

Shaking so hard she could barely hold the steering wheel, Darla headed to Sara's, determined to do everything she could to make things right.

She arrived at Sara's just as Jeff had. Just looking at him had her knees shaking so hard she feared they'd fold. But when she later walked outside and saw Nathara on her red phone, Darla, who had never in her life fainted, had seen spots before her eyes and her head went light.

Nathara glared at her. "What's wrong with you?"

What wasn't? "I'm fine." She looked pointedly at the red phone still in Nathara's hand. "Everything okay?"

"We have a week. With Nora out of the way, we shouldn't need it." Nathara frowned. "You did take care of Nora."

Darla nodded. "I told you I did."

"Pity she put things together." Raven took in a slow breath. "She always was bright. An emotional fool, but bright."

Darla stared at Nathara.

"What?"

"She was your sister."

Nathara's condemnation remained unspoken but annoyed anyway. "I'm aware of that. We are twins."

"Yes." Darla's expression cooled and she stepped back. "Do I have further orders?"

"Indirectly." She looked beyond Darla to Tack Grady, who joined them. "Ah, good. You're here."

He nodded, the brim of his baseball cap shading his eyes.

His grim expression frayed Darla's nerves, and she prayed to be smart enough to live long enough to tell Beth and Jeff the truth. Doubt that she would clawed at her.

"I don't like what I'm hearing, Tack." Nathara glared. "The villagers are working too hard to find Nora. Don't these idiots know people don't get involved anymore?"

"Nora is beloved." Darla shrugged. Nathara was cold and ruthless but not as smart as she thought or she'd know people would search forever for Nora. Guess that made her smart on some things, but she sure didn't understand people or tender emotions, and she sure didn't understand her sister.

"Why?" Nathara seemed genuinely perplexed.

"Nora loves unconditionally and cares for those who have no one else." Darla shrugged again. It was like explaining love itself. Or what happened with her awakening to God. It defied words and required heart. Nathara's heart had been blackened by the evil she'd let run wild. She couldn't grasp what she couldn't grasp—not without divine intervention. Evil was like that. It smothered everything good until it became alien. Until even if you sensed or witnessed it, you had no concept of what you were sensing or witnessing.

"That's the trouble," Nathara said. "People rely on someone else to take care of them instead of taking care of themselves. She's to blame for that. They should hate her, and instead the idiot sheep adore her." She grunted. "This search could complicate matters for Phoenix." Focusing on Tack, she added, "It's time for the next phase in this Dead Game mission."

Tack looked stunned. "But the election is two months away."

"We can't wait."

Darla asked a question she feared hearing answered. "Can't wait for what?"

Tack shrank back, stuffed his hands in the pockets of his cargo pants.

"For Hank Green to die of seminatural causes and Phoenix to step into the mayor's job." Raven revealed the original plan in the mission. "That would have ended the complications we've encountered. Unfortunately, my sister ruined it."

Tack looked taken aback. "I'm running for mayor, not Phoenix."

"I'm aware of that."

The lines alongside his mouth deepened to grooves and his jaw went tight, but no heat carried over into his voice. "If they find Nora's body they'll stop searching." He looked to Darla. "Where'd you dump her?"

Darla's stomach dropped to her knees. *Please, don't let them see the truth in my face.* "In the woods."

Impatient, Nathara pushed. "There are a lot woods here. Where?"

"Near Three Gables." Darla thought fast. "I figured if they found her body quickly, then their attention would be diverted."

"I'll get people looking in that direction." Tack turned away, reaching for his phone.

"No." Nathara lifted a hand. "Let them continue searching. It'll diffuse focus."

Darla's heart beat hard and fast. "From what?"

Nathara gave her a smile that chilled her blood to ice. "Plan B."

What did that mean? Darla had seen that look on Nathara's face before— when she'd ordered Nora's death—and didn't dare utter a word.

Tack did. "Plan B?"

"We're going to clear the deck for Phoenix." Not a sliver of emotion evidenced on Nathara's face. "Kill Sara Tayton."

Shock rippled through Darla. "What?"

"Don't make me repeat myself. You wanted out of jail, I got you out of jail. I want Sara Tayton dead. Handle it." Nathara shoved the phone into a pocket on her dress. "Tack, keep your village idiots away from Three Gables. I don't want Nora found yet." Nathara pivoted her gaze. "Darla, do the hit tonight. Tomorrow morning, I want word spread far and wide that Sara Jones-Tayton is dead." Nathara headed around the side of the house toward the driveway. "I'll be at Nora's. Surely those Crossroads do-gooders have the place habitable again."

Knowing Lisa, Mel, and some of the church ladies were waiting for clearance from the police to help Annie do just that, Darla stayed quiet and watched Nathara leave. The crafty look on her face as she departed made what was going on in her mind crystal-clear.

She owned Darla. NINA owned her, and Darla couldn't turn on them.

But she wanted to turn, and the way Nathara's eyes had closed to slits proved that to her, wanting to turn made Darla even more dangerous.

Nathara couldn't kill Darla—yet. The truth was so obvious now. She had to live to take the blame for Masson and Nora's deaths—and, the way things were going, for Sara's and possibly Beth's.

Fearing she'd be sick before she made it to the patio, Darla hurried. Blamed for all those deaths. Lance would probably lose his mind. Darla could just see the headlines...

Darla Green—Serial Killer.

21

D arla?" Beth shook her arm. "Answer me. Where's Nora?"

"At Three Gables, hiding in one of the cottages." Darla shuddered. "You were right, Beth. I couldn't kill Nora, so I hid her where I knew she'd be safe. Raven doesn't know it or I'd be dead."

"Who is Jackal?" Jeff asked.

"And Phoenix?" Joe added.

She twisted the tissue. Sniffed. "Jackal is Raven's boss. I don't know him, but she spoke Rumantsch to him. It's prominent in an area of Switzerland."

"What about Phoenix?" Joe persisted.

"At first I thought he was Karl Masson."

"No, he was Gray Ghost." Joe looked at Jeff. "We picked that up through other venues." He glanced back to Darla. "You said *at first…*"

She glanced at Sara and held her tongue.

"Darla." Beth claimed her attention. "We know you and Nathara knew Robert before he came here. We have photos of all of you at the Martins." Beth looked at Jeff. "Nathara posed as Nora there."

"Who are the Martins?" Sara asked.

Beth spared her a glance. "Where's your inhaler?"

"I don't need it."

"They're your in-laws."

"Martins?" Sara asked, not seeming at all stunned. "So Robert isn't Robert." She looked Darla right in the eye. "Robert is Phoenix, isn't he?"

"I wasn't told. Raven doesn't tell anyone more than she has to tell them."

"But you believe he is," Sara said. "And like a phoenix, he'll rise from the ashes." Sara glanced at Jeff. "She doesn't have to say it. I see it on her face. Robert's alive and he's in neck-deep with NINA."

Jeff didn't comment, just turned the subject. "Did Karl Masson pull the club attack?"

"He planned it, but he wasn't in Seagrove Village then. Phoenix executed the plan."

"After he was supposedly kidnapped," Beth said. And Jeff had suspected her of that awful deed.

"The minute I saw the missing groom, I knew he was connected," Sara said. "Not whether he was a victim or in with them, but involved." She looked at Beth. "They've been pushing for classified information. I refused."

"They, who?"

"NINA, through Robert. He told me they'd kill him if I didn't cooperate. I figured the kidnapping was to convince me, but when all the blood proved he was dead, I thought, well, he couldn't have been working with them—and I'd be next."

"So you told Margaret to pull your clearances so you couldn't get any information."

"Months ago. When he first started pressuring me." Sara nodded. "It was the best protection I could manage."

Joe frowned. "You should have reported it to the OSI. They could have helped you."

"I'd have been signing my death warrant, and maybe Beth's too. I tested them and planted some false information. NINA got it. There's a mole inside OSI headquarters, Joe. I don't know who it is, but Mark might have more information for you on that."

"It's resolved, buddy." Mark sent Joe a level look.

Joe didn't ask questions, but Beth felt sure they'd come later, privately between them. The sting of betrayal turned Joe's expression grim. "Sara, what did Robert do to push you into helping him?"

She looked away.

"He worked over her feet with a golf club." Jeff's voice trembled.

Shock pumped through Beth. "That's what was wrong with your feet? It wasn't the new shoes that had you hobbling?" No wonder the paramedic had looked at Beth as if she'd lost her mind. "Was he the reason for the hospital visits too?"

Sara nodded, anger burning in her eyes. "Just getting away from him wasn't an option."

That she didn't have to explain. Her intense interest in helping the abused moms took on new meaning. "You didn't know whose side he was on, but you thought if you disappeared, they'd come after me." The truth slammed Beth with the force of a sledge. "You stayed to protect me."

Sara shrugged a shoulder. "I got us into this, hooking up with him in the first place. With NINA, there's nowhere to hide, Beth. We all know it."

"So the kidnapping was to coerce you into giving them what they wanted?"

"Yes." Sara lifted her chin. "I still refused."

"So they killed him," Jeff said, then looked at Joe. "Or did they?"

"They didn't. The blood was cold." Joe turned to Sara.

"I'm not sure."

Beth wasn't either. "Darla, why don't you just tell us?"

"I would if I knew. If he's not Phoenix, I have no idea. If he's Phoenix, he's alive—or he was, last I heard from Raven. She was planning on making him mayor."

Sara gave her a fierce scowl. "Over my dead body."

"Yes." Darla nodded her agreement. "Which brings us to our most immediate problem and the reason I called this meeting." Darla looked at Sara. "Brace yourself."

"What?"

Jeff moved closer to Sara, placed a steadying hand on her shoulder.

"Raven ordered me to kill you, Sara. Tonight. It's supposed to signal Phoenix to surface."

Sara paled but her breathing stayed even. Jeff lightly squeezed her shoulder and she placed a trembling hand atop his. "That pretty much proves Robert is Phoenix."

"If you're not dead or if Nora surfaces, we're all going to die."

"Define all." Joe pressed Darla.

"Me, Nora, Sara, and Beth." Darla dared to glance over. "I'm so sorry, Beth. I wanted to start fresh and build a life worth something."

"You still can. You didn't do it, Darla. Instead, you warned Sara and you're helping all of us, telling the truth."

"You're so good but so naive. I love that about you." Darla sighed. "I'm going to die anyway."

Jeff seemed untouched. "I'm hopeful you won't, and Beth's right. You've confirmed a lot for us."

Beth focused on Sara. "Jeff thought I kidnapped Robert and Nora was Raven."

"Guilty." Jeff's face flushed. "I had to explore every possibility."

"It's his job, Beth. He's conscientious." Sara told Jeff, "I understand. Proving who isn't leaves who is."

Relief washed over his face. "Yes."

Darla pulled a resealable plastic bag from her purse. "This is a mask I found in my living room. I think I was supposed to find it." Nathara might not understand people, but she understood temptation. "Nathara knew I'd have to try it on. Who could resist seeing if it really was a likeness? I did, so my DNA's on it." Darla frowned. "But so is Nathara's. She killed Masson—or Tack Grady did. I'm not sure which—they were there together when I got home."

Jeff stiffened. "How's Tack Grady hooked into this?"

"He's a minor NINA operative," Joe said. "NINA planned to make him mayor—"

"That's what they told him, and they did fund his campaign," Darla said. "But I suspect he'll be dead or underground long before the vote."

"Why?" Jeff asked.

"My guess is they wanted Phoenix installed—he's tight with Jackal—but from the snips of conversation I caught, Raven determined Phoenix couldn't stand the scrutiny. When they installed Tack as caretaker in my home and I heard he was running for office, I knew they had no intention of making him mayor. He was my keeper, to make sure I stayed in line."

Jeff took the bagged mask. "When did you find this?"

"The day I helped with the phones at Crossroads." She looked at Peggy.

Peggy nodded. "Same day."

"As what?" Beth asked.

"The day I think Karl Masson was killed on my terrace." Darla glanced from Joe to Beth. "Tack's shoes had dried blood on them. He pressure-washed the terrace—he'd just done it the week before. When word broke that Masson was dead, I knew it'd happened there that day."

Mark's eyes glinted. "It fits without conflict."

From Joe's relaxed stance, Beth figured he agreed. "So one or the other of them killed Karl Masson."

"No one else was there," Darla said. "From the mask, they wanted Masson and anyone else who might see anything to think I was the shooter."

"Nathara shot Masson," Joe said to Jeff. "I knew the shooter wasn't Darla—too heavy—I just wasn't sure who she was until now. DNA on the mask should back that up."

"Why would Nathara plant a mask of Darla at Darla's? Seems foolish."

"It's diabolically clever," Mark said. "Who masquerades as herself to commit murder?"

Sara looked more confused.

"It created doubt," Joe said. "Raven could spare Darla with it, or hang her as smart enough to pull off all that's happened."

Maximum flexibility. Beth wanted to cry. "Nora's going to be devastated. Her sister ordering her death." Nathara was all Nora had left of family, and just losing Clyde… How that snake of a woman could do this to anyone was beyond Beth, but to her twin?

"Actually, Nora took it pretty well." Darla sighed. "Better than I would have. She figured out Nathara was Raven and tried to call Mark. That's when the hit was ordered. She wasn't surprised. Embarrassed and angry, but not surprised."

"Nora will be fine." Peggy cleared her throat. "She's a survivor—and she's never had any illusions about her sister."

"She's ruthless," Mark said. "We've seen the evidence firsthand."

Jeff stepped away and called Kyle to collect the mask and run it to the lab. When he returned to the group, Joe asked, "Do you have Nora's DNA on file?"

"Why?" Beth asked.

Joe answered. "They're identical twins. Identical DNA."

"There's conflicting thoughts on that."

"I know, Beth," Joe said. "It can be resolved, but it takes time that we don't have right now."

Darla frowned. "Won't this put Nora at risk?"

"Actually, it'll clear her," Joe said. "Her fingerprints will be different. Surely we'll lift one off the mask."

Resentment dragged at Beth. "Nathara meant for everyone to think Nora was Raven."

"And I thought my family was bad." Joe nodded. "Cold, huh?"

"Ice is warmer." Beth frowned.

"Darla." Joe crossed his arms. "You know they're going to kill you."

"No doubt whatsoever." She blinked hard.

"So why are you helping us?"

"It's a God-thing." She glanced at Beth, a serene smile curving her lips. "Beth said I wasn't so far gone He couldn't find me, and she was right."

Beth's chest went tight. "I'm glad."

"So did you kill John?" Jeff asked.

Her smile faded. Remorse slithered over her face.

Peggy told Jeff, "That's been legally addressed. Darla was convicted and jailed and after Johnson confessed, turned loose. Now she's risking her life to spare Nora, Sara, and Beth. You know NINA wants all of SaBe and its assets, not just Sara's portion. At the moment, we've got enough problems." Peggy looked at Darla. "Later's soon enough to deal with that."

Darla nodded. "I do think I could help more here right now."

Mark folded his hands atop the table. "If we can keep you alive—and I believe we can, because all your NINA connections are exposed, dead, or anonymous—then I propose you address the John issue with authorities later. Right now we need you here. You have insights to NINA we don't have."

Darla lowered her lashes. "When you say it's time is soon enough for me."

Mark nodded. "I'm sure the authorities will take your actions in all this into consideration. Helping us with NINA, refusing to execute its kill orders on Nora and Sara, plus sharing your insider knowledge of the organization—it all makes you valuable in the government's war against NINA. A lot more so than your being in jail."

Darla looked at Jeff. "Are you all right with this?"

"Yeah, I am," Jeff said. "Mark's right. We need your insights."

Sara sat back, her jaw tight. "Sorry, but I have an issue with this."

"Settle it with me," Jeff said. "Because of her, you'll have the chance. You won't be dead."

Sara closed her mouth.

"Sara, I'm not going to duck responsibility. You have my word on it. I know I have to pay for what I've done."

Beth didn't say it, but she figured Darla had been paying for it.

"I know you all must hate me. I'm so sorry." Darla looked at Beth. "Especially you. You believed in me."

Beth had. She'd stood up for Darla. Discovering she was guilty stung. "I don't hate you. I do want to know why."

"It was John or Lance. They wanted their man as mayor so they could continue operations here. John had to go. I either helped them or…"

"They'd kill your son," Beth and Peggy said simultaneously.

Darla nodded, tears streaking down her face. "I made mistakes. I did bad things, and I won't say I didn't. I considered asking for help, but this was NINA.

No one could protect us from NINA." She gathered control. "But if I live, I promise I will do the right thing. I am different now."

What would Beth have done? She couldn't be sure. No one could. In the end, Darla had lost John and Lance. The authorities would sort it out. "Yes, you are different."

Clearly considering that situation resolved for now, Joe asked, "So how do we prove Robert is Phoenix?"

Darla faced Beth. "We fake Sara's death tonight."

Sara said, "If he's alive, he'll surface for the money."

"No," Beth said. "He'll surface for the money *and* for access to the classified information NINA wants."

Jeff got himself a glass of water. "And if he doesn't?"

"He will," Sara said. "For Robert, I've always been about money and NINA."

Beth looked at Joe. "This was your plan."

He nodded.

"You're good." Beth sighed, offered Sara the chance to be honest. "I hate to ask, but I need you to sign this." She pulled the papers from her purse.

"What is it?"

"An agreement. If something happens to you, Robert stays out of SaBe..."

Sara looked Beth in the eye. "It's redundant. Henry Baines has one on file. I signed it after the first hospital trip."

Beth smiled. "Thank you for protecting me, Sara." All their lives it had been the other way around. Sara had been the fragile one. But not anymore.

"I tried." She shrugged. "I'm not very good at it, but I'm a rookie."

Beth swallowed hard. "You're not fragile, Sara."

"Not this time." She seemed pleased. "I think, no matter how fragile or vulnerable we might be, we all have chances to see for ourselves who we are. I saw. Being fragile was easier. It was definitely more comfortable—I've always been that way. It was expected of me. But this time was different. I was different."

"You wanted to be more," Joe spoke softly.

She nodded. "When Robert hurt my feet, I thought of that murdered mom whose son called 911. She wanted to be more but chose not to because she was scared of being killed, and then she was killed anyway. I never feared death. It was life chained to Robert that terrified me."

"Why couldn't you pray?" Beth asked.

"I was lying to everyone I loved. How could I pray? But God loved me through it—"

"Grace." A smile touched Peggy's lips.

"Yes." Sara sniffed. "But it appears I'm still chained to the monster."

From his expression, that terrified Jeff too. "One hurdle at a time."

"Right." Sara drew in a shuddered breath. "So, how am I going to die?"

Jeff answered. "Darla is going to kill you, as ordered."

Sara reached for Beth's hand. "I want a lovely funeral. Tell Annie to handle it. Nora can't, of course, because she'll be dead with me. Shall I go to Three Gables too?"

"Absolutely," Ben said. "It's the only place Mark and his team can keep you two safe."

"Thank you, Ben." She looked back to Beth. "I'm sorry you'll have to mourn."

"Faked mourning, I can handle." Beth would do it well. She had to, to not give away that Sara was alive.

Sara let the truth shine in her eyes. "I've spent too much time in my life shutting people out so I wouldn't be hurt again. I want everyone there."

"That's probably not a good idea," Jeff said. "NINA could try another attack."

"After two failed attempts? Doubtful. But if they do, stop them, Jeff." Sara smiled up at him, touched his cheek, and dropped her voice to a whisper. "Will you cry for me?"

"I will." The tip of his pug nose turned red.

Beth sighed. "Oh, but I wish things could have been different..." She clasped a hand over her mouth. "Did I say that out loud?" Her face burned.

Everyone hid smiles. Beth cringed.

"Oh, forget it." Peggy gave her chunky necklace a tug. "We all wish things were different."

"They are what they are," Jeff said. "But I'll say this, so everyone's clear. No matter how all this shakes out, Sara, I'll always be here for you. You understand what I'm saying?"

He loved her. He wouldn't give her the words; he didn't have the right and she was in no position to accept them. But the truth was clear.

Sara teared up. "I understand."

Beth looked at Joe and lost herself in her feelings for him. What a privilege it was to have them, and to be able to express them. Too tender, she went to the sink for a drink of water.

"What?" Joe stepped close, lifting her hair at her nape.

She spun to face him, felt his warm breath fan across her face. "I am totally crazy about you, Joseph." There. She'd said and meant it.

"You're not running anymore?"

"No." She touched a hand to his chest.

"Why not?"

"What I saw in there…" She paused, then tried again. "Relationships are messy."

"That isn't exactly the response I was hoping for, Beth."

"I'm not done yet."

"Then please continue."

She clasped his face in her hands. "There are worse things in relationships than fear of heartbreak."

A lazy smile caressed his lips. "Still falling short, sha."

"It's a process, okay?"

He smiled, placed butterfly kisses to her eyelids. "You keep working on it, gorgeous. You'll get there."

She would. Not get there; she was there. It was admitting it that was hard.

"I don't want choke marks on my neck." Sara's voice carried over to the fridge.

"Let's go direct this death or they'll be debating it till tomorrow." Beth smiled.

Joe joined the others saying, "Break her neck, Darla."

"Will that leave a mark?" Sara asked.

"No."

"No."

"No."

Mark, Ben, and Jeff all answered at once.

"That'll work then." Sara stood and squared her shoulders. "Break my neck, Darla."

"This has to be the craziest conversation I've ever heard in my life—and with my whacked-out family, that's saying something." Joe shook his head.

"Get used to it." Beth patted his back. "Odd is kind of normal around here."

"Whoa, wait." Jeff looked at Sara. "I want every detail planned. Then Darla can break your neck." He scanned the group, then stopped on Beth. "You'll find her body—and it goes without saying, no one outside this room is to be told anything about this. One slip could blow it all apart."

Darla wrung her hands. "It could, and then Nora, Sara, and I really will be dead."

"And Beth." Jeff motioned to her. "Sara and Peggy are right. NINA wants it all."

Beth's knees wobbled. Fear set in. Darla said this was operation Dead Game. But it didn't feel like much of a game. Beth had seen what NINA could do, what it had done.

It was real. NINA was lethal.

And all of them, Joe included, were already on its hit list.

∽

At 11:00 p.m., Beth found Sara's body and phoned police.

Jeff arrived, called in forensics, and by midnight, the first of the reporters arrived outside the gate.

By dawn, the street was full of them, and flowers had begun to appear along the fence.

Sara was stashed with Nora at Three Gables under heavy guard. Peggy and Annie were at Crossroads, planning Sara's funeral. And Beth and Joe were at Sara's, which was less vulnerable than Beth's. Even NINA wouldn't enter a crime scene swarming with FBI agents.

Beth didn't have to fake upset; stress was thick with all who knew the truth, and the grief honest with those who didn't.

Sara's funeral was set for Tuesday, and when it finally arrived, Beth was emotionally drained. Robert still hadn't surfaced. Margaret, Nick Pope from Legal, and Henry Baines were in a world of hurt over losing Sara. It'd taken all Beth could muster not to tell them the truth.

Joe stayed by Beth's side, helping her through touchy times. Peggy was first to note that not one of Robert's friends had been by to express condolences. Beth never liked them. They were Robert's, not Sara's, friends, but Sara being alone and lost in their circle crushed Beth. Didn't they know how special Sara was?

Apparently not, and that hurt so deep Beth spontaneously broke into tears every time she thought of it. She prayed hard, but how God could get Sara from where she was to a place she'd be happy, Beth couldn't imagine. Seeing no way upset Beth all over again.

She thought about it while dressing for the funeral in a simple black sheath and pumps. While seated in church during the funeral service. While riding to the cemetery in the limo, and while seated before Sara's coffin waiting for the funeral to be over. Sara had fallen in love with a man who'd lied, betrayed, and beaten her. A man who'd used and abused her. A man who wanted her money but couldn't have cared less about her, much less her heart. She'd loved him with all she'd had. But her all hadn't been enough.

And then she'd discovered his duplicity and been trapped.

Emotionally divorcing him and finding the love of a good man in the tragedy seemed like adding insult to injury. A man who loved her so much he pledged his devotion forever—regardless of whether or not she was ever in a position to return his love.

Tragic. Tragic. Tragic. And so unfair. Hot, fat tears rolled down Beth's face, soaked her tissue. Sara deserved to be happy. After all that had happened to her, with all that was to come, how could she ever be happy?

Beth cried in earnest…and Joe seemed to innately understand what she was thinking and feeling. He curled a protective arm around her. "Have faith, sha. Greater eyes than ours are watching over her."

Grateful for the comfort he offered, she leaned into him, and he held her while she cried.

ᘒᘓ

"It's been two days, Joe." Beth's nerves strummed. "How long will he wait?"

"Not long." Joe looked across Crossroads's entrance. Mel at her desk on the phone. "All the insiders think he'll move quickly, before you make any major changes."

"I thought Nathara being at Sara's funeral was hard to handle. But it was nothing compared to this waiting."

Joe swept her hair back from her face with a gentle hand. "You're doing fine, sha."

She wasn't doing fine. Her nerves were raw, like they were on the outside of her skin. "We need to go to SaBe and check the freezer."

"It's too soon. You can't show up at the office yet."

Ben, Mark, and Jeff agreed with Joe. It'd tip their hand to NINA. Still, standing idle was driving Beth up the proverbial wall.

"Roxy took a quick look."

He hadn't told her. "Did she find anything?"

"No, but she was interrupted. Others arrived. She had to get out or be discovered."

The evidence was there. It had to be. Robert wouldn't trust anyone else with evidence on him. No way. "Did Jeff pick up Tack Grady?"

"He's under surveillance. They all are."

That was reassuring for her and Sara, Nora, and Darla. "I can't keep avoiding my home. They're going to find that odd."

"You're right. But with it on the Gulf, there's no way to guard it."

"So what do we do?"

He thought a moment. "Fake an injury here at the center. Trip over a rug. Then we can keep you here and no one will think a thing of it."

"And tonight? What then? You think on it and call Jeff. I'll go fall."

"We'll take you to Three Gables too. Easier to guard you all together."

"How do we explain—I know. Jeff can arrest me for Sara's murder."

"No way. Damaging consequences to SaBe."

"I wasn't thinking." She rubbed at her head. "The problem is I *can't* think."

"Nora would blister your ears for that." Joe curled his arms around her, kissed her. "You need to get away for a few days."

"Perfect." She dragged a shaky hand through her hair. "If I have to see my mother crying one more time, I'm going to lose my mind."

"She loves Sara."

"Yes, but it's more than that. I told you she and Dad always have dreamed of living in Europe for a few years. They've been waiting for Sara and me to *get settled* so they can go without worrying about us. Mom's known something was up with Sara, and she's been nagging me to find a good man and settle down."

"So she's kept her dream on hold because even if Sara wouldn't tell her what was wrong, her intuition warned her Sara was in jeopardy?"

"Exactly," Beth admitted. "With all this NINA and Robert craziness, she's been scared to death for us both. Now that Sara's dead, she's a basket case over me."

"How could she not be? She loves you, sha."

"Exactly." Beth lifted a hand. "Seeing her upset, mourning and blaming herself… I can't stand it."

"Why is she blaming herself?"

"She's a mother." Beth sighed. "Anytime anything goes wrong with your kids, you feel as if it's your fault."

"But she had nothing to do with—"

"I didn't say it was logical, Joseph. I said it's the way moms react. Dads do too. Parents protect their kids. Period. It doesn't matter if they're grownups; they're still your babies and you're still supposed to protect them. When you don't, it's your fault. It doesn't matter if it's a freak accident or an evil man or an internationally feared terrorist organization. It's your child and your fault."

"Explains a lot about my mother. I never looked at it like that before, but I see it. Unfortunately with my family, she's had tons of chances to take on guilt that wasn't hers."

"I just can't do all I have to do, knowing she's mourning and crying her heart out."

"You'll know it no matter where you are, sha."

"But I won't have to watch it. Maybe we can focus on ending this so she can stop."

He nodded, pulled out his phone, then dialed. "Jeff, we've resolved what to do with Beth. Put the word out she's getting away for a few days. You know where I'm taking her."

"Got it. I happen to be at Ruby's, and Megan is working."

The village grapevine would get the word in warp speed. "We'll consider the word spread then."

Beth hugged him hard.

⚬⚬⚬

Beth tumbled over the waiting room rug. Lisa Harper bandaged her up, Mel insisted she take crutches, in case she needed to whack somebody to defend herself, and Joe got her into her SUV passenger seat. "You okay?"

"Fine."

He slid in behind the wheel and cranked the engine.

"Drop by Sara's. I forgot my purse at her house."

Joe turned, and at the gate came to a dead halt. Two cruisers were in Sara's driveway. "What's going on here?" He whipped out his phone and dialed Jeff.

"I was about to call you," Jeff said. "Robert's returned."

"Do I come in with Beth?" Joe asked. "Is Mark there?"

He trusted Mark, but then he would. They'd placed their lives in each other's hands many times. "He's here and he says, yes, bring Beth inside."

Beth's stomach roiled in revolt. She thought she was ready, but Robert standing in the living room with his back to her... She wasn't ready. She'd never be ready to see him again.

"Think steel, sha."

Joe's whisper had the desired effect. She stiffened her spine and her resolve. "Robert?"

He turned. His face was scraped, his right arm in a sling. "What are you doing here?"

She hobbled over to the dining room chair and picked up her purse. "Forgot this."

He glared at her. "You found Sara's body?"

"Yes." Beth glared back. "Where've you been?"

"Kidnapped."

"I know that. I paid your ransom." She paused, but of course he remained silent. "I mean after that."

"They threw me out of a moving car." He lifted his bum wing. "I didn't fare well."

"Apparently not. Sara was devastated. You knew she would be, yet you couldn't call?"

"I called. That's when I discovered my wife was dead and you had buried her."

She bit her lip, teared up. "I did."

"Did you kill her too?"

Anger surged through Beth and radiated off Joe. Jeff tensed up. Beth schooled her voice. "No, I didn't. Did you?"

Robert lost it. "Get out of my house!"

She could push, reveal that it wasn't his, but a glance from Jeff warned her this wasn't the time. She started toward the door, paused, and looked back at him, then at Jeff. "Detective, has the judge signed that restraining order to keep him away from SaBe?"

Jeff picked up the carrot Beth hoped would force Robert to move quickly. "It will be ready by ten tomorrow morning."

"Restraining order? Against me?" Robert scowled. "You can't do that. I own half of SaBe now."

"I can and will." Beth walked out Sara's front door and went straight to the SUV.

Joe got inside, started the engine, and slapped at the gearshift. "Am I going to have to muzzle you to keep you alive?"

"What?"

"If he's Phoenix—and I'm sure he is—he's going to kill you for that."

"No, he's not. He is going to do whatever he's planning to do before ten tomorrow morning, though." She frowned at Joe. "Jeff got it, why didn't you?"

"I got it, okay?"

"So why are you ticked off?"

He backed out of the driveway and drove to the stop sign before answering. Then he frowned at her. "Because I love you. I can take NINA wanting my head on a platter. It's been there a long time. But I can't take them wanting your head on one. I can't take the thought of—"

Beth touched his face. "You're not going to lose me, Joe."

"I could. You just put a target right between your own eyes."

"Honey, it was already there. I just gave our side a clue when he'd strike."

Worry flooded his face. "I wish I could put you in a cage somewhere safe. I wish I was sure I could protect you."

"I don't believe what I'm hearing." Beth stilled.

"What?"

"You actually care about me." The truth settled in and refused to be rebuffed. "Why?"

"I'm asking myself that very thing."

He looked so disgusted with himself that Beth couldn't not laugh. That insensitive reaction earned her a withering look that would have swept her off her feet had she been on them.

"Do you not see how much danger you're in?"

"I do." She coughed to hide a chuckle. "Really. It's just…"

"What?"

"Worth it." She let him see her surprise, her awe. "You care about me. One day, you might even come to love me."

He stomped the accelerator, leaving half her tires on the street. "Sha, right now I don't even like you."

"I like you anyway." Beth checked her watch. It'd be dark in an hour. "Let's get some coffee at Ruby's and then go check SaBe."

"It's been checked."

"Roxy was interrupted."

"No Ruby's. We'll go to Three Gables. Nora is having a fit to see you and Sara's worried the fake mourning's been too much for you. You can have coffee with them, then we'll go to SaBe. I need privacy to get some backup in place."

"That'll work." She leaned over and pecked a kiss to his cheek. "Get over your snit soon, okay? I like my calm, cool Joe."

"I don't do snits."

"'Course not." She smiled. "What was I thinking?"

He pursed his lips. "She's going to drive me nuts the rest of my life. I can see it now."

"But she's crazy about you."

He guffawed. "Still falling short, sha."

"Growing into it, Joseph." She pushed her sunglasses up on her nose, hiding her eyes. "Quit complaining and just drive."

22

O h, my girl, I'm so glad to see you." Nora enveloped Beth in a fierce hug, her whole body shuddering.

"No happier than I am to see you." Beth hugged her back, then looked into her face, saw the pain in every crease and line. "I'm so sorry, Nora."

"You know about Nathara?" When Beth nodded, Nora sniffed. "Can't choose your family, dearie, you're stuck with them. I did better picking my own—Ben, you, Sara, and my boys."

Beth blinked hard. "You're loved and you know it."

"I'm a lucky woman. I told Mark not to even think about doing anything to Darla Green. If that girl hadn't had the guts to stand up to NINA, I'd be pushing up daisies."

"They've given her immunity." Beth looked at Sara. "You okay?" They hadn't spoken since Robert's return. Who knew how Sara was handling it? She wasn't holding her inhaler. That was a good sign.

"I'm fine." She nodded toward Nora. "Not that I'd be indulged in being anything else."

Beth smiled. Nora did have a low tolerance level for anything that smacked of self-pity, but good grief, with all this, Sara had earned it. "What are you going to do, now that he's back?"

"I'm weighing my options."

"He'll be in jail a long time," Nora said. "No need for Sara to rush into any decisions. His hands are tied tight. She'll have plenty of time later to decide what to do."

Beth knew what Sara wanted. But wanting and getting were two different things. "It'll work out."

"Yes, it will." Sara smiled. "I don't know how, but it's on the altar. I can't think long-term or even next-week-term right now."

Sara was praying again. Beth choked up. "I'm very glad to hear that."

"I'm very glad to be able to say it."

They went into the cottage. Beth and Nora had coffee and Sara a cup of Earl Grey. After catching up on the news and details on what happened to whom, the conversation turned to Robert's blood.

"I haven't seen anything remotely like that at home." Sara accepted a slice of chocolate cake from Nora. "But I know now why Jeff searched my freezer."

Nora set a plate in front of Beth. "Robert was playing it both ways—where he could seize control through Sara or you, Beth. He's put that evidence where it'd hurt either of you girls." She stilled, scrunched her lips. "Got to be at SaBe."

"He doesn't have keys." Sara paused, her fork in midair. "Unless he stole them."

Beth finished her cake.

Joe stuck his head in the doorway. "Beth, we need to go."

"Where are you going?"

"To SaBe to look for evidence." Beth winked at Nora.

She glared at Joe. "You're taking her there tonight? What are you thinking, my boy?"

"Robert doesn't know she'll be there. He has no reason to go there, Nora."

"He'll do it because he can—before the restraining order's in place." She seemed exasperated. "You know the man's an arrogant fool, bless his heart."

"Nora's right. Don't go, Beth. I have a bad feeling."

Beth didn't. "It'll be fine. Worst case, he shows up. What's he going to do? Nothing. He doesn't want SaBe tied up as a crime scene. He wants access, remember?" She put her dishes in the sink. "Right now, SaBe is probably the safest place on the planet for me."

"She's got a point." Nora looked at Sara.

Sara stilled a long moment and then caved. "She does. But I still don't like it."

Beth didn't like any of this, but it was the best opportunity they were going to get and they needed to seize it. Robert could destroy the evidence. Then where would they be?

Nora hugged her. "Be careful, my girl."

"I will." Beth prayed being careful would be enough.

∽∾

After Joe parked the SUV in Beth's usual spot, he ran a perimeter check while Beth chatted with Margaret, who was leaving for home.

"His majesty phoned here looking for you. I told him you were at police headquarters, hoping that would knock him back on his heels," Margaret said about Robert. "I had no idea when or if you'd be back."

"When was that?"

"Right before I left the building." She scrunched her nose. "He pushed me again for the financial records. I told him they were in the vault and I'd request them, but since I didn't have authorization, we'd have to wait until Henry gave it before either of us could get them."

"Bet he wasn't happy to hear that."

"No, he wasn't. If cold tones could kill, I'd be six feet under."

"Where was he when he called? Did he say?"

"No, but I heard background noise. My guess is he was in his car."

"Red Hummer, right?" Joe asked Beth. When she nodded, he scanned the parking lot again.

"Margaret, did Robert ever come to SaBe when we were all gone? Maybe nights or on weekends?"

"A week ago, I'd have said no. But Glenn from security told me not two days ago that he guessed Robert wouldn't be coming here for peace and quiet anymore."

"Peace and quiet?"

Margaret nodded. "That's what he told Glenn. He came here to write because he couldn't take all the noise at home."

"What noise?" With just him and Sara, there was no noise.

"Logical question. He had an entire house in a gated community and restricted traffic with a guesthouse office and a backyard on the cove, for pity's sake."

Joe faced the hot night wind funneling in under the overhang. "Looks like you were right, Beth."

"About what?" Margaret parked her glasses atop her head, her car keys jangling.

"Nothing significant." Adjusting her purse strap, Beth shifted her weight. "Just Robert running away from home every chance he got."

Joe started to correct her, then caught her gaze and knew she didn't want to share. No sense worrying Margaret needlessly. From the smudges under her eyes, she wasn't sleeping.

"I've got to get going." Margaret turned for her car. "Game night at my house. I have to get the munchies ready. It won't be the same without Nora. I do wish they'd find her."

"Me too." Beth waited for Margaret to get into her Tahoe, then told Joe, "That woman is a walking contradiction."

"Yeah, she is." He waved as she drove past. "I like that about her."

"Me too." She tipped her chin and touched a hand to his chest, then noticed his puzzled expression. "What?"

Joe frowned. "Why didn't you ask her about Robert and the blood? You know Roxy was here. Margaret's probably already looked."

"Roxy wouldn't tell her what she was looking for, and if I'd told Margaret, she would have stayed to help us look. She's exhausted and needed to go home."

Joe took a long look at Beth. "You didn't want her here because you were afraid Robert might come after you and she'd be at risk."

The security lights and streetlamps came on. Dark had officially fallen.

"Anyone in Robert's path is at risk." A body need look no further than his parents for proof of that. Beth shoved her hand in her pocket, curled her fingers around her cell phone. "But I figure we're safe here."

They entered the brick building, took the elevator up, and entered the office. The lamps were on in the reception area, and Beth didn't bother with the overhead. Slashes of light streaked down the hallway and they walked straight to the kitchen.

Joe turned on the light.

Beth opened the freezer door and they looked inside. Thin red streaks were on the right side of the inner wall. The bottom had a few flecks of ice here and there but no tinges of red. "Joe, Roxy wouldn't have missed this."

He called her, spoke briefly, then told Beth, "She never got the door open. There were people in the kitchen, and not knowing who was and wasn't with NINA, she didn't want to tip our hand on knowing Robert was alive."

Feeling better with that explained, Beth pointed to the traces on the inner wall, then scooted over so Joe could position to see them. "Sliding the bags in." He removed the ice bin, started to put it back, but stopped and pulled it out all the way.

Beth glimpsed the curled edge of something. "What's that?" She looked closer. A corner of the little piece of paper stuck to the back of it. "It's blank."

"Doubtful, sha. Can you peel it free without tearing it?"

She did, then flipped the paper. "Not this time." Her heart rate soared, her gaze collided with Joe's. "It's Robert's handwriting. I'm sure of it."

"What does he mean by that—not this time?"

"He says it all the time, always meaning he comes out on top. Remember, the Martins mentioned it too?"

"I remember now."

"In this case, he means he wins and I lose. Well, me or Sara. However it worked out." She stepped away.

Joe set the bin back into place, bagged the note, and then started digging through the drawers and cabinets.

"What are you looking for?"

"If he pulled units of his blood here with the idea of blaming you or Sara for it, then he probably stashed what he needed for that here too."

Beth shut the freezer door and helped Joe search.

He paused and reached for his phone. "Jeff, it's me. Yeah, you'd better get to SaBe with forensics. Yeah, we found something in the freezer."

"And here we have the rest of it." Beth backed away from the bottom cabinet, under the sink. "Behind the trash can."

"We were right. He did it to himself and planted the stuff here to tag anyone at SaBe. Yeah." Joe closed his phone, bent down, and looked. "Jeff's on his way."

"It's all there—blood bags, tubing, needles—everything he needed."

A woman's voice carried into the kitchen. *"No. No, I won't do it."* She cried out. *"Please, don't!"*

23

Beth went still, felt the blood drain from her face.

"Beth?" Joe whipped around, whispered, "Who is that?"

"Sara." Beth ran toward the voice.

"No, Beth. Wait! It's not her."

Beth didn't slow down. Robert must have found her at Three Gables, forced her to come here. She ran toward the voice, into Sara's office. "Sara?"

The television was on. No other lights, no movement, just the television. Beth's skin crawled. She walked through the darkness to the set; someone had set the timer. It could have been done weeks ago. No one was ever here this late.

On the screen, Sara screamed.

Beth instinctively backed up and saw Robert hitting Sara with a golf club. Hearing he had done it was awful, but seeing it... "Oh, sweet mercy."

Joe stopped just inside the door. "Beth, you okay?"

She swiped at her face. It was wet with tears. "Someone set the timer."

"Please, Robert. Stop." Sobbing, Sara had begged him. He used the club like a baseball bat, striking her feet until she collapsed on the floor.

"That's the rusty shed. He took her to that awful place?"

Beth remembered the stench that stole her breath. "She's chained, Joe. He chained Sara in that awful place and he beat her."

She turned to face him. "You warned me on the terrace. You knew then that he did this to her?"

"No. All I was told was that she was in trouble and she wasn't in the hospital for her attacks. I thought if I warned you, you'd confront her and she'd tell you."

"She stayed and put up with this to protect me." A sob broke in Beth's throat.

Joe curled an arm around her shoulder. "She's fine now, sha. Remember that. She's fine now."

"You are going to give them what they want, Sara," Robert said. His face wasn't on the screen, but his voice was clear and unrelenting. *"You won't do it for me, but you will do it. They'll kill us both."*

Sara looked up at him, her swollen face red, streaked with dirt and tears. *"Why are you doing this to me? I loved you."*

"You're forcing me to do it. I don't want to die, but you'll let them kill me. For what, Sara? Some noble sense of patriotism?" He grunted his disgust. *"No. No, you're protecting her, aren't you? You stupid woman. You think you can save her?"* He laughed, hard and deep. *"You can't save her or yourself. Now tell me where you moved the money."*

Sara clamped her jaw shut.

"I said"—he swung the stick and the sound of it hitting Sara's foot reverberated through the office, through Beth— *"tell me!"*

Sara screamed in pain. The shrill peal curdled Beth's blood and a wrenching mewl broke loose from the back of her throat. She wanted to turn away, to throw something through the screen to make the horrific images go away, but it was like passing a car wreck, she had to look. She had to know exactly what this monster of a man had done to Sara.

"No." Sara pulled herself to a sitting position, and then struggled to her feet. They were raw and bloody and crusted with dirt. *"You will* not *get that too. I don't care if you kill me. Please, do it. I'd rather be dead than married to you."*

"Oh, you'll tell me, Sara." He motioned with the tip of the club. *"You'll tell me or I'll beat you to death."*

Sara didn't move.

Robert tucked his chin, slid her a warning look that dripped venom. *"Make the call."*

Her voice cracked, her chest heaving, shoulders shuddering. *"I don't understand why you're doing this."*

"It's what I want." He stilled her with a stare so ice-cold it chilled Beth.

She rubbed at the goose flesh peppering her arms. Sick inside, Beth covered her face with her hands and turned away. "Turn it off, Joe." She pressed her hands against her roiling stomach and opened her eyes. "I—I can't watch it. I can't—Joe?"

He lay on the floor, deathly still.

"Joe!" What happened? She hadn't heard anything. How had he ended up on the floor? Beth ran over to him, dropped to her knees. He was bleeding. His chest! He'd been…shot? She'd heard nothing.

Silencer.

"Oh no. No." Her fingers trembling, she positioned her fingers at his throat. He had a pulse. A strong pulse. He was alive. She reached into her pocket to get her phone and call 911 while tapping his cheek. "Joe. Joe, answer me."

"Dead men don't talk, Beth." Robert Tayton stepped out of the shadows, pointing a gun with a silencer at Beth's head.

Terror pumped through her veins, clamped her chest, paralyzing her.

"Get up." Robert backed away and motioned with the barrel of his gun.

Beth didn't argue. He thought Joe was dead. If she kept his attention diverted…

"Despite what you see on the screen, Sara learned to do what I wanted, when and where and the way I wanted." He sniffed. "You're going to regret not following her lead."

She hadn't. Sara had fought him and won. Hand still in her pocket, Beth swiped at her face with her free hand to claim his attention, silenced her cell phone, and dialed 911. *Thank you, Joe. Thank you for insisting I keep the special phone on my body at all times. Thank you.*

She swallowed hard, stiffened her spine. *Think steel. Jeff and forensics are on the way. They'll pick up the 911 call and rush. Just keep Robert talking and you might live. Joe might live.* "Sara didn't listen to you." Beth contradicted him. "Not about the money. Not about NINA. She told you nothing because she knew nothing." Beth grunted. "Even now you have no idea where her money is, do you?"

"Soon enough. It's my money now." He clicked on Sara's desk lamp. "You and Joe—why don't you call him Thomas? No matter. He's dead, you'll die, and Margaret will be blamed. She has been handling my finances for Sara. It was easy to manipulate transactions so it appears she wanted full control of all assets. A nice little paper trail leads directly to her." He winked. "Always have a backup plan for your backup plan."

So that's why he chose SaBe and not their home or Beth's. So Margaret could be in position if needed. "Why Sara? She was a good person who never hurt anyone. Why did you do this to her?"

"Actually, she was my second choice. My first had more class and was totally at ease in my social circle." He pulled a sour face. "Sara was horribly inept—a social cripple."

"The widow you took advantage of that caused the split with your parents? You rushed that man's death so you could marry and control his wife and her fortune. But what you'd done was discovered, so you found another victim. Sara."

"You've been busy." He hiked his eyebrows. "Surprisingly resourceful, Beth."

No remorse. None. No regret or even acknowledgment that he'd deliberately inflicted suffering on another human being. According to Joe's sources, the man was terminal and Robert had withheld his medication, fed him vitamins and aspirin in its place. Of course, the truth wasn't discovered until the autopsy, but his widow was suspicious and so Robert disappeared and they'd been searching for him ever since. Was Robert psychotic? No, no, he knew what he'd done was wrong. He could differentiate between good and bad. "Why Sara?"

"NINA chose Sara. It was her or you, and Sara was, shall we say, more malleable? I was fine with that. Still, she required incredible patience. Tedious work. Sara was inept, awkward, drearily clingy, and oh-so needy, but she was very, very rich. That made up for a multitude of flaws." He hummed. "Hers was the perfect murder."

He hadn't killed her but he'd planned her murder. He was Phoenix.

"Sara was easy to control until I pushed her on Quantico." He lifted a hand. "Even after I died, she was too ashamed to tell you about me. You, her best friend and partner, the one person in the world she trusted." He laughed. "That was amusing."

"She wasn't ashamed. She was disgusted. And while she didn't protect you, Robert, she did protect me."

"Her mistake, wasn't it? Considering she's dead and all."

Sorely tempted to dispute him, Beth bit her tongue. "What kind of monster are you?"

"No kind at all." He shot her a scathing look. "I warned Sara not to restrict my spending. I warned her NINA would kill me, and she still refused me. Me! So she got what she deserved."

All of Sara's odd behavior and reactions, her warnings, made sense. She really had mentally divorced him. Sara couldn't stand the sight of him.

"Sara's inability to act guaranteed my success." Robert stepped around Sara's desk. "You would be in jail for Sara's murder and, of course, my abduction, and I'd have her personal fortune, half of SaBe's assets and full run of your half and future earnings." He smiled broadly. "Sweet, eh?" When she didn't answer, he added, "Now you'll be dead and Margaret will be blamed for everything, including killing you and Joe, and I'll still have it all."

Robert walked over to where Joe lay in a heap on the floor, still out cold. "This is all his fault, really." Robert gazed back at Beth. "He should have stayed out of Georgia and away from you."

The television screen went blank; the background turned solid blue. Robert clicked off the set with the tip of the gun barrel. "Everything still would have been fine, but you two just wouldn't mind your own business, and then you found my parents." He paused a few steps from Beth, the lamplight pooling at his feet, glinting off his watch. "How did you do that?"

She didn't answer. Just stood silently, not sure how much more of this she could take—the images of Sara on that screen replaying in her mind, Joe so still on the floor—and... *Oh, please let Jeff get here soon!*

"You were foolish to try to come between me and what is mine." He lifted a hand. "How dare you try?"

"You're threatening to take my life, and you ask me how I dare?" He was crazy.

"Oh, I'm not threatening, Beth. I am going to kill you." Robert said that with the same ease of saying he'd played eighteen holes of golf. *Chilling.* "I considered killing you a year ago—if Sara hadn't agreed to elope, I would have. But now, after all the trouble you've caused me, well, of course you must die."

Stall! Stall! He's winding down and you need more time. "What about Darla Green? Did you have to kill her too?"

Surprise flickered across his face. "I wasn't aware she was dead." He stilled, digested. "Ah, you knew that. It was a little test. Aren't you the clever one?" He rubbed his fingertips over his chin.

"Clever enough to know you wanted Sara alive and under your control. You didn't plan her death." Joe was conscious; Beth saw him blink. *Thank God.*

"Would I dirty my own hands if it wasn't absolutely necessary?" Cocky, Robert looked at her down the barrel of the gun. "But you've been a thorn in my side since day one."

"You've already said you're going to kill me. What's left to threaten me with?"

"There are worse things than death." He squinted, closing one eye. "Sara would agree."

Beth spotted the tip of a shoe at the door. "I'm sure she would, Phoenix."

His jaw tightened. "Enough. I win, you lose." He took aim. "Say good-bye, Beth."

Multiple shots fired.

Robert slammed back, hit the floor with a thud.

Choking back a scream, Beth stared into his sightless eyes, at the gaping hole in his chest, and said the one thing that ran through her mind. "He's bleeding on Sara's carpet…"

Joe holstered his gun. "Clear."

Jeff and Roxy came in, their guns still drawn. They'd all shot him. All of them.

"He's dead now."

"You okay, Joe?" Blood stained his shirt.

"Fine. The bullet just grazed me. For all his evil, Robert was a lousy shot."

Beth didn't seem to hear him. She just stood, staring at Robert's body.

"Get her out of here, Joe," Jeff said.

"Joe, he's bleeding on Sara's carpet." Beth clutched at the front of Joe's shirt. "He can't be dead on Sara's floor. Not after what he did to her. I've got to get him out of here. Can you help me get him out of here?"

Roxy answered. "I'll take care of it, honey."

"Okay." Beth stood there, unsure what to do. "Okay."

"It's all right, sha. Everything is going to be fine now." Joe wrapped an arm around her and led her out into the hallway.

"Okay." She wrung her hands. "Okay."

"Let's get you some fresh air." He led her downstairs and then outside.

24

Jeff joined Beth and Joe outside. "You all right?"

"Yeah," Joe said. "We're fine. Beth just needed a few minutes."

She cleared her throat. "I—I never saw a man killed before—I mean, in person."

"It's different than viewing clips on the computer," Jeff said. "I understand."

She nodded. "There are a lot of police here."

He swiped at the sweat sheen on his forehead. "Everyone responds to a 911 call."

"What about Nathara and Tack Grady?" Joe asked.

Beth gave him a slow blink. She couldn't feel her feet or her fingertips. Joe rubbed little circles on her back and slowly the numbness was subsiding and feeling returning. She slumped against him. "Thank you for not being dead, Joe."

"You're welcome, sha." He gave her a lazy smile that made her feel safe and secure, beloved.

"You're really okay, right?" She looked at Jeff. "They bandaged his side but he wouldn't go to the hospital. Does he need to go to the hospital?"

"I'm not hurt." Joe clasped her upper arms, held her steady. "Everything is going to be okay now. Understand?"

She nodded, sniffed.

Jeff claimed their attention. "Nathara and Tack are in custody. She actually tried to pass herself off as Nora. That lasted about two seconds."

"It's over." Something in Beth snapped. "It is, isn't it, Joe?"

He nodded.

Admiration lit in Jeff's eyes. "You handled Robert well, Beth." When she nodded, he asked, "Did he say anything about Jackal?"

"No. Not a word." She frowned. "We shouldn't have killed him. He might have told us something."

"No choice, sha. He was going to shoot you."

"But now what he knows is lost to us."

"There's always another Jackal," Joe spoke softly. "No matter how many we take down, there's always another one behind him. We do what we can, when we can, as best we can, but there's always one more."

"That's why you think steel."

Joe nodded. "You seem okay now. Are you?"

"I will be." She nestled closer to Joe. "Jeff, those films of Sara. I don't want anyone to see them ever again."

"But they're evidence, Beth."

She glared at him. "Sara did nothing wrong and she lost everything. Don't you dare take any more from her. I mean it."

Jeff looked away. "I'll do everything humanly possible to keep them private. You have my word on it."

Joe stroked Beth's back. "Trust him. Jeff will take care of it. He loves Sara too."

"I should have known Robert was hurting her, and I didn't. The signs were all there." Tears blurred her vision and Beth swallowed hard. "I think Maria suspected it, but she wasn't sure, and I just didn't see the signs."

"You're not to blame. Only Robert is." Joe forced her to meet his gaze. "Let it be over."

It was over. But the women around Robert Tayton paid a steep price for being close to him. "Oh, his poor parents." Beth thought of the Martins. "They're going to be so...hurt."

"Yes," Joe said.

"I wish..."

"I know." He pressed his fingers over her lips. "No one wins in these situations. Everyone loses and that's just a fact. But we found the truth, sha. Sometimes, the truth is as good as it gets."

She closed her eyes for a brief moment. "It helps to heal."

"Yes." He passed her handbag, then circled her waist with his arm. "Let's get you home."

Beth leaned into him, calmer, working toward peace. The healing would come with time and grace. For now, she was content for Joe to be with her, knowing he would be with her from now on in good and hard times. "We need to go to the cottage."

"Jeff is on his way to tell Sara."

"I know." Beth sighed. "But she's going to be told she's a widow. I need to be there."

"She won't have an attack, Beth."

"No, she won't. She'll be relieved and devastated. She once loved him, and considering the kind of man he proved to be, she'll be really confused by that."

"Sara will work through it. You said yourself, she's not fragile."

"No, but she is human. She'll need her best friend." Sara and she had taken Robert's worst and won. They had survived his Dead Game, but not unscathed. "Wounds were suffered."

"And survived." Joe squeezed her hand, seated her in the SUV. "We'll go to the cottage. But let's give her and Jeff a little time before we arrive."

Thoughtful. Beth smiled at him. "I believe you owe me a cup of coffee."

"I brought it to you at Sara's, remember?"

"I do remember." Her smile broadened. "So I have a question. You answer it, and I'll buy."

"Intriguing offer." He hiked his eyebrows. "Your question?"

"What is your real name?"

"Thomas Edward Scoffield."

Beth hugged him hard. "You trust me."

"Totally." He hugged her close. "But you'll have to keep calling me Joe."

"I'll do my best."

"That's more than enough." He pulled back. "Now that I've passed the trust test, you ready for Ruby's?" He gave her that smile, the one he reserved just for her, that melted her knees and turned her mind to mush. She thought she just might like having a mushy mind. "I'll go anywhere with you."

"Wow. Tell the woman your name and she's putty in your hands. If you'd just let me in on that earlier, you could have spared me a lot of anxiety."

"I didn't want to spare you. I was too busy trying to spare me."

"Ah. Max, eh?"

Surprise streaked through her. "I never told you his name."

"I know. That worried me, so I asked Mark."

Joe refilled her goodness well, and after the confrontation with Robert, it had been drained nearly dry. Images of the shooting flashed through her mind. The horror on Jeff's face. "If I tell you I'm glad you shot Robert, will you think I'm an awful person?"

"He was going to kill you. I had no choice."

"I'm glad you and Roxy shot him at the same time Jeff did. It'll make it easier on Jeff."

"Killing a man, even an evil NINA operative, isn't easy."

"I didn't say easy. I said easier."

He spared her a look.

"He'll never have to second-guess himself, wonder if he shot Robert because he'd hurt Sara—so Sara would be available to him. Doubt could have nagged him for a long time."

Understanding dawned. Joe tapped the turn signal with his little finger. "He and Sara will be fine. All they need is a little time."

"Will we be fine too?" Her voice sounded weak, unsure. She hated that.

Joe kissed the back of her hand. "You love me, gorgeous. How could we not be fine?"

No uncertainty from his view. "Interesting response."

"What?"

"I said I was crazy about you. I said I adored you. But I don't remember ever saying I love you."

"You've said it, sha. In a million ways."

She had to ask. Had to do it. Had he told her in a million ways that he loved her? Beth's mouth went dry. "Um, Joe?"

"Mmm?" He didn't look away from the road.

The words wouldn't come out of her mouth. She wasn't that brave. "Never mind."

☙❧

Jeff found Sara on a porch swing outside the cottage. Her hair was down, loose and teasing her shoulders, and her feet were bare. The swelling was going down, the bruises fading. She swung the porch swing by toeing the concrete. "Sara?"

She smiled. "Jeff." Her eyes sparkled. She looked peaceful.

He hated to be the one to shatter it, but he didn't dare wait. Word was already spreading through the village. "It's over, Sara."

She stopped swinging. "Beth?"

"She and Joe are fine."

Sara let out an enormous sigh. "Thank God."

Jeff's stomach flipped. He had to tell her not only that Robert was dead, but that he'd shot him. "Robert showed up at SaBe."

"He went after Beth." She stared up at him. "Is he in custody?"

"He's dead, Sara." He paused, gave her time to absorb that.

"Did Beth…?"

"No. He was going to shoot her, so Joe, Roxy, and I shot him."

"All three of you?"

"We had no choice. It was kill him or he'd kill Beth."

She stared off into the night for a long moment, almost as if waiting for something. Should he say more? What more could he say?

"Come sit by me." She patted the swing at her side.

Jeff sat down. "You okay?" Stupid question. Who would be okay?

"I'm fine." She offered his arm a reassuring pat. "I wish I could be sad, and in a way I am. But not as a wife would be." She looked through the twisted limbs of the giant old oak. "I'm sad for the shattered dreams of a woman terrified to love and trust, who dared to anyway and was crushed."

Jeff covered her hand on her thigh with his. "You'll heal and dream again, Sara. I promise."

"Will I?" Her smile was sad, bittersweet. "Can you ever be as blindly trusting as you were before you were betrayed?"

Jeff thought a long moment. "Probably not, but maybe that's a good thing. Maybe seeing flaws and faults and knowing things can go bad and daring to dream anyway is better. There's nothing reckless in it. No abandonment. You know the risks and choose to take them. Nothing blind in that. Wisdom. You lacked it before, but it's there now. Takes a lot of courage to trust with wisdom."

"I guess it does."

"You guess?" he challenged her.

"Okay, it does."

"Why?"

She looked into his eyes. "Because you know what a rare gift being loved is. How much richer it makes your life. Holding someone's heart is a precious treasure. Hearts are sturdy and strong and capable of enduring a lot of pain. But they also hold love, and when you love them, they're fragile too."

"I'm sorry for what happened to you."

"I'm not." She hiked her chin, let him see the truth. "I hid my heart my whole life, Jeff. After my parents died, I couldn't let myself totally love anything because losing it just hurt too much."

"Then came Robert."

"Yes, and look how that turned out." She paused and pulled in a deep breath. "But I will never hide my heart again. That wasn't a life. It was the shell of a life. I want it all. The good and bad and indifferent."

He smiled. "I'm glad."

"But for right now, I just want to be relieved."

"I understand. I'll go now and give you some privacy." He started to stand.

She held him in place with a hand on his thigh. "Stay."

"Are you sure?"

She nodded. "I've had privacy and I've done my mourning. Can we just sit here and swing and be…normal? I've missed being normal."

He held her hand, laced their fingers. "For as long as you like."

"Careful." She squeezed. "Not today, but someday I'll tell you that I fell in love with you my first day in the village, which you probably don't even remember."

She'd fallen in love with him then? Then? And he hadn't seen it? *Moron.* "You got run over by that tourist on the bike and landed flat on your backside." She had looked so stunned, sitting there on the sidewalk.

"You do remember."

If she loved him then, there was hope for the future. "I remember…"

∾

In the shadows of Ruby's parking lot, Beth stepped out of the SUV and Joe enveloped her in a hug so tight it hurt her ribs, cupped her face and kissed her soundly, then hugged her even harder. "Easy, Joe. Ribs. Ribs."

"Sorry." He gentled his hold a fraction, his whole body shaking. "When I saw Robert aiming that gun at you, I thought I'd die."

"Me too." She smiled. "But like you said, we survived. We'll be fine." A lump formed in her throat. "Thank you for everything. I couldn't have gotten through this without you."

He hesitated, then rubbed gentle circles on her cheeks with his thumbs. "I love you, sha."

"I love you too." She never thought she'd say those words, especially not to a man like him, but they tumbled out of her mouth with ease on a rush of strong emotion and truth. She couldn't not say them.

"Finally, she gives my heart the words." He smiled. "I was beginning to wonder, I have to say."

"You weren't."

"I was."

"You're a woman magnet and you're trying to tell me you were worried?"

"Very worried."

"Joseph."

"It's true, gorgeous." He crossed his heart. "Attracting women isn't me, it's them. The woman I want is here, right now, in my arms. And I want her there. But that's her choice, not mine."

Beth snuggled closer. "It's where she wants to be—but we've still got a lot of talking to do."

"I knew there'd be a *but*."

"It's a little one." She smiled. It was, and it was fading fast. "For now can I be relieved we're alive and kiss you instead?"

"Absolutely." He tilted his head and his mouth descended to meet hers.

Beth sighed her content. Sara and Nora were fine. Everyone was fine. And Beth was in love. In her mind's eye, she saw Robert, heard him whisper through the chambers of her mind: *I win. You lose.*

No, Robert. Not you, not Nathara, and not NINA.

Not this time…

Epilogue

෴

A thick envelope arrived.

"Tell me that's not a bill." David Dawson smiled at his wife.

"It's from Beth." Millicent returned his smile.

"Well, hurry and read it. About time that girl remembered she had parents."

"She hasn't forgotten." Since they'd moved to Europe after Robert's death, the girls had been getting their feet and finding their way in the world. "She's let us adjust to our new nest."

Millicent walked outside, looked out on the breathtaking coast. She loved Italy. She'd always loved Italy. Living here had been her fantasy, but with Sara married to Robert, Millicent had feared she'd never live to see a time when she felt comfortable doing it.

So much had changed...

She sat in her rocker, watched David weed a flower bed, and opened the letter.

Dear Mom:

It dawned on me that today it's been two years since you were home. I couldn't believe it. So much has happened in Seagrove Village, and I know you've got to be settled into your life there now and ready to hear news of what's happening here. Nora says I'm late sharing, but Sara and I discussed it, and after the gray hair we've put in your head with everything, we decided you needed a good, long stint of stress-free time to decompress. Well, it's officially over now. I can't contain myself any longer.

Nora is doing well. She had some new experimental eye surgery, and it seems to have helped at least a bit. She still can't drive or anything, but Darla takes her out to Magnolia Branch every other Sunday after church. She puts flowers on Clyde's grave and chats with him awhile. Mark and Joe put a couple benches out there, so they have comfortable places to sit while they visit. Nora still hasn't been to Leavenworth to see Nathara, who's under maximum security, where Nora says she belongs. No one has any illusions that the woman is less dangerous in prison than she was out of it.

Ben and Kelly Walker married right after the Dead Game incident was over. They decided they'd waited long enough and they're now the proud parents of a beautiful baby girl. They named her Susan, in honor of Susan Brandt. Crossroads was her dream, and it's been such a blessing to so many. I think Susan would love that.

Peggy Crane is still running the center and playing Cupid to Nora's Rambo. I can hear you chuckling about that but, you know, something about it works. I think I told you on the phone, but in case I didn't, Lisa and Mark married Christmas Eve in the Crossroads chapel. All of Mark's old team came, and security was tight because of it, but what a wonderful group of men they are—especially my Joe.

Mom, you won't believe the changes in Sara. She's blossomed into such a strong woman. It's been amazing to watch. Once she discovered she could be strong, she has been, and for the first time ever, when I look at her there's no sadness, no hint of feeling alone in her eyes. She's vibrant, Mom, and she and Jeff are head over heels in love. It looks good on her. You know that right after Robert's funeral, she emptied her house down to the last stick of furniture and totally redecorated—Sara-style. It's gorgeous. Warm and welcoming, and just as beautiful as she is. Maria helped her, and it's finally a happy house again. Sara's radiant—and apparently impatient. That's why I had to write you now.

Last week she told me she was tired of waiting for Jeff to pop the question, so she's arranged a special evening and she's proposing to him. Isn't that wild? Sara? Our reserved and conservative and so-shy Sara is going to propose to Jeff? I'm laughing out loud as I write this. He won't say no, but if he did, the whole village would blister his ears. Sara's recruited everyone into helping her set him up for the proposal. It's tonight, and I can't wait to see what happens. I'm betting she won't get down on her knees, but I'm definitely in the minority on that. Even Joe's betting she will.

Hank Green is doing a good job as mayor, and Darla worked up her courage and asked him and Lance for a meeting. I don't know what was said, but I have the feeling she told them everything. They've treated her differently since then, and though it took awhile, the three of them meet for brunch at the club every other Sunday. Well, Darla and Hank do, now that Lance is away at college. Peggy says that's a good sign, especially since Darla and Hank never got along, and I guess it is. I know she's doing everything she can do to make a difference. God has to be pleased at the way she's turned her life around.

We broke ground on the new cottage development for the moms on Airport Road. Sara has been as persnickety about every detail to do with it as Susan Brandt was in building Crossroads. Anytime someone puts that much love into something, good just has to come out of it.

Mel, the receptionist at Crossroads, is living proof of what love can do. I don't know if you remember it, but there was a time when she was a teenager on her own. Her mother fell to drugs and Mel showed up at the center. Everyone embraced her, opening their arms and their hearts. Well, this spring she'll graduate from college, and she's going to stay on at Crossroads. Not as a receptionist, but running a program she designed specifically to help troubled teens.

All the girls—Kelly, Lisa, Sara, Nora, Peggy, Mel, Annie, and I—

had a baby shower for Roxy Talbot. She's retired from the FBI now and she and Harvey are expecting their first in less than a month. She's not complained at all about swollen ankles or morning sickness or any of that (which just isn't human, is it?). Actually, I guess her training taught her to deal with worse and a lot more. She does get emotional easily, which frustrates her, but the rest of us find it endearing. Even Nora, and you know how she is about that kind of thing. Anything tender sets Roxy off like a fire hose. I love that. If a woman needs to cry, she should just cry. It rattles Mark, but Harvey doesn't bat an eye, and Joe totally gets it. 'Course, he always has had an uncanny insight to women.

Oh, Mom, I still have to pinch myself sometimes. Who could have imagined that a man like Joe would love me? It boggles my mind. And to think that if not for Crossroads and NINA, I never would have met him. I definitely do not want to imagine that.

After Roxy's shower, we all went to the center and stood before Susan's portrait. Taking turns, we each told her how her dream had changed our lives. Crossroads was her dream, but oh, are we blessed to have been a part of it. Peggy Crane tagged us as Susan's Ripples. She says she's getting us pink T-shirts and sun hats. Imagine Nora in a T-shirt and sun hat. Hilarious, isn't it?

I'll happily wear the shirt on my beach runs. I don't know about the hat, though Nora says we could start a Pink Hat Society. That could be fun, so we'll see.

You know, Mom, Susan's dream was born in sadness, but look how God used it to create so much good. A lot of happiness has been found through those walls—and not the fleeting kind. The kind that lasts. When I think about it, it just awes me. I know it does you too.

Now that you're settled in, stay in touch. Sara and I miss you. All your friends here miss you too. And while we want you to have your dream, we expect to see you on visits. Know that you have nothing to worry about here. You left us in good hands. His hands.

We're content, Mom. Blessed. Life is good.

Much love to you and Dad,

Beth

READERS GUIDE

1. Beth was betrayed by Max and sees herself as too ordinary for a man like Joe to be genuinely interested in her.[1] Have you experienced things that changed the way you see yourself? The way you see others?

2. Joe had a rough childhood that drove him to church so he could find someone to go home with to get a meal. While there, he found God.[2] How did you find God?

3. Most would consider Joe's youth, caring for his brothers, a horrific burden, and yet it prepared him for his future. He acquired needed skills and knowledge.[3] Have you experienced a hard time or challenge that proved later to be beneficial to you?

4. Sara was deemed fragile, and she stayed with that path because it was comfortable and expected. Yet there came a time and a situation when

---

1. To see what the Bible says about these things, you can begin by reading the following scriptures from the New International Version: "For he chose us in him before the creation of the world to be holy and blameless in his sight" (Ephesians 1:4).
2. "She gave this name to the LORD who spoke to her: 'You are the God who sees me,' for she said, 'I have now seen the One who sees me'" (Genesis 16:13).
3. "And we know that in all things God works for the good of those who love him, who have been called according to his purpose" (Romans 8:28).

she couldn't take the easy way anymore.[4] Have you experienced that—where you wanted to change and knew you had to change, but were torn because you didn't want to leave what was comfortable or expected and step into the unknown? How did you cope? How did it work out?

5. NINA will do anything to anyone for money. What are your thoughts on that? Have you ever been tempted to bend your principles to get what you wanted?[5]

6. Beth feels torn about helping Sara when the beneficiary is a man she considers evil.[6] Have you experienced torn loyalties? How did you work through them?

7. Darla has committed terrible acts, but through her own choices, she makes an effort to be a better person. And through grace she is redeemed.[7] Do you believe that no one is beyond redemption? That everyone can be redeemed? Why or why not?

---

4. "Who shall separate us from the love of Christ? Shall trouble or hardship or persecution or famine or nakedness or danger or sword? As it is written: 'For your sake we face death all day long; we are considered as sheep to be slaughtered.' No, in all these things we are more than conquerors through him who loved us. For I am convinced that neither death nor life, neither angels nor demons, neither the present nor the future, nor any powers, neither height nor depth, nor anything else in all creation, will be able to separate us from the love of God that is in Christ Jesus our Lord" (Romans 8:35–39).
5. "I can do everything through him who gives me strength" (Philippians 4:13).
6. "But store up for yourselves treasures in heaven, where moth and rust do not destroy, and where thieves do not break in and steal" (Matthew 6:20).
7. "Keep your lives free from the love of money and be content with what you have, because God has said, 'Never will I leave you; never will I forsake you'" (Hebrews 13:5).

8. Beth has always protected Sara. Now Sara and she are at deep odds, and Sara distances herself from Beth and won't explain why.[8] Have you been in this position? Have you trusted the judgment of the one distancing and been bruised and hurt because of it? Did you accept the distance decision in the absence of a reason? How did you resolve it? Did it resolve?

9. At one point, Beth feels lost and afraid and forced to step into the lions' den.[9] Have you ever felt that way? What gave you the strength to do what needed doing? Was it as bad as you expected? How did you cope?

10. Joe doesn't like to talk about his past. He's ashamed of it. After he does discuss it, he would naturally perceive slights that just aren't there—the result of his feelings about himself. The remnants of that shame he'd carried with him growing up.[10] What remnants of your past are you carrying with you? Are they constructive or destructive? What must be reconciled to put them to rest in the past?

11. People who know Beth well regard her with suspicion when Robert disappears. When a similar situation arises with another, Beth refuses to suspect and considers that person innocent only to later discover

---

8. "Yet to all who did receive him, to those who believed in his name, he gave the right to become children of God" (John 1:12).
9. "If we confess our sins, he is faithful and just and will forgive us our sins and purify us from all unrighteousness" (1 John 1:9).
10. "So do not fear, for I am with you; do not be dismayed, for I am your God. I will strengthen you and help you; I will uphold you with my righteous right hand" (Isaiah 41:10).

that person was guilty.[11] Have you been a victim of misplaced suspicion or misplaced your trust in another? How did it impact you and your other relationships?

12. One of God's promises is to turn what evil is intended to harm us into good.[12] Beth and Joe experience this in several ways. Have you had an experience where someone did something intending it be harmful to you, but it was turned and used for good?

---

11. "In him we have redemption through his blood, the forgiveness of sins, in accordance with the riches of God's grace" (Ephesians 1:7).
12. "'You intended to harm me, but God intended it for good to accomplish what is now being done, the saving of many lives. So then, don't be afraid. I will provide for you and your children.' And he reassured them and spoke kindly to them" (Genesis 50:20–21).

Dear Readers,

At some point in our lives, many, if not most of us, have been betrayed. We've also experienced torn loyalties. Situations where we must act, and no matter what we do, someone is hurt. And many if not most of us have been falsely accused of saying and doing things we did not do.

These are the challenges raised in *Not This Time* that had to be addressed as well as the physical challenges of danger and deception. When we try to live seeing the good in others, it's often difficult for us to accept that there are those who just embrace the bad because they choose to embrace it. But those people do exist and in our denial of it is danger. Not just physical danger, but emotional and, most important, spiritual danger.

If the whole duty of man is to fear God and keep His commandments, and we are charged by Christ to love one another, how do we love those embracing evil and stay true to walking in faith and not be harmed by the actions of those embracing evil? It can present quite a puzzle. One that confounds us and tests us to the limits. Yet we need not despair. We've heard what to do when we reach the end of our rope. To reach for the hem of His robe. It is in that reach that we find our answers and the courage to do the right thing for the right reasons. To take that leap of faith and dare to trust again, to be loyal without being an enabler fostering evil.

I followed Beth and Joe—you met them in *Deadly Ties*—through their trials, and I have to say I was intrigued and on the edge of my seat. Every time I thought things were about to work out, something else happened or something was revealed that made me look at things differently, or showed me that what I believed was true wasn't. It was at times chilling, at times heartwarming. And in the end I discovered that there is a way to endure indignities and wrongful accusations and broken trust and torn loyalties without becoming bitter or dis-illusioned. His way.

May you enjoy their journey as much as I did, and may your own journey be eased in some way for having made it.

My most humble gratitude to you for traveling through the Crossroads Crisis Center series with me from *Forget Me Not* through *Deadly Ties,* and now in *Not This Time.* I pray we're all richer for the experience.

Blessings,
Vicki Hinze
Florida

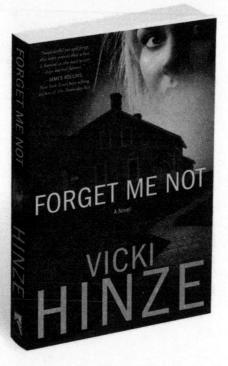

HER ENEMY WILL STOP AT NOTHING FOR CONTROL...SHE WILL RISK EVERYTHING FOR FREEDOM

Lisa struggles to save her mother from an abusive monster. Mark fights to save Lisa from certain death. Together they must stop an international conspiracy and in the process find love and true faith.